We Feel Your Pain

SO YOU DON'T HAVE TO

Sam Hawksmoor

Hammer & Tong

First published in 2020 by Hammer & Tong – also available on Kindle

Text copyright © Sam Hawksmoor 2020

The right of Sam Hawksmoor to be identified as the author of this work has been asserted.

All rights reserved. No part of this publication may be reproduced, stored in a retrieval system, or transmitted, in any form by any means, electronic, mechanical, photocopying, recording, or otherwise, without the prior permission of the author.

1 3 5 7 9 10 8 6 4 2

Publishers Note: This is a work of fiction. Names, characters, places, incidents and dialogues are products of the author's imagination or are used fictitiously. Any resemblance to actual people, living or dead, or to businesses, companies, events, institutions or locales is entirely coincidental.

Book Layout © 2016 BookDesignTemplates.com

We Feel Your Pain/Sam Hawksmoor– 1st ed.
ISBN-13: 9798699087693

Acknowledgements:

To Kitty Thomas, Roxy West, Walli F. Leff, Allen Cook, Dean at University of Bridgeport and Rosemary North for their generous insights, encouragement and support.

WE FEEL YOUR PAIN
So You Don't Have To

At the Jirdasham Institute we believe you don't have to live with pain. For years Doctors have ignored the underlying causes of pain – prescribing opioids and other painkillers that often lead to complications, or addiction, leaving a patient in far a worse situation.

We Feel Your Pain - So you don't have to

We will strive to take your pain away *forever, with a drug-free treatment that really works. We make no claims about curing cancer or healing rheumatics. Our Jirdasham method is not a 'cure', but we promise to remove your pain and let you get on with living again.

Can't live with pain? Get rid of it. Forever.

Thousands have already taken up this offer. Imagine your life without constant pain – isn't that worth paying for? Contact us now for a free one-hour consultation
Available to Berg City Residents only at this time
See us on on-line and make an appointment.

* Terms and Conditions apply. Pain treatment subject to diagnosis to a specific problem. Multiple or subsequent new health issues may require more than one treatment. Note: this is not a cure, but a pain management process and you will need to consult with your doctor for ongoing treatment for any underlying health issue.

All pain teaches us something -
it is for you to understand what that lesson might be.
- Guru Gurajani

CHAPTER ONE

Morning rain

Somewhere a dog was barking. A shutter repeatedly slammed hard against a window. Ahead, freezing wild rushing water was coming straight towards him. He didn't know why he was standing in a river or have any idea of how he got there. He desperately scanned the riverbank for a way out, but it seemed so far away. He could barely stand on the cold slippery stones. That dog was still barking. He turned his head to see where it was but immediately lost his footing and began to flail backwards into the icy waters.

Delaney woke with a start, gasping for breath. He opened his eyes, aware of a cold breeze on his face and pounding rain on the zinc roof. He tried to shake off the vivid images of the rushing water and regain reality.

He groaned as he pried his fingers open. The shutter slammed again. Damnit, he thought he'd fixed that catch already. He looked at his watch 6.15 am. Rufus was barking, most likely excited by the tumultuous roar of the rain.

He was very much awake now. Delaney painfully raised his right arm to get it mobile and naked, crawled from his bed and made it to the open window and fastened the shutter.

The city desperately needed this rain, the trees and plants were buckling under the unexpected deluge. He inhaled the sweet smell of fresh rain on bone-dry grass mixed in with the scent of honeysuckle and mint. If not for the incessant maddening pain in his arms, this moment would be proof enough that he lived in the best city in the world.

"Rufus?"

He headed to the bathroom first. It always seemed to take a while to get his circulation going. He reckoned he was getting no more than three or four hours sleep a night. Never enough. No physician, osteopath or witch doctor he'd ever consulted had the slightest idea of how to treat his pain. They all had excellent theories about what it might be, but no damn cures. "Stress," they often concluded, "practice mindfulness. You're still in your early forties, it will go in time."

Needless to say, time was late in showing up. He peed. Rufus was still barking. He went to see what the problem was.

He'd left the patio door open; a pool of water was forming on the living room tiles. A roof-shaking rumble of thunder added to the drama outside. A wet nose poked his leg. He looked down and Rufus yawned, clearly agitated, then sniffed the air.

"It's rain. Go out there. Go pee. I know you need to."

Rufus turned to stare at the rain but wasn't in the least bit keen to go out in that. He looked up at Delaney questioning this request.

"Go on, you'll love the rain. Go pee, dog."

Rufus' eyebrows danced with worry as he indicated his concerns. It was too early; he was not an early riser at the best of times. Besides he wasn't well.

"I'll go out with you," Delaney encouraged him. "You probably need a shower."

He walked out onto the grass and Rufus reluctantly inched forward, rain splashing on his face and making him sneeze.

"Jesus." Delaney hadn't quite prepared himself for just how bloody cold the rain was. It was a shock. Behind him Rufus had a moment of madness and dashed around him, barking at the sky and sliding on wet grass. Delaney turned his face to the heavens and drank it in. Goose pimples covered his arms and torso. He felt the rain harden. He headed back to the house as rain abruptly turned to hail. Rufus beat him to it and stood there dazed, drenched.

"Don't shake." He commanded, as he shut the glass door.

He shook. Water sprayed everywhere. The once red but now faded sofa was used to it.

Delaney quickly headed for the shower. He needed to get warm again.

The hailstones fell like rocks on the roof and he briefly wondered if it could pierce the zinc. He remembered something about recent giant hail punching holes in aircraft wings at the city airport.

"Feels good, right?" He yelled at the dog who'd

followed him into the bathroom. Rufus shook again and rubbed his face on the bathmat. He was less than impressed by rain.

"We're going to have to get your tail looked at, Rufus. That infection isn't looking good, boy."

Rufus ignored him and furiously began licking his tail.

CHAPTER TWO

Asha & Zuki

Asha opened her eyes. Her tongue felt thick and she had a mild headache. Zuki lay beside her, her mouth agape. Still wearing her clothes and make up. They'd both drunk too much and she couldn't let her drive home. "Hey wake up, slug. I've got a job to go to."

Zuki pretended not to hear as Asha headed to the bathroom.

"I can't move my head," Zuki protested.

"I'm sorry girl, but you're out of here. Breakfast at Harry's OK? They make magic smoothies and there's fresh sourdough."

"Only if you're paying, I'm broke till I get a new job," Zuki drawled, struggling to open her eyes. "God, what did we drink? I feel like death."

"I think you drank most of it."

"Shit. Why did you let me drink Tequila? I can't handle that stuff."

"You need coffee."

"I need a job."

"Harry's are hiring."

Zuki exhaled. "So that's why I have a degree in Applied Artificial Intelligence."

"AI isn't hiring humans these days; they don't need us anymore. Come on. Get up. I'm late."

Zuki reluctantly surfaced, shaking her hair loose as Asha reappeared.

"Go pee. Your toothbrush is where you left it. No time to shower. We've got to go."

Zuki headed towards the bathroom, eyes barely open.

Asha opened her cupboard and sighed, wondering what to wear. She normally had everything decided the night before. Making a choice in a hurry wasn't her way.

"You take your job way too seriously, Ash." Zuki announced on her return, squinting at her phone. "Hell, man, it's only seven."

Asha frowned. "I start early. If you had a job, you might notice the traffic in the morning. No one uses the bus anymore since the virus. Reality check, girl. If we don't leave now it will take an hour or more."

Zuki struggled with her shoes. "You just got lucky. All you had to do was that little thing you do with your nose and he was toast. Older men are such suckers."

Asha shook her head. She remembered the interview well. It had been a disaster. She'd turned up late. Got lost navigating the back corridors of the old office block. Got his name wrong. Told him she didn't like dogs and she'd spilled coffee on his shoes. Working for a small agency surviving on outsourced work from City Hall meant the salary wasn't great, not everyone would put up with that. But it was a job and she had desperately needed it. Mostly it had been his gentle smile that had made her accept the role when he called up with the offer. That and how he obviously needed someone to take care of his office. If there was one thing, she was good at, 'focusing' was it. Others might call it obsessing, but in the right circumstances it could work. Luckily Rufus had made it easy for her to overcome her antipathy of dogs and he provided enough distraction for her not to become too focused.

"I'm going to start my own agency one day." Asha told Zuki as they went down in the elevator. "I'm probably doing at least three people's job now."

Zuki smiled and rooted in her backpack for her car keys. "You will. If anyone will, it's you. Don't you have to take exams and stuff to be a detective?"

"We're not detectives. We're representing the Office of City Oversight. We investigate anything the City might be involved with, scams, illegal permits, disputes with contractors, stuff like that. Mayor wants an 'independent' eye on City business."

"As long as you don't look at what he's doing, right?"

Asha shrugged. "So far he's proven to be pretty legit. But I guess we'll find something embarrassing one day. Delaney reminds me of that every day."

"You'll be sorry," Zuki said, rolling her eyes. "Politicians can't help themselves. Your boss is 'Delaney' now? What happened to Mister Delaney?"

Asha didn't register the sarcasm. "He doesn't like

being called Mr Delaney. Anyway, he can teach me a lot. He's got years of experience and ..."

"He hasn't tried to get into your panties? Single, lonely guy with a cute dog? Bet he hired you to get into your panties. It's a #metoo minefield, Ash."

The doors opened and they walked into the lobby.

"He's not like that. Besides he's in pain most of the time. You can see from the way he moves. I keep thinking he's going to have a heart attack, but he says his heart's fine."

Zuki adjusted her hair in the lobby mirror. "It's a weird job and a weird situation."

Asha was looking at the glistening streets. Her heart leapt. It had finally rained. She loved the rain. Living in the sunniest city on the coast was great most of the time, but every year the rain seemed to come later and later, or sometimes not at all. This would clean the air and fill the reservoirs. She felt happy all of a sudden.

"Shit, rain." Zuki complained.

Asha sighed. She and Zuki were such opposites. They didn't seem to agree on anything. "I'll ride with you. I can walk to work from Harry's."

"You'll get wet."

Asha grinned. "I know."

CHAPTER THREE

The Scam

The waves were quite spectacular at the beach that morning. Big rollers were breaking hard against the rocks, driven by a fierce westerly wind. The rain was easing slightly but no one else was out there walking dogs this early. He watched Rufus run along the sand jumping the surf as it swept in. It was their usual routine. No matter how busy he was he always made time for the dog. Rufus definitely wasn't right though. He kept stopping to urgently lick his tail and when the surf swamped him, he didn't dash off as normal and yelped as the saltwater covered his tail.

Delaney caught up with him pulling him away from the waves. "Easy boy. Let me take a look."

Rufus didn't want to cooperate. The sore was driving him mad and Delaney could see it was much worse than he'd thought.

"You're going to see the vet, dog. No amount of licking is going to cure this."

Rufus looked doubtfully at him, then went back to frantically licking his tail.

It was a struggle to get him back into the car. Delaney realized that he couldn't lose this dog. He'd lost so much in the last three years. Rufus had no idea how important he was to keep him together. It was possible he'd been bitten by a rat and was rapidly going septic. He had no idea when it had happened but watching him obsessively lick the wound wasn't good. There was a risk he'd lose the tail and he wasn't sure Rufus could take the humiliation. He was very proud of his magnificent tail. He didn't care that he was a mixture of Ridgeback and Collie. The lucky result was one good-looking dog who was devoted to the guy who'd found a pup yelping for dear life in a dumpster behind City Hall and taken him home.

He left Rufus at the vets. The dog had looked at him with such surprise and sorrow when he'd taken him in, only at the last second recognizing the vet's iron gates with horror. This was betrayal in his eyes. Hard to tell a dog that it's for his own good.

"Two days tops. Then you'll be home, I promise." Delaney had told him, but that tail between his legs and the whining told him that he didn't believe him. You don't forget being abandoned – ever.

The car park was half empty. So many layoffs in the city, everyone was doubling up on jobs whether they knew what they were doing or not. Everything was blamed on the virus and if not that, the last administration that had perfected corruption on a grand scale. He wasn't convinced the new Mayor was the savior he pretended to be, but thus far his little agency had flown under the radar and the contract was being honored. His office was running with three people, but one, Alice, was off with stress. He had to keep paying her under employment law, but it was getting harder to carry the cost. He grabbed his mask but didn't put it on. An easy rebellion when no one was around.

He saw the 'Out of order' sign on the elevator and sighed. Third time this month. Cutting back on maintenance was a false economy, but it was the same all over the city. People were nervous of spending in case things got worse.

Asha was standing on the balcony wringing out the rain from her hair when he arrived. She looked soaked but didn't seem unhappy about it.

"Rain. Don't you just love it?" She called out as he headed towards the kettle. No way he could start his day without a decent coffee.

"You got something dry to wear?" He asked, as Asha moved towards her desk. He tried not to look too closely as her clothes clung to her perfect trim body. But he couldn't help noticing how she made his heart run a little faster. He should have hired the obese girl with dandruff to be safe. Too late now.

"It'll dry. Can't even remember the last time it rained."

"April 10th. I had a blowout on the Eastern highway. Took about an hour to get the damn wheel nuts off. I caught a cold, remember? Did you get the almond milk? I forgot."

Asha nodded pointing behind him. "Where's the dog?"

"Vet. Tail got bitten somehow and it's septic. Rufus is very proud of his tail."

Asha made a face. "You're very proud of his tail. He's just a lucky dog with a besotted owner. And if you're going to ask me how wonderful my weekend was, stop right now."

Delaney rolled his eyes and heaped coffee into the French Press as the kettle steamed. He briefly glimpsed an image of his wife holding her morning coffee cup with two hands and inhaling the aroma before starting work in the morning. Funny how it's the small things you recall about a person.

Asha was looking at her computer screen. "Got a weird one for you today. What would you pay to get rid of the pain in your hands?"

Delaney poured a dash of almond milk into the coffees and took one over to Asha.

"This one of your hypotheticals?"

Asha smiled. "How much would you pay to fix that annoying kid who used to live with you? God she was the most self-centered girl I ever met, but I guess I'd be grumpy too if I broke my back."

Delaney thought about the money he'd spent on Maria's injuries. Nothing had helped. She and her mother had thankfully walked out on him three months ago and his finances were only just now recovering.

"Since you're asking, I think I'd need money-back guarantees. The pain would have to be gone forever. I'd pay a great deal for that."

Asha nodded. "But you didn't actually come up with a figure. Would you sell your nice little house with a view of the harbor?"

Delaney wrinkled his nose as he considered it. "That's a pretty big ask. But some days, when the pain is really bad, I'd probably consider it."

"Serious?" Asha asked, her eyebrows raised.

"Until you've been in pain constantly for months or years, you can't know how desperate you can get, Ash. Money-back guarantee, I'd go for it."

Asha was impressed. Until this moment she hadn't appreciated just how bad his pain really was. "Well then, I guess you are the exact right person to interview our first contestant this morning."

Delaney grinned. This is why he'd hired Asha. She had a sense of humor and understood possibly how pointless most of what they did was half the time.

"Mr Abrams. Ten o'clock. Spent thirty grand at 'Jirdasham - We feel your Pain – So you don't have to.' And now he wants his money back."

Delaney almost laughed. "He did what? How much? Who?"

"'We feel your pain – so you don't have to.' You haven't seen the Insta ads?" Asha rolled her eyes. Of course, he hadn't, he didn't do social media.

"Seriously, this is a thing? Thirty grand? Is this even in our purview? It has to be medical surely and the Health and Safety department would handle this. If City Hall still has one."

Asha shook her head. "This was Alice's stuff. She dumped it on me. It's a scam and guess who investigate scams – us. She made an appointment for you."

"But what has this got to do with City Hall?"

Asha read from her computer screen.

"Jirdasham: 'We feel your pain' is the most innovative and promising organization I have seen that deals with drug-free pain control. If we are to get on top of the scandal of people dying from opiates, legal and otherwise, we need to work with organizations like 'Jirdasham Pain Control.' Mayor Caesar Stoll. Quote - unquote." She adjusted her seat before adding, "it was in all the papers months ago."

Delaney groaned. "And how much was he paid to say that? Shit, Ash. This can't be true. He's pushing some scam artists and what happens if we expose them?"

"I guess we look for new jobs." Asha replied shrugging. "But who knows, Chief. They might be genuine. Ye of little faith."

Delaney sipped his coffee. "It stinks. No one can fix pain. I know. I've tried them all."

Asha read more. 'The Jirdasham Method is 100% natural with no dependency issues."

"Don't buy their shares just yet, Ash."

"As if. Alice was looking into this. There's a whole lot

of complaints."

Delaney rolled his eyes. "Well that's a surprise." He didn't need this. Of course, it was a scam. No one could get rid of pain without addressing the causes of pain, like Maria's fractured spine.

His desk phone rang. He just hoped it wasn't the Mayor.

"City Oversight. Delaney speaking."

"Mr Delaney. Forgive me for this late call but I believe we have a ten o'clock appointment."

Delaney hoped he was cancelling. "Mr er ..." He'd forgotten already.

"Abrams. If I may request that we meet at my store, Mr Delaney. I'm in too much pain to walk today and I can promise you an excellent coffee for your trouble. BookBank. You know it well, if I'm not mistaken."

Delaney smiled with recognition. "I've spent many hours browsing in Bookbank, Mr Abrams, even bought a few books and your excellent coffee."

"Then you'll know that I wouldn't ask you to come if I could avoid it."

Delaney glanced at his watch – six blocks, all uphill. "Make it 10.15, Mr Abrams. See you then."

Asha was watching him. "He owns BookBank? Tragedy about his daughter, Lily. I used to worship her. She was quite an activist for the environment. So sad she killed herself."

Delaney frowned. The beautiful Lily was dead? He made a note in his screen diary. All his appointments had to be accounted for in case of audits from City Hall.

"She's really gone? I didn't know. I hope Mr Abrams doesn't remember me. I used to haunt his bookshop when I was young. Had such a real crush on Lily. Tall, brown, with vivid green eyes and the best smile ever."

"You didn't know she was gay?"

Delaney frowned. "No way. All the guys worshipped her."

Asha laughed. "Typical male. So, you didn't know she married the women's champion tennis player Sinca Fermind?"

Delaney drew a blank. He hadn't really thought much about Lily since he'd gone to University and found girls more amenable to his attentions.

"She taught African History at my college and I know for a fact that she had affairs with some of the girls. Even though she was older, she always looked great. She had wonderful style and that amazing voice."

Delaney felt a twinge of disappointment. Lily had meant so much to him once and he'd lived for her brilliant smile.

"I find it hard to believe someone like her would kill themselves. She got me reading stuff I would never had tried, just so I'd have a chance to discuss them with her."

Asha was looking at Delaney in a new light. He was a romantic. Sweet.

"She had cancer. I guess didn't want to suffer. I can't believe you don't know all this."

Delaney glanced at Asha and nodded. He'd been in Europe for eight years before starting this agency. Things had changed, people moved on, or died. Perhaps he was too wrapped up in his own pain and Rufus to catch up. Poor Lily. Poor Mr Abrams. He'd been devoted to his beautiful daughter.

"I'm going. Don't sign us up for anything else this crazy today, OK?"

CHAPTER FOUR

Mr Abrams Regrets

BookBank was on the corner of Bight and Mill streets. The building a former bank built in 1853 – all imposing granite to reassure customers the bank was 'solid'. Now it was three floors of books and a coffee shop. The coffee shop was bigger than Delaney remembered and there were a lot of things on sale that weren't books. It was the last surviving bookshop in the city. He'd be sad when it finally succumbed to 'progress'. He slipped his mask on.

Classical music floated in the air and he found Mr Abrams sitting at a desk surrounded by new titles writing potted 'reviews' to make it easier for customers to make decisions. He'd lost weight, wasn't wearing a mask. Lost most of his hair too, but wore a well-cut suit and immaculate shoes, just as he always had. A portrait of Lily Abrams hung on a wall behind the till, just as he remembered her. Those luminous green eyes watching, the questioning smile.

"Mr Delaney. You're taller than I remember."

Delaney stuck his hand out to shake but then remembered you don't do that anymore. Mr Abrams smiled. "I don't miss shaking hands. Hurts too much to shake. I can see from your hand that you're in trouble too."

Delaney hated it when people noticed how bent his fingers were now. Hell, he was only forty-two, what would they be like when he was older?

"We all have our pain to remind us that we're human." Delaney said. His late unmissed father's words. He'd had heart problems and luckily for him passed away in his sleep at fifty-five.

"Indeed, we do. Some of us are more human than others, I think. You still sail, Mr Delaney? I still remember your victory in that Two Oceans race. You were so young to be skipper I recall. Lily always said you'd go far."

"I doubt she remembered me." Delaney said. "I'm so sorry for your loss. I only found out today. I was working away for eight years in Europe."

"We all miss Lily. She was very fond of you y'know. I remember you used to sneak in and peek at her. Those books you bought at a special price. Lily's way of saying she liked you."

Delaney had no idea she'd known how much he'd admired her.

"I remember she said that you were too polite for your own good."

"She was right. Luckily sailing changed all that. Politeness can get you drowned."

"And now you have an investigative agency in our fair City."

"What's left of it. Tough times, budget cuts. Something brought me back, Mr Abrams. This is still the best small city in the world."

"I'm glad you still believe that. When I'm gone that will be it for books in this city. I don't really like all the changes." He shifted in his seat with obvious discomfort. "Last time we met you were sailing to South America. You were still a boy. Can't believe so much time has gone by."

"You can't sail if you can't use your hands," Delaney remarked. "You're a liability to the crew."

"Must have been quite a wrench for you to give it up."

Mr Abrams waved an employee over. He smiled at the approaching girl. "Lucy, get Mr Delaney a coffee. How do you like it, sir?"

"Americano, one shot, almond milk if you have it and no sugar."

The girl spun away, and Delaney leaned up against a bookshelf observing the old man.

"You're lucky you can still drink the stuff, goes right through my bladder." Mr Abrams said with a heavy sigh.

Delaney smiled. "That it does."

"You ever marry, Mr Delaney? If you don't mind my intrusion."

Delaney hated the question and the inevitable explanations. He sighed.

"Yeah. I did. One of my better decisions in life." He paused, wondering whether to reveal the rest of it. But he and the old man went back a long way, it wouldn't do any harm. "My wife, Denise, was killed in a terrorist attack in Paris. She was French. It's over three years ago now. She was just sitting at street café waiting for me to join her after work. I was stuck in traffic and missed the explosion by minutes." He paused, closing his eyes. "There was nothing left to identify her except by her shoes. She died but took me with her. I was devastated, Mr Abrams. Nothing would console me. That's when I quit Europe and came home. Part of the healing process, I guess. Denise was an illustrator. Pretty good one, you've probably got some children's books on sale here she worked on. I try not to think about her now to be honest. It still hurts."

"Denise Malbure? She illustrated some wonderful editions. I am so sorry to hear she's gone. In such terrible circumstances too."

Delaney shrugged. Normally he'd never mention it.

"Talk to me about this 'We feel your pain' thing. I was pretty skeptical when I heard about it today and even more surprised that you were taken. Lily always said you were the smartest guy in town. Or tightest, I can't remember exactly now."

Mr Abrams laughed, then sighed. "Should be 'We feel your wallet' Mr Delaney. I paid a lot of money to them. Hubris doesn't cover it. Lily I'm sure would have said 'tightest' but things change. Some days I'm in so much pain I can't dress myself. It's embarrassing. I can't leave my bookshop to Lily anymore – all I have now is pain. Twenty-four hours a day pain." He moved back into his chair and winced. "They promised me a pain-free existence. They have testimonials, even one by your Mayor Caesar Stoll himself. 100% pain-free, or your money back. That's what they promised."

"And you paid up."

"Thirty grand."

"And it didn't work."

Mr Abrams smiled as the coffee arrived. The girl put it on the desk next to a pile of books. Delaney removed his mask, glad to be able to breathe again.

"Thanks, Lucy." Mr Abrams said. She swiftly left them too it.

"You're wrong in that assumption, Mr Delaney. It worked. For one month I was pain free. I felt it was the best thirty grand I had ever spent. I was a new man. I was happy. Ask anyone here. They were talking miracles. I could walk, drive my car, and visit the park. How I used to miss strolling under the trees by the ocean. Now I could do it all again and listen to the waves. The best month of my life."

Delaney frowned. He hadn't expected this. "I'm confused. You paid. It worked. That's the deal, right?"

"And suddenly it stopped working." Mr Abrams lifted an arm to demonstrate and you could see the pain swirl over his face.

"Ah. But I imagine they have clauses in the contract to deal with that. Do you have the contract to hand?"

"Yes. It's somewhere here."

"Naturally you contacted them and complained."

Mr Abrams spasmed a moment and closed his eyes.

"Yes, I complained."

"And their response?"

"They could repeat the cure. A top-up for another fifteen thousand."

Delaney whistled. "And you paid this?"

Mr Abrams chuckled. "You might think me foolish, but I'm not insane, yet. That would mean I would have spent forty-five grand and who is to say the pain would not return again? A man is only made of so many thousands and this man is running a bookshop that survives mostly on the coffee we sell."

Delaney understood. "But I suppose some people will keep paying."

Mr Abrams nodded. "I'm sure they do. Pain never takes a day off. Never. I could pay them if I took out a loan. But I would be forever waiting for the pain to return."

"And who's to say it isn't new pain?"

"Which is Clause 14A," Mr Abrams informed him. "My lawyer couldn't believe I'd paid them anything. Technically if you experience just 24 hours pain free, they have fulfilled their contract and any pain thereafter is new pain. I won't tell you what my lawyer said to me – it wasn't polite."

Delaney could guess. "A fool and his money, right. We hear a lot of scams at the office. Especially people who claim to be calling from City Hall – telling people that their house is built on city land and there is a ten grand fine or face demolition. If they dare to challenge it, the fine will double."

Mr Abrams seemed surprised. "People fall for that?"

Delaney nodded. "All the time. One: all land and legal occupiers' records are held on a digital database. Two: they'd have to go to court to demolish anything. Three: they don't call people up. They send red-lined letters that look pretty scary."

"But people believe City Hall is scamming them."

"Exactly. No one trusts anyone anymore."

"So, you don't condemn me for paying them?"

"My first boss in Paris used to tell us, 'Never look under the hood – just keep driving. Hit your targets.'" Delaney paused a moment to savor his coffee, appreciating the kick. "They arrested him for major fraud about two months after he told me that. Everyone seemed to be surprised about that except me. I'm a kick the tires type of guy. Pretty impressive coffee Mr Abrams. I must buy some."

"Ask Lucy when you leave. You didn't answer me. You think I'm wasting your time."

Delaney examined his left hand, the disjointed fingers that had killed his sailing days. "My colleague, Asha, asked me how much I'd pay for all this pain to go away. I've no idea how much, but if I knew for sure it was real, I'd pay, Mr Abrams. I'd pay."

Mr Abrams inhaled and wiped moisture from his eyes. "I was stupid. All their talk of this Guru and his disciples swayed me. They even introduced me to former clients who are now pain free. I was convinced they could help. They seemed so professional and welcoming. Now they just threaten me if I try to sue."

"What exactly would you like us to do, Mr Abrams?"

The old man leaned forward with effort. "Expose them. I can't be the only one who's fallen for this. It's a lot of money. It's fraud. An elaborate fraud and they are preying on the old and taking them to the cleaners. The Mayor sings their praises, so you have to think he's on the take. If you fear for your job, Mr Delaney, I will understand. I've been fighting corruption in City Hall for years."

"At least you got a month pain free," Delaney pointed out.

"That I don't regret. The pain returning was like being run over by a tank. My Lily killed herself because she didn't want to go through with the treatment. Pancreatic cancer can't be easy on anyone. She was already at stage three when they diagnosed it. I didn't condone it. She didn't consult me. She knew it would cause me to suffer and I do, daily, but I totally understand her choice. She watched me decline into this wreck, Mr Delaney. Lily, beautiful Lily was never going to be a wreck. She didn't hesitate. Once she knew what she was facing – she held a big party to say goodbye and that was it. It takes a lot of courage to kill yourself. I'm not sure I have it, even now."

Delaney finished his coffee. "Email the contract to me, any digital receipts, doctors notes, if you're willing to share. I'll look into it. No promises. Caveat Emptor, Mr Abrams and all that. But, like you, I've tried everything. Acupuncture, physio, quack ointments, meditation, drink no dairy, eat no meat, I'm not even supposed to drink coffee, but nothing, absolutely nothing works."

Mr Abrams blinked. "Which makes you exactly the right person to expose them, Mr Delaney."

Delaney smiled, remembering Asha had said the same thing. Perhaps. Perhaps not. "I'll let you know what I discover. But don't get your hopes up. Even if we find fault, you may not get your money back."

Mr Abrams leant back in his chair. "That is a given. But if you can save others from them, then at least it won't be a waste of your time."

Delaney was on his way out when he saw a small display of children's books in the window. He recognized the distinctive Crow and Fox on a large illustrated book immediately. It was the very last book that Denise had been working on. She'd often complained that life was full of too many fairy tales but loved illustrating them. He went back inside to buy a copy. It was the least he could do for her.

CHAPTER FIVE

Little ironies

She had no idea what time it was, or even what day. How long had she been lying here? Stella Palmer tried to move her head to make herself more comfortable, but it was hopeless. She was so very cold. So stiff.

She'd been almost amused at first. The irony of finding herself in this situation, sprawled on the marble floor in her designer kitchen and unable to move was typical. Her phone was up on the counter of course, well beyond reach. She could hear the phone ringing again. Mostly likely it was Paulo, the hairdresser wondering why she hadn't turned up for her four o'clock appointment. Or Dr Vitch, puzzled she hadn't appeared for her regular physio. Or perhaps it was Edith; annoyed she hadn't come by to take her shopping, as she had promised to do.

The phone ceased ringing and she was again reminded of her thirst. The steady drip of the kitchen tap did not help any.

Stella tried once again to inch herself towards a chair but just couldn't move. She knew her leg was broken, possibly her hip too. She'd slipped on something and fallen hard on the damn marble. Perhaps if she'd been younger, certainly thinner, it might have been possible to get up again, but hauling her weight anywhere now with good legs was hard, never mind with a broken one. At least she wasn't in pain. She laughed at the very thought. That was exactly the problem. If only she hadn't heard of those people at 'We feel your pain.' If only she'd not sold her mother's empty apartment and had the cash to hand earning no interest at the bank. That was what had made the decision to finally deal with her arthritis.

"You won't feel pain anymore. You'll be able to walk again. Go back on the golf course you love so much." They told her. The devil had placed temptation in front of her and she'd seized the chance to be pain free. They hadn't lied. Here she was sprawled on the floor with a broken leg and couldn't feel a thing. How was that for a testimonial? She'd seen the Mayor was promoting the company and called in to complain about the cost. The Mayor had no right to promote something that only the very rich could afford. It wasn't right to tell people to use it if he wasn't prepared to pay for the treatment. Stella was a diehard liberal. She felt guilty living well; perhaps that was why she'd got rid of the money so easily. But now she was paying for it.

Her mouth was dreadfully dry. She tried to remember how long she'd been lying there. She'd fallen on Sunday, or was it Saturday? And what day was it now? Was there anyone due to visit? Even if they did, they would most likely go away if she didn't come to the door. She couldn't think of anyone who'd come. No one at all. Of course, it was her own fault. How happy she'd been to get divorced five years ago. Finally rid of James and his rotten gambling habits and obsession with porn. How lucky she'd thought herself to be living alone; just pleasing herself. No one to mock her weight every day, even though she knew only too well that she needed to lose at least fifty pounds and how hard that had proven to be.

She cried a little. In the background she could hear Henrietta moving around, wondering why she hadn't fed her. How long before she would consider nibbling her leg or arms? She was small, but always hungry. Stella was strongly aware that a terrier had only loyalty to her stomach when it came right down to it. Someone would finally find her gnawed to death. It was almost funny. Almost.

That dripping tap was killing her. What she would give for a simple glass of water.

CHAPTER SIX

A Few Complaints

Asha was eating a rice salad when he returned to the office. She looked angry.

"Another cut back at City Hall. They're closing the Environmental unit. Companies must publish an environmental impact statement annually instead."

Delaney frowned. "They're supposed to anyway. Who will police it?"

Asha shrugged. "Not us. They probably don't want anyone to oversee anything. So, we just cross our fingers and hope they don't poison the rivers and kill the forests."

Delaney had known this was coming. "How long before he sells the parks to private developers. You're right, Ash. Time to start looking for opportunities in the private sector."

"You want some salad?"

Delaney shook his head. "Grabbed a sandwich on the way back."

"How is Mr Abrams?"

"Old, in pain and a lot poorer."

"You going to follow up?"

Delaney flipped on his desktop computer. "What about all the other complaints about that company. I need to see them."

"I forwarded them to you."

Delaney opened his email, then sighed when he saw a long list of names and groaned. "How many?"

Asha giggled. "Maybe this was why Alice went off with stress."

"There's some Guru involved. We have a name?"

Asha pointed to a pile of papers on her desk. "Guru Gurajani."

Delaney frowned. "The tea man? God my mother used to swear by his Rooibos magic blend. He must be like ninety-years-old now. No way he's running a scam like this. It's too big."

Asha finished her salad and stood up. "I guess it's a

place to start. I have to go. That zoning complaint. Remember?"

"Trees. The developers promised to plant trees. Make sure they have a commitment to planting trees, watering them and a definite date to comply."

Asha nodded. "You sure you don't want to go? You're the chief."

Delaney shook his head. "I'll only get angry and piss people off again. Trees, Asha. The City wants a binding commitment to parkland around the project. Make them aware that we hold the cards for their permit. Trees first, development later."

Asha grabbed her notes and left. She had to save the trees.

Hours later Delaney was toiling through a damn list of names.

"Mrs Tate?"

"Who is this? How did you get my number?"

"We represent the Office of City Oversight. You made a complaint about the Jirdasham Method. The Zero Pain Company..."

Delaney heard her breath suck in. Clearly, she hadn't expected a return call.

"That was months ago."

"Well we're making investigations and I ..."

"I withdrew my complaint. I definitely withdrew it."

"So, you're no longer in pain, Mrs Tate?"

"I told you people I withdrew my complaint."

"Would you describe yourself as a satisfied customer?"

The phone abruptly disconnected. Delaney dutifully crossed out her name from the long list. He dialed another number.

"Mrs Orfang?"

"Who is this?"

"Delaney. We represent the Office of City Oversight. You made a complaint about the Jirdasham Institute. The Zero Pain Company on March 29th this year. I suspect you paid them a lot of money."

There was a momentary silence. Delaney could hear a TV on in the background. "I told someone there. I withdrew my complaint."

"You're completely satisfied with ..."

"I withdrew my complaint. Didn't you hear me?" She disconnected.

Another name to cross off. People were so damn rude these days. He looked at the clock. Another half hour and he could leave. It was his choice to start this agency, walk away from the big salary in Paris. He'd told himself that he could bury himself in the minutiae of city life back home and the pain in his heart would disappear. He had forgotten just how petty and demeaning representing City Hall could be. He'd been happy to get the contract, it paid the rent, but it wasn't quite what he'd planned for. And this, calling up complainers, was supposed to be Alice's job. So easy to go off with stress and get your full salary paid for three months. Not as if she did much when she was at work. Perhaps the Mayor was right. Privatize the whole thing. Hire staff motivated to work hard for their salary. He shook his head, it was difficult to get his old life out of his system. No one in City Hall would survive a week in his previous company, except Asha.

He dialed another number.

A little later Asha returned from the meeting wearing a new hat. She was grinning, looked so pleased to be alive.

"Still raining. I'm so happy for the trees and flowers. Shit, Chief, you look frazzled. How's it going with the army of pain junkies?"

"Not good so far. You hear the rumor there's going to be another garbage strike?"

Asha flung her soggy hat to one side. "And guess whose son-in-law owns a private waste company. The Mayor's been wanting to privatize waste collection since he got into power."

Delaney sighed. "Might be you're a tad cynical, Ash."

Asha nodded. "My generation. We know everything's fucked."

Delaney couldn't argue with that. "How did the meeting go?"

"They made promises. I made them strongly aware that they can't start the development unless they layout the park in first. They tried to squirm, but Mabuza from Parks and Environment was there from City Hall and he beat them up good. He's told me that he thinks we're doing a good job"

Delaney laughed. "That usually means they're about to terminate our contract. No one wants us to do a good job in City Hall, Ash."

"Now's who's the cynic."

Asha glanced at all the names crossed off on the printout. "Wow, you've been busy. Alice would have made that list last a week."

"Almost all of them claim to have withdrawn their complaints, or they want to complain about something else entirely unrelated. None of them are what I would call 'nice' people.

"All withdrawing? Isn't that just a bit strange?"

"You think? Got two who haven't responded. I'll check on them tomorrow. Most hang up on me, but no one will say why they've changed their minds."

"Normally people love complaining in this city. You should see the feedback online. It's like City Hall is Satan incorporated."

"Maybe they are. Have you ever to tried getting through to any department on the phone?" Delaney asked. "Impossible." He picked up his list again tapping at the names and sighed. "It's almost as if someone knew these people complained to us."

Asha frowned. "I could call Alice. She should have logged them withdrawing complaints. You think we've been hacked?"

"You seriously think anything we do here interests anyone?"

Asha laughed. "I suppose. Must be quite a come down for you working here. Alice said that you were used to handling millions back in Paris. I bet you never thought you'd be slumming it back in Berg City."

Delaney placed his hands behind his head and tried to exercise his neck. He was stiff from making calls. He looked down for the dog, then remembered Rufus wasn't there. Damn he missed that dog.

"When my wife died, I made a choice to walk away from that life, Ash. I wasn't in a good place. Thought I could start a small agency and see where it goes. I was lucky we got the City Hall contract, but perhaps they weren't counting on us actually turning anything up that would embarrass them.

The Mayor, I sense, doesn't quite appreciate the idea of 'oversight' as much as the taxpayers in this city do."

Asha smiled. "At least I know you take what we do seriously."

Delaney smiled, unlocking his fingers. "Always take what you do seriously, Ash. Learn what you can here and take it with you for your next job."

Asha shook her head. "I don't want to move on yet. I like working with you."

Delaney scribbled two addresses on his notebook. "I'll be in late tomorrow. I'm kinda curious now about this 'We feel your pain.' scam."

"Not a scam if everyone withdraws their complaints, right?"

Delaney stood up and arched his back. He'd spent too long in one position. "Maybe I wasn't going to take it seriously in the beginning, but now I'm interested. A lot of the people I called were genuinely scared that we'd follow up on their complaints. That has to be worth investigating, don't you think?"

Ash nodded. "What can I do?"

"Trace the owners. I want to know who benefits and whose endorsing them, aside from the Mayor. You know the rules. Follow the money."

Ash grinned. "On it. See you tomorrow, Chief."

Delaney's iPhone rang. He answered and glanced up at Ash with a grin.

"Tonight? You sure? Great. I'll be there in half an hour."

Ash looked at him quizzically.

"Rufus is OK to come home. They've cauterized his bite; injected antibiotics and they want him to recover at home."

"You can leave him home tomorrow?"

Delaney shrugged, pulling on his jacket. "He can sleep here just as well. Got to go. There's a dog needing his supper."

Asha watched him go, fascinated at how happy he seemed to be collecting his dog. She kind of envied him. What was it about dog people?

She grabbed her hat and followed him out.

CHAPTER SEVEN

The Return of Maria

"I still hate you."

Delaney stared at Maria with bleary eyes and tried to recall if her mother had mentioned that she was staying over.

"And good morning to you, Miss Sunshine."

Maria narrowed her 13-year-old blue eyes and gave him the death stare. It wasn't working. She winced as she shifted on her stool.

"I don't remember you arriving. What do you want for breakfast?"

"You don't have anything but fucking muesli."

Delaney shrugged. "Fucking muesli is what keeps your gut healthy. You want everything laced with sugar poison you've broken into the wrong house. I've got pineapple juice, bananas and quite possibly rye bread to toast. Your choice, Maria."

Maria wrinkled her nose. "You're such a loser."

Delaney shrugged. "Listen kid, without us losers there wouldn't be winners. We play a big part in their success."

Maria stuck her tongue out. Delaney noticed it was white. Not a good thing. He hadn't expected to see her again. Dating her feckless mother had been a stupid moment of weakness on his part. He pondered how to play this situation.

"I'm not hungry."

"Of course. It's always best to go to school hungry. I know how much it helps with the concentration."

Maria sighed. She hated his irony.

"I'm pouring you juice and if you get down on your knees and beg I'll make you a smoothie."

"I'm not going to beg," she snorted, then realized he was baiting her.

"Just as well, as I have just remembered your mother stole my blender."

Maria glared as he poured her a glass of juice. He cut two slices of bread for her too and didn't object when he popped them into the toaster.

"Any particular reason you're here? I swear I remember you and your mother moved out three months ago now and you were pretty definite about how crap I was. Not heard a word since."

Delaney scooped out some muesli for himself and poured almond milk on it.

"She's dating. He's a complete moron."

"Naturally. But why are you here? I swear I changed the locks."

Maria smirked. "Didn't fix the back door though."

"You let yourself in, or did your mother drop you off? You're lucky Rufus isn't well. He might have bitten your head off."

"Rufus loves me. He wouldn't hurt a fly. Where is he?"

"Sleeping. I haven't woken him yet. He's on some strong pills and off his food. He got bitten and it went bad."

Maria looked genuinely concerned. "Poor Rufie."

The toast popped up and she helped herself, lathering on some jam. "You're out of dairy-free spread."

"Duly noted. Tell me, why are you here?"

"Rafe, the moron doesn't like kids. Specifically, he doesn't like me."

"Your mother dumped you here?" Delaney asked, with growing annoyance.

"No."

"So, you just thought you'd come back."

Maria shrugged, crunching on her toast.

Delaney began to eat his muesli and thought some more about this 'situation'. "I'll call her."

Maria said nothing.

"It's OK, Maria. You're safe here. You know that. Just promise me you'll keep your room tidy."

Maria stared at him as if contemplating the offer. She was tough, growing up with a mother who couldn't stay with any man for more than a few months made her fatalistic. But just hearing him say 'your room' meant more than he could ever know.

"How's your back? Delaney asked.

"Same."

"The acupuncture didn't help?" He'd paid for six appointments.

"No. Nothing helps. I got needle scars to prove it."

Delaney raised his eyebrows as she showed him a rash on her side from the needles. "Ouch. That's not supposed to happen. You complain?"

"She wouldn't give the money back. Ma bitched her out but ..."

Delaney cut himself a slice of bread. He noticed Maria watching his hands.

"Still swollen. I know. Doc says it could be arthritis or fibromyalgia. The needles didn't do anything for me either."

"Maybe it's all this healthy food." Maria suggested, smirking. "Won't fix your hands and it sure as hell won't fix my spine."

"You're not back on painkillers, are you? You know what I think about those."

Maria rolled her eyes. "If I wanted to be a zombie, I'd take em. Plenty of people do. Rafe the moron wants me on them. He gets sick of me being a pain. Rafe the moron is a male nurse at Liberty hospital. He says he can get me any drugs I want."

"This does not fill me with joy, Maria. Male nurse, huh. Quite a catch for your Ma."

Maria smiled; she knew he was being sarcastic. "He's ten years younger than her too. She's like giggling all the time, makes me vomit. He's so going to dump her when he finds out she's thirty-eight."

Delaney nodded. "That he will. Just don't take anything he offers. OK? You're the strong one; remember. You fractured your back, but time will heal it. You're young and things will mend without opioids."

"It's taking too long." Maria said with a heavy sigh. "I'm sick of being the school cripple. I'm sick of all the mean shit they say about me." She remembered about the dog. "Can I see Rufie? I missed him so much."

Delaney smiled. "Now we get the real reason you're here. He's on antibiotics. Nearly lost his tail."

"Nooo. He'd be such a freak without his tail. Shit,

we're all like broken dolls or something. You with your hands and me the spaz, now Rufus is sick. Bad karma, Delaney."

Delaney laughed. "Karma? What do you know about karma? Your mother into crystals now and all that stuff?"

"I know about karma. Fate. Everything happens for a reason."

"Hmm. That day you ran off to the cliffs?" Delaney asked. "You think it was karma you fell and fractured your spine?"

It had been one hell of a day. Her mother screaming that she wanted out of the relationship and yelling at Maria because she'd locked herself in her room to block out the screaming. He'd done his best to remain calm and even offered to pack for her, but she'd wanted money to get her own place and the argument got ugly.

Maria pouted. "Rufus found me, remember? I love him and he came looking for me. That's karma."

Delaney accepted that. It was true Maria and the dog had bonded quickly. That day Rufus had increasingly behaved oddly and wanted out, throwing himself at the door and then the garden security gate. Delaney had thought it was the screaming that was driving the dog mad. When they discovered Maria had disappeared, he'd finally let Rufus go and he'd dashed straight up the hill towards the cliffs. It had always been a complete mystery to him as to how he knew she'd be there. Took three hours to get an emergency crew down there to hoist her up. All those months in a back brace hadn't exactly improved her moods, add a shitty mother always having to move each time she left another man, Maria was surprisingly resilient and sane.

"Can I stay until Rafe dumps her?"

Delaney shrugged. "I'll call her. Not up to me, you know that."

Maria knew that. She had no control over anything. Being thirteen totally sucked.

Delaney's phone vibrated on the counter. They both stared at it as it spun around. "That will be her, my guess." He picked it up and put it on speaker.

"She's here."

"That little bitch. Didn't even leave a note. I've been worried sick."

"She's fine. Having breakfast. I'll take her to school."

There was a rather overlong pause. They could both hear her 'thinking'. Maria made a face and Delaney knew exactly what she was thinking.

"She needs a break from me and ..."

"Maria can stay. She's no trouble."

"You sure?" They both could hear the 'relief' in her voice.

"Her room is still here. She'll be fine. She'll need clothes and stuff."

Maria smirked. She knew her mother was trying not to sound yippy skippy about this.

"It will only be for a few days."

Delaney knew different. "It's fine. Leave the stuff she needs by my delivery nook, OK?"

Maria frowned; her mother would choose all the stuff she hated to wear.

"Yeah, yeah, of course. Later today. I've got an interview."

"Happy to hear it." Delaney said, noting that she hadn't asked to speak to Maria. They could hear someone shouting something in the background.

"Got to go." She disconnected.

Delaney stared at the phone a moment. "Rafe sounds nice."

Maria snorted. "Moron. He's probably gay."

"Just because he's a nurse doesn't make him gay."

"He's got a moustache."

Delaney frowned. "Remember our talks about tolerance of other people." She rolled her eyes. Delaney decided this was a battle for another day. He finished his toast. "We're leaving in five. At the risk of you hissing venom at me – may I suggest your hair could be brushed. Your toothbrush is still in the guest bathroom."

Maria wrinkled her nose. "I do not hiss venom."

Delaney grinned as he rinsed his glass. "Well that's an improvement. Five minutes. I've got to get Rufus up and fed."

Maria stood slowly, testing her back and went downstairs towards her room. Delaney realized that he'd missed her, despite her moods. How strange was that. Nevertheless, he made a note on his phone to change the back-door lock.

CHAPTER EIGHT

A Dog's Breakfast

"Don't shit on the sidewalk, dog. It's a two-grand fine in this neighborhood." Rufus glanced up at him, his eyebrows knitted together. That's the thing about dogs; understand what the eyebrows are saying, and you've got dog speak down pat.

"I hear you. A dog's got to do what a dog's got to do. I only got three shit bags left, you got more in you, put a cork in it."

They were standing outside a fancy white timbered cottage with a ten-year-old Jaguar on the drive. Nothing looked amiss, the lawn was dutifully manicured, the surrounding homes were all in the three to five million bracket and Delaney look a bet with himself that none of the neighbors knew each other. Average age of the residents would be 60 plus, the perfect target for a company looking to make money out of their aches and pains. His mother used to play Bridge with some people on Herzog Avenue; he wondered if any were still alive after the virus swept through this enclave. He remembered working a hot summer painting houses nearby when he was student to pay his tuition fees. He sure as hell couldn't do that now, not with his hands the way they were.

"Leave your tail alone, Rufus. Let the bandage do its work."

Rufus growled at his tail. But reluctantly obeyed.

His phone rang. "What's up, Ash? I'm at the Palmer house now."

"Guess who's a shareholder in our scam show?"

"Oh, some saint in the business world no doubt."

"Gus Huissan."

Delaney blinked. "Isn't he..."

"In jail for tax fraud. Took the City for thirty million in the stadium disaster."

"Keep digging, Ash. Good work. I wonder if our Mayor knows."

"I bet he does. I'm digging. Call me when you've seen Mrs Palmer. She's one of the few who haven't retracted their complaint. Hell, I hope she's still alive."

Delaney looked at his phone a moment. He hadn't really contemplated that.

"I'll see you later."

"Tomorrow. I've got tennis practice remember."

Delaney disconnected. He hadn't played tennis for such a long time. All the damn things he couldn't do anymore.

"You staying or coming?" He asked Rufus.

The dog gave up on sniffing the bushes.

A pile of newspapers lay scattered on the porch. Not a good sign. The mail slot was overstuffed with flyers and when he pressed the bell – no one came. He didn't really expect them to. Of course, anyone could go away for a few days and forget to cancel the papers - not that anyone seemed to get the papers much anymore. That was his first surprise when he'd returned from Europe. No one was selling the papers at street corners. People either just read their phones or ignored the news altogether.

"Let's take a look around, Rufus."

Rufus leapt away. He knew the drill.

Delaney pushed open a side gate. It resisted but wasn't locked, why would it be, this had to be the safest neighborhood in the city.

He heard barking. Rufus had met opposition.

The white fluffy thing looked terrified as Rufus towered over it. The rear French window was ajar. Could be the place had been burgled if Mrs Palmer was away, but Delaney's sixth sense told him it was something else entirely.

He scooped up the little dog. Rufus swept inside, fearless as always.

Mrs Palmer lay unconscious on the kitchen floor in a puddle of urine. Her phone rested on the kitchen counter; an upended dog bowl seemed to have been the culprit to cause her fall. He called emergency services. He felt her wrist. She was alive at least. He found something to put under her head and as she came around, he gave her water to sip.

"I've called an ambulance, Mrs Palmer. Are you in any pain?"

The woman stared at him in wonder, clearly disorientated, and then laughed, choking on the water. It was quite disconcerting.

He fed a dog that was quite desperate for its dinner and Rufus helped himself as well. It was quite a kitchen. He wasn't the marble and gold edging type himself, but clearly Mrs Palmer hadn't stinted herself on the place.

He had to wait for the ambulance, so he made sure Mrs Palmer kept drinking water. When the woman seemed to have regained some of her composure, Delaney tried to get her to talk.

"Is there anyone I should call?"

Mrs Palmer shook her head. She was getting control of herself now. Had no idea who the man was, but she was very grateful he was there.

"I'm so sorry," she kept saying, aware that she stank of piss.

"You sure you're not in pain? Your leg is definitely broken, Mrs Palmer. I'm not moving you, but you have to be feeling something."

Indeed, Mrs Palmer could plainly see her leg was spread at an awkward angle and her ankles were excessively swollen, but she simply could not feel a thing.

"I'm not in pain." She answered at last, licking her dry chapped lips. "That's the whole problem. I can't feel a thing anymore."

"You had dealings with the Jirdasham Institute. The 'We feel your pain' people."

Mrs Palmer shook her head in sorrow. "You don't understand. I was in such pain." She began to cry. "But now I can't feel anything. It's not right. It really isn't right. And who will look after Henrietta? She's a very particular dog."

Delaney reassured her that arrangements would be made. He took some notes but wanted to know more.

"So, it didn't work the first time?"

Mrs Palmer sipped some more water and sucked on the ice he'd given her to soothe her chapped lips. "Oh yes, it worked, but not for long. I was so upset. I wanted to kill myself when the pain came shooting back, Mr Delaney. You have no idea how shocked I was. Devastated. Thirty thousand it cost me, and it had all returned after just two weeks."

"Then they offered you a booster."

"It was so expensive. I resisted at first, of course."

"Naturally."

"But then they said if the booster didn't work, they would refund me everything. I considered that honorable."

Delaney nodded. "Entirely reasonable. Then you paid for the booster."

"Yes. Reluctantly; but yes, I paid. And it worked. But it worked too well. I burned myself on the hotplate and didn't even notice until too late. Now look. My leg. They said I wouldn't feel pain and they're absolutely right, but Mr Delaney, I can't feel anything at all. This can't be right. It's unnatural."

"And who did the treatment, Mrs Palmer? Do you remember?"

Mrs Palmer stared at him as if he was talking nonsense.

"The Guru, of course. I demanded it. It was a lot of money. A disciple treated me the first time, but I wanted the best if I was paying again. He laid on his hands and sang to me. It was strange, but I mean you expect that, he's the Guru. He's the one who started it. He personally guaranteed that I would never feel pain again."

Delaney smiled. "It's good to know a company that keeps its word, Mrs Palmer. I hope that when they fix you up that you take precautions in future."

The ambulance crew arrived finally and took over. Delaney promised to lock up and leave the keys in a safe place. She wouldn't be back home for quite a while he figured.

"Promise me you'll call my friend about the dog." Mrs Palmer pleaded before they shut the ambulance doors.

"I promise." Delaney replied, aware that after all that had just happened to her the dog was her main concern. Who would care for little Henrietta, who hadn't eaten her after all?

CHAPTER NINE

Back Trouble

She was sitting on the school steps all alone reading a book. He was almost an hour late. She looked so vulnerable. But he knew she was good at protecting herself, a natural survivor. Delaney lowered the passenger side window. "Sorry. I hope that book's more interesting than what I've just been reading."

Maria looked up and was going to give him a mouthful for being late but swallowed her words. He'd come for her as promised. He didn't have to. She could have used the bus.

She gathered her things and ambled towards to his Discovery. Then broke into smiles as Rufus stuck his head out wagging his tail.

"Don't wag, Rufie. I don't want you to break your tail."

She climbed into the back seat with him and hugged him.

"I can't believe he let a rat bite him. I hope he bit back."

Delaney kind of hoped not. Who knew what diseases that rat was carrying?

"I'm going to swing by the Deli on the way home. Anything you fancy for supper? You're still semi-vegan right?"

"Can we have lentil and quinoa burgers? I have a thing for those."

Delaney grinned. "We can, but don't share with Rufus. He's liable to explode if you give him lentils."

Maria laughed and buried her face into Rufus's fur. "Poor Rufie." Then she looked at him in the driving mirror. "I guess you're rounding up all the strays today."

"Had to find someone to take care of a dog. Not as easy as you think. Dare I ask how school is going or do I get the usual 'ugh'?"

"Shit, worse than ugh. The principal came to our class today to talk about career choices. I told her what you said."

"Uh, oh, what did I say?"

"That AI is going to take all the jobs. That humans will

be redundant."

"Well that happens to be true. What did she say?"

"She said 'Own the robots'."

Delaney laughed. "She's not wrong. Smart woman."

Maria looked thoughtful. "It's hard to get motivated about school or jobs if you think robots are going replace all of us. That's what you said, right?"

"An A Star for listening. The trick is to try and stay one step ahead of AI. Figure out jobs they can't do - yet. Caring for instance."

"Wiping asses. Rafe the Moron does that. Looks after old people."

"Robots will not be cleaning our assess anytime soon, I think. But then again, if no one has jobs, who can pay to get their ass wiped? You see the dilemma."

Maria rolled her eyes. "You fill me with such hope."

"Prepare for the revolution, M. Join an Army. You'll get fed."

"And get killed. I've seen that movie."

"That's another AI proof business. Burying the dead. You see how life is full of possibilities."

Maria buried her head into Rufus again. "I'm not going to be an undertaker. Got any careers that don't involve asses or dead bodies?"

"Well AI will be taking most of the teachers' and lawyers' jobs, doctors' too. With luck it will also solve climate change and all our economic problems. There's going to be millions of people with a lot of spare time. My guess is you could keep them entertained."

"Great, clowns. You want me to be a clown."

"The Great Bellucci. I can see you terrorizing kids with water cannons."

Maria laughed. "Now you're talking. Water Cannons. Fucking Ace. That has possibilities. I should practice at school. Some bitches need taking down."

"Wasn't quite what I was thinking. When was your birthday? I missed it, right?"

"Two months ago. Thirteen. Welcome to the worst years of my life."

Delaney smiled. "Doesn't have to be. I took up sailing at thirteen and you couldn't drag me off the water after that.

Made some good friends too."

Maria didn't comment. "I'm going to need new shoes. These are falling apart."

"Noted."

"Rufus needs a shower. He's pretty stinky."

"Tomorrow maybe. Not whilst his tail is bandaged."

Maria settled back, checking Rufus's face. "Tomorrow, dog. Your date with destiny. I know how much you like that blow dryer."

Delaney grinned. Maria was good for Rufus. She was so lost. He wondered how long her mother would leave her with him. Still couldn't believe he'd started up with her. What had he been thinking? Tried to tell himself that he had to move on from Denise, but why he picked on someone so insecure and unstable he had no idea.

He pulled into the Deli car park. "You staying in the car or coming with?"

"Staying." She looked up at him a moment. "You ever miss my mother?"

"Not for one second. Missed you occasionally, but her? Not once."

Maria nodded. "I bet all the guys say that."

Maria didn't appear for breakfast the next morning. Delaney felt aggrieved by this. She knew the routine. If she wanted a ride to school, she had to be ready and eating breakfast by 7.30. He sent Rufus down to fetch her, but then he didn't return either. He frowned. Maria wasn't a kid who enjoyed missing school; she'd missed too much already and didn't want to fall behind.

He walked to the top of the basement stairs. "Mia? Rufus?"

Rufus appeared at the bottom of the stairs and made worried sounds. Delaney was attuned enough to know Rufus meant for him to come down and look for himself.

"OK, I'm coming down. What's the problem?"

Rufus didn't wait and disappeared back into Maria's room.

Maria was sitting on the bedroom floor, her pj's stained with wee. He could see she'd been crying. She didn't look up at him.

"Can't move. Can't fucking do anything," she spat out,

angry at herself and the fact that he had to see her like this again.

Delaney made no comment and went to work. He knew the drill. He'd had to do this many times after her fall.

"Your back or your hips?"

Maria looked up at him angrily. "I don't know. Just can't move."

"You should have called me. The bell is …" He glanced up and saw the bell was sitting on the window ledge, out of reach. His fault. He thought she'd moved out forever.

"I'm going to lift you."

"I stink. I'm sorry. I don't mean to do this."

Delaney said nothing. He knew it was best to be as calm as he could and not get hysterical like her mother. Ignoring her sodden pajamas, he got behind her to lift the way he'd been taught to do.

"No sudden movements. Yell if it hurts. Take a deep breath – now!"

He got her standing. "Test your legs, M."

She knew what to do.

"Pins and needles, ow, ow, ow…"

"Pull up your toes. Stay focused. It's just the blood circulation starting up." He waited a moment. "I'm going to walk you over the shower. You OK to stand in the shower? The railing is still there. Or did you want me to find you the stool?"

Maria gritted her teeth, the pain was excruciating, but far worse was the humiliation. She hated not having control over her own body.

"Stand," she whispered. Not so tough right now.

Delaney got her to the shower, turned it on and waited until the hot water was flowing. He walked her into it, getting soaked in the process, but let her grab the rail and slowly ease herself upright as the hot water helped ease the pain.

"I hate this."

Delaney was about to go to give her privacy.

"Stay. Take them off. I can't bend yet."

He knew the last thing she wanted was for him to stay or see her naked, so she had to be in a lot of pain. He helped her out of her pjs and then dribbled shampoo on her hair and squirted soap on her back. She gingerly washed herself, one hand firmly gripping the rail.

Delaney noticed how thin she was. "Your mother feeding you at all? You're eating, right? I mean, you've got the broken back badge; you're not going for the slimmer of the year award too I hope."

Maria swore, which Delaney read as a good sign. "She went on some stupid diet. No protein, no carbs. Rafe the Moron likes her thin."

Delaney winced. OK, she hadn't been eating. Also noted.

Once dried, he wrapped her in his old dressing gown and carried her upstairs and put her in the high-backed chair he'd bought for her months ago and so casually abandoned when they'd moved out. "You can sit OK?"

She nodded.

"Breakfast in a moment. I just have to get dry first." He turned around to the dog and Rufus was close by as ever. "Take care of her, all right?"

Rufus laid his head on her lap and Maria gently pulled at his soft ears. She couldn't believe her back had just given way like that. One slight movement the wrong way, her back seized up. This was not what they had promised at the hospital.

Delaney returned a few minutes later and found her leaning back into the chair, her eyes closed. Rufus still keeping guard.

"I called the school. New principal. She's very understanding. She thinks you're very brave and a good student."

Maria opened her eyes. "I miss the team. You're like nobody if you're not on a team."

"Well I guess you're not going to be running anytime soon. Any other teams you can join?"

"What? Chess club? Bring your own wheelchair."

"I was thinking of something that expressed your wonderful 'personalities'."

Maria lowered her head, but he saw that he almost got a smile out of her. Delaney made breakfast. She didn't protest when he pushed the muesli under her nose.

"What happened to that magic crème you got from New York for your hands?"

Delaney poured them both glasses of juice and tossed

Rufus a dental chew to keep him busy.

"The thing about magic crème is that you have to believe in them to make them work. Frank's Crème held so much promise. It's a miracle in a tube. $300 bucks of belief, in fact. Want to try it? It does work for around fifteen minutes or so."

"Fifteen minutes sounds pretty good right now."

"I'll get it after I've had my coffee."

Maria ate, tried not to breathe too hard as it hurt.

"Did you fall or what?" Delaney asked as he put marmalade on his toast.

Maria shook her head. "Didn't do anything. I just swung my legs out of bed to go to the bathroom and that was it. I couldn't move. Just before that I was dreaming that I was in a cage. It was so weird."

Delaney shrugged. "Sounds like muscle pain. Remember when I couldn't even put my jacket on, couldn't lift my arms it hurt so much. That was before the pain went to my hands. I haven't decided if that's an improvement yet. But yeah, sometimes being in pain feels like you're in a cage and if only there was some way to open that door, you'd fly away free from it."

Maria looked at him curiously for a moment. "I thought you'd kill yourself actually. It's like pain controls you. I want this to be over, Delaney. I want to be normal again."

Delaney smiled. "You might be pain free soon enough, girl, but normal? Not you."

Maria stuck her tongue out him; but didn't object. She knew what he meant.

CHAPTER TEN

The Guru

An hour later he was at the office. He'd left Rufus with Maria to take care of her emotional needs. He hoped she'd study, but then again there was always the temptation of daytime TV.

Asha was working at the computer. She looked up and smiled.

"How's the brat? I can't believe you let her back in."

Delaney shrugged. "She's in a lot of pain and angry. She's been pretty much discarded by her mother. Maria's almost too tough for her own good."

Asha sipped on her coffee. "But you're the sucker who cares for her. She'll get all comfortable with you, then spit in your face again."

"You're too hard on her. She's scared she won't get better."

"You're too soft. Rufus knew a sucker when he saw one."

"You have it wrong, Ash." Delaney returned to his desk, booting up his computer. "Rufus rescued me. You have no idea what black hole I was in after my wife died. Couldn't find my way forward at all. I was lucky Rufus was there needing help." He glanced over at her. "You might think you don't need anyone. I was like that once. I'm pretty sure I was an arrogant bastard too, but I was the skipper and took responsibility way too seriously. I can't even remember that person now."

Asha shrugged, turning back to her screen. "I've made some progress I think."

"Oh?"

"Spoke with Mina in the tax office. My last and worst temp job ever. Jirdasham is registered to an offshore shell company in Panama, it's just a number, no name, and they in turn license the 'healing' process to Jirdasham. Everything is rented – all the staff are self-employed. Perfect gig economics 101. The Guru is listed as a consultant, even though from reading their stuff you'd think he was running it all. Mina says it's unlikely they pay any corporate tax either."

"If anyone tries to sue to get their money back – there's nothing there."

"The money probably goes straight out of the country the moment it's paid."

"But the staff must get paid here."

"The rent is paid locally. They probably keep a token amount in the city. No assets. Almost as if they were expecting to get sued."

Delaney nodded. "I would so like to track down the Guru. Mrs Palmer told me that he personally treated her."

Asha frowned. "I don't get it. They probably have thousands of clients, right? No way this ancient Guru is treating all these people. Did our client get treated by the Guru as well?"

Delaney couldn't recall. "I'll ask him. It's a good point. Let's say he treats two people a day five days a week. We're talking what just over five hundred people a year. They've only been operating what…?"

"Almost three years, max." Asha answered. "Fifteen hundred customers. Of which 308 initially made complaints this year."

Delaney was thinking. "If everyone is paying what Mr Abrams paid, that's around…"

"Forty-five million." She whistled. "Did I get that wrong?"

Delaney shook his head. "That's a lot of money to not pay any tax on. Don't forget they're also charging clients for boosters when the first session doesn't work."

Asha stared at her screen. "We are definitely in the wrong business, Chief."

Delaney smiled. "We most certainly are. It's also a lot of money to process every year without raising red flags with the IRS. We need to tread carefully. Which bank are they using? Who are their accountants? They'll be very protective of such a cash heavy outfit."

"I wonder what kick-back the Mayor is getting?"

"You can be sure his next election campaign is fully paid up. I definitely need to speak with the Guru. Do we have any clues on how to find him?"

"Not yet. Have you tried their clinic?"

"Not sure how to approach this without alerting that we're looking at them. They're based in that old restored shoe factory on Wharf Street, right?"

Asha nodded. "I could go." She made a sad face. "On behalf of my dear mother who's crippled with pain."

Delaney looked at her quizzically. "Isn't your mother really sporty?"

Asha shrugged. "Yeah. We don't talk, that's all. She married the most evil guy in the universe and wonders why no one will visit her. She's the fittest forty-five-year-old in the city. Plays tennis almost every day. Used to be a local champion actually."

"There's enough real people in pain we could send their way if we need to, I'll go, give them a peek at my jazz hands."

Asha glanced at his hands as he waved them in the air. "Well at least you wouldn't be faking it." She sighed. "Actually, I doubt my mother could feel pain even if you put a stake through her heart."

Delaney stood up to go. "Let's find the Guru, he'll be the key to everything. I'll talk to Mrs Palmer and Mr Abrams perhaps they know more than they realize. Where are you going today?"

"Following up on all those testimonials from physios and chiropractors they have on their website. You would think they wouldn't want the competition."

"If they could charge thirty grand to treat someone they damn well would. But they can't promise zero pain. But you can guess they get paid well for a referral. Tread carefully, Ash. Maybe make it sound like your keen for your mother to get treated."

Asha nodded. "Yeah, will do, Chief." Her watch beeped. "Time for my jog. Trouble is with all this jogging I get so hungry. I swear I put on weight after every lap around the park."

Delaney smiled looking at her. "I doubt there is a scintilla of excess weight on your body, Ash. "

She snorted. "There better not be. The moment I can't wear my old skinny jeans I'll have to kill myself."

Delaney stood up, looking for his car keys. "You ever hear of a company called Slam Cakes?"

Ash narrowed her eyes. "You know I don't allow the

word 'cake' in the workspace."

"Actually they made the best healthy cupcake in the world."

"Healthy cupcakes? That's a thing?"

"All-natural ingredients, fat free, gluten free, vegan, so guilt free. Eat as many as you like and never get fat."

Asha laughed. "Yeah right. Let me guess, they lied"

"They went from one store to fifty in a year. Everyone swore by them. Lines around the block. Then someone wrote an article on-line saying they weren't vegan, or gluten free and probably had more calories than a ten-tier wedding cake."

"No shit. I guess that was the end of Slamcakes."

Delaney nodded. "The woman who wrote the article exposing them neglected to mention she was a silent partner in a rival cupcake company. This only came to light when she got sued."

"But meanwhile Slamcakes was toast (so to speak)."

"Turned out that the cupcakes were healthy after all, but of course the damage was done."

Asha frowned. "And you're telling me this because you think our client is working for a rival company?"

"Or Mr Abrams has an agenda. I'm not saying he has, just that here's a company apparently doing miracles and we don't want to come at them headfirst in case they have achieved the impossible."

"You confuse me sometimes, Chief."

Delaney shrugged. "Sometimes I just like to believe in miracles. Ask anyone in long-term pain. That's what they want most of all."

Asha grinned. "Like healthy cupcakes."

"Yep. A miracle in a paper cup." He glanced at his watch.

"Catch you later. I'm going to see the Commodore. He's always got his eyes and ears open."

The patient sat upright on the chair; bare feet planted squarely on the floor as instructed. He was dressed in a pale blue hospital gown and seemed nervous. His hands lay in his lap and he was aware of each painful throbbing finger. He could almost sense the gristle growing in his pinkies, distorting them ever more out of shape. He hated his hands now and how he kept dropping things, he could barely get a firm grip on his paintbrush anymore.

The Guru was studying him from across the room, his disciple, Rafael standing beside him. The Guru knew that Rafael fancied that he would one day replace him, despite the fact that he seemed to have little spirituality about him and even less empathy with the patients.

The patient was trying the deep breathing exercise that the Guru had asked him to do. He'd agreed to the disciple being at the session as he got a small discount on the price and every cent mattered to him. He'd given Jirdasham his entire life savings so far and was pissed that the first all-day session had given him no relief at all. Thirty grand flushed away with all the anti-toxins they had made him swallow. He'd insisted that if they wanted more, the Guru himself had to treat him and finally after months that day had come. If it didn't work, he'd seriously considered ending it all. Had they no idea how fucking desperate he was? What kind of artist couldn't pick up a pen without being in agony? How was he supposed to concentrate?

"Can you raise your arm, Mr Alexander? Your left arm," Rafael asked him.

He raised his arm, but only as far as being level with his shoulders, he couldn't go further.

The Guru's expression didn't change. Rafael thanked him.

"Did you list your diet as we asked you to?"

The patient nodded. "Yes, I eat fresh fish mostly now. I live by the harbor at Jarrick Bay. I won't touch meat."

"And alcohol? Wine, beer, whisky?" Rafael asked.

"Not anymore. I can't drink wine; it makes my toes hurt. I think it's the sulphur."

Rafael walked around the back of the man. "Yes, it's acidic, no other alcohol?"

"No."

"How long?"

"Four years."

"And no meat?"

"Ten, at least."

"You're aware that a high fish diet may contain mercury?"

The patient made a face. "I have to eat something."

Rafael put pressure on the man's neck and asked him to raise his arm again. He managed to raise it just a little higher than the previous time.

Rafael told him to lower it. He looked over at the Guru.

"His spine is out of line and needs cracking. His hands are at second stage osteoarthritis and he has virtually no mobility in his neck." He glanced at the patient. "You spend long periods of time doing one task I think."

"Yes, it's true, I'm an artist."

"You need to do these neck exercises" Rafael demonstrated turning and lowering and raising his head to get the maximum flexibility. "Often."

The Guru slipped off his chair and came closer to the patient. "Good assessment, Rafael. Now take hold of his hands."

Rafael came around to the front and took up Mr Alexander's hands.

"Rafael is going to apply positive energy to your hands. I'd like you to consider giving up fish for a whole year. None. Eat only vegetables, especially cruciferous vegetables. Cauliflower, broccoli, kale, spring greens, radishes, these can prevent DNA damage and help with your liver."

Rafael was holding the man's hands, rubbing the bony growths on the pinkies. "These must be sore."

The patient winced. They were sensitive to touch.

"Rafael will now apply positive energy directly through the hands. Rafael, focus your energies directly into his fingers like so." The Guru demonstrated with his own hands and Rafael followed him, closing his eyes to concentrate and channel his energy into the crippled hands.

The Guru watched keenly and smiled encouragement at the patient. "Any heat? Can you feel a tingling?"

The patient thought about it a moment, then shook his head.

The Guru frowned. "No heat at all?"

The patient shook his head again. The Guru tapped Rafael on the shoulder and bade him release the man's hands.

"Rafael, it's all about empathy. You must meld your mind with his; feel your way to his energy flow. You need to work on channeling." He took the patients hands into his own and laced his fingers between the patients.

Rafael backed away a little, annoyed that whatever the Guru did, he could not. They had tried this before, and he still couldn't generate any damn heat. He knew his way around the human body, but unless you were generating friction, there was no way to create heat in his book.

The Guru reminded the patient to relax. "Think of something beautiful, a place, a memory, a moment." He pressed their hands together with more force.

The patient began to frown; he could feel the beginnings of heat. He tried to think of the ruins at the base of the sand dune he'd been painting. How he'd paint it repeatedly, each time minded of the immense presence of the mountain of sand poised to engulf this building, but for some mysterious reason had remained in this symbiotic state of constant threat for countless years, ever threatening, never consumed.

The heat is his hands was intense, he wondered if he should yell to stop it, but this was the 'cure', this was the Guru and more importantly, this is what he had paid for. He wanted that cure; he wanted his hands back. He became aware that the Guru was singing. Rafael reluctantly joining in the mantra of joy, only he could tell that Rafael was faking it, the Guru was radiating joy and he could feel it engulf him, like an x-ray maybe, heat him up from the inside.

The Guru abruptly let go, he smiled as he stepped back and fell back onto his barrel chair.

The patient closed his eyes; he was almost vibrating.

"Place your arms straight out in front of you," the Guru gently asked him. He complied, his arms tingling, his hands still warm.

"Wiggle your fingers."

He wiggled and opened his eyes in astonishment. He was actually wiggling his damn fingers, that hadn't wiggled in nearly five whole years.

"Raise your arms." Rafael asked him.

He raised his arms. They both went well above his head with no pain.

The Guru giggled. "Enjoy your life now. Remember this isn't a cure; we have simply removed the pain. Eat cruciferous vegetables. Exercise your neck, keep the blood flowing."

The Guru left the room. Rafael asked him to go behind the screen and put his clothes back on.

The patient felt immensely happy, he had never really thought he could experience happiness ever again. It had cost him everything but finally he was cured.

"He's amazing," the patient declared.

Rafael shrugged as he headed for the door. "Don't forget to sign the forms on the way out." He left aware that the Guru had once again failed to show him the trick. It had to be a trick. There was no way he was channeling some mystery heat. Somehow, he was able to fool the patients into thinking they were cured. Whatever it was he wanted to know how, one way or another.

CHAPTER ELEVEN

The Commodore

He got through to Mr Abrams on the third try as he drove down to the harbor. Seemed he was well protected by staff decidedly unkeen to pass a call through to the boss.

"You're still working on it?" Mr Abrams asked when he finally came to the phone. "I wasn't sure you'd follow up."

"It's crazy but interesting, Mr Abrams. I met a woman who'd been treated by the Guru and she couldn't feel pain at all, even though she'd broken her leg and hips."

"I'm almost jealous," Mr Abrams told him. "I'm barely able to move my arms at all today and struggled to make it in. But if I'm not here, they lose motivation. Good people, but they need direction."

Delaney negotiated a roundabout and slowed for the security guards at the harbor entrance.

"Were you treated by the Guru himself, Mr Abrams?"

"No. His second-in-command, as it were. Calls himself Rafael. One of the disciples. I suspect not his real name."

"Did you ask for the Guru?"

"Yes, but he was busy treating others. I was guaranteed that Rafael was just as good, if not better."

"Hmmm. Ok. Well I'm trying to find the Guru. If you can think of anything that might trace him."

"He has a sister. She's an odd one. Jasmina. I have no idea where she lives but she's in Berg City somewhere. She's a spiritualist I believe. Should be possible to find her if you ask around."

"Thank you, Mr Abrams. I'll get back to you if and when I have something to report."

"I look forward to hearing it. Meanwhile, accept a case of wine from me. I wasn't sure you'd follow up but I'm happy your taking it seriously."

"I take pain seriously. Wine isn't necessary."

"I think you'll find it is, Mr Delaney. I'll have it dispatched to your home."

Delaney disconnected. Wondering how the old man

knew where he lived, but then again, he hadn't changed address in this city since he was 21. Anyone could find him. He was pretty sure that it broke professional investigators rules, but what the hell, he wasn't going to move over a case of wine.

The Commodore poured himself a generous slug of whiskey and offered the bottle to Delaney. Delaney shook his head. "Sticking with juice, Frank. Got a kid to feed later and need to keep sharp tonight."

The Commodore shrugged. "Luckily I'm all over that family stuff. Wife took the kids ten years ago and I didn't put up much of a fight. Never really liked 'em." He laughed, then winced as he coughed. "I don't suppose they'll turn up for my funeral anyway. I'm leaving what's left of my money to the Yacht Club."

Delaney could see he had aged considerably since his last visit. "You planning on dying soon?"

The Commodore waved his hand in a dismissive manner. "They say six months to a year. But I beat it last time, so I could beat it again. Whiskey has magic properties I'm told."

Delaney looked around the yacht club. It was nearly empty and in need of repair. Once this place had been his life, but it looked like it fallen on hard times. Everyone had grown so old whilst he'd been away. The Commodore was nearly sixty, but they'd already taken one lung and he'd only just given up smoking. Hard core. Six months looked optimistic.

"So, you're looking into these pain cowboys. Pity Jen Webber isn't here. He paid them a ton of money for his arthritis pain."

"It work?"

"So he said. But then it suddenly didn't. He blew his brains out at home. He was always a bit dramatic, but a great yachtsman. Can't take that away from him. His name is on the board forever."

Delaney looked into his pineapple juice and frowned. "That's what so crazy about this. It's a scam that works. They probably offered him a booster."

The Commodore reached for some nuts. "They did. He wouldn't pay. Don't blame him at all. His pension was with Accaton. Remember them? They deliberately loaded up on debt and then walked away from the pensions. Ruined about 50,000 people's lives. Just so two bastards could get filthy rich. He should have shot them, not himself."

"Yeah, few private pensions are safe now. You never get around to thinking about them till too late. You ok?"

The Commodore laughed. "You think I have a pension? Property is the only thing I invested in. I'm dying and even now I'm too scared to cash out and put it in our banks. Nothing's safe anymore. When I'm gone, they can sell, but right now I need the rents. Doctors cost a fortune. Can't afford to live and can't afford to die. How the hell did we get into this situation in this city, Delaney? Thirty years ago, we were the envy of the world. Our hospitals first class."

Delaney shrugged. "We get the politicians we deserve I guess."

The Commodore swore. "Maybe so. We're saddled with the Mayor now. I hate ambitious bastards like him. Goes everywhere in an armored limo. He's got his fingers into everything."

Delaney nodded. "The Mayor is one of the boosters for this pain scam actually."

The Commodore laughed. "Of course, he is. You know who bankrolled him? The Jaywaller woman. What was her name? She used to be a model. Was on the covers of all the magazines. She probably doesn't mention her time crewing here, not to mention screwing here."

"Veronika Jaywaller?"

The Commodore nodded; take a sip of his whiskey. "Hard bitch. On her third husband already, although I hear they're separated. Contributes to the 'party', if you know what I mean. Her first husband was the mining magnate. Met him here I recall. Heart attack. Serves him right for marrying a girl thirty years younger than him. Somehow his kids were written out of his will and she got the lot. You look under the rigging and you'll probably find her behind this scam. Never enough. People like her always have to have more."

"I remember her. She was pretty but hard to please. She crewed for the Rio mob."

"Of course. Which is how she caught her first husband. Pretty girl, bikini, knows her way around a yacht, bound to catch someone's attention. We're too down-market now. She goes with the international set and sails on the Med in July. She's the kind of woman you glimpse at a society event.

Y'know, surrounded by over-zealous people who hope to extract money from her for a good cause."

"Which they skim to keep their Beemer payments going," Delaney interjected.

"She was just Ronnie to us, remember. Until she got that swimwear contract, then there was no stopping her. I warned her first husband that she was only out for the money, but he just said I was sad because I couldn't get it up anymore. Which was true, even worse." He laughed again, sipping his whiskey. "I thought you'd go for her."

"We disagreed over politics, if I remember." Delaney said, remembering a juvenile fumble on some stateroom bed. "She told me that she could have any man in the city she wanted. I guess that much was true. I met her a few years ago again at a wedding. She looked pretty impressive I remember."

"I went to the first husband's funeral. After all he was a member. She told me she was heartbroken. But I knew she was already seeing the man who'd become number two. Poor bugger. Probably thought he was onto a good thing. The golfer. Pete somebody. He was the PGA champion that year. She ditched him pretty quick and took him for ten million or so."

"What makes you think she's involved with this pain scam?"

"I know nothing, Delaney. But I remember Jen Webber telling me that he'd met her at some function or other and she'd been keen to get his 'pain' sorted, had mentioned these people. Just putting something together here. Doesn't mean I'm right."

"Hmm, interesting. One thing I can tell you, Jirdasham generates a lot of cash."

"Naturally it does. Whilst my generation still has money, they're going to either tax us to death or bleed us dry in the hospitals. They're bloodsuckers, Delaney. But watch your step. If Veronika Jaywaller is behind this, she won't welcome an investigation."

"Yeah, I get that. People who complain about the treatment suddenly retract."

"My advice, for what it's worth. Go back to Europe. Berg City is finished. Just full of corpse-feeders now. I know you had a hard time when your wife was killed, but civilization here is just a veneer. How many murders in this city last year? Over a thousand. Don't try anything on your own."

Delaney drank his juice and stood up. "Advice taken. Good luck, Commodore. I hope the magic works."

The Commodore shook his head. "If only. Take care, son. There's always a billet for you here if you need it. Your name's still on the board."

Delaney grinned. "Thanks. Take care."

"I won't. But you should. Tell whomever you're working for that there's nothing doing and quietly give their money back. I have a bad feeling about this. Remember what happened to Jen Webber."

Delaney left him to his whiskey and momentarily paused by the open sliding doors and surveyed the moored yachts and beyond them the churning ocean. He missed the open water, the challenge, the peace, but his throbbing hands made him turn away. He had no business being here anymore.

CHAPTER TWELVE

A Casual Mistake

Asha didn't know exactly when she decided she'd take him home with her. Perhaps when he told her he couldn't accept her offer of a drink because he was a poor medical student and couldn't possible return the favor. Or his disarming smile that made her want him, made all the easier by his lean fit body that she found irresistible. She was a bit shocked at herself really. She'd spotted him at the bar and something about his eyes had drawn her in. Zuki, her regular bar companion, had warned her, not once, but twice, that he was a taker not a giver, but she was already on her third glass of wine and caution disappeared under a cloud of giggles as he told her stupid jokes about med school.

As she left with him on her arm Zuki gave her once last chance to escape but Asha wasn't listening. A night of uncommitted sex beckoned, and she needed it. Or the wine did, either way she was taking him home. She even gave him the car keys because she didn't trust herself behind the wheel.

"You'll be sorry," Zuki told her as they left.

She figured Zuki was jealous because she'd spotted him first. Zuki got married and divorced when she was seventeen, so she was always down on any guys that showed interest in either of them. Sometimes you just have to go with the flow.

Asha woke suddenly and looked across her empty bed, realized that he'd gone already and swore. She looked for her phone and swore again when she saw the charging wire lying on the floor. "Bastard."

Naked she leapt out of bed and ran to her dining table. Her laptop was still there at least. She looked across at the bowl where she kept her car keys, then screamed.

"No. No. No. What a stupid bitch I am. I can't believe I fell for that bastard." She affected a whiny voice. "My girlfriend just dumped me. Well no shit Sherlock, what with you being a fucking thief."

Asha angrily tossed her bedding across the room.
"Don't cry, Ash. It's just a phone – just a car. Pull yourself together girl."

She headed to the bathroom and loudly kept on swearing. Didn't solve anything, but at least made her feel better.

An hour later, Delaney was listening to her with a sympathetic expression on his face. Rufus was sprawled on the floor by his feet, his tail still bandaged.

"Bastard played me. I was feeling sorry for him and he was really fit, y'know. Zuki warned me off him, but I just thought she was being a bitch because she fancied him too."

"Can they get into your phone?"

"Password protected. I guess someone really smart could get in, but it's an iPhone. Good luck on that. My car he can definitely sell. There's always someone who knows how to fiddle the paperwork. I'm truly pissed, Chief. I loved that little car."

"You insured?"

"Yeah, but it was old. Over 100,000 miles. I loved it, but it wasn't worth much. If I claim, I know I'll be penalized for my next car. They always do that. Stupid is what it all is."

"And you sure he can't access the cloud and grab all your personal stuff. I know you bank on-line."

"No. They can't. I already talked to the bank. It's just such a pain to have replace all the apps and my music – shit."

"I'm sorry. I can lend you some money for a replacement phone if you like. Actually, I think I have an old SE in a desk at home you can have."

Asha smiled. "Thanks. I might take you up on that until I can afford a new one. If I'm late in for a few days I'll be blaming the bus, right? If I ever see that guy in the bar again, I'm going to kill him."

Delaney nodded. "Stay angry. The Commodore seems to think that Mrs Jaywaller is involved with our pain scam. You might want to follow that line of investigation, but tread carefully, Ash."

"Veronika Jaywaller? She can't need the money. Has to be like the richest woman in this city."

"It's always about money. She's dangerous and well connected." Delaney remarked. "I've got a line on the Guru.

Well, his sister at least. She might know where I can find him. She lives in Ashridge, near the lower road."

Asha made a face. "I know it's urban cool now, but be safe, Chief. Some scary people live around there."

Delaney paused at the door. "You sure you weren't targeted?"

Asha thought about it. "You think?"

"It's possible, but it's early days. We haven't really stirred anything up yet. Might just be opportunistic."

Asha frowned. "He said he was a med student. Seemed to know a lot about infections. I don't know why they'd target me and not you."

"You're right." He remembered Maria suddenly. "Maria's at the hospital today. I've arranged for her mother to pick her up, but don't be surprised if she turns up here later. She's very vulnerable right now."

"And you're not? You're way too nice to that girl."

Delaney made a face. "I'm thinking she might be our gateway to clinic staff. They don't have to know I'm not going to pay the thirty grand." He called the dog. "Rufus. Come on. Work to do."

Asha didn't think involving the little brat in anything was a good idea; but didn't say anything as she watched the dog sleepily stretch his back legs and then follow the Chief out.

Moments later there was a knock on the door and Zuki walked in.

"You're not answering your phone." Zuki said, as strolled in and perched on Asha's desk giving the office a once over. From her sour expression, Asha knew she wasn't impressed.

Asha sighed and leaned back in her chair, jealous as ever of Zuki long brown legs. "You were right. He was a sleazebag. Fucking stole my phone and my car. I was stupid and dead wrong, consider me well punished."

Zuki laughed, but then mussed Asha's hair in sympathy. "He wasn't a medical student either. Professional conman. Tully says that his modus operandi is to get a girl drunk and then take her for what he can get. Did you happen to notice your debit card is missing?"

Asha's face went into panic mode as she dived for her purse. It wasn't in the drawer where she normally kept it.

"My purse! Don't tell me he got my cards. Please not that. Oh my god, Zukes, I'm so screwed. God knows what he's spent by now."

Zuki waved her purse in the air. "You are so lucky, girl. You were so keen to get into bed, you left everything behind. How did you get into work without an EzRider card? I know they don't take cash on the bus."

Asha thought about it. "I was so angry I just showered and left. Got a ride into the city with one of the residents. I have no idea what I was thinking this morning except of ten ways to kill that bastard."

Zuki handed her over her purse and stood up, smoothing her short skirt. "Next time I tell you the guy's a jerk, you gonna listen?"

Asha investigated her purse and was relieved to find everything intact. "I may have to give up alcohol forever."

"That might be too drastic. Come on, buy me coffee. I never come down to this old part of town anymore. Used to go the dance studio over the way, remember? The coffee place still there, you think?"

"Yeah, it is. Not changed a bit except the tables are a lot further apart." Asha stood up, gripped her purse and gave Zuki a big hug.

"Thanks, Zuki. I'm sorry I didn't listen to you. Don't let me drink more than two glasses in future. Men seem so much more interesting when you're drunk."

Zuki frowned. "I think I'd need two whole bottles before that happened." She grinned. "This office is like something out of an old movie. I kind of expect ancient typewriters, piles of paper everywhere and men smoking cigars."

"It was built in 1880. Used to be part of an Engineering College. Come on. Coffee, cake, whatever you want. I can't go out for long. I have work to do."

"Ah yes, the great detective must detect." Zuki laughed and headed towards the door.

CHAPTER THIRTEEN

The Insights of Mrs Rama

Delaney worried about parking his Discovery. It was the kind of street where you couldn't be sure you'd still have wheels when you returned. Ashridge gentrification was in progress, but the older owners and tenants were resistant to change. Some were sitting out on the pavement on battered car seats and vaping huge clouds of some stinky mix. Rufus eyed them suspiciously and didn't need to be told to guard the vehicle with his life.

Delaney hoped the open window was wide enough to let Rufus get in a good bite if anyone tried anything.

The house was nothing special. Patchy whitewash, iron bars on the windows and a half-dead pit bull sleeping in a sunbeam on the porch. It began to bark with a distinct wheeze as he approached and rang the bell. He heard nothing inside but maybe the dog was enough of an alert. He was looking at the crumbling cement around the windows thinking that if you were the sister of what had to be a very rich man by now, you'd think he'd have moved her into a better neighborhood.

The door inched open and tugged against a tight chain.

"Mrs Rama?" He held up his company ID. "David Delaney representing the Office of City Oversight. I called earlier. Wanted to talk to you about your brother, the Guru."

One misty brown eye gazed at him from the crack in the doorway. She was obviously weighing up whether to admit him.

"I won't take much of your time."

The door closed a moment and he heard her fiddle with the chain. He waited patiently as the dog gave up on wheezing and settled back down to his sun patch, job done.

"Come." She beckoned. "Good boy, Ben."

Ben momentarily wagged his little tail.

Delaney found himself in a dark hallway filled with the

acrid stench of a curry in progress. His skin prickled as the spices penetrated every pore.

"Something smells good," he lied, his eyes beginning to water.

"For the meeting tonight," she muttered. Which was a polite way of saying she wasn't offering any.

Delaney realized that she was quite tiny and strangely wore silver ballet slippers. And she was so very old. He could see someone was in the kitchen doing something, so at least she had help.

She led him into the inner courtyard, half lit with sunshine. Delaney loved these old houses. 19th Century builders knew what they were doing. No garden outside, but an inner sanctuary safe from prying eyes and here was an old Jacaranda tree in flower with a crumpled wicker chair under it. Mrs Rama made her way over and sank into it on a pile of purple cushions. Delaney regarded each wall around him painted in different vivid colors. Blue, pink, yellow and something burnt orange. It was wonderfully charming. No wonder people wanted to buy these old places when they came up.

"I thought you was one of those property jackals. Always wanting me to sell up. Here I was born. Here I'll die. Soon enough most likely."

"And beautiful it is Mrs Rama. I was happy to see the old bakery is still there. My Dad used to come here to buy their fresh bagels late on a Saturday night. He used to run the old furniture factory on Lower Main street."

Mrs Rama studied him and nodded. "Factory's closed down. All changed. There's a market there on Saturdays. My niece sells chocolate there."

"I've been looking for your brother, Mrs Rama. He's not listed anywhere and well I kind of hope you're in touch with him."

She leant back against the tree and sighed. "I haven't seen him in two years. He's a stupid fool for living in that big house all by himself. They work him hard, night and day and he's far too old to be doing this. They'll use him up and spit him out. I told him. You can't trust them; you can never trust them."

Delaney watched a ginger cat stroll across the tin roof and jump to the tree before deftly slipping down the branches to the old woman's shoulders. She pulled it down to her lap and began to stroke it vigorously as it stared at Delaney with curiosity.

"My mother used to swear by his teas and herbs. Every damn headache I ever had she'd make me swallow the Guru's herbal teas."

Mrs Rama laughed showing a perfect set of natural teeth. "And some of them worked I'll bet. Another business he was swindled out of. Could start something, but never hold onto it. Borrowed money to expand and they took it all from him. Just left his name on it. A fool never changes. Every time I see a jar of Guranji curry sauce I want to smash it. He should be a millionaire."

"But he does live in a big house." Delaney pointed out.

She spat, alarming the cat. "What does a man his age need a big house for? He's got a room here. I never changed a thing since he left. He was born here, and this is where he should be. I told him. You're not one of them. You don't need to live like rich people with a swimming pool. He hates water. Can't even swim. He'll be 88 next month. Why does he need all this? Who is he going to impress? He doesn't talk to us and all he does is see his patients and never rests. Never sees me, his own flesh and blood. Sends me prayers and chocolates. What am I supposed to do with chocolates? My niece sells them. I can have all the chocolates I want."

Delaney wiped the sweat from his face. The curry spices were really getting to him and he needed to get out of there.

"You think your brother can really cure pain?"

Mrs Rama regarded him with surprise.

"Of course. Ever since a boy. You ask Ben outside."

"Ben?"

"He was gone. I was waiting for someone to come and bury him and Ansolm comes home and just strokes him and sings him a little song and Ben woke up. It's not right, of course. Dog like him shouldn't live so many years, but he's twenty now and I think will carry on whether he wants to or not."

Delaney smiled. "I'm sure Ben is grateful."

Mrs Rama shook her head. "He's never expressed an opinion but as long as he gets fed, he's happy."

"Is that the only time you've witnessed his talents, Mrs

Rama? We've had a lot of people complaining that they've paid and not been cured..."

"Nonsense," she protested. "Impossible. You ask anyone in this street. If he lays his hands on you your pain will go. Doesn't cure people. He would be the first to tell you that. He just makes pain go away and that's all that people ask. You speak to Reverend Hasper. He was all for having Ansolm locked up. He was telling everyone that only God could cure pain, but then his wife got ill and whom do you think she called for? He was bitter about it, but Ansolm took her pain away and she died peacefully. You can't ask more than that. When Farnie went through his windscreen and was all in agony with stitches and could barely see – Ansolm went to the hospital and fixed him. Once the pain's gone, you can concentrate on healing. That's how it works. God works through him to make people better. God didn't tell him to live in a big house and not see his family."

"Perhaps God has plans for him."

Mrs Rama swore. "Now you sound like her. The witch. She came here. Told him how much she had loved his teas, flattered him, charmed him so he couldn't hear me anymore and said he could cure so many others. She would make him rich beyond his dreams."

"A woman?"

"Ach, you know her. She's always on TV and in the magazines, showing off her beautiful mansion by the ocean. She turned his head. How could such an old man be so easily fooled? Just help a few people she said and now he's her personal slave. A witch if ever I saw one. He walked out of here and never came back. Promised me he'd look after me, but never did. Only thinks of her. They'll kill him with work. I know it."

Delaney could believe it. "I'd like to speak to him. You know where the big house is?"

Mrs Rama looked away and he could see her face saddened. "Never been to it. Never invited. He's ashamed of me, of what I do. He doesn't want me embarrassing him in front of his new friends. But I'm his sister."

"The house?" Delaney asked again.

"On the hill. Kennet Avenue. Big white house with gates, lots of tall trees on the drive. Fool, living like a king and leaving all those who love him behind."

"Happens all the time. One day he'll realize his mistake." Delaney remarked.

Mrs Rama shook her head. "She won't let him. Not till he's dead and even then ..."

Delaney stood and wiped his eyes again. One taste of that curry and he was sure he'd be dead too.

"When I see him, I'll tell him to visit you. It's not right, Mrs Rama. I'll make sure of it."

She closed her eyes momentarily. "I can hear in your voice that you mean it, but I shan't hold my breath." She touched his arm to console him, then abruptly seemed quite alert. She gasped and crossed herself several times.

"She misses you terribly, y'know. My Lord, how did I miss that? She's all around you."

Delaney frowned and began to protest but Mrs Rama held up her hands to silence him.

"She had a terrible death. But she's found her way to your side and she's with you now. She worried about a child. Not yours, or hers, but she's definitely trying to tell me something..." She appeared to be listening, her head cocked to one side.

Delaney blinked. He wasn't prepared for this.

Mrs Rama could see the alarm on his face. "People come to me for comfort all the time. I can see you're afraid, but don't be. Ask anyone around here. If you want comfort or miss a loved one, they all come to see Mrs Rama."

Delaney was feeling a little bit groggy. Part of him was happy to know Denise was with him, but the other, rational part was trying to reject it.

"My wife died far away from here ..." he began, but she cut him off.

"Yes. Paris. Terrible, but she felt nothing. It was instant. She wanted me to tell you that. But more importantly, the child is thinking of killing herself. She is thinking of death all the time. She wants me to tell you that she wants you to take her to see my brother."

Delaney was stunned. Perhaps this was a con. Here she was pushing her brother but then again, she never saw him, never benefited from anything from him.

"I'm afraid your brother charges thirty thousand for his 'cure', Mrs Rama. There's little chance I can afford such a high price."

Mrs Rama stared at him as if he was a demon.

"Thirty thousand? Are you speaking the truth? Thirty thousand when he would heal the pain for the price of a chicken or even an orange one time because they were so poor. You are serious? The witch makes him do that?"

Delaney considered her surprise genuine enough. "Yes, it's true. Big houses cost a lot of money."

"Then he's nothing but a thief. I want nothing more to do with him. God would never approve of that. Never in a thousand years."

"I'll tell him that too."

Mrs Rama struggled to rise, and Delaney pulled her up as the cat jumped down.

"Your wife says she will be with you always, but you must help the child."

"I am trying."

"I'll see you out."

"I should pay you," Delaney suggested, realizing that she probably did this for a living.

Mrs Rama shook her head. "You didn't know. I was caught by surprise, that's all."

"My wife was very beautiful, a loving woman with a lot of talent, Mrs Rama. I think about her every day."

"She knows."

Mrs Rama ushered him towards her front door. "My brother can heal pain, but he can't fix a broken heart. That stays with you forever."

Delaney knew that already.

Rufus seemed agitated when he opened the car door but at least all four wheels were still in place. He realized he'd been clenching his fists with the tension and he prized his fingers loose again. He didn't normally give credence to such a thing as talking to the dead, but she hadn't known who was coming to see her, certainly couldn't know about the bombing in Paris and for a brief moment, if he dared admit it, he had felt Denise's hands kneading his shoulders like she used to do and blowing on his neck to calm him. For one second she had really been there.

He opened the car door. "Let's go, Rufus. We're looking for a big house on the hill."

It wasn't just a big house on the hill. It was the biggest house on the hill. The kind of place a banker might live in to show how much he loves your money. Delaney counted six windows either side of the Roman portico complete with tall stone Doric columns and lions on plinths. All a tad pretentious and not what you'd expect from an old man from Ashridge. The driveway gates were chained, but a small gate to one side was open for deliveries in the 'Tradesman's Entrance'. Rufus took this as an invitation and Delaney followed.

He had no expectation that the Guru would admit him and most likely had staff to deter questions, but it was worth a try. He looked up and saw no faces at the windows, no sign of life and the vast garden looked neglected. He rang the bell and stood with his back to the house to survey the sweeping view of the city. You could see the old 19th Century University towers and beyond that the glittering ocean where a freighter was leaving port. The contrast between this place and his sister's home was stark. No one, not even a banker needed a place as fancy as this.

Rufus looked expectant. "Go take a look around the back. No one's coming."

The dog took off and Delaney casually followed. He didn't exactly expect to see the Guru floating on his back in the swimming pool sipping cocktails, but you never knew.

Rufus was quickly searching in and out of any available space. He could be relied upon to bark if he found anything interesting. The pool water was brown, and algae were growing on the sidewalls. Delaney looked inside the house as he passed windows and was surprised to see every room was empty. He'd either moved out or hadn't moved in.

Rufus barked once.

"What have you got there, boy?"

Delaney walked around fallen pool chairs and found himself in a little pool house changing room. There was a single bed with two crumpled rugs and a stained pillow. Some unwashed pots and pans and a bowl of dying fruits covered in flies. Maybe the Guru let someone stay to protect the place, or it was a squatter. Either way it wasn't what he needed.

Delaney only noticed the security cameras when he was leaving. He wondered if they were switched on. Rufus gave chase to a fat pigeon that only just made it into the air.

"You need to be faster, dog." But he was glad he hadn't caught it, didn't want him choking on feathers.

He checked his watch and wondered how Maria was getting on at the hospital and if her mother had remembered to collect her. He reflected on what the Guru's sister had told him. Was Maria really thinking about killing herself? It didn't tally. Sure, she was angry she was taking so long to heal, but suicide? He needed to have a serious talk with her but realized he lacked parental skills. She had always considered herself baggage when living at his place before – even though he'd done his best for her, taking her side in the many arguments with her mother. Child Psychology 101 was missing from his oeuvre, not that his own father ever had any skills in that direction. They'd stopped talking when he'd informed him that he wasn't going into the furniture business selling stuff no one could afford at a ridiculous interest rate.

His phone vibrated. Asha.

"I've got a kid here who's pretty pissed no one came for her at the hospital."

"Ah. Give her a job to do. Make her feel included."

"Sure. Short of filing I'm not sure what though."

"Think of something hard. Or suggest she does her homework."

"Oh I get it. You're more devious than I thought, Delaney."

Delaney grinned. "We're eating lentil and something burgers. If you're up for that you're invited."

"I think that falls under employee abuse. Pass. But Rufus is out of Dentastix."

"Noted. So, you do like dogs."

"I just prefer dogs with good dental hygiene."

Delaney disconnected and turned to Rufus who was inspecting the dirty bandage around his tail. "Remind me about dental sticks dog, and the rest. Your appetite back yet?"

Rufus looked up at him from the back seat with surprise. *Obviously, my appetite is back. You know nothing.*

CHAPTER FOURTEEN

Mr Nice Guy

He cooked the burgers on the griddle with onions and shitake mushrooms. Maria played with a very clean looking Rufus.

"Don't let the sweet potato fries burn," Maria shouted.

Delaney checked the oven; they were almost done.

"We're eating outside. The table laid?"

"Oops. On it."

"There's ketchup in the fridge. You feed Rufus?"

"He was hungry. Record time tonight. He's showered and he's fine."

Rufus did look kind of fluffy. "How's his tail looking?"

"Gross. They shaved his hair, but it's healing. I put the ointment on, and it stinks."

"Supposed to stop him from licking it."

"Working so far. He keeps looking at it and making growly noises."

Delaney smiled. "Probably itches. If he starts scratching put more bandage back on. The hair will grow back in time. I think we're done here."

Delaney served up, then went to the fridge and looked inside. Only cider to drink.

"You drink cider?"

"It got alcohol in it?"

"Yes."

"Then I drink cider."

Delaney frowned. He should probably water it down. It was definitely against the rules; but what the hell, he hadn't got anything else.

They ate on the stoop. Maria staring down at the ships in the harbor and listened to the wind in the pine trees nearby.

"So your mother didn't turn up." Delaney remarked.

Maria made a face. "You really think she would?"

Delaney shrugged. "What did the hospital say about your back? You saw Dr Puli, right?"

Maria sighed and dipped her fries into the ketchup. "He said it was a muscle spasm. They made me go on the treadmill and do leg exercises."

"It hurt?"

Maria rolled her eyes. "Duh."

"So, what's the advice?"

"I had another scan and he thinks maybe the 'plates' aren't back in position or whatever. He was pissed mother wasn't there. He's sending something to you. I told him I was back here and he said he was happy about that."

Delaney didn't comment on that. "Plates? Not discs?"

"Something about alignment. Don't ask me."

"I'll call his office."

"He wants me to go swimming regularly."

Delaney nodded. "Good idea. Low impact exercise. We can go Saturday. Early, before the crowds."

Maria ate some onions and regarded him carefully.

"Why are you being nice?"

"Aren't I always nice to you?"

Reluctantly she nodded. "But why. I don't deserve it."

Delaney didn't think you had to explain this kind of thing, but clearly, she was in the mood for talking.

"My Dad never spoke to me after I took up sailing and told him I wasn't going to work in his factory."

"What never?"

"Not a word. Didn't see me win any championships. Didn't come to my graduation from school or university. Refused to come to my wedding and wouldn't let my mother come either. He died just after that. I nearly didn't go to his funeral, but I guess I had to."

"He was an asshole."

"Yep."

"Now you're nice to me because your father was mean to you."

Delaney took a slug of his cider. "I'm nice to you because your mother is an asshole and you've got no one else, except Rufus. It all comes down to Rufie. If he says you're ok, you're ok. I'm nice to you despite your language."

"And my shitty attitude."

"That too."

Maria grinned and drank some cider, making a face. "Strong."

Delaney nodded. "Which is why you only get half a glass."

"You think my back will ever get better? What if it's out of alignment and I've got a twisted spine now and I'll be a cripple forever?"

Delaney realized this was the real issue. "You won't be. You can walk. If need be, they'll get a large hammer and knock you straight. Dr Puli is one of the best in his field and you're lucky you're on his patient list. If he thinks swimming will help, it will. We'll make a schedule. There's no way you're not going to be fit again, Maria. Think of the progress you've made since you left this house. You were in a wheelchair remember?"

Maria digested that and finished up her meal. "Asha says I should be nicer to you. She says you're sad all the time because of your wife being dead."

Delaney leaned back in his chair and sipped his cider. "I'm not so sad today. Weirdly I met an old lady, she's got a gift. I was talking to her about another matter, but she suddenly told me that Denise is with me."

Maria's eyes opened wide. "Like a ghost?"

Delaney nodded. "That spook you?"

Maria shook her head. "Does it spook you? Is she here now?" She looked around, as if expecting to see her.

Delaney shook his head. "Kinda gives me comfort actually. I've tried so hard to forget her because it hurts to remember she's gone. But if she's here, even if I can't see her, I feel stronger. That too strange for you?"

Maria swallowed more cider, seriously contemplating this. "Bet you were nice to her too."

Delaney laughed. "I used to come home, and she'd be frantically trying to finish some drawings and she'd always be on an impossible schedule. I'd make her some supper and pour a glass of wine and just watch her working. She was a perfectionist. Never quite satisfied with her work, but it was always brilliant. I loved her very much, every bit of her, even the callus on her pen finger. She knew how to make me happy and I think I made her happy too."

Maria regarded him with wonder.

"I still can't believe you dated my mother. She hasn't a clue how to make anyone happy, let alone herself."

Delaney laughed and began to gather up the plates. He looked across at Maria suddenly. "M, never feel you can't say how you're feeling to me, ok? I know you get frustrated and angry, but there's nothing we can't overcome and make your life better. Understood?"

Maria stared at him a moment as Rufus put his head on her lap. He could see she wanted to say something.

"Sometimes I can't see a future for me."

Delaney carried the plates into the house. "I'm sure there's a ton of platitudes I can say, but believe me, I know you have a future girl. You won't always be stuck with your mother. Your back will get better and in no time at all you'll be that annoying sarcastic girl that knows she's smarter than everyone else around her.

Maria frowned. "What if I don't want to be that person anymore?"

Delaney came back to finish his drink. "I wasn't always this 'nice' person, M. When I was sixteen, I went all out to be the best sailor in the country. Won all the championships and later on I was the youngest skipper in the Two Oceans race – From New York to Rio and back. Which we won I might add in record time. Nothing was going to stop me. I think the crew knew that and I drove them to extremes, just to satisfy my ambitions. I didn't care if they liked me or not. I wanted to win at any cost. In fact, I'm pretty sure a lot of people hated me. I didn't suffer fools gladly and I might have gone on like this all my life."

Maria was listening.

"I had an accident. Skiing. My second time in the Alps. Went with a group from London. We went off-piste and there was an avalanche. Only five of us survived. I was in hospital in France for weeks and couldn't move my legs or make my hands works properly. They said it was shock, but although some of the pain left me, I never really got back my strength. I couldn't sail anymore, my fingers were pretty damn useless, especially in the cold and it's often cold out there on the ocean. I had to rethink my whole life.

"I went back to university, did an MBA (that's business studies) and I ended up on the finance side of the insurance business. It was the complete opposite of everything I ever wanted. Part of me seemed to have died."

Maria understood that only too well.

"The aggressive 'winner take all' side of me had gone and I was depressed about it until the day I met Denise."

"How did you meet her?"

"She came to the opening of a gallery we were sponsoring. She just woke me up, made me laugh and I was suddenly on a rocket to Mars. I knew I had to make my move right away.

"We were married in a month. I moved to the Paris office, learned French and became Mr Nice Guy."

Maria narrowed her eyes. "Ha. I guess you told me all that because ..."

"Because just when you think you have life figured out a ton of bricks can fall on your head."

"Or you fall off a cliff," Maria reminded him.

"And survive. Hold on to that thought. You survived for a reason. Rufus found you because you have a purpose. What that might be is in the future."

"I thought the future was wiping people's asses."

"That's not your future, girl. No way. Come on, let's wash up, you've got school tomorrow."

Maria scooped up the last two fries and gave them to Rufus.

"Naughty." Delaney admonished.

"He's been good. Didn't beg once."

After supper Delaney regarded his back yard with outsider eyes as Rufus lay near his feet. He'd always considered the front of the house with the stoop and view of the harbor the best part. The back yard looked neglected. A neighbor who wanted to build a bigger house had offered him a good price for half of it ten years ago. It had come to nothing, but he was glad he hadn't sold.

There was almost half an acre of trees and bushes that looked pretty spectacular in spring but overgrown the rest of the year. Somewhere out there, buried under the brambles, there was a fully equipped tool shed, big enough to build a boat in. He felt guilty for neglecting it. Rufus had been digging holes all over the place and the hardy plants he'd put in seemed distinctly off color. The herb garden had gone totally wild, but he kind of liked that and mint seemed to have colonized half of it. It was all well and good living in a house for sentimental reasons, as well as the view, but letting the garden go showed a lack of respect.

He tried to remember the first time he moved in. At twenty-one he was the youngest of his circle to own a house. No mortgage, no debts. The Two Ocean prize money had bought him that privilege. He'd bought this tin shack for a song at a time when the housing market was tanking. Friends who understood money better than he did back then all told him to tear it down and build new ready for when the market was strong again, then he could move up to bigger and better. But he'd known, almost from day one, that he'd never want more than this. Aside from the amazing view that no one could take from him, he always loved the sound of rain on the zinc roof, the simple whitewashed walls, the old Cypress tree out front that said here lies two hundred years of history. You don't mess with that.

All in all, this was his home and even though he'd lived in at least fifteen others over the years, as work and sailing had taken him all over the world, everything else was temporary. He'd never let it out, had no plans to make it pay, there was nothing to treasure except the log fireplace he'd installed, nevertheless, the sum of the whole was home, his anchor and he'd always hoped that Denise would eventually come to live with him here. He smiled. The first thing she'd said to him when she finally saw it, 'when are you going to finish the garden?'

He decided he'd plant a lemon tree for her. She loved lemons.

"Delaney?" Maria was behind him in her pjs. "You ok?"

"Yeah, fine, why?"

"You're staring at the garden."

"Thinking about what we can do with it."

"Water it," she told him. "I heard plants need water."

Delaney laughed. "Girl you just got yourself a job."

Maria groaned. That hadn't worked out too well at all.

"Bed, girl. It's late." Rufus trotted over to Maria's side. He'd been ready for bed for hours.

"I'm going. Night."

"Night."

He watched as Rufus leaned close into her legs as they walked back inside. She really had captured that dog's heart.

CHAPTER FIFTEEN

Penance

Asha was already in the office when he arrived with Rufus.

"I hope there's coffee ready. It was bitter cold on the beach this morning."

Rufus aimed for the water bowl as Asha walked towards the cafetière.

"I just made some. The bus was a nightmare. We're all standing jammed in staring at each other's masks. It's gross. No distancing at all."

Delaney took off his coat. "Remember that stuff your Dad used to tell you about bringing home strangers?"

Asha put her hands up in surrender. "I messed up. I know. I drank too much, I can't drink more than one glass and I'm gone. He was cute, played me a lot of attention and I got kinda hot."

Delaney smiled. "Next time scan his ID and maybe put some ice in your pants."

Asha stuck her tongue out. "Was that what your mother used to tell you?"

"My mother was worried that I was gay because I never seemed to bring a girl home. She didn't quite realize that there's quite a few places to bunk down at the yacht club and a lot of girls. And yes, there were times when I wish I had put ice down my pants."

Asha smirked. She poured them both coffees and went back to her desk, opening up her screen. "If I'm honest, I'm sort of worried about what we're getting into here."

Delaney added almond milk to his coffee and went to his desk picking up a small exercise ball for his hand.

"Well, we know they don't have a cash problem. I went to the Guru's house on the Hill."

Asha's eyes widened. "Kennet Avenue. The Hill?"

Delaney nodded. "Big white house with Roman columns out front with a view right across the city to the ocean."

Asha scrolled through some pages and then went 'Ah ha' and turned her screen around to Delaney could see it. "This little old house?"

Delaney looked surprised. "It's on-line?"

"It's part of their publicity material."

"You'd think they'd want to keep it secret."

Asha laughed. "The thing about scams is that you have to show you're successful. Big White Mansion on The Hill says our scam works. Your money is safe with us."

"Hmm, you're right. But the Guru doesn't live in it. It's empty. I paid a visit."

Asha shrugged. "I guess they don't care where he lives. Just as long as the whole thing looks wonderful."

"It's weird, Ash. Everything about this scam is off. It works, then it doesn't work. There's no way a guy of 88 could be healing the number of people they are treating and how many other people in the whole wide world would have the same skills as the Guru?"

Asha sipped her coffee as Rufus turned circles on his daybed.

"Perhaps the Guru is a front."

"Probably, but Mrs Palmer swears by him. He genuinely removed all her pain."

"Maybe it only works on some type of susceptible people?" Asha suggested. "Anyway, I put together a list of the Guru's endorsers. A Celeb Z list if you will. Ex-sportsmen and women mostly. People who are now fifty plus and got a whole lot of pain."

Delaney saw the logic in that. "Senior Brand Influencers."

Asha smiled. "Well done. You just past the test."

"Don't be smart. I am not a dinosaur – yet."

Asha grinned. "It's aimed at middle class woke people who are using info on Facebook to self-medicate themselves. Cheaper than seeing your doctor and there's lots of drugs available on-line that will cure practically anything. If you believe the hype."

"None of which work, but then again, your doctor probably is only prescribing opioids, so if you're woke, you want to avoid that trap."

"There's a lot of people just like you, Chief. Got pain

issues and want a solution."

Delaney threw Rufus a treat. He caught it and ran to a corner to eat.

"Actually, I'm beginning to think we should hand this over to the cops."

Asha narrowed her eyes. "You seriously think they would know what to do?"

"The Cyber-Crime unit is good, I hear."

"And short-staffed due to them paying only a fraction of the salary of private Internet companies. You'd earn more in the Amazon call-center in Malmsbury Grove."

"We'd probably earn more working there." Delany told her. "You think I should go talk to the Mayor. At least warn him that this could blow up in his face?"

Asha shook her head. "He must know what's happening. He's the one promoting it."

"Then what? How do we proceed, Ash? You tell me."

"We need backup. Lawyers. We need a team behind us when we expose them."

"We might be torn to shreds."

Asha paled. "Torn to shreds. Is that for real?"

"Trashed in the media, shunned. I told you the yacht club commander says Veronika Jaywaller is involved right?"

She nodded. "I haven't found her name on anything yet. We have any proof of her involvement?"

"The Guru's sister says a rich white woman came for treatment to the Guru and was so impressed she wanted to set up a business with him."

"There are a lot of rich white women in this city, Chief."

"Not ones who host that property show on TV. 'Style your home' I think it's called. She's in all the magazines with those "How does she look so great at 40?" articles."

Asha rolled her eyes. "Money helps and a personal trainer, no doubt."

"Anyway, I was getting some treats for Rufus and there she was on the cover of Career Woman. I took it back to the Guru's sister and she identified her immediately. 'That's the Witch,' she says and spits."

Asha was impressed. "Veronika Jaywaller is like the Ice Queen in this City."

"Now maybe, but I remember when she was just a teen hustler in a push-up bra at the yacht club."

"You know her?"

"She's younger than me, but she knew how to target rich men. I doubt she'd remember me now, but you didn't cross Ronnie then and you don't now. Nothing gets between her and money."

"So I'm right. We need legal backup."

Delaney nodded. "Call Goodman and Clay. Speak to Nicolas Goodman. Tell him what you know so far and ask if he's interested. There might be a group lawsuit he can put together from all those who complained (if we can make them change their minds). Then again, he might say that because we are subcontracted by the city, we're compromised in some way and we need to walk away. He's smart. We were at University together."

Asha made some notes. "And you?"

Delaney glanced up at the ceiling a moment. "I'm going to talk to the Deputy Mayor. He's ambitious and probably keen to replace the Mayor any chance he can get. Leverage is all in politics remember."

"He's hard to find, I hear."

"I know where he hides."

"Ok, Chief. I'm going to try and find a connection between Ms Jaywaller and the Guru. There has to be a trail of some kind."

Delaney nodded. "Cover your tracks. Record everything and back it up."

Asha nodded. "Always do. Same for you, Chief."

Delaney told Rufus to stay. "Don't let him lick his tail."

Asha glared at Rufus and he quickly went back to eating his snack.

CHAPTER SIXTEEN

The Deputy Mayor

If you are deputy mayor and you don't want to deal with all the crap the Mayor doesn't want to deal with either, you hide in the Green Oasis coffee shop just behind Market Square. It had good wi-fi and was pretty dark inside for perfect anonymity.

Delaney ordered an Americano and took it to the corner table where the DM was reading stuff on his iPad.

The man looked up surprised, then nodded as Delaney slid onto the opposite bench.

"What deep shit has the Office of City Oversight dug up now, Mr Delaney?"

"You sure you want to know?"

Delaney stared at the big-shouldered black former football player with a broken nose to prove it. He looked nervous, but then again it might have been the dim lights.

"Jirdasham."

The DM frowned, then shrugged. "Doesn't ring any alarm bells."

Delaney sipped some coffee. "We feel your pain, so you don't have to. Ringing any bells now."

The DM laughed, exposing huge white teeth with two gold implants. Another souvenir of his sports career.

"That's for real? I mean, I've seen the ads on-line, but how the fuck is the city involved with this?"

"The Mayor highly recommends them. Says it's a good cure for opioid addiction whilst he's about it."

The DM narrowed his eyes and pulled on his earlobe. Delaney almost smiled. Two tells. The guy not only knew about it but also was about to lie.

"I'd like to see a cure for these opioid victims. Hell, our hospitals are full of them if they aren't lying in our doorways."

"Well, if I told you that they were a crooked outfit who pay no taxes to the city and could be turning over fifty million in the last three years, you wouldn't be concerned."

The DM made a face. "How much?"

"You heard. And how much do you think the Mayor is getting to recommend them?"

The DM looked around the coffee shop for other ears and was satisfied no one could hear them. "You're making quite an assertion there, Delaney. We pay you if I recall."

"You pay me to check the City is playing straight and flag up potential problems. My guess is he's getting enough to pay for his re-election next year."

The DM was clearly annoyed. Delaney wasn't sure which part of the information was rubbing him the wrong way though.

"What else?" The DM asked. "There's always a second shoe dropping with you."

"They target the old and the rich promising to take all their aches and pains away forever. Thirty grand a pop. If that doesn't work, fifteen more for a booster."

The DM was suddenly interested. "Forty-Five grand per victim?" He whistled.

"I'm not sure how many 'clients' they have on their books, but it generated three hundred and eight complaints to our office this year alone. Three hundred and six of those clients suddenly withdrew their complaints when I called them. If that doesn't raise a red flag – nothing will."

"And you want to shut them down."

"One of the shareholders is Gus Huissan. He gave them start-up money I suspect."

"He's in jail for Christ sakes. I put him there."

"You didn't find his money. I guess he put it to work whilst he's inside."

The DM was clearly upset now. Perhaps he hadn't understood how much cash this scam was generating and suddenly realized he wasn't getting enough. Delaney fiddled with the salt-cellar.

"Look, I know you can't stop people doing stupid things with their money, but at the very least with the Mayor endorsing them, you're liable. We could at least look at the tax angle. Audit them. Their website carries no certification from any health outfit except a homeopathic association. But if someone dies from their treatment, the Mayor won't look too good when it blows up in his face."

The DM finished his coffee and Delaney considered what the man might do.

He was clearly pretending to be shocked. He obviously knew more than he was saying.

"Can you get evidence to me?" He asked. "Who are their accountants?"

"No information yet. Whoever it is they'll have a lot of cash to hide. They have no tangible assets or liabilities here that I can see."

"Other than Huissan, who else is behind it?"

Delaney stood up. "Veronika Jaywaller mean anything to you?"

The DM shook his head. "No, no, no. Don't go there. She's untouchable. The Mayor is crazy about her."

"Does his wife know? Does that mean you want information so you can do something, or do I go play on the beach with my dog. It needs policing. But I guess the Mayor might not see it that way."

The DM looked directly at him. "How many people know all this?"

"Just me and my dog," Delaney answered. He left Asha out of it.

"Keep it that way for now, Delaney. There's a few people in the City who don't like you Delaney. In fact, they were only asking yesterday to have your office shut down."

"Anything to do with planting trees, by any chance? Or the ones looting the city treasury for all they can carry?"

The DM frowned. "You know we have a handle on the corruption now. Those days are over. Don't worry. I have your back."

Delaney now knew for sure he had to worry. He just planted a target on it.

"Then I'll keep digging," Delaney told him and walked away.

The DM watched him go with a look of real concern on his face. He picked up his phone and made a call.
Delaney waited across the road, partially hidden by a delivery truck. He didn't have to stay long. The DM came out of the coffee shop and seconds later a black BMW pulled up to collect him. It took off in a big hurry.

"Interesting." Delaney muttered to himself as he took

a photo of the license plate and headed on back to his office. He knew he'd pulled a trigger and wondered where the bullet would land.

CHAPTER SEVENTEEN

A Good News Day

Asha was happy to see him as Rufus ran up towards him and rubbed up against his legs.

"Zuki found my car!"

"Zuki? Where? Is it a wreck?"

"Left outside the Happy Mart in the bay. Zuki saw it when she was out riding her bike."

"And it's ok? Have I met this Zuki?"

"My best friend and no, you haven't met. She's a bit hypercritical. I didn't want to lose my job in case you took offence. No keys in the car but she says no visible damage. She's staking it out in case that creep returns and tries to drive off. Zuki has a black belt in karate. No one messes with her. I'm going to get my spare key and go there shortly. That alright with you?"

"I'll take you. I have to pick Maria up from school."

"Cool. But don't make any arrangements for tonight. Guess who's doing a book signing tonight at Oyster Point?"

Delaney looked nonplussed. He didn't know any writers.

"Our very favorite Guru Gurajani."

"He writes books?"

"He writes spiritual books. The Oyster Point bookshop is full of them. You must have been there. You need a candle to ward off bad vibes, that's where you go."

Delaney smiled. "And I guess I'm going there tonight. What time?"

"Seven. You might need to wear robes or get your hippy outfit out of the closet."

Delaney laughed. "I'll be sure to put some flowers in my hair."

He showed a photo to Asha on his phone. "Can we trace that number? The Deputy Mayor was very keen to get into that vehicle after my little chat."

Asha noted it down. "How did it go?"

"He pretended not to know anything, but then he also hinted that people want us shut down and he's got our backs."

Asha grimaced. She knew what that meant only too well.

"Trust no one, Ash. Tell no one except Nicolas. Did you call the lawyer?"

"He's sort of interested. Especially when I mentioned the money."

Delaney nodded. "Yeah, that would get his interest. Meanwhile if anyone asks, you know nothing about Jirdasham and I'm handling it, not you."

"Ok." Asha understood.

Delaney thought of one more thing. "Assume someone is going to be listening to what we say, who we call and what we write down from now on, Ash. Come on. Let's get your spare key and find you my old phone. I can't have you cut off from the world. You might want to change your lock at home too."

Asha grabbed her bag. "They're changing the lock today. I hope he didn't mess up Boo-Boo."

"Boo-Boo?"

"My car. Daddy bought me that little Fiat 500. It was one of those 'Never ask me for any money ever again deals.'"

Delaney smiled. "I'm sure that's not true, Ash. You are way too cute for a Daddy to cut you off entirely." He gave her a friendly nudge. "Anyway, your thief probably just wanted to get home and was too polite to wake you up."

"Or mention he stole my phone. Bastard."

CHAPTER EIGHTEEN

The Road to Oyster Point

Delaney was preparing to leave for Oyster Point.
"You sure you'll be ok on your own, M? I could call your mother."
Maria rolled her eyes. "Like she'll come running. I don't think so."
"I'm taking Rufus to guard the car. You sure you'll be safe?"
Maria looked exasperated. "It's your house, of course I'll be safe."
Delaney sighed. "Alright, I've left you Asha's number in case. You'll do your homework?"
Maria gave him her 'As if' look. "Oh, let me see, homework or Netflix, hmm I wonder."
Delaney grinned. He wondered if he'd have done any homework if Netflix had existed when he was thirteen. No way. "Did you like the samosas by the way? If you didn't, blame Asha."
Maria nodded. "You can definitely buy those again."
"Good. Asha seems to know all the cool veggie places in the city."
Maria cocked her head to one side. "How come you aren't dating her? She's like amazing and clearly likes you."
Delaney was caught by surprise. "I'm almost twenty years older than her for starters and she likes fit guys without scruples."
Maria blinked. "No way you're twenty years older. I have no idea what scruples are, but you clearly aren't picking up on her signals."
Delaney laughed. "Maria's dating tips. Luckily no one cares how old you are after twenty-five, but it's a rule that you never date the girl you just hired. When it goes wrong, it can go very wrong indeed."
Maria shook her head. "She likes you though. I can tell."

"She likes having a boss who lets her do what she likes. Ok. I'm going. Remember to go to bed. I won't be back till very late. Oyster Point is about two hours away."

Maria cleared her plate away, but he noted she didn't try to wash it up.

Rufus followed him to the front door. "Don't forget to lock, but don't slide the bolt over or else I won't be able to get back in."

"I won't. 'Bye Rufie. Come back safe."

The Coastal Highway was one of his favorite driving roads in daylight, slightly more precarious at night with a sheer drop one side to the ocean and steep cliffs on the other. A heavy cloud was obscuring the moon and it was chilly, winter hadn't quite released its grip. There was very little traffic. He guessed not many people travelled to Oyster Point at night, it being mostly a retirement village by a small fishing harbor.

He thought back to the last time he'd been there. Denise sitting beside him in the hired car; feeling nauseous most of the time. Three months pregnant and she could hardly eat anything and didn't travel well at the best of times. She was scared she'd lose the child, he remembered. Two weeks after they got back to Paris, she'd come down with chicken pox and lost the baby. He couldn't recall who'd been the most devastated about it. She blamed her mother for not having her vaccinated when a child and she blamed him for taking her to his home city where she swore she'd picked up the virus. He'd had no choice as he'd gone back for his mother's funeral. It was her idea to join him and take a brief vacation there.

Denise had talked of buying a cottage at Oyster Point she'd liked it so much.

He tried to force the memories from his mind. No wife, no child, little inclination to start over. Perhaps that was why he was being nice to Maria. A need to be a parent, to care for someone. Could be. She was right of course, he did like Asha, but carefully kept his distance. No need to complicate things or risk embarrassment if she found the idea too weird.

The sign indicated Oyster Point – two miles. He turned off the highway and headed down to the cove. He wondered what he'd say to the Guru and how responsive he'd be.

The Guru was in the Spirit Garden illuminated with lanterns hanging from the cherry trees. A tiny man, he stood on a plinth as he read from his book. The crowd was attentive and surprisingly young. The man had a curiously hypnotic voice. "Happiness is a consequence of daily exercise and healthy eating. It's no accident that a moment of depression can be relieved by a simple walk in the park."

Delaney surveyed the bookshop, the inevitable exotic candles and homeopathic cures that promised relief for just about any ailment. If only.

The Guru's book on 'Taking Control of Your Body' seemed relatively normal. There was a photo of him smiling out of the cover. Chapters included – 'Master Your Pain', 'Don't trust the drugs', 'Say No to Meat and Dairy.' Delaney realized he could have written this book himself. Less likely to get the exorbitant price he was asking for it, however. He had to buy a copy so the Guru could sign it later.

Delaney noticed the minder only when the Guru stopped speaking. He'd been lurking in the shadows - his dark suit and tie looked out of place in these surroundings.

People asked questions. The Guru answered in his giggly style, possibly all part of the act. There was a lot of talk of God and how he worked through his hands, people seemed to buy into it anyway.

Finally came the book signing. Delaney made sure he was one of the last in the line. The minder was attentive for the first few but grew bored and when it had dwindled to the last five, he left to get the transportation.

Delaney leaned in close when it was his turn. "Your sister misses you Ansolm. Wants you to pay her a visit. One mustn't neglect family."

The Guru looked up at him with surprise, his eyes so old and cloudy.

"I'd like to talk to you about Jirdasham when you don't have a minder around. Perhaps when you visit your sister."

The Guru stared at him trying to enter reality. He'd been on automatic for so long. He blinked and nodded his head.

"My sister's birthday perhaps," he whispered.

"Nothing to be afraid of," Delaney assured him. "Just need to know how an old man like you can cure so many thousands of their pain. It must be exhausting."

The Guru was smart enough to hear the hidden threat behind this.

Delaney smiled. "You sister will call me if you show up." He indicated where he could sign as he saw the minder returning.

"Make it out to Maria. She fractured her back and it's not healing well."

The Guru resumed his beatific smile. "I should see this girl. Back pain is one of hardest to treat."

The minder returned and leaned in to tell him it was to go.

"Namaste," Delaney said with a little bow as he retrieved the book.

"Namaste," the Guru replied, as the minder helped him up off the chair. Delaney noticed the tattoo on the minder's wrist. A tiny red Jackal. The minder was definitely ex-cop. All beefed up on hormones with cropped hair. The tiny gold earring was a bit off, but you didn't mess with the Jackals, current or ex. Clearly Jirdasham were serious about keeping the Guru under close guard.

Delaney watched him being led away. The Guru briefly turned his head to glance back at him before disappearing behind the trees. He wondered how many book buyers would find their way to Jirdasham and part with thirty grand. This was the soft sell part of the scam.

Delaney glanced down at the inscription and saw what the Guru had written. 'Help Me.'

Delaney pondered that as he drank some pungent hibiscus tea on the terrace. Did he mean it? The Guru liked a little joke, but then again, there was the mirthless minder to consider. They were working the old guy hard. Maybe he really did need help. He made a note to find out when his sister would be having a birthday.

It was going to be a long drive back. Maria would be anxious. She seemed tough; he knew she would have been happier if he'd left Rufus behind. He sent a text to Asha to say he'd met the Guru. It hadn't exactly been a productive meeting. He really needed to get to speak to the Guru alone.

He took the dog for a walk on the beach by the harbor. Six small fishing vessels were being prepared to go out to sea. A half-moon was finally visible through the clouds. Rufus found a stick and they played catch for half an hour.

'Help me,' played on his mind. He wondered if the man was ever able to get to his sister's house. Perhaps they let him out once in a while unsupervised.

"Time to go, hound. Long way back."

Delaney didn't remember exactly when he realized he was being followed. For a while he thought it was just another car on the road. But when he stopped for Rufus to have a pee, the other car stopped too, at a distance. It wasn't exactly subtle.

"We have a tail, Rufus. Not sure what to do about it. After all, if they know who I am, they'll know where I live. No need to tail me at all."

Delaney continued driving, speeding up a little to see if he could lose them, but not too much. At night the tight twisty coastal highway was dangerous, and he was on the ocean side of the road now. They maintained the same distance. They meant business. He guessed the minder had made a call to one of his friends. At some point they would make a move. He stepped up the speed a little more.

"Hold tight, Rufus. This could get a little awkward."

He tried dialing Asha but couldn't get a signal. He was worried about Maria. He didn't want them going to his house frightening her. Should have told her to bolt the damn door.

Maria switched the TV off, aware it was late, scared of Delaney coming in and finding her still up. There it was again. A noise. Someone was outside the house. They'd climbed over the gate.

She flipped the light off and ran towards the front door. It was locked, but he'd distinctly said leave the bolt undone.

It definitely wasn't Delaney. Rufus wasn't impatiently scratching on the door like he normally did to get in. Biting her lips, she was hesitant. If it was a thief, she was vulnerable without the dog. Why oh why hadn't he left the dog behind?

As quiet as possible she slid the bolt into place. Someone was definitely out there; she could hear footsteps. Maria pictured every room in the house and couldn't think of a single safe place to hide. It was dark without the light, but she felt safer without it on so they couldn't see inside. But what if they got in?

She grabbed her fleece off the hook and ran towards the kitchen door. Made sure that was locked and bolted. She moved into the laundry room. The window catch was faulty. If they found it, they could force it open easy. If they got into the house any other way, she could at least get out by this window.

Her heart was racing. She heard pounding footsteps running at the back of the house. The security lights from next door were triggered and she heard someone curse as they tripped and fell hard, probably in one of Rufus' holes. Then they were running back, right past the laundry room swearing loudly. The other security light flashed on and now the whole house was bathed in a bright light. Maria held her breath praying they wouldn't get in, clutching one of the dog's sticks for defense.

It went quiet. Finally, she heard a car drive off at speed, tires squealing. Maria grabbed some old sheets around her and stayed put. She didn't dare leave the laundry room. The bolt would have to stay on the front door until Delaney pounded on it to let him in. She promised herself that she wouldn't sleep. How could she sleep? Someone had been trying to get in.

CHAPTER NINETEEN

Eyes in The Dark

Officer Kosik slowed down on the Coastal Highway. There was broken glass in the middle of the road and the ocean side crash barrier was broken and bent out of shape. His headlights briefly picked out the gleaming eyes of an animal. When he stopped, he found a wounded dog on the side of the road. Nothing too unusual about a wounded animal on this stretch of the coast highway, but it was after midnight and a long way from any settlements.

He left the headlights shining on the animal as he approached. The dog was whimpering but made no attempt to move. Some of his colleagues might have just driven on by but he was a dog person and besides, needed a piss. It had been a long drive back from Oyster Point and he still had five hours left to patrol and keep the world safe. He liked the night shift patrols on weekdays. Weekends inevitably ended up being busy booking speeders or drunks, but this had been a no-nothing kind of night so far.

The dog flinched, didn't like him touching, his left flank was bleeding. Hit by a car maybe, then, what the hell was he doing out here?

"Hey, calm down. I'm not going to hurt you. Someone throw you out, dog? Is that what happened? You barking too much for their tastes? Lucky you've got a collar boy. Maybe someone will be happy to know you're alive."

The dog stood uncertainly, lifting its back leg to relieve the pain. His hair was matted with blood and there were cuts on his head and back.

"Leg doesn't look broken. Fancy a ride home?"

Rufus whined some. Wanted to explain what had happened but it was impossible.

Officer Kosik was taking a leak listening to the ocean when he noticed a flashing emergency light way down below.

He finished up, checked the curbside barrier to his left and could see it was smashed in two places. The vehicle had hit the barrier at speed. It was one hell of a steep slope to the ocean below. He wondered how the dog got up here with a bad leg. Or had it been flung clear? It was too dark to make out anything much, but he called it in. Someone would have to go down there and see if anyone was still alive. He didn't hold out much hope.

He shouted in case someone was conscious down below, but the ocean was too loud and swallowed his voice.

He scooped up the dog and carried him to the car, gently putting him on the back seat. Rufus protested some, didn't like the smells, but wasn't about to try and get out again.

Officer Kosik grabbed his flashlight and went looking for skid marks and broken glass. It didn't take long to find scorched rubber tracks and broken plastic. He gathered up what he could before it all got trampled by other traffic. He wondered how long ago this had happened. The only witness wasn't going to be very cooperative on that score. He contemplated on finding a way down the cliffside but decided against it. He'd look a total idiot if he couldn't get back up and someone stole his vehicle.

His radio squawked. Tow truck wouldn't be available until the next shift. No ambulance crew equipped to go down a cliff would be available until early morning at the earliest. His instructions were to tape off the incident area, leave traffic hazard lights and move on. There was fire in the bay area, and he was needed there. He was reluctant to leave the scene. The sky was clear, the stars were out and far below he could hear the ocean waves. Most likely whoever was driving that vehicle was dead on impact. Nothing but boulders down there.

He sighed as he got out the hazard lights and switched them on. A car drove on by but didn't stop. No one ever thinks to stop to lend a hand. He briefly wondered if they ever did.

Asha woke suddenly from a deep sleep, slowly coming to realize the phone was vibrating on the bedside table. She grabbed it and answered croakily.

"This better be an emergency. It's...," she glanced at her phone, "almost four am."

"Good morning, Ma'am. Sorry to call so early. Office

Kosik here, BPD."

"Police?" Asha sat up in bed. She couldn't recall ever getting a call from the cops.

"I'm in possession of a wounded dog. Got two phone numbers on the tag. One of them is this number. This is why I'm calling."

"Rufus? Brown and Black Ridgeback/Collie cross-breed?"

"That's the one, brown and black with a white ruff. Not sure about the breed however."

Asha wasn't going to argue the provenance of the dog.

"Where are you? Why do you have it? Where is David Delaney, the owner?"

"You happen to know if Mr Delaney owns a Land Rover Discovery?"

Asha heart leapt. "Oh my god, what's happened? Is Delaney all right? Where are you? I'm coming right over."

"City precinct. Speak the desk sergeant; he'll know where I am. Do you have any idea why Mr Delaney was out on the Coastal Road last night?"

"Is Delaney alright"?

There was an awkward pause.

"I'm afraid we found the vehicle, but we're unable at this time to access the area of the accident."

"What? I'm coming. I'll be there as soon as I can."

Asha blinked. Delaney had texted to say he'd met with the Guru but said nothing else. What about the girl at his home? Was Rufus all right? She dashed to the bathroom. Her mind a total jumble.

CHAPTER TWENTY

Saving the Chief

Asha walked out of the police precinct confused. Sure, she was happy to have Rufus on the lead, even if they hadn't bothered to clean the blood off him. He limped beside her happy to be with someone he recognized. Asha couldn't believe they hadn't even gone back to the crash site and sent someone down to investigate. What if Delaney was still in the car slowly bleeding to death? The Cops promised to get a tow truck out there to winch it up, but they'd been overwhelmed by the fire downtown during the night and short staffed. Tow trucks were busy clearing burned out vehicles from the streets. They had priorities clearly; she realized they had decided that Delaney was dead.

Her phone rang, and she struggled to answer, unused to Delaney's old phone.

"He didn't come home, Asha." Maria informed her in an unusually small voice. Asha tried to remember that she was just a kid and was probably scared.

"There's been an accident, Maria. I'll be honest with you; Delaney hasn't been found yet. His car went over a cliff."

"A cliff?" Maria squealed. "And Rufus?"

"I've got the dog. He's cut up and bruised, but somehow, he got out of the car. I'm bringing the dog to you. You can take care of him?"

"Yes. Bring him here. Poor Rufie. I won't go to school if he's injured. Is Delaney...?" She didn't want say dead. Her life was about to change again if he was.

Asha didn't know what to say and Delaney would be annoyed if she didn't go to school. Nevertheless, the dog was certainly traumatized and needed a lot of love and attention. Such a pity Rufus couldn't tell her what had happened.

"Asha?"

"Yes?"

"Someone tried to get into the house last night. Delaney told me not to bolt the door, but I had to. He shouldn't have taken Rufie. I was scared they'd get in."

Asha's alarm bells went off. "You sure they were trying to get in?"

"Yeah, absolutely. They had to climb over the wall to get into the back garden. They tried all the doors and windows. All the security lights came on, both sides. I heard them running at the back."

Asha didn't like the sound of this at all. "Maria, I'll be with you soon. I'm going to sleep over tonight until they find Delaney. OK? Don't worry."

"You promise?"

"I promise."

Rufus looked up at her and sneezed, then yelped, as it must have hurt.

"Don't worry, dog. Maria will take good care of you."

A short while later she'd managed to down a coffee and eat some toast, still angry no one was going to look for Delaney. Maria was staring at her, wiping a tear away.

"Promise me you'll go and find him, Asha. Please. I know you don't think I care but I do. He's the only person who has ever given a shit about me. He can't be dead. What if he's trapped in his car and bleeding to death?"

"It's ok. I'll go. I'm as worried as you are."

She pulled on a warmer sweater from Delaney's wardrobe. Rufus was happy to be left with Maria but whined piteously if anyone touched him. He would get good care and cleaning him up would keep Maria distracted for a while. Clearly, the girl had been shaken up by events and desperately didn't want Delaney to be dead.

Asha put on her shoes and grabbed her keys. "I'm going. If anyone other than cops come to the door, do not let them in. Bolt the door, Maria."

Maria nodded. "Will you call me when you find him?"

"Yes. Lock and bolt, girl. I'm going now."

Maria raised Rufus' head from her lap and quickly went to lock the door, sliding the bolt over. She looked back at Rufus and saw him yelp as he tried to get more comfortable. She felt tears welling. If Delaney was dead, she'd have to run away, but in all the imagined scenarios of running away, she'd always had Rufus at her side. Now he could barely walk.

Asha drove towards the coast road angry. How could the cops just leave him down there? Maria was right. They had no idea if he was alive or dead. Someone had to go down that cliff and it might as well be her.

Asha parked up on the side of the highway, leaving her hazard lights on. The only sign that there had been an accident was a lone flashing cone and police tape flapping in the wind by a gap where the crash barriers had been. It was a gloomy morning, the sun well hidden behind thick clouds.

She examined the crash barrier with interest. They were designed to deflect a car away from the edge, yet his vehicle had hit it with such force it had completely given way. She peered down over the edge and could see the back of his Discovery and one hazard light weakly flashing as the battery ran down. It had to be at least a hundred and twenty feet straight down. He'd have hit the rocks really hard. It would be a bitch to winch up. She wondered how Rufus had found a way up, especially injured like he was. Her eyes followed the scrub and wildflowers clinging to the cliffside. There was a bit of a ledge heading down. She checked her watch and wondered where the cops were. Surely, they'd come back and investigate properly. Officer Kosik had reassured her they would, he seemed to be a man of his word.

She went back to her Fiat and dug out her old walking shoes, a small bottle of water and a fleece. When she turned around, she could see skid marks where Delaney must have braked hard. There was broken plastic on the side of the road, which had to be from his rear lights. But if anything was going to break, surely it would be the front glass headlights, not the rear? This was no accident for sure.

She crossed the road and gingerly made her way down along narrow ledge, trying hard to ignore the sheer drop if she made a mistake. Sure enough, about thirty feet down she found blood and crushed vegetation. This had to be where Rufus had been thrown clear. So, had the rear door burst open or a window smashed before the car had plummeted further down?

Asha slowly made her way down towards the smashed vehicle, glancing up only once when she heard a truck go by. Hell, it was steep. If Delaney had survived, he couldn't have climbed back up in the dark. She wasn't even sure she could get back up. Below her the ocean seemed calm. Soft waves gently broke on the shingle shoreline. She wondered how the vehicle hadn't ended up in the ocean.

She stood on a boulder to get a better lie of the land. To her left it was limestone cliffs. Seagulls cruised around her, curious as to why she was there. To her right she remembered there was an abandoned Christian community that must have been cut off when they built the new coastal highway. Fishwake Village. Quite how she had remembered that she had no idea. Something about a scandal maybe or a murder. It had lodged in her brain for some reason.

To her immediate right a mountain stream emptied into the ocean; given how rough the terrain was, an injured Delaney couldn't have gone far. She steeled herself for the worst. She dreaded finding him squashed against the wheel and very dead.

She jumped down to a flat rock. The vehicle was squeezed between two boulders pincering the Discovery in place. The vehicle had stopped six feet short of the shoreline, literally pinned into place by the boulders. She'd been right about the right-hand rear light cluster. It had been smashed. There was a trace of red paint easily visible on the Discovery's polar white metal.

Heart in mouth she peered inside. Delaney wasn't there, but there was a whole lot of blood everywhere. The windshield was missing. She winced. Had Delaney been thrown out? She couldn't get the door open. The interior was a mess; the passenger airbag had opened, but curiously not the driver's side. She managed to squeeze through the open window half-way and retrieve his phone from between the seats. She found the Guru's book on the dash and dragged that out as well. There was a tell-tale spray of blood on the roof lining and the roof itself was dented badly. She was no accident expert, but this looked to her like Delaney was shunted off the road. They must have deliberately chosen this desolate cliff edge to do it. Chances of his surviving the crash were pitifully small, even if he did have a tough vehicle. This had been deliberate; she was sure of it.

There was blood on the back seat. The right rear passenger window was shattered. Rufus had been cut by glass or thrown against the doors. The dog must have escaped through the gap. He wouldn't have been strapped in like Delaney.

Which must have saved his life at least. Rufus had a good survival instincts.

She found more blood all over the seatbelt buckle, which told her that he'd been conscious enough to release it and get the hell out of the car. This was a good sign. She grabbed the ignition keys; his house key was on it and she'd need it.

Asha dropped down to the narrow shingle shoreline and narrowly avoided some broken glass. The water was pretty deep here. Could Delaney have been propelled out of the car into the ocean? She couldn't see a body floating anywhere, but then again, it was tidal, he could have drifted away.

She glanced back at the vehicle and saw blood smeared across the hood. He'd crawled out through the smashed windshield for sure. She should be able to track him. Indeed, there were blood traces on the shingles and the direction was towards Fishwake.

How bad was he hurt? Would she find him before he bled to death? She dropped the Guru's book and only then saw the inscription. 'Help Me'. She did a double take. A joke; or for real? Only Delaney would know the answer to that.

Asha took the positive viewpoint. He'd got out of the vehicle, so he was definitely mobile. But how badly injured? She surveyed the shoreline towards Fishwake. No way, injured or not, was he or she going to get there climbing over the huge granite boulders that had come down from the mountains. Delaney would have had to swim around them. It was low tide now, so it had to have been high when he crashed. She removed her shoes and tucked her dress into her underwear with memories of being six years old at gym class at school. She waded out into the freezing ocean, quickly finding herself waist deep. She held his phone, the book and her shoes up above her head to keep them dry.

She aimed for the remains of a broken jetty. Above her she could hear morning traffic passing but none slowed. Still no sign of the damn tow truck.

Like Rufus, Delaney would have natural survival instincts, after all he'd sailed the Pacific. He would have swum if he could, he'd know the cold saltwater would slow the bleeding or at least wash his wounds and disinfect them. She wondered if that was true, she remembered being taught it as a child, but so much her father had taught her turned out not to be true, or at least, less than useful.

She made it to the jetty; but struggled to find a way ashore. The rocks were sharp and slimy with seaweed and she swore violently when she stubbed her toes.

Asha found another route to the shore. She had to take her dress off after all and wring it out. Her sweater and fleece were soaked too and altogether she felt cold and miserable. It must have been easier to do this at high tide. She tucked his phone into her bra to protect it. She wanted to dry off, but it was too cold to sit around. Only when she finally got her shoes back on over her wet feet did she spot fresh blood on the old dock stone paving. Her heart leapt. He'd reached this point. She looked along the coastline. It was about a mile to the old settlement at Fishwake. He had to be there, just had to be. She felt more confident now. Delaney was tough. Yes. He was alive for sure.

CHAPTER TWENTY-ONE

The Small Print

Delaney woke abruptly. He discovered he was lying on a small bed by the side porch of a wooden shack; a makeshift blanket was strung up to protect him from the wind. There was an overwhelming smell of cat pee, but given his disorientation, he was grateful he was somewhere. He looked at his wrist and wondered where his watch had gone. He had no idea how he'd got to this place, but he knew he'd been in an accident. His clothes were torn and damp, his legs had been bleeding and his head hurt like hell, now wrapped in a tight cloth. He dimly remembered getting stitches and passing out. He had no idea how long he'd been there.

He suddenly remembered Rufus. Where the hell was Rufie? Please God, let him not be dead. It was worrying that he wasn't with him. Rufus normally stuck to him like glue. He tested his limbs, taking each one in turn. Everything about him was sore, like he'd been repeatedly hit with a baseball bat on every extremity. But his toes and fingers seemed to move ok and that was pretty remarkable in itself.

He heard talking on the porch and he was going to call out, but something about the tone of the conversation stopped him. He tried to listen.

"Did you see him?" A woman was asking.

"He's coping," a man replied.

"Coping? You seriously think he's coping? He's been screaming night and day. The pain is killing him. You said it couldn't kill, but it is."

"Pain, of itself, can't kill," the man replied. "It's a medical fact. Your husband doesn't have cancer, no matter what he thinks he has. It was all agreed in the contract."

"Agreed? He agreed, not me."

The man began walking along the porch. "Nice place for the children to grow up in, Janice. You must be very proud of your husband."

"Proud?" She questioned.

"As I remember, you were living in a derelict school bus when we found you. Talk to him, Janice. You have a safe place now, the rent is paid, and the kids eat. Your husband did this for you."

"But he wants out of the contract."

The man laughed, Delaney registered it was quite sinister and mocking.

"As I mentioned before. He can terminate the contract, but if you examine the sub-clause 16E/1 you'll note that you must give six months' notice. You think it is easy to find healthy volunteers? Time, money, persistence, we're looking for reliable volunteers all the time. Try to remember how desperate you were to sign the contract. Your husband is a hero in our eyes. And will be well compensated at the end of the contract. Don't forget – when he makes it to the end he can re-sign and get a bonus. That could be a year's rent on an apartment in the city, a new car or holiday for you and the kids."

"Gerry doesn't care anymore. He's not eating. He's threatening to starve himself to death."

"Well, that would be most unfortunate, Janice. It would incur a penalty on your part. Read Section 7. 'Any attempt at willful termination of the contract you will forfeit all monies owed to you from the start of the contract.' You'd owe us double what we would be paying you. You really don't want to be in debt to us, Janice. You might have to decide which one of your children would have to take your husband's place. Think on that, won't you? You really want your kids to suffer like that? We test quite thoroughly for natural causes. Any suspicion of suicide and your life would not be worth living. Dispel any notions of termination. Your Gerry must see it through."

"But ..."

"We will send one of our people out to talk to him, Janice. There might be something we can do to make the pain more tolerable. Don't worry – it's all part of the care package. It's the least we can do."

Delaney heard the man walk off and moments later a car starting up. He thought he heard the woman sobbing. He called out, but she didn't come to see him. He tried to move but he still felt dizzy and he thought better of it. How the hell had he got here, why was there seaweed on his trousers? He couldn't make sense of the conversation. Her husband was participating in some medical trial and wanted out? Was that it? If only he could stand. Where was Rufus? What time was it? He urgently needed to make calls. Asha. He needed to call Asha.

Asha cursed her leather shoes that were chaffing her heels and she knew they would be bloody sore when she took them off. She was disheveled and ravenously hungry despite that hurried round of toast with Maria earlier. She had arrived in what remained of Fishwake, a forlorn collection of wooden homes that at first sight looked abandoned, but on more careful inspection were inhabited, or at least some of them were.

The first house had rotted out, the roof fallen in. The second was empty, but sported new timbers, so someone cared for it. The new highway may have cut this place off, but there was a narrow track and she could see a small pick-up parked outside one house, so there had to be access.

There was nothing for it, she'd have to knock on every door and hope someone had seen Delaney. She was surprised he'd made it this far. He had to be here somewhere.

She knocked on the door of a much-neglected house with peeling blue paint. Salt encrusted windows didn't give her much hope, but it had faded curtains and she could see smoke coming from the chimney.

The door opened and the women looked at her as if she was the devil in person come calling. She wore a kaftan far too tight for her obese frame and her blackened toes protruded out of pink fluffy slippers.

"No strangers here. Didn't you see the sign?" She barked.

Asha stared at the woman's yellow teeth. "I'm looking for..."

"I told you. No one here. No ever comes here. No strangers."

"You think one of your neighbors might have taken someone in?" Asha asked quickly.

The woman's face contorted into a mask of hate. "This is a Christian Community. We don't take strangers in. Go away."

She slammed the door in Asha's face. The whole

house shook. She briefly wondered about that bit in the Bible about shunning strangers, but then again Delaney might have escaped a worst fate. She backed off the porch and warily walked towards the next house. There was a guy fixing the roof. It had to be his pick-up. No way Delaney was there either as some side walls were entirely missing.

The fifth house looked more promising. A woman was hanging out washing. Asha braced herself for rejection.

"Excuse me?"

The woman looked at her with surprise and spat out the peg in her mouth. She was clearly unused to anyone approaching her.

"I'm sorry. I'm looking for my boss. He crashed his car up on the highway last night and I've been following his blood trail ..."

The woman relaxed and pinned up the last sheet. Asha noticed bloodstains.

"Is he here? If he is, he has to be badly injured."

The woman brushed her hair from her sweaty brow and picked up her empty basket. "You seen his dog? He's been rambling about his dog for hours."

Asha breathed a sigh of relief. "Rufus made it out alive. Cuts and bruises mostly."

The woman nodded and seemed happy to hear that. "He'll be relieved. Never seen anyone so anxious about a dog before."

"Can I see him?"

"He's sleeping."

"I can wait."

The woman clearly didn't want her there. "You got a car? I don't see any car."

Asha nodded. "Left it up on the highway."

The woman led her towards her house. She had very prominent blue veins in her legs and extraordinarily red hands. But Asha didn't get any bad vibes from her.

"You're lucky that I took him in, young lady. Others around here wouldn't have. Strangers aren't allowed. This is a strict Christian community."

Asha felt that she had already picked up on that. "I didn't know this place was still occupied. Must be hard being so far from the shops and stuff."

"We get by. We grow food. People used to do that y'know."

Asha was aware that there were pear trees in blossom and the more she looked she could see rows of vegetables planted out in rows.

She was impressed. "Old school."

"No school. Home school. Kids are out fishing somewhere right now. It's too far and there's no buses out here."

Asha appreciated that. Her absolute idea of hell, but clearly the woman was in her element.

She hadn't lied. Delaney was sleeping. His head was wrapped in a bloody tea towel. His shoes were blood soaked and wet.

The woman glanced at her wet clothes. "You swam here?"

Asha nodded. "Waded at least. Picked up his trail at the old jetty."

"You must like your boss a lot."

Asha hadn't thought about it that way. Delaney was her boss but somehow her friend too. Perhaps the desperate look on Maria's face at breakfast had spurred her to do it. Either way, she'd found him, and he was alive, contrary to her earlier expectations.

"I had to stitch him up. He was cut deep. Don't worry. I know what I'm doing. Had to do first aid at school. I was a teacher before I met my husband. Curse the day that happened. He crashed down from the highway? Not many people would survive that, I'd say."

Asha nodded. "I figured he used up a few lives. You call an ambulance?"

The woman shrugged. "Look around you, girl. No electricity. No telephones. You wouldn't come here unless you had to."

Asha got the distinct impression that she had to. She leant forward and stroked Delaney's face. He barely stirred. "Did you give him something to sleep?"

The woman shook her head. "He needs to sleep. He lost a lot of blood. The body knows what to do."

Asha pursed her lips turning towards the woman. "Thank you for taking care of him. I'm going to go and get my car. It's quite a walk. He'll be ok here?"

The woman nodded. "It's a Christian's duty to help a

stranger in trouble. Even if he was trespassing. You got any money?"

"Money?" Asha queried. She'd left home in a panic without her purse.

"He bled on my sheets. Sheets cost money. I don't mind feeding him, that's the Christian thing to do, but sheets and food costs money. Look around you, money doesn't exactly grow on trees around here."

She was poor. It wasn't an unreasonable request, Asha reasoned. Someone was calling her from inside the house. A man who sounded in pain. The woman ignored it. "Don't listen. There's nothing to be done about it."

Asha frowned. What were the odds of two people being in pain in the same house? Was it safe to leave Delaney here? No way he'd be able to walk back to her car.

"You find Delaney's wallet?" Asha asked. "It's usually in his back pocket."

The woman narrowed her eyes. "I'm an honest woman, young lady. I'm not going through a man's wallet. Some might around here, but not me, not my kids."

Asha smiled. "I didn't think you would. I'm going to fetch my car. If he wakes, tell him Asha came. Tell him Rufus made it out alive."

"You can tell him yourself when you come back. Make sure you come back mind. I can't keep feeding him."

Asha followed the narrow track out of the settlement. Sixteen wooden houses in all. The faded sign at the entrance read 'Fishwake Christian Community. Strangers not welcome.' Not kidding either. She couldn't believe Delaney had made it there. Talk about luck. Finding someone who knew how to stitch a wound. Asha didn't even know how to sew, let alone stitch a bloody wound. Then again, if you're going to live so far out of the city, you'd better know how to do a whole lot of things for yourself.

The sun finally came out and she was almost dry by the time she got back to her car. The road was busy, but there was still no activity on getting Delaney's Discovery winched up. If he hadn't got himself out of the vehicle he would have bled to death. Asha discovered that she cared about that, a lot. Delaney was soft-hearted and got all these mysterious pains in his hands, but the woman was right, somehow, he'd become an important part of her life. How weird was that.

Delaney was awake when she returned. He was drinking tea and seemed very happy to see her. "Ash, Jesus H, how the hell did you find me?" He held up the Guru's book and his phone. "I was just wondering how these got here."

Asha grinned. "Did she tell you Rufus survived?" Asha went forward and gave him a hug. Delaney winced with pain but hugged her right back like he meant it.

"Rufus made it? Janice didn't say anything about that. My God, I can't believe he's alive. Hell, I can't believe I'm alive."

Asha broke free laughing. "Me either. I've seen your Discovery. Six foot more and you would have been in the ocean at high tide, Chief. You're a very lucky guy."

Delaney gripped her hand. "I don't know what to say. Thank you for coming. Janice said someone had come by and been following my blood trail. I think I lost a lot, right?"

Asha nodded. "A lot. But somehow you swam to the jetty. I don't know how you did it. How's your head?"

Delaney touched the tea towel and made a face. "I don't remember much, but I do remember her pinning me down and stitching my head. I think there was a kid holding me down too, but I can't be sure."

"You have to buy her new sheets." Asha told him.

Delaney winced. He felt guilty. "She's been a bit weird, won't allow me into the house. I had to pee in the garden. Is she here?"

"She's inside somewhere. I can hear a man yelling."

Delaney nodded. "I heard that too. Talk about that later. Maria?"

"She's looking after Rufus. Skipped school, with my permission. She was quite upset you didn't come home."

"That makes two of us." He sat up in bed, wincing a little. He was still a little dizzy, but so happy Asha was there. "Can you get my wallet out? I can't quite manage it."

Asha was looking at his hands. "My god, Delaney, they're scraped all over. You're going to be so sore."

Delaney wrinkled his nose. "Had to smash out the cracked windscreen. Harder than you think."

Asha dug into his pants and fished out his wallet.

"Seventy-five."

Delaney nodded. "Give it to Janice. She saved my life, Ash. Can we go?"

Asha nodded. "Lots to tell you, Chief. They haven't winched your car up yet. They didn't even send anyone down to look for you. It's pretty disgusting actually."

"Did you take photos? Probably need it for the insurance."

"Yeah, before I climbed down. Were you driving too fast for the bend?"

Delaney blew air out of his lungs. "I couldn't remember anything at first, but now I can. I was followed back from Oyster Point. He must have patiently waited until we got to this area. He fucking shunted me off the road. I couldn't do anything about it. Went clean through the barrier."

"I saw. And I picked up your taillight pieces."

Delaney stared at her. "He definitely wanted me dead."

Asha smiled and stroked his face. "Actually, you look pretty close to dead to me, Chief. Come on, let's get you checked out by a proper doctor and get the towel off your head. Although I think it's kinda cool."

Delaney felt his head. "That's what this is?"

Asha helped him up as Janice returned looking flustered. She looked relieved that Delaney was leaving.

"Here, I'll take the other side. Don't put stress on your ankles. You're going to be black and blue tomorrow, Mr Delaney."

Delaney knew that already. "Thank you for your kindness, Janice."

Asha pressed the seventy-five into Janice's raw hands. "For the sheets."

Janice nodded, appreciating it. "Didn't always live like this. I might have become head of school if it wasn't for meeting my husband. And having kids. I was too old to have children really. Too late to send them back."

"Your husband sounds pretty sick," Asha remarked.

Janice shrugged. "He'll live. Next year we'll move back to the city and live like proper people. I might get a teaching job."

"I hope so," Delaney told her. "Thank you. I hope

your husband finds relief soon."

Janice made no comment as she helped maneuver him into the Fiat. Delaney could feel every single bone as he folded into the front seat.

"Belt up, Delaney. It's a dangerous road up there."

Delaney acknowledged that with a smile. Asha quickly drove them out of the settlement. Delaney turned his phone on.

"No signal out here. Save your battery." Asha told him.

When they got to the highway access, they could see a tow truck had finally arrived at the scene of his crash. Two guys were scratching their heads as they looked down the cliff.

"You think I should tell them you're ok?" Asha asked. "How the hell are they going to winch it back up? It's a sheer drop. You were so lucky to survive, Chief."

"I still don't know how I did. Seatbelt cut right into me. I was jerked upwards and hit the roof really hard. My neck is killing me. Did the airbag deploy? I don't recall. I don't remember much, just knew I wanted to get the hell out of the car. I'll have to speak to the cops and make a statement anyway when we get home."

"Not today. I'm taking you to see your doctor, Chief. I need to know if you've had concussion."

Delaney closed his eyes, happy to let Asha take control.

CHAPTER TWENTY-TWO

Pizza

Maria was organizing dinner. It had mostly involved ordering pizza and the toppings, but Delaney wasn't going to argue, and Asha wasn't in the mood for cooking either. The log burner was kicking out heat and the dog was spread out in front of it soaking up the warmth, his legs twitching in his dreams.

Delaney disconnected his phone with difficulty. He leant back on the sofa nursing his wounds. His head and hands were bandaged, ugly purple bruising was appearing on his neck and arms. Asha was opening the wine as Delaney disconnected.

"What did the cops say?"

Delaney sighed. "They're officially happy to hear I'm alive and have no excuses or apologies as to why no one came to look for me. My vehicle has been taken care of." He wrote down the incident number given to him for the insurance company, wincing as he directed the pen.

"They want me to make a statement, in person, when I'm ready for it. They want a breath sample. Apparently, it's an accident black spot."

"I guess they don't offer house calls."

"My Doc did a breath test when he took blood samples. It will show if I have alcohol or anything illicit in my system. For my protection, he said. I get the distinct impression the cops were annoyed I'd survived. Creates more paperwork I imagine."

Asha nodded. "I got the same feeling. What now?"

Delaney glanced up at her. "You going to pour that wine."

Asha laughed. "Sorry, got distracted. You didn't take any painkillers, right? You can't have wine with painkillers."

Delaney smiled. "No pills. I can't believe the doc went straight to the codeine. I told him I wasn't going to take them. He seemed surprised."

"I guess people expect them. No one likes pain."

"When's the pizza coming, M?" Delaney asked.

Maria was pouring herself some juice. "Twenty minutes."

Delaney rubbed his head. His whole body ached. He was grateful to be alive and genuinely happy Rufus was OK. Asha brought him a glass of red wine and squatted by the fire stroking Rufus's hot flanks. He didn't stir.

"Oh yeah. A journalist called from The Star. Heard a rumor you were dead, and did I want to comment on the Mayor wanting to close down our office and bring it in-house."

Delaney almost smiled. "I guess they too will be pissed I survived."

Asha nodded. "You think they'll try again?"

Delaney shrugged, as he tasted his wine. "Hmm, nice. That the Caracal blend?"

Asha nodded. "There's a whole case of it."

"Gift from Mr Abrams. Hell, Ash, we might not get paid. We might be shut down, but at least we can drink something to drown our sorrows."

"You really think they'll shut us down?"

Delaney nodded. "We were safe as long as we were looking at things like environmental compliance or that stupid bus contract, but there's a lot of money in this scam. Makes sense to bring it all in house and bury it."

"Kind of makes a mockery of City Oversight though."

"Yeah, but the rule is 'kill the messenger' right?"

"You're not going to get the guy who ran you off the road?" Maria asked, suddenly paying attention. "He tried to kill you, Delaney."

Delaney glanced across at her. "I'm sorry you're having to go through all this, M. Must have been scary for you last night."

Maria held his gaze. "What were they looking for? You think they'll come back?"

Delaney raised his eyebrows. "Might. But I think they will consider me sufficiently warned. They don't want us anywhere near the Guru, that's for sure."

Asha placed another log into the burner and shut the door. "But we're not giving up, right?"

Delaney raised his glass. "To our crusade. They will close us down, but we will do our damnedest to expose them."

Asha raised her glass and drank. "No idea how I'll pay

my rent, but here's to fighting back."

"We haven't had formal notice yet. They would have to pay us an early termination fee. Panic next month, alright?"

Asha smiled with relief. "So, what's the plan?"

Delaney felt a momentary spasm shoot through his head. He pressed a hand to the back of his neck and closed his eyes.

"You ok?" Asha asked.

"Shooting pain. It'll pass. The Doc said I should expect some aftershocks."

"You need to take it easy for the rest of the week, Chief. I mean it."

Delaney smiled and lowered his hand. "I'll be fine. When I was lying on Janice's porch, she had a visitor. I was pretty out of it, so even though I heard everything, I can't exactly remember all the details. But I swear there is a connection between Janice and Jirdasham."

"Her husband was making a lot of noise. He must be in agony."

"He's undergoing some medical trial. Janice didn't want to talk about it. But she did admit that six months ago the whole family was living on a derelict bus down by the old stadium after her husband lost his job."

Asha frowned. "She's pretty resentful about her husband. Regrets her marriage, that's for sure."

"Anyway, the people doing the trial are paying her rent, which can't be much out there for god's sake, and if he goes to the end of the drug trail, he's in line for a big bonus. Enough to pay rent on a city apartment for a year they said."

"But whatever they are giving him isn't working." Asha remarked, suddenly remembering something. "You know, I saw a poster up in the Market Street toilets. They were looking for volunteers for a drug trial. Could be the connection. A lot of homeless people use it to get clean."

Delaney looked at her with surprise. "You used the Market Street toilets?"

"Eww," Maria exclaimed. "I had to use them once. It's full of junkies. I've never been so scared in my life."

Asha made a face. "I had an emergency. It happens. No details."

"So, what? We assuming they are recruiting desperate

people for a drug trial. But what are they testing? I can't see a connection to the scam, but I swear there is one."

Asha thought about it. "Maybe they're training people to take the Guru's place. They need volunteers."

"Yes, but we're talking about removing pain, not causing it."

Asha drank some wine. "We definitely need to talk to the Guru."

The doorbell rang. Rufus attempted to bark but yelped with pain when he tried to move. Maria squealed with fright.

"Pizza," Delaney announced. "Suddenly I am very hungry. Get the door, M."

It was only after Maria had gone to bed that Asha and Delaney continued the conversation. The fire was dying down, but the house was still cozy.

"Help Me," Asha said, remembering the Guru's book. "He actually wrote that in front of you?"

Delaney was staring at the Guru's book. "He did. He had a very officious minder, so there wasn't much time to talk. Ex-Jackal. I saw his tattoo."

"And you think he's being held captive by them."

"I wouldn't say captive, but certainly controlled. I suggested we meet at his sister's house and he told me that she had a birthday coming up."

"So, you're hoping to meet him there without the minder."

Delaney nodded. "Yeah, I'll call her tomorrow and I'm sure she'll cooperate."

"Maybe the Guru isn't the bad guy in all this."

"He's certainly out of his depth and they're certainly working him hard. But the business model doesn't work unless there are others like him."

"Others that are using tricks to make people believe their pain has gone temporarily. Hypnosis? Could that work?" Asha suggested.

"Maybe, but how long would that last? When they complain the pain's returned, they get the option of the real thing for a fifteen-grand booster."

"So, all those people who withdrew their complaints are the ones who didn't want to or couldn't pay more? That would make sense."

"And were threatened. They certainly sounded scared."

"And our wonderful Deputy Mayor is in on it." Asha said.

"I suspect he made the call to have me shunted off the road. Never prove it, but ..."

"The Mayor is just as guilty, after all he's the one endorsing it." Asha declared. "He's selling it as a solution for the opioid epidemic. They're offering them these drug trails. It gets them off the streets and out of our doorways."

Delaney considered that. "Maybe that's what this is. Scam the rich and get the poor off the streets. Maybe they're thinking that they're Robin Hood."

Asha gathered up the wine glasses and plates. "Elections next year. So, if you can claim to have got all the homeless housed someplace and off the streets ..."

"We might be attributing too much milk and kindness here on behalf of our City Fathers. It is costing them money."

"But only a fraction of what they're getting up front," Asha pointed out. "Is it legal?"

Delaney shrugged. "Probably. Is it ethical? I doubt it. Did you ever find a connection to Veronika Jaywaller?"

"I've been a bit preoccupied with saving my boss's ass."

Delaney smiled. "That you did and I'm beyond grateful, Ash. You sure about staying over?"

Asha nodded. "I drank more than the limit, so I can't drive, and I promised Maria. I'll take her to school tomorrow. You need to rest."

"You like her any better yet?"

Asha shrugged. "She's looking out for herself. Knows how to push your buttons, that's for sure."

Delaney stood up uncertainly and then took Asha's hand. "Thank you for finding me. It took courage to go down that cliff."

Asha grinned. "Hey, I needed you to sign my salary cheque. It's going to be my last one."

Delaney laughed. "Tough cookie, aren't you, Ash."

"Did I mention I was Captain of the Soccer team at University? We were deadly."

Delaney leaned in and kissed the top of her head. "I don't doubt it for a moment. I'm going to crawl to bed. Bolt the door."

Asha watched him go, amazed he could move at all. The outside rear security light flicked on and her heart leapt. She cautiously went to the window only to see a cat walking across the wall. Panic over. She made sure she bolted the door. Rufus stood up stiffly from the hearth and licked his wounds.

"You feeling as rough as me, Rufus? You're one lucky dog to get out of that car alive, y'know."

Rufus glanced up at her, then flopped back down to sleep again with a huge sigh.

CHAPTER TWENTY-THREE

Volunteers Wanted

It took three days before Delaney was able to get out of the house again. Every step was an effort, but he forced himself to do it. Rufus was reluctant at first and still very sore but gamely joined him as they waited for the Uber. He wasn't going to be left behind.

At the beach a biting wind cut right through Delaney's jacket. Rufus limped along ahead. He showed no interest in chasing seagulls or jumping the waves. Definitely was not himself. Nor was Delaney. If anything, he was more uncomfortable than the day before. The bruising was coming out and his hips ached. He called it quits early.

"Come on, let's get a coffee."

Rufus gratefully turned and headed towards the rocks and the seafront cafés.

"Wait at the road."

Rufus knew the drill. He was waiting at the curb as Delaney caught up and together, they crossed to Café Blue Horizon. A welcome refuge for such a grey day.

Delaney sat at the corner table and Rufus crashed down at his feet with a huge sigh. The waitress walked over and looked at them in alarm.

"You guys been hit by a bus? You look pretty bad, Mr Delaney."

"A big bus, Davina. I'm taking it easy for a few days."

"You should. That's one mighty purple bruise on your neck."

"Hands got wrecked too. Your boyfriend ok?"

She nodded, pleased he remembered. "Could have broken his leg. I hate him going on that motorcycle weaving in and out of traffic. I won't go with him."

"Don't blame you. The statistics aren't in his favor, that's for sure."

She walked away to get his coffee and a biscuit for Rufus. Delaney left the dog whilst he popped to the restroom.

Chilly weather and his bladder didn't mix.

As he was pissing, he came face to face with a poster calling for Medical Trial volunteers. Compatible volunteers will be lodged in our research facility and after successful completion could be remunerated for a minimum of five thousand... Delaney noted the words 'compatible' and 'successful completion'. It had to be the same poster Asha had mentioned. He snapped a photo and returned to his table.

His Americano was waiting, Rufus happily chomping on a biscuit.

"Hey, Davina. How long has that poster been up in the John?"

"Poster?" She looked confused.

"Looking for volunteers for a medical trial."

"Oh that. Some guy came in and said it was important to find people. An antidote to painkiller addiction I think. It's a big problem in this city. Couldn't say no, could I?"

"You sure that was what he said?"

"Absolutely, Mr Delaney. I told Bryan about it. Y'know, the guy who always come around begging and I have to chase away."

"He take it up?"

Davina tilted her head as she thought about it. "Must have. Haven't seen him around for a month at least."

Delaney nodded. "Thanks."

"You volunteering? You don't need the money, I'm pretty sure. Italian boots. I have a thing for boots and shoes."

Delaney looked at his boots and realized that he had bought them in Italy.

"Well spotted and no, but like you, I'm thinking that's there's someone who needs the money I know, it could help."

Davina smiled. "Got to help people who need it right?"

"Right."

"I hope you've got a good lawyer for whoever was driving that bus. They drive so fast along here, no thought for pedestrians."

"Yeah, Rufus got hit pretty bad. He's a bit depressed today."

"I can see that. Poor thing."

Delaney dialed the number on the poster. It went through to a recorded message.

> *'Welcome to H&J Research Centre. If you are calling about volunteering for medical trials, we are still taking names. If you want to participate please leave your name, a phone number and an address where we can reach you. We will endeavor to get back to you within twenty-four hours or three days if by letter and discover your suitability for this opportunity to help others and participate in ground-breaking pain treatment. Leave your message after the tone*:

Delaney disconnected. He guessed a lot of people would hang up, but the desperate would leave a number or address, if they had one. A homeless guy or woman would need to have a reliable mail drop – the toughest part of rough living. He guessed there wouldn't be many places where they could be sure to get any mail.

He remembered to call the Guru's sister. It was a long shot but worth trying. Then he had to call his car insurers. He counted his blessings for no-fault insurance cover. Meanwhile he would need a loan vehicle.

He decided to take a swing by the Stanley Street homeless shelter on the way home. The Uber driver couldn't get out of there fast enough. The Mayor wouldn't admit it publicly, but this part of the city was pretty much abandoned.

The building was a former brick Elementary school built in 1897. It still showed the old signs for Boys & Girls over separate entrances. It was in need of a whitewash and perhaps the tall windows didn't used to have iron bars across them, but it was still serving the community, fulfilling a purpose. Two tall oak trees cast shade over the building and the playground was surrounded with barbed wire to keep people out.

He had to show his City ID card to persuade the Warden to open up the highly secure metal gate. She seemed pretty damn hostile, judging him to be little better than the bums outside the building, listlessly waiting for her to open up. She stood glaring at him with extreme wariness. Hair tightly pulled back, wide shoulders, overtight elasticated jeans that didn't flatter her any, she could probably stop a charging bull with a mere flick of her black-eyed icy glare and puckered lips. The sort of woman who wasn't ever going to take any sass from anyone, ever.

"I don't like dogs," Ms Crabtree told him. "I don't like the City coming around here either. They've not done me any favors lately."

"You wouldn't deny a man his emotional support dog, would you?"

"You don't need a dog, Mister. You need a full-time carer from the look of you. You get beat up or something?"

"Something." Delaney rubbed his sore arms as he talked. "How many people you got coming here to feed and get cleaned up?"

"I'm up on all the inspections, if that's why you're here."

"I'm following up on complaints about the mental health of some homeless people at an experimental treatment center. H & J Research Centre. Ring any bells? You might have seen their posters up on public facilities."

"The City can go fuck itself. It doesn't support us, it's six months behind on payments and frankly the Major doesn't give a shit about these people. Won't fund the drugs we need to get them off the shit they inject. It's a miracle we're here at all."

Delaney glanced back at the line-up of people outside the shelter, anxiously waiting for the soup kitchen to open and a chance at the small number of billets that would be available that night. He was surprised at just how many women were out there waiting.

"How many people do you usually handle per night?" Delaney asked.

"A hundred get food and a voucher for a mattress to sleep on and a shower. The other three hundred or so, will get a basic meal before being shoved back out onto the streets. Any more questions, you'll have to pay. You think feeding these people comes free? Money on the table now, Mr Delaney. I'm not kidding. No visitor leaves here without contributing or volunteering. House rules."

Delaney took out his wallet and pulled out two fifties. "I'll need a receipt."

She snorted contempt but went over to the corner of a desk and produced one, stamping it, clearly very used to extorting 'Visitors'. "Thank you for your generosity, Mr Delaney. That will feed forty people tonight." She wasn't being sarcastic, just pragmatic.

"If someone is willing to enroll these people in some scheme to get them off the streets and straight, then I'm happy. I know they're taking my people and I'm all for it, Mr Delaney. I reckon at least a hundred and fifty have taken up their offer, maybe a lot more. You want to be a volunteer to feed 'em or hose 'em down tonight, feel free. If a few more people working for the City came here and saw what I see every night, maybe they'd show a bit more compassion. Maybe even pay me what's owing."

Delaney couldn't help but agree but knew as well as she did that it was unlikely to ever happen.

"You ever meet any of these people recruiting 'volunteers' for the research?"

The Warden shook her head. "No. But I know they're out there on the streets looking for the right kind of person. Not everyone can be helped, if you know what I mean. You want information, they're all out there in the line-up, Mr Delaney, waiting for food. Talk to them, not to me. I only know what goes on in here."

Delaney did just that, keeping Rufus on a short leash. After an hour of trying to get people to talk any sense, to him, for good or bad, Delaney left with a better understanding about what was going on and an urgent need to shower. He had to walk a mile or more to a safer area to finally find a taxi willing to take him home. He discovered he was utterly exhausted. Should have rested like the doc ordered.

Rufus stared at his dinner bowl about three hours too early as Delaney hit the shower to clear his mind. He fitted a plastic bag over his hair to protect his stitches, heeding his doctor's instructions. He really needed to wash away the hopelessness he'd felt talking to so many desperate people. A lot of those people had once lived good lives, had jobs, families, all of it taken by the damn virus or opioids. For some it was just an excuse, but he knew from their stories that for many Covid-19 was the beginning of a downward spiral. Lose your job, get evicted, end up homeless, depressed, broken.

He felt more himself after the shower and found his way to the sofa to make a call. Asha answered on the fourth ring.

"Dial this number and listen to the answer phone message. Then call me back."

Twenty minutes later Asha finally called back.

"Shit, we finally have something to go on. H & J Research, Chief. It's registered to Huissan and Jaywaller. Gus Huissan's in jail, so I guess your Mrs Jaywaller is running the show. You were right."

"What is H&J Research, Ash?"

"Believe it or not, it's a registered charity for the betterment and welfare of the homeless."

Delaney smiled. "Well done. Finally, we have a tangible connection. And she connects to the Guru – so you can assume that she's running both shows. Question is; what the fuck does she get out of it? Other than the Mayor thinking she's a saint."

"You get anywhere with the Guru's sister?" Asha asked.

"She's called Jasmina Theresa Hoffman."

"The Guru's sister is German?"

"Her husband of thirty happy years was a schoolteacher at the German school in Berg City. He died of pneumonia on a school trip to the lakes. She goes by the name of Mrs Rama. I have no idea why."

"And you're going to her birthday party."

"Only if I bring Maria along."

"Maria? How the fuck does she know Maria?"

"Long story, but she's very keen to see her. She's very concerned about her."

"How is this possible?"

"Trust me, it's weird, but I'm going along with it. More importantly, I went to Stanley Street hostel today."

"You were supposed to be resting."

"Rufus needed a walk."

"To the shelter? I'm surprised you got out of there alive. Wasn't there a shooting there last month?"

"Apparently that's a regular thing, along with knifings and overdosing. Cost me a hundred to get out actually, but it seems the medical trials have worked wonders there. The Warden, a Ms Crabtree, emphasis on Ms, swears that well over a hundred and fifty regulars were signed up by H&J Research and she hasn't seen any of them since."

"Wow."

"You might be interested to know that almost half of them were women. I don't know if that's relevant or not, but sadly there's always new homeless people arriving. She seemed pretty pleased they are getting a chance to earn some money, have a regular place to stay and get cleaned up."

"So far so wonderful. Mrs Jaywaller is bucking for the Nobel prize," Asha said.

Delaney smiled. "Well perhaps. I was leaving when this guy hustling for cash came over. He wasn't worried about Rufus, although Rufus was pretty sketchy about him. He claimed he knows where all the volunteers are lodging. He couldn't remember the name of it, but he knows the building. I gave him a twenty and promised more if he'll take us there tomorrow."

"They'll let us in?"

"Maybe. Maybe not. We're still the Office of City Oversight, Ash. This is city business since they are sticking their posters up on city buildings and whatever."

"It's a stretch, but I'm with you. I'll pick you up at seven-thirty. Maria's got to get to school ... oh shoot; it's Saturday. No school."

"Maria can look after Rufus. She likes doing that. He wasn't himself today."

"You're not yourself. Still no word as to whether we are still in business by the way."

"It would have to go through the committee. That takes time. Let's hope someone makes an objection."

"And lives to tell the tale."

"Quite. Got to go. I'll pick Maria up by taxi shortly. Come by my place around breakfast. Say eight-thirty. My guess is that homeless guy won't be an early riser. Twenty bucks buys a lot of damage on the street."

"I'll bring my own yoghurt. Maria was very complimentary about your muesli yesterday."

"She's such a tease. 'Bye Ash."

"'Bye, Chief."

CHAPTER TWENTY-FOUR

Saint Joe

They parked about a hundred meters from the shelter and waited. Around them homeless people slept in doorways or shuffled around, some smoking, others standing staring at nothing in particular as sunlight filtered through the trees. Most of the houses around here were boarded up and covered in graffiti.

"He's not coming," Asha declared, searching for her mask, she didn't feel safe here one bit. She was a bit embarrassed to be carrying Delaney around in such an untidy car to be honest. She was annoyed at working on a Saturday and having to hang around this district that stank of piss. The flies bothered her too.

"Don't they clean the streets anymore?" She complained.

Delaney glanced at her as he rubbed his sore neck. "Just be happy you'll never end up around here, hey."

Asha sighed. "I guess the first injection of whatever paradise you can get doesn't always tell you this is where you'll end up." She studied their ravaged faces as they shuffled by. An emaciated woman was wearing a deep blue Prada jacket and red crocs. Someone got lucky in a charity dumpster. She checked her door lock again.

"I once drove across the States with Denise," Delaney began. "She wanted to see Arizona and then go to Santa Barbara, because of some children's writer she was keen to work with. I wanted to go because that's where Raymond Chandler lived."

"Who?"

Delaney smiled. "A different writer. Anyway, the point is, we were excited to get there and when we reached the harbor there was the longest line for a soup kitchen I had ever seen."

"Isn't that where Meghan and Harry moved to? Santa Barbara soup kitchens, really?"

"Meghan aside. The thing is, every one of those desperate guys and women queuing for food probably set off thinking they were heading for paradise and everything would work out once they got there."

Asha looked confused.

"Pacific Ocean. They couldn't go any further. You either walk back to where you came from or wait for soup. Everyone here in this street right now thought they could probably beat whatever it was that destroyed their lives. The Virus, booze, pills, heroin, it doesn't matter. I guarantee no one thought this is where it would all end."

Asha looked across the street at two guys sprawled asleep in a doorway.

"I didn't know it was this bad. I heard stories but..."

Delaney checked the door locks once more, trying not to alert Asha to how nervous he was at bringing her here. "These people are the few who are awake at this hour. Ms Crabtree told me there's at least two thousand on the methadone list and there's a wait list for the Naloxone antidote to Fentanyl. Or Suboxone, which is rarely available either. There's no budget for any of these drugs, so effectively no one is getting treatment." He sighed and tried to loosen his stiff neck, awkwardly tilting it from side to side.

"For everyone taking Oxy or Fentanyl, the drug deposits itself in the fat tissue and it's a slow release into the body. The antidotes only work for about 30 minutes, so you either have to keep on giving the antidote or accept defeat. No one has the kind of money needed to beat this shit."

Asha stared at him. "I had no idea you knew about all this."

"I lived in Paris. You want to see real poverty and social chaos, buy a ticket for France. Denise's place was right on the edge of it, but she liked it. Me, not so much. Now here we are in Berg City downtown and it looks bad. Now add the suburbs and the shanties by the airport where they're in the grip of Spice or Benzos, you are looking at a quarter of million people in desperate need of a fix, a drink, anything, rather than face the shit they've got themselves into and running between them are the little kids, maybe their own kids, selling the shit for the gangs. All this on our doorstep."

Asha looked away from a woman squatting to piss right by the car with no self-consciousness at all.

"I guess I never wanted to know." Asha said quietly.

Delaney nodded. "Me either. No one does."

"What's this guy we're looking for look like?"

Delaney had to think about it. "Mousey hair, a vivid red scar on his left arm – knife wound."

"Nice."

"I'll give him ten more minutes," Delaney muttered.

Asha closed her eyes and made a list of things she needed to do. Cancel her gym membership being high on the list. Find a new job; think about renting a cheaper place or at least sharing it. She hated thinking like this. She liked working with Delaney. It felt they were making a difference.

"Don't worry about them closing us down, Ash. I'm thinking of working with the lawyer Nicolas Goodman, starting a proper agency. He's expanding and he needs investigators with a good knowledge of finance and cyber-crime. I'd like you to be a partner in that. Think about it anyway."

Asha was about to reply when Delaney slapped the dashboard and put on his mask. "There he is. Stay in the car, lock the doors."

Delaney leapt out and made his way towards a guy staggering out of a doorway.

Asha watched as Delaney caught him, held him up and got him to focus. Clearly, he'd forgotten his promise, but Delaney was walking him back towards the car, trying to get him to cooperate. She screwed up her face in revulsion. The guy's chest was covered in bloodstained vomit. She really, really didn't want him in her vehicle. "Oh my god," she kept repeating as she stared at the guy's bloodshot eyes. She lowered her window. "Please tell me he's not coming with us."

Delaney grinned at her discomfort. "He's a bit stinky. Drank two bottles of something pretty vile and wants to do it all over again." He held up a twenty note. "Michael you should eat. Your liver needs food, not more rotgut."

Michael's attention was on the twenty, nothing else. He cared nothing for food.

Asha winced when she saw his knife wound, all the way from his wrist to his biceps. He'd been sliced open.

"Does Michael know where this place is?" Asha asked. Delaney nodded. "St Joes."

Asha had no idea what it was. There was a saint called Joe? She doubted this. Then remembered her father swearing about Jesus, Joseph and Mary whenever something went wrong. Usually when attempting DIY at home.

"St Joseph's, a private school that went bust about eight years ago. I spent a good ten years there. Tough discipline but was very empowering and a bit radical."

"St Joes," Michael was repeating, his stained teeth seemed to have been sharpened or decayed to points. "They're at St Joes."

Delaney gave him the twenty. "Eat Mike, drink later. Grab a pie at least, man."

Michael snatched the note and staggered towards a wall to throw up again. Asha tried not to look as disgusted as she felt, pleading, "Can we go now?"

Delaney came around the car and she unlocked the door for him. "Michael's the reason St Joes went under." Delaney remarked as he belted up.

"He is?" She squirted some sanitizer on his hands.

"Well, people like him. Believe it or not when I was a kid this was a really nice place to live. The virus recession didn't help, I guess. So many foreclosures and then there's the gangs. Tough place to survive in."

Asha drove them out there. "Where to Chief?"

"Straight, then take second left and go up the hill to Riley Park."

"You're kidding. The shooting gallery?"

Delaney laughed. "You don't get down here much do you."

Asha made a face. "I resolutely steer clear."

"Riley Park was once a really nice place to go on a Sunday. Concerts, even opera in summer. I used to cycle to the café just for the homemade ice cream. I swear, I always thought I'd own a home around here. Go slow, ok."

Asha slowed, glancing at the old 19th Century homes, once painted in bright colors that were now unloved with peeling shutters and rusted railings. Bougainvillea was running riot over the tin roofs. She could almost envision that it must have been a desirable neighborhood at some time in the distant past.

"You should buy around here, Ash. They're going cheap, they all have quite big back gardens and if they ever clean the junkies out of the park, you'd make a killing."

"You saw the size of Michael's knife wound, right? What are the chances of my car lasting one night on these streets?"

"Seem to recall your car was stolen from inside a high security apartment complex not so many days ago."

"Ouch," Asha nearly blushed. "You're mean, Delaney."

Delaney smiled. "See those gates and the arch covered in ivy?"

Asha looked at where he was pointing.

"St Joseph's Prep School."

"Nice, right across from smackhead park. No wonder they closed."

"Find somewhere to park. Maybe one block over by the Co-op might be safer."

Asha did as she was told; relieved to see that other cars more valuable than hers were parked in the next street. Obviously, this was where the city divided. One block over from hell. She was pleased to see a vegan restaurant she didn't know as well. It was as if they'd come through an invisible wall.

"Where the aubergine goes – the rest will follow," Delaney remarked mysteriously.

Asha concentrated on parking, finally switching her engine off. She turned to Delaney. "We should be making the Mayor rescue that park."

"Yep. You have to recapture the spaces one block at a time."

Delaney led her back up the hill and into an overgrown alleyway strewn with vehicle parts and wildflowers thriving on neglect.

"Where are we?" Asha asked.

"Behind St Joes. Kids used to smoke weed in the old coach house."

"You smoked weed?"

Delaney grinned. "No need to look so shocked. You didn't when you were thirteen?"

Asha shrugged. "Yeah, but only once or twice. I was

trying to be cool, but I didn't like it much. Besides I played soccer remember. Any drugs and you were dropped ASAP. No appeals."

"Same on the sailing team, although the coach didn't have the same rule for booze. I think rum and coke was the big thing for us kids then."

"We're like two saints. I try to make it a rule only to drink on weekends now. Otherwise it makes you fat."

"I hope not. I have a cellar full of wine that needs drinking."

"Don't blame me when you bloat, Delaney."

Delaney laughed and led her through a small gap of overgrown ferns and snapdragons growing between the cracks in the stone. Delaney indicated that they were to remain silent. They emerged into a small courtyard where a filthy minivan with flat tires was parked.

"Back stairs lead to the dormitories," Delaney whispered.

"You spent ten years here?" It didn't seem possible.

Delaney leaned into her left ear. "It was co-ed. I really liked a girl called Shannon. We never really got past kissing stage before her father was posted to Nairobi. I think my heart broke on that step right there. We stayed friends for a while when she returned later, but by then we'd both moved on."

Asha looked down at a turn in the stone staircase and she could almost see a young Delaney crying his heart out.

Delaney put a bandaged hand up. "Listen."

Asha heard moaning. A lot of women were groaning, as if they were in labor. It wasn't a good sound. There was a strong smell of disinfectant and piss in the air. They climbed up further and came to two double doors with reinforced cracked glass windows. Asha looked in and it was like a medieval nightmare. Forty - maybe fifty beds. Women screaming, some writhing in agony, others standing like zombies staring into space. Harassed staff were cleaning up a mess on the vinyl flooring and swearing at the woman who'd made it. Delaney took his turn but made no comment.

He pulled her away from the doors and they climbed up to the next floor. Another dormitory, this time filled with men. Some screamed in pain, others rocked crazily from side to side. Delaney was counting beds. "Fifty-five. There's another dorm on the other side of this." Two beefy male nurses were holding a man down whilst a doctor or nurse injected something. Asha saw that many of the men were strapped down onto the beds. Others walking up and down had the look of lost souls. All were emaciated.

Asha heard something and pushed Delaney into the shadows. Moments later a medical orderly came out of a small door pushing a cart laden with ampoules and needles. She knocked on the doors and waited. She didn't look left or right, if she had she would have seen Asha easily.

A bolt was slide aside and the door opened. "You're late." Someone called out from inside. "They're going crazy this morning."

The orderly pushed her cart in, and the door was quickly bolted again.

Delaney was breathing heavily into her neck. "We'd better go."

Asha was happy to leave. She was going to have nightmares about this place.

They were just about to run across the courtyard when a delivery truck arrived, and they again hid as the driver dropped off many trays of groceries and bread. When he was done, he banged on a small metal door and got back into his truck, backing up as there was nowhere to turn around.

Delaney signaled Asha and they dashed across the courtyard before anyone came for the food.

Neither one of them said anything as they walked back down the alley. Only when they got onto the street and there were people around did Asha feel safe.

"At least they're feeding them," she said weakly.

Delaney made no comment at all. Asha guessed he was more disturbed by what he'd seen than herself, if that was at all possible.

She dropped him home. Delaney turned to her before getting out.

"I've got no idea what they're doing, Ash. But it will be a hell of a long time before I forget what I saw."

"Or the screaming," Asha added. "Did you see many of them were strapped down?"

Delaney frowned. "Perhaps they've got a different

definition of the word 'volunteer' to what we have."

Asha chewed on her bottom lip. "Their faces. They looked so scared. Is that better than living on the streets?"

Delaney exhaled. "I don't know. We don't know how long the trials are or what the hell they're giving them, but I wonder how many of them last to the end pot of gold?"

Asha shook her head. That thought had occurred to her too. "Shit, to go through all that pain for nothing."

"As you said, at least they're getting fed. See you Monday, Ash. Go out, enjoy yourself. Don't pick up any strays."

Asha affectionately squeezed his arm. "You rest, ok? Don't push yourself so hard."

"I won't."

Asha drove off, her head filled with images of horror.

CHAPTER TWENTY-FIVE

A Sunday Walk

Sunday came around and Delaney discovered the swimming pool was closed for renovations.

"A whole month?" Maria protested. "How am I supposed to exercise if the pools closed?"

"You know there's an ocean out there, right?"

Maria rolled her eyes. "No chance. I'd freeze to death."

Delaney wasn't going to push it. "Ok, it's Sunday, I'm sore, your stiff, Rufus is whining, we all need exercise, so we're going to walk down to the old harbor for lunch."

"And walk back up the hill?" Maria protested.

"That's the plan. Person or dog that complains the most has to do laundry."

"You're mean."

"So, I hear. Rufus?"

Rufus stuck his head around the kitchen door.

Delaney smiled. "He's got a very guilty expression. What have you done, dog?"

Maria investigated and squealed. "He's got my rug again." She wanted to scold him, but he looked so guilty she gave him a hug instead. "I know it's chilly and you're not feeling well. But it's my rug, you've got one in your basket, Rufie."

Delaney grabbed his coat and the lead. "He definitely needs a walk."

Maria found her fleece and hat and Rufus showed some signs of interest as they opened the gates. "Don't forget the treats and do-do bags."

"Got 'em."

They walked down the steep slope towards the old harbor keeping between the old tramlines. The wind whipped Maria's hair so violently she scrunched it up under her hat, praying it would stay on.

Delaney looked at the clouds. "Might rain later."

Maria took the dog lead from him because she could

see it was hurting his hands.

"Can I ask you something?"

Delaney glanced at her and saw she had her serious face on. "Yeah."

"What if I didn't want to go back to my mother? Once he's dumped her."

"You know that's not in my control, M. You can't make those kind of choices until your eighteen, if I remember the law correctly."

Maria frowned. "But if she stays with the moron, she won't want me back."

Delaney placed a hand on her head momentarily. "I'm not kicking you out, kid. You can stay as long as you like or until she demands you back. I know how hard your life is with her. What's brought this on?"

Maria looked away a moment as they passed two kids sailing a huge yellow kite. Delaney stood and watched, but then thought better of it as he wasn't sure they had much control as it swooped crazily over their heads.

"They tried to kill you." Maria said suddenly. "You were driven off a cliff. I thought you were dead. You're the only person who ever cared about me. I've been pretty disgusting and rude to you and never really ..." she struggled to think or say what she meant. "I guess you matter a lot to me. I don't want to leave again. I don't want to be screamed at because I was born and how inconvenient it has been for her to have to keep putting up with me. I don't want to feel like shit every day because 'I'm such a burden, I'm ruining her life.'"

Delaney reached across to her hand and squeezed it. "I'm not stupid, M. My second thought after I crashed was who the hell would take care of you."

She glanced up at him. "What was your first thought?"

Delaney squeezed her hand. "Rufie, where the hell was Rufie?"

Maria took back her hand and wiped a tear from her eyes. She nodded. "I'd have done the same. Rufus is like a rock. I sometimes hold him just to keep from drowning."

"I promise you can stay with me as long as it's allowed and if your mother doesn't want you back anytime soon, you're safe. As long as you tidy your room."

Maria scoffed. "My room is tidier than yours. House

rules go both ways, Mister Delaney."

Delaney grinned. He pointed to a yacht coming into the harbor. "That's a real oceangoing vessel. See the tall mast? She could cross the Atlantic really easy. We'll go and see them. Find out where they've been."

"You can do that?"

"Sailors like to talk, M. Rufus, come on, long way to go yet."

Maria took Delaney's hand again and felt safer than she had for a long time.

CHAPTER TWENTY-SIX

The Slap

Asha was driving in early Wednesday morning traffic cursing the heavy rain and how drivers seemed paralyzed by it. She wanted to scream at some woman who wanted to turn right on a no turn lane.

She was suddenly aware of the driver to her left nodding his head in time to the incredibly loud beat on his sound system. With a shock she realized it was him, the bastard who'd stolen her phone and car. She wondered if he'd stolen the Golf he was driving. She quickly snapped a photo as he turned left.

"Got you, scumfuck." He was going to get a nice surprise when that image anonymously showed up on Insta with 'THIEF. DO NOT TOUCH THIS SLIMEBALL' attached. OK it wasn't going to get her phone back, but it would give her some satisfaction and mess with his life. She sat in traffic some more and felt a tad less bitter.

Delaney showed up at the vehicle pound with Rufus. Even he was impressed about how much shorter his Discovery was. It was sitting there like a huge concertina.

"Seriously, you walked away from this?" The car pound guy was asking as he wiped oil off his hands.

"We both did." He noticed Rufus was reluctant to go closer. "Tough machine. I might get another one."

"You don't survive something like that twice," the guy said, hunting for some paperwork.

Delaney looked for his notebook, but it seemed to him that someone had picked the interior clean. He wondered whom. Rufus sneezed and whined, didn't like being here with all the oily smells and hung back.

"Did the insurance guy turn up to take a look? He said he would."

"Yeah. He signed the release form. You have to initial it too."

"Release form?" Delaney queried.

"To be crushed. Look around you. No room here. Used to be they stacked everything up for evidence and shit, but now everything gets crushed as soon as it gets released."

Delaney was looking at the dent at the rear of his vehicle and the streak of red paint. He guessed no one wanted to investigate that. He remembered the sudden thump of the impact as he was cruising around the bend. Must have been doing sixty at the time. One tap would be all that was needed to send him over the cliff at that speed. He looked back at Rufus and wondered just how he'd survived. He had no memory of the actual crash at all.

"I guess we were lucky guys." Delaney remarked signing the form.

"Not many get the chance to see their coffins when they end up here," the guy told him. "Shame the alloy wheels are wrecked, I could have done a good deal."

"Sorry," Delaney mumbled as he left. "Careless of me."

He decided to walk Rufus back to the office along the Lower Main Road passing all the ethnic traders, antiques, coffee shops and vaping stores. He quite enjoyed the relaxed atmosphere and the well-preserved shop fronts, a total contrast the sterile Mall in the city. He wasn't ready to face things just yet. He wasn't sure at this moment he was ever going to get behind a wheel again. He needed fresh air real bad to steady his nerves.

"Come on. One day, dog, tell me how you got out of that car alive."

Rufus stuck close. It had unnerved him to see and smell the crashed vehicle.

Finally, back at the office Delaney opened an internal letter and sighed. It was a note to tell him that they had formally tabled a motion to bring the Office of City Oversight in-house. He looked at the date. The meeting would have been the day before. No need to wonder at the outcome. There was no 'thanks for your service' included and he noted that he'd not had a call from the Mayor or his Deputy. Not even about his 'accident'. When you are on the out, you're out.

He guessed Asha had gone for a run or something, she

probably wasn't expecting him to come in. He left the letter for her to see. No doubt there would be another before the day was out. He left Rufus in charge and went to his lunch meeting with Nicolas Goodman at the Imperial. Five Star hotels were a bit rich for him, but it was adjacent to the lawyer's office and he liked to live well.

Nicolas had selected a table in a nook where it was hard to be overheard and arrived only minutes after Delaney. He went bald at twenty, struggled with his weight but was still a hard guy to beat on the squash court. They'd been on sailing teams together when young and they'd remained friends. He didn't bother with the menu when the waiter came by.

"Seared tuna salad. Dressing on the side."

"Falafel salad for me," Delaney told him.

Nicolas' eyebrows shot up. "Don't tell me you've gone vegan, Delaney."

Delaney smiled. "It's not so hard giving up meat. Besides I still eat fish when no one is looking. It's better for your health, Nick."

"You don't exactly look a picture of health, if I may say so. You drove off a cliff on the Coastal Highway I hear."

"Shunted off actually. I could prove it, but no one is interested, apparently. I guess that's the problem with no-fault insurance."

Nicolas drank fresh squeezed pineapple juice. Alcohol at lunch was no longer acceptable. "The same thing happened to Mike Anders. Remember him? The Electronics guy? His wife wanted a divorce and he was reluctant."

"She drove him off the road?"

"Someone did. She's now a very rich widow."

"Well I guess I disappointed whoever tried it with me."

Nicolas dipped some warm sourdough into the balsamic vinegar.

"So, your office is going in-house. Which means no oversight from now on?"

"They're claiming it's going to save money."

"Will it?"

"They'll hire the Mayor's third idiot cousin and lock the door."

Nick smiled. "Of course, but did you expect anything

else? Asha filled me in on this Kirdasham thing."

"Jirdasham. Slogan 'We feel your pain, so you don't have to'."

"Genius," Nicolas declared, laughing. "And you think it's a scam."

"It's something. Selling a pain cure, which sort of works, and then you have to pay again and probably ad infinitum. Whether it's legal or just plain unethical we haven't quite figured out yet."

"The pharmaceutical industry has been getting away with this for decades. Why sell a complete cure when you can keep them coming back forever to mask the illness?"

Delaney acknowledged that to be true. "Well at the very least they are exploiting the vulnerable with this 'cure'."

"And this campaign to get the homeless off the streets and into medical trials is what exactly? Apparently, the Mayor loves this scheme."

"It's evil and unpoliced." Delaney leaned in to speak quietly. "We have seen hundreds of homeless people strapped down onto beds, being administered drugs and screaming in agony."

"At St Joes?"

Delaney nodded.

"And you want to me to do what?" Nicolas asked.

"That's the problem. If you tried to shut them down, you'd have a ton of critics who'll say you're taking food out of the mouths of the homeless and preventing them from starting a new life."

"And we wouldn't want to be doing that."

The food arrived and conversation stopped. Delaney ate without pleasure, his jaw ached with every chew. Nicolas ate quickly, reluctant to talk and eat. Only when he leaned back in his chair was he open to conversation again.

"I'm not really sure of the way forward with this, Nick. Exposing their cruel methods with the homeless would be just. Exposing them for exploiting the old by promising them a pain free existence and fleecing them has to be worth an investigation, but as you will no doubt say – caveat emptor and you can't stop people from being foolish with their money."

Nicolas nodded, giving the matter some thought.

"Gus Huissan wouldn't be a problem to expose. His reputation is already trashed. If you wanted to go after Mrs

Jaywaller, well taking her on would cost us on contracts elsewhere. We'd need deep pockets and to be frank, fighting on behalf of the homeless only wins brownie points, not cold hard cash."

Delaney knew that. "I'm still investigating."

"Be careful. You already had a taste of what they're capable of. You know we need investigators. Especially cyber-crime. I know you're thinking that you could probably come over to us, but I'm not so sure."

"We wouldn't come cheap, Nicolas."

"We don't want cheap. But remember this, you'd be working for our clients and sometimes you won't like them, or their morals, most of the times I should think."

"Hmm, that's the price isn't it."

"You want to start up an independent investigation unit, do it, you'll do it well. We'd hire you when our morals coincide, but my job is defending my clients, no matter what."

"I appreciate your candor. Re Jirdasham and the scam...?"

"Bring me evidence of an actual crime. Find me evidence of financial fraud. Not the fact that they aren't paying tax. That's for the taxman. Get me stuff so I can pin the Mayor and his pals to the door, and I will take the case. The money might be overseas, but Veronika Jaywaller isn't, and she has assets, not all of them financial."

Delaney nodded. Nicolas signaled the waiter.

"Link her to the scam and the scam to the homeless and I'll make sure you get a good payday. That a deal?"

Delaney smiled as Nicolas offered his hand. They shook on it. Nicolas immediately took out a small bottle of hand sanitizer from his pocket and offered it to Delaney. They performed the cleansing ritual without comment.

"I hope the hell you get in better shape soon and come visit us out on the lagoon. You haven't seen Kris and the kids for an age."

"I will."

"You still live in that tin shack overlooking the harbor?"

"I was offered two million for it and the land at the height of the boom."

"You should have taken it. It would be half that now."

Delaney shook his head. "I love that house. The Two Oceans race bought it. Still got the original zinc roof."

Nicolas took the bill and indicated he'd pay it. "This is on me. Get me evidence, Delaney. Then I can go to town." He took out his wallet. "By the way, Shannon was in town last month. She's on her third husband. She runs a workspace empire now. Way out of our league these days."

Delaney felt little for Shannon. It was all so long ago. Three husbands already? Three more broken hearts.

He was leaving the men's room when he heard an argument just off the hotel lobby by the cloakroom. Some woman was really laying into the man she was with. Delaney hung back; he didn't want to get involved. The man said something in reply, and he heard a resounding slap.

"You ever say that to me again and you are a dead man." She shrieked.

"I didn't..."

"You're such a big man, deal with it, or just fuck off out of my life. Show some guts big boy."

Delaney pretended to be waiting for a coat. The cloakroom girl looked up at him expectantly.

"Ticket?" She asked.

Delaney half turned as a good-looking woman angrily swept past him towards the ladies' restroom. He would have recognized her anywhere, Veronika Jaywaller. She was dressed to kill and clearly been working on that body.

"Sorry, I forgot I wasn't wearing a coat," he told the confused cloakroom girl and he quickly moved towards the domed lobby with its expansive marble floor. He glimpsed the Mayor walking out of the hotel rubbing his face. Proof positive that the Mayor was working with Mrs Jaywaller or was it a lover's tiff? He almost felt sorry for the guy. There's always someone who thinks they can melt an ice queen's heart.

Nicolas appeared at his elbow suddenly. "I think I just saw Veronika Jaywaller heading to the spa room."

Delaney nodded. "You did. She just gave the Mayor a dressing down. Sounded very personal."

Nicolas smiled. "His wife is the Governor's sister. She has ambitions for our Mayor to go a lot higher. Must be a difficult choice for him. Ambitious wife versus rich society dame looking for husband number four. Lot of calculations to be done, don't you think?"

Delaney walked out of the hotel with him. "I'm not sure I'd go for the rich dame in that scenario. If I can pin stuff on her, I will, Nicolas. Give me a bit of time."

Nicolas gave him a brief salute and they went their separate ways.

Delaney's phone suddenly sent him an alert. Time to get his stitches out and worse, his second Covid vaccine booster was due. He groaned. He'd completely forgotten. He turned around and headed towards the medic center, wondering, not for the first time, if all his hair would grow back.

CHAPTER TWENTY-SEVEN

Dixon

Asha decided initiative was needed with regard to Mrs Jaywaller. The old building on Stelli Street was practically derelict, the last redoubt against the onward march of gentrification. She had to step over two homeless men sleeping in the stairwell and the stench of piss was overpowering. If they felt safe enough to sleep here at night she figured if had to be safe enough for her at midday.

The stairs were covered in a sticky carpet, but she could see most of the offices were occupied and the third floor seemed to be full of semi-naked women smoking in the corridor. She guessed someone was running an online porn outfit here. The women glared at her with hostility as she made her way to higher floors.

Dixon had the whole top floor to himself. She followed the wiring up the last set of narrow stairs, past the fire escape door that was blocked by a stack of chairs and assorted debris.

"Dixon?"

He didn't answer of course. He never answered, hoping people would just go away.

"Dixon, I'm coming in. It's Asha." She entered, squeezing past some empty Amazon boxes into a vast loft space. It was hot up here; a bank of servers cooled by a primitive air-conditioner didn't help much. An electric fan pushed hot air around and there were wires and cables everywhere.

Dixon stood stripped down to his underwear holding some wires together. He barely looked up at her. Thinner than she remembered, premature balding in progress, but he still had the chiseled features any guy would die for.

"Hold this," he said, thrusting wires into her hands. "Stay still, there's a live wire on the floor near you somewhere."

"You have fire insurance?"

"You think this building could get insurance? The

owner is praying I'll burn it down so he can get a permit to build apartments."

He took the wires from her one by one and installed them into a junction box. When the task was completed, he set it down and flipped a switch. Asha couldn't see anything happen, but she guessed it had worked.

Dixon finally acknowledged her. "Asha Knight, the girl who spurned me."

"Dixon you're gay, get over it."

"I wasn't then."

"You were always gay; you just didn't acknowledge it."

Dixon didn't bother to dress. "If you've come to see me you must be desperate. I'm not hiring. One-man band, only way to be safe."

"I have a job. Correction, I have a job for the next few days at least. We got too close to the fire."

Dixon sat down in front of a row of computer screens. "What fire?"

"Veronika Jaywaller."

Dixon laughed. "You thought you could take on her? She's like the big spider that got the whole city wrapped in her fucking web. Please tell me she doesn't know your name."

"Just my boss."

"That's bad enough. What do you want to know?"

"Company is called Jirdasham. Pain management scam, that's taking a lot of old people for a very expensive ride. Thirty grand a pop."

Dixon shrugged. "One way to even things up, I guess."

"Well yeah, but it's all going to her. Millions in fact."

"You want to steal it back?" Dixon looked interested for one nanosecond.

Asha grinned. "Tempting, but we just want to know where it's gone. We're guessing Panama or the Caymans. So, I thought of you."

"And you want to know this for free?"

Asha pursed her lips. "I was hoping for a favor."

"Like the one you did me and drove me into the arms of Philippe?"

Asha wrinkled her nose. "Philippe was pining for you for months and you never even looked at him."

"Because I was looking at you."

"I thought you were looking at Louis."

"Louis was very pretty. What did you do with him? Is he gay now too?"

"Louis went to Hollywood and he's a junior doctor on a soap and judging from the photos on Insta he's very popular with all genders."

"Yeah, that was always going to happen. Let's hope he's miserable at least half the time."

"Hollywood suits him, he always lacked commitment."

"I sense a note of sarcasm. He hurt you. I hope so."

You're horrible, Dixon."

"I know."

"Is there anyway of tracking money going into Jirdasham and going out without the bank or anyone knowing?"

Dixon scratched his ass and thought about it. "I can track it from their main account, but if it's left the country it gets harder. There's always a digital trace but it doesn't mean it's genuine. And if she's going into bitcoin or any other digital currency, you'll never find it. You know her personal bank here?"

"Finchbank."

Dixon went to the keyboard and began to work. "Of course, bank of choice for all nefarious operators and politicians."

Asha watched as he went straight into Finchbank and by-passed their security.

"Spell Jirdasham." He asked.

Asha called it out. "I couldn't find a trace of Mrs Jaywaller to connect her to them, but we know she owns it."

"Company address?"

Asha told him; impressed he had got into the system so quickly.

Dixon glanced up at her. "I'm no genius. Just so happens Finchbank got me to test their security and I did a clean-up last month. Best paycheck I've ever had. I found a back door that I thought it might come in handy."

"And that's not monitored?"

"Not by them anyway." He smiled.

"God, what's safe?"

"In banking? Nothing. Get a mattress or stuff your cash under the floorboards. Not these floorboards. If I don't burn it down, the porn guys downstairs will. They've got so much electronic stuff; they must be using half the power in the city. I'm using the other half, so god knows what keeps your apartment lit at night."

He showed her Jirdasham's accounts and brought up Mrs Jaywaller's accounts alongside.

"That's a lot of money flowing in. It doesn't go to her personal banking. See, she's pretending to be cash poor for the benefit of the taxman. Jirdasham money seems pretty normal, it goes to salaries, and lots of regular payments into numbered accounts."

"Payoffs to the Mayor and his Deputy and some of the Jackals." Asha told him.

"Makes sense. Keep them all sweet so you can keep the operation going." He brought up another set of outgoings. "Fuck, that's a lot of money. It's gone to some accounts in Hann Bank. Numbers again. But that's millions, Ash. That's as far as I can get. Hann Bank has the best security in the world. My guess is that she's leveraged it. That's their specialty. Y'know, put a deposit down on a $100 million Picasso and sell it on five years at twice the price. You profit the difference."

"Sounds easy put like that."

"It is as long as the bottom of Picassos doesn't drop out."

Asha frowned. "I'm looking for Picassos?"

Dixon snarled. "It was just an example. But yes. If she wants her money out of the country legally, take it to London or better yet, Monaco and sell it to some other guy who stole a lot of money."

"So, all I have found out is ..."

"That the money is most likely still here with a nice frame around it."

Asha leaned in and gave Dixon a kiss. "You're a star."

"I know, but Ash, do not go near that woman. She is lethal. Emphasis underscored. Now piss off, I have work to do. And don't even glance at the Ukrainian women down there, they get angry fast."

Asha was looking at the all wiring snaking around the loft floor. "What do you do with all this cabling?"

"I needed extra power. Don't ask. You really don't want to know and don't ever put your savings in a bank."

Asha got up to leave. "You need some sun, Dixon. You are way too pale."

"No time for sun. No time for anything."

"Thanks anyway."

"Next one costs, Ash. Dixon has to make a living."

"Absolutely."

Asha was standing by the printer when Delaney returned nursing his sore head and arm. Rufus ran up to him and greeted him like he'd gone a month.

"Hey, Chief, didn't think you'd be in today."

"Had a lunch meet with Nicolas Goodman. Plus, I had to visit the vehicle pound. Rufus was a bit upset to see it. I just can't believe either of us survived."

"Me either. I still have nightmares of finding you crushed behind the wheel."

Delaney looked at his bandaged hands. "Remind me to carry a hammer to smash a windscreen with. Just in case there's a round two. I just had the stitches out. And my Covid booster. Feeling a tad sore all round."

"Ouch. Sorry. Hey, that number you asked me to look up before you crashed."

"The Mercedes that collected the Deputy Mayor. Right."

"It's unlisted."

"Fake plates?"

"It's the Jackals."

Delaney blinked. "Jackals? Police? Shit. I knew it."

Asha nodded. "I guess we're not going to take it further."

Delaney groaned. You didn't take on the Jackals. The force within the police force – elite cops so called, although some would say they were the law above the law. Untouchable. No wonder his car was going to be crushed so fast. It also confirmed his suspicions about the Guru's minder being ex-Jackal.

"You're just lucky they screwed up," Asha told him.

Delaney rubbed his neck. "I feel lucky every day. Anything else?"

Asha nodded. "I saw the letter you opened, guess what? We got final notice from the committee about an hour ago. Termination without prejudice they call it. We've got a week to vacate the office, but we will get six weeks termination fee. I'm making sure we submit expenses now in case."

"Good thinking. And sorry. I was hoping we'd last a bit longer."

"I'm just glad I didn't order the shoes I wanted."

"Well hold off on that for a while. There is a plan."

Delaney sat down and pulled out a document from his inside pocket.

"One, we finish this case. Two, we make sure we take the coffee and biscuits with us and everything else that's ours when we move to Copper Street."

"Copper Street? Down by the harbor?"

"Big office over the Steamship Bar & Grill."

"Noisy at weekends." Asha wrinkled her nose. "I used to go drinking there when I was a teenager. It was called the Pelican Pub then."

"It's gone up market now. Surf, Turf & Pizza. They've got a genuine wood-fired pizza oven in the back. There's parking, which is amazing, and we get the roof garden, although the plants look pretty dead to me. The rent is good. They didn't know what to do with the upper space as it isn't zoned residential or for restaurant use."

"How did you find it?"

"Maria found it. You know how much she likes pizza. We were walking Rufus and looking at the yachts. Got talking to the pizza guy at the Steamhouse."

Asha's heart was racing. What did this mean for her?

"What's the plan, Delaney?"

"We're a team, Ash. Delaney and Knight Investigations."

Asha opened her mouth to say something, but nothing came out.

"You have to finish the course you're on to get certified and ok, you're not putting in anything, but you'll be liable for half the bills as well as half the profit, assuming there will be any. Not giving it to you on a plate, Ash. I'm relying on your IT skills, your name will be on the lease, just in case someone else tries to run me off the road."

"Do I get to say no?"

Delaney shook his head. "You have a better offer?"

"No."

"Then congratulations. You're now a chief too."

"Jesus. Chief. You work fast when you want to."

"Yeah. The good news is that the Guru's sister called. Birthday party tomorrow. Any idea what a woman of 83 wants for her birthday?"

"New teeth? A Zimmer frame?"

"I'm thinking flowers."

"Go with flowers." Asha decided, rolling her eyes. "By the way, I paid a visit to a friend at lunchtime. He's pretty good with IT security, although I wouldn't necessarily trust him 100%. Dixon is a bit flexible with morals."

"And?" Delaney asked, curious now.

"We got a look at Jirdasham accounts. He thinks the money is still here. Leveraged or invested in art. Something portable maybe."

"Interesting. Makes sense, if you want to hide some money, borrow more, so all people see is the debt."

"He was talking Picassos." Asha said.

Delaney shook his head. "Too obvious, too traceable, but good work, Ash. See you're already running the show." He stood up. "This guy's not going to run to Mrs Jaywaller, is he?"

"He thinks we'll get burned by her. He did it as a favor to me."

Delaney frowned. "Well we need allies if we're ever going to bring her down." He turned to the dog. "Take care of Rufus. I'm going to fetch my loaner and order a new vehicle. I'd like electric but ..."

"I thought you were keen to save the planet, Chief."

"Too much range anxiety for me. When they can do 500 miles on one charge, I'll be ready."

Asha remembered Maria suddenly. "I'm taking Maria swimming after school. That ok with you?"

"That's very ok. Thanks Ash. She'll appreciate that."

"It will help her back."

Delaney smiled and gave a wave. "It will. I'll return for Rufus in an hour."

Asha's mind was a whirlwind. A partnership, she had never expected it. She had to call Zuki, but then remembered calls could be monitored. She grabbed the old iPhone and stepped outside onto the balcony.

Maria studied Asha as she sliced through the water. She wondered how she'd learned to do that. She tugged at her costume and turned around in the water, kicking off, waiting for the pain to grab her. She began to crawl, kicking harder, snatching breaths on the roll, just like Asha. With each stroke she gained confidence that she could beat the pain.

She reached the far end and flipped over, heading back again. Asha was suddenly at her side in the next lane matching her pace. Maria tried to go faster but she didn't seem to make any headway. Asha was ahead again. She concentrated on her roll and the sweep of her arms and suddenly she was back at her starting point.

Asha was smiling at her as she grabbed the wall. "Nice action, girl. Don't kick too hard, it actually slows you down, keep a steady rhythm."

Maria pushed her goggles up and wiped her mouth. "You cut through the water like a knife. I'm so messy."

"No, you're fine. You're only just back in the pool. Your muscles need toning, that's all. We do this regularly and you'll be strong again. How's your back?"

Maria bent over; the pain was still there but not acute as before. "Fine."

"Low impact. It's the best exercise for you now."

Maria nodded. "Thanks for bringing me here. Can't believe you live somewhere where there's a pool."

"Not everyone uses it. Place like this needs to be used. I doubt I'll be here much longer though. Rent's high and I'm going to be broke."

"That sucks." Maria stood and stretched out her arms. "I'm going to do my twists. Doctor says I have to stretch my tendons."

"Well, ok. I'll do them with you. Don't overdo it. This is only your first time."

Maria smiled. She twisted and stretched; she could feel it hurting but she knew it was the right thing to do. She was determined to beat this.

"Back stroke now. Just one lap." Maria declared, falling back in the water. She kicked off and swept her arms back. It hurt like hell. Asha followed her and stayed close worried she'd overdo it.

Maria was in a talkative mood in the changing room. She was sore but felt as if she'd been in control of her pain in the water.

"You think Delaney will let me stay? He says I can."

Asha stepped out of the shower and began to towel dry her hair.

"Of course. I didn't realize how much he likes you until this week. I'm only just getting used to him myself."

"He wants you to stay." Maria told her.

Asha wrinkled her nose. "He's lucky to be alive. He wants me to become his business partner. My pal Zuki says it's too soon, but it might be the right move."

"You have to stay. He needs you. You saved his life."

"He saved himself. I just drove him home."

Maria shook her head. "Uh-uh. You saved him. I know you like him more than you're saying."

Asha stuck her tongue out and laughed, she was not going to discuss that. "And what about you, Maria? What do you really want?" Maria pulled on her sweatshirt, wincing with pain as she pulled it down. "I never want to go back to my mother. I never want to see her again. That's what I want."

Asha began to dress. "You've had it tough."

Maria shrugged. "I've seen her drunk so many times. I have look after her when she gets beaten up by the assholes she brings home. You don't know all the things I've seen. The guys look at me like I'm next. They grope me and I've felt their stinky breath when they try to stick their disgusting tongues down my throat. One guy wanted to pay me to go down on him and he smashed the bathroom door down when I locked myself in. I never, ever want to go back. You think they'll make me?"

"Who?" Asha asked as she pulled on her jeans.

"Child services. She wanted to put me up for adoption; you know that? Turns out, no one wants to adopt a thirteen-year-old kid with a bad back. Not cute enough. Then she was thinking foster care. Susan, she's in my class, is on her tenth foster home because no one likes her attitude. Ok, Susan isn't cute, and she doesn't wash so much, but no one gives a shit about her. All I know is; I don't want that to happen to me."

"So, you came back to Delaney."

Maria bit on her lip. Asha could see something else was bugging her.

"You worried I'm going to take him from you?"

Maria shrugged. "You could. You might. But I'm keeping Rufus. You can't have Rufus."

Asha grabbed her and hugged her close. "Never be afraid of what I might do, girl. You made a good choice. Delaney won't let you go. Believe it or not, you're his family now. You're lucky."

Maria rested her head on Asha's chest. She wondered if that was true.

"Come on, let's go get you some cake."

Maria broke free and grinned. "Cake solves so many problems."

Asha laughed. "It does. It really does."

CHAPTER TWENTY-EIGHT

The Birthday Party

Maria was puzzled as she ate breakfast. "No school?"

"Not today."

"And we're going to an old woman's birthday party?"

"We are, although I suspect it might be a bit short on balloons and jellies or party games."

Maria snorted. "You think that's what happens at parties?"

Delaney grinned. "I seem to recall bringing you home from a party where you were vomiting out the window the whole way back."

"I can't drink vodka." Maria protested.

"You can't drink a whole bottle of vodka and swallow whatever else there was at that party. Remember how you told me how gross it was to have someone stick their tongue down your throat."

Maria blushed. "I have no memory of this. It didn't happen."

"Sure. Your mother was hysterical for a week praying you weren't pregnant."

Maria looked at him with astonishment. "I was only twelve. What did she think I did? She's so stupid. There was only one boy there. He was terrified."

Delaney laughed. "I'm sure. Anyway, today we have to keep our heads down and keep in the background. It will be extremely boring, so bring any homework you need to do."

"I really have to go? Can't I go to school or stay with Rufie?"

"Not today. It's important you come along. How's your back?"

Maria shrugged. "Great as long as I don't bend or pick anything up. I couldn't pick Rufus up last night. He was most offended."

"Did the swimming help?"

"Yeah, but I'm pretty sore today. Asha can swim like a

fish. It kills me to roll in the water and crawl, but I swam. She's cool."

"And your Pilates?"

"I'm doing my exercises. Why the third degree? Am I in trouble?"

Delaney ate some toast and topped up his coffee. "You might meet someone today who could help your back, that's all. I can't guarantee he'll show up or help, but ..."

Maria scowled. "At an old lady's birthday party."

"Stranger things have happened, M. And if it doesn't, we'll just concentrate on the swimming."

Maria drank her juice as she contemplated him. "You're being weird today. What about Rufus?"

"Quick walk first; then he's guarding the car. You think his limp is getting better?"

Maria called Rufus in from the backyard, he wandered in expecting a treat. "Yeah, he's moving a bit better. Still tender though. He hates being hugged right now."

Delaney tossed him a treat that he caught and swallowed whole.

"What did I tell you about chewing first, dog? You're a brave dog. How the hell he got out of the car and found his way up the cliff still puzzles me."

"He's smart." Maria declared. She glanced over at Delaney. "What do I wear?"

"It's a come as you are party. You look fine."

"Delaney, I'm wearing my pjs."

Delaney looked at her more closely.

"School uniform?" He suggested.

Maria's expression nixed that.

"Wear something colorful," Delaney decided. "She loves colors."

Maria nodded. "Black it is."

Delaney shook his head; he wasn't going to win this one.

They handed over a huge bunch of African Daisies to the housekeeper who grumpily didn't think they had a vase, but Jasmina, the birthday girl was delighted. She let out a huge shriek of happiness. "Flowers. No man has brought me flowers in twenty years or more." She turned to the housekeeper.

"Of course, there's a vase. Look in the shed, girl. I must have ten at least. My husband always brought me flowers on my birthday. Thank you, Mr Delaney. Thank you and thank you for bringing Maria. I have so wanted to see you child."

Maria gave Delaney a panic-stricken glance as they were sucked into the inner courtyard where many well-wishers had gathered. Everyone was drinking some coconut-flavored punch, and some were singing. It was only ten in the morning, but a party had definitely started.

Maria found herself sitting with two other kids her age, a boy with scars, the other a girl wearing a headscarf that hid orange hair. The old woman was certainly popular. She was sitting regally in a wicker chair under the courtyard Jacaranda tree.

The flowers were brought out to sounds of oohs and aahs as the housekeeper put them on display on a table laden with cakes and snacks. The atmosphere was friendly and most of the people seemed to know each other. Delaney found himself standing next to a white guy of about fifty, who seemed familiar.

"Funny how people find their way here," the guy remarked as he sipped on the coconut juice.

Delaney suddenly remembered him. "TV. You used to do the nightly news. I remember you."

The man smiled. "That was a long time ago. Before the bombing."

Delaney blinked. Couldn't believe he'd forgotten the attack on the TV station about ten years back. Armed terrorists stormed the studio demanding justice for some political crook on trial for corruption. It was this newsreader's bad luck that he was live on air when they broke into the studios.

"You never came back?" Delaney asked.

"They missed my liver by a millimeter, but I never really recovered, then someone told me about Jasmina here. She gave me more in one session than seven years of therapy ever did. I teach journalism now. It's a lot safer."

Delaney nodded. "Yeah. Well I'm happy for you. No one really comprehends the collateral damage violence can cause."

"Yeah. Very true."

"Maria?"

Maria looked up to discover Jasmina was calling her

over, beckoning for her to sit on the stool in front of her. She would rather die than go over, but all eyes were on her, some slightly jealous that she'd been called and not them. Maria briefly glanced at Delaney, but he just gave her the thumbs up and she went forward, bracing herself for total humiliation.

The stool was strange with a twisty stem so you could raise or lower it. She sat down facing Jasmina with all the sensation of someone awaiting a death sentence.

Jasmina placed her hands upon her head and closed her eyes to concentrate.

Delaney watched from his corner wondering if the Guru would show.

"Don't be alarmed, Maria. Just relax. Nothing bad will happen here. I've been waiting to meet you. You don't know this, but you have been to see me in your dreams. Your bad dreams. I felt them coming towards me, like ripples in the ocean. They came over me and I knew that one day you'd come here. This is a place of healing, girl. Do not be afraid. You are in good company. The boy, Cedric you were sitting next to, he witnessed his father being shot right in front of him. They shot Cedric too. You can imagine what terrible dreams he had. And Simi, the girl you talked to, lost all her family to a rare sickness. They have all faced their fears and survived, my girl. You aren't as alone as you think you are."

Maria felt embarrassed now. She'd experienced nothing like that. No one had been shot or died, although she realized Delaney had come close and no one knew how sick she had been when Asha told her he was missing. She would never admit it either.

Jasmina pressed her fingers deeply against her skull. She learned forward almost whispering. "Listen well, Maria. Think of the one who loves you. Relax and think of him. And yes. I know it's a dog."

Someone laughed but Jasmina held up a hand to silence them.

"Maria here knows nothing of her father. Not even his name. No one else here today has been so deprived. So do not belittle the love of a dog. Sworn to be loyal and faithful to a girl who is devoted to him. Maria has a mother...," Jasmina shuddered a moment, "a woman who has never for one moment thought of what is best for her daughter. We all know what happens to a daughter whose mother doesn't care. The streets are full of the unloved. I know. I see them every day. They think they can get by, but they have been robbed of the one thing that can help them survive. A mother's love is second only to that of God."

Maria felt the hairs rise on the back of her neck and for some reason she could feel Rufus was lying across her feet but clearly, he wasn't. She took comfort from it anyway.

"There is such unhappiness in this person," Jasmina was saying. "The dog is here. I can feel him. His spirit has travelled with her here today. Can you feel him Maria?"

"Yes," Maria answered hoarsely. "He's at my feet."

The crowd murmured, as if they too could see Rufus.

"It was this dog that found you when you had that accident." Jasmina declared, then stopped, her head cocked to one side as a piece of information clicked into place. "Only ... we know it wasn't an accident, don't we, Maria."

All Maria's alarm bells went off at once. The voice in her head was shouting 'No. No. No. No one must know this.'

"You never meant to survive. I can see that now. The cliff; the biting cold wind, the deep ocean and terrible rocks below. You were filled with darkness and despair. I can almost taste it. Anger. Your mother had made you angry. Threatened to destroy your happiness and you, in that moment paid a terrible price for it.

"The dog knew. I can tell you that even now he's anxious you'd do such a terrible thing again."

Delaney stared at Maria with shock. She had jumped. He had always wondered why she had gone out without Rufus to protect her. He vividly remembered that day. The screaming from her mother; who had threatened to move out, move on. Maria had been throwing up almost every day for a week with anxiety and he'd never even considered that she would want to take her own life rather than move out. How had he missed that? Too preoccupied with the stress of dealing with her mother and her moods he supposed.

'I ..." Maria began, but hot tears were flowing now, and she couldn't form words.

"We don't blame people here," Jasmina was saying. "We are here to tell you that there's not just a dog that loves you. Your life matters, Maria. You have a bright future. I know you don't believe it right now, but you do.

"Everyone in this room knows that. Mrs Laider over there, came to me with just weeks to live. She was told she had the cancer. That she must say goodbye to her three children. Imagine that. I told her that they were mistaken. To see a different doctor and he would know how to cure her. And here she is today, her children all grown up. I saw a future for her, and I see one for you girl. Look at me."

Maria looked up at Jasmina, surprised to see the old woman's eyes were still closed, but tears were running down her cheeks too. "My brother is here …"

Indeed, a breeze swept through the courtyard and all heard a door firmly closing. The Guru had arrived and stood inches by Delaney's side as he took in the situation.

"My brother, Ansolm will take your pain away, Maria. But you must repair your heart. Believe me, when I say you have a future, it is true. You despair of returning to your mother and I understand that. I truly do, but this will not happen. You have a home and sometimes it might be awkward, never known a home yet where everyone gets their own way all the time." Some people in the crowd murmured their agreement on that particular point, but Jasmina held up her hand for silence. "You, my girl, will come to realize life is worth living and one day, a long time from now, you'll be walking on a beach holding the hand of another who loves you and will never betray you."

Jasmina opened her eyes.

"Brother come. Embrace Maria."

The Guru entered the open space to general affectionate murmuring, a smile on his face as he studied Maria who stood up to greet him. He enfolded her in his arms and began to sing in a strange hypnotic voice. Jasmina waved to Delaney to join them and he reluctantly left the shadows. Moments later he found himself in the circle of many arms wrapped around Maria. The Guru was pulling him in ever closer. He smelled of cinnamon and beans. Jasmina pressed all their heads together and joined in the singing.

A cry went up from the assembled crowd and they too began to sing and sway as they clapped and made exclamations of joy.

Delaney's mind was clouded. He could distinctly hear Denise's voice in her distinctive French accent telling him to live, to enjoy his second chance, that she was right with him and had been with him in the car when he'd crashed and woken him.

And then, quite abruptly it was over. The housekeeper was announcing coffee and cake.

The Guru was hugging his sister and she was crying with joy as Maria sheepishly turned to Delaney taking hold of his hands. Delaney almost withdrew them from habit, fearing pain but she saw his expression change.

"What?" Maria asked.

"My hands. The pain has gone."

Maria squeezed his fingers harder and normally that would have made him yell.

"Nothing. No pain. Amazing." Delaney told her, withdrawing one hand to wipe the tears from Maria's face.

"I feel like I'm about to fly," she whispered. "I feel so light. You might have to hold me down."

Delaney pulled her towards him and held her. Something he never did. She never ever allowed it.

"You're sure you're ok?" He asked.

Maria shook her head. "I'm sorry."

Delaney smiled. "Nothing to apologize for. I didn't know this would happen today, like this, but I'm not sorry I know what happened to you now."

Maria buried her face into his chest. "It's true. I did want to jump. She was going to leave you. I couldn't leave. I couldn't leave Rufus, or my room, my home, even you." She took a deep breath. "I just felt this blackness come over me and then I slipped. I promise it was an accident but ..."

Delaney hugged her harder.

"Rufus knew. I don't know how, but he just threw himself against the door and wanted out. I couldn't stop him once I opened it."

Maria pulled back and stared at him. "You're not angry?"

"I'm not sorry your mother left after your accident, but I always missed you."

"I know that now."

Maria turned her body one way and then the other and then stepped back and bent down to touch her toes. She stood back up her eyes full of wonder.

"I can't feel any pain. I can't feel any pain, Delaney."

Delaney smiled with genuine happiness for her as Maria turned to the Guru still hugging his sister.

"Thank you. Thank you, Jasmina, thank you both. I don't know what you did, or even why but ..."

Maria suddenly sat down on the stool and sobbed.

The Guru put out a hand to her head. "The pain was in your heart, not your back. My sister was right, as always." Jasmina beamed in his praise.

Delaney pulled Maria up and led her away to the kitchen so the Guru and his sister could have some time together.

The two kids, Cedric and Simi took Maria over and they went into another room. Delaney watched them go with wonder. The TV news guy nudged him and offered him coffee and cake.

"Breaks your heart every time."

It took some time before Delaney could get the Guru to himself. So many of Jasmina's regulars wanted to reconnect with him and tell him their stories. He patiently listened to all and Delaney realized that part of his skill was this ability to listen. Jasmina wouldn't leave his side but agreed to let Delaney ask questions.

"How long have you got before they'll come for you?"

The Guru glanced towards the way to the door. "Another hour perhaps. I never get much time." He reached out and touched the vivid purple bruises on Delaney's neck. "You look a lot worse than when I saw you last."

Delaney could feel his hot fingers brush his skin; it was a strange eerie sensation.

"I hadn't been driven off the road then."

The Guru stared at him in surprise. He nodded and pursed his lips. "I apologize if that was my fault in any way."

"They were doing their best to silence me."

"May you have ten lives," the Guru intoned.

Delaney smiled. "I sense I might need them. Did you fix my hands just then? The pain has gone and ..."

The Guru shook his head. "You did that. Taking in the girl. In any case my sister Jasmina is much more powerful than me."

"Well whatever happened, I hope it lasts."

The Guru merely shrugged. "Nothing lasts but stone, and even stone wears away to sand."

Jasmina muttered agreement. "True, so very true."

"Tell me about you and Mrs Jaywaller, Ansolm."

The Guru laughed, but it was mirth filled with bitterness. "She stole my gift. Stole my life."

"I appreciate that you have a gift, but I don't understand how this scheme works. You have assistants?"

"They call them disciples, which is blasphemous. I can teach them the 'way of Jirdasham' but none have the gift. Only God can bestow that."

"So when they use the disciples to do the cure..."

"They cannot," The Guru snapped. "It is a lie. They can only use the method to help a patient manage their pain, relax them, but it cannot work for long. Some people respond better than others, some not at all."

"So that's when you step in. The so-called booster. They get the real thing if they pay the booster."

The Guru squirmed; he was uncomfortable with these questions. "They use me. I am exhausted. I have not the capacity to be used like this."

"My client, from BookBank was desperate to be rid of his pain, but he said it came back within a month. He declined to pay for the booster."

The Guru frowned. "I know Mr Abrams. He kindly stocks my books. I never saw him."

"Was he right to decline the booster?"

"If his pain went away for a month, then his problem has a solution. I doubt the disciples had any role in making it go away. There is an element of auto-suggestion."

"But if he paid the fifteen grand you would be the one to perform the task and his pain would go."

The Guru shrugged. "If I treat the patient, the pain will go. It is God's will. But this is a criminal use of my time, an abuse of God."

"Tell me about your big White House on The Hill. It's empty."

The Guru sipped coffee and sighed. "Why would I live in such a place? I have never set foot in it. I won't."

"Then where do you live?" Jasmina butted in, unable to stop herself.

"I sleep in the pool house behind her house. I would

not call this living. She thinks I must do her bidding at all hours, but I need to pray, to sleep, to eat. She seems to do none of these things."

"But you went into business with her."

The Guru stared at his sister with a guilty expression. "Jasmina told me not to. She said I know nothing of the business world but after my tea business was taken from me, I wanted to prove her wrong."

"Does she pay you, Ansolm?" Jasmina asked. "Is that big white house yours?"

The Guru looked down at his feet. "They say so. I have seen a bank statement. There is a lot of money deposited in my name, but I have no ability or need to spend it."

"I'm presuming they have a bank card to allow them to spend it on your behalf. Are they putting aside money for tax?"

Jasmina was shaking her head. "That was what happened before. He never thinks about tax until they come banging on the door."

"Mrs Jaywaller is a very powerful woman," Delaney said. "It must be hard to say no to her."

The Guru nodded, took his sister's hand. "I know I have been a fool, but there are things..."

"What things?" Jasmina asked.

He shook his head. He didn't want to say.

"Tell me about St Joes, Ansolm."

The Guru looked up at him with surprise.

"I have been there," Delaney told him. "Tell me about men and women screaming in pain all day and night. Don't pretend to me that this is for their own good. We're getting the homeless off the streets and promising them money. You and I know they'll never last long enough to be paid. Tell me about a family that were living on an old bus, suddenly given a roof over their heads, as long as the husband screams in pain all day long. A promise of a year's rent paid in the city if he lasts. Tell me this pain isn't killing them."

The Guru shifted in his chair. He hadn't expected this.

"I want to help you, but you need to make me understand what is happening. How it happens."

Jasmina understood better than Delaney.

"No. You didn't. Tell me you didn't." She turned to

Delaney with anger flashing in her eyes. "They're keeping the pain alive."

Delaney frowned. Not immediately comprehending.

"Explain. Keeping it alive?"

The Guru sighed, stood up and took a stem of African Daisy from the vase. He returned to his seat and grabbed Delaney's right hand. He glanced at his sister. "What was the girl's name?"

"Maria?" Jasmina asked. "She broke her back."

The Guru nodded and closed his eyes as he held the stem in one hand and Delaney's hand in the other.

"You wanted to know if the pain has gone forever. For you and the girl." The Guru told him. "Watch."

Delaney watched the Guru and the flower. A strange intensity flowed across the Guru into the flower stem and it began to wilt, then after a moment, shrivel in his hands. He let it drop to the floor.

"You and the child will never have this trouble again," the Guru declared, his voice wavering a moment, as if the effort had exhausted him. "Maria will recover quickly now. Your pain is gone, but you haven't shed the source of your pain."

"The source?" Delaney queried.

"Your wife. She is gone, but you can't let go. The pain you feel is guilt. It's punishment you have given yourself because you didn't die with her."

Delaney said nothing, but the truth of it pierced his heart. How the Guru knew this he had no idea.

"It is easier to dismiss the pain of a healing broken back, but only you can take your pain away forever. Only you can forgive yourself."

The Guru let go of his hand and immediately it was as if he was carrying hot coals. Delaney was tempted to blow on his hands to cool them.

"The flower died, Ansolm." Delaney remarked.

"As will Maria's pain."

"But the other people in St Joes, their pain is still alive."

The Guru didn't want to say it, but his sister knew. Delaney glanced at Jasmina and clearly, she was wrestling with the morality of this.

"Who will take their pain away, Ansolm?" Delaney

asked. "Or do I have it backwards."

The Guru looked away. "They told me it would help them. The suffering is only temporary. It will not kill them. They are no longer sleeping on the streets. They will get clean, eat hot meals and ..."

"Bullshit, Ansolm. You're transferring the pain from paying clients to the homeless. And you're trying to say you're helping them. It's disgusting. It's immoral, not to mention crazy."

The Guru looked to the ceiling but found no help there. "Mrs Jaywaller made me do it."

Jasmina swore. She was clearly shocked. "No one can make you do anything, brother. No one."

The Guru visibly shrank from the wrath of his sister.

"At first it was just a few. Keep the pain alive so she could put it to work."

Jasmina was visibly distressed by this admission. "You know the rules. You know it has to be given to the plants. You can't play with mercy, Ansolm. Remember how upset Mamma was when her beloved plants would die. She always blamed the soil."

Delaney put a hand on the Guru's arm.

"You alone do this, but there are so many victims. You have to be seeing ten people a day or more."

The Guru closed his eyes. "They always bring the volunteers to the clinic. They wash them, feed them, treat them with kindness. I ask each one if they understand what will happen."

"No one can imagine pain, Ansolm. They cannot understand what it will mean to them."

"The pain is not the disease and they will be paid." The Guru protested.

Delaney shot him down. "I don't understand why you'd even consider doing it. What the hell has that woman got on you, Ansolm?

Jasmina shook her head. "You must stop this, brother. God will punish you severely."

The Guru clapped his hands to his face. "It's too late, too late. Far too late."

"Can't you take the pain away from those people in St Joes? And elsewhere. I'm sure there's more elsewhere."

Delaney asked.

The Guru's eyes were darting around the room as if he wished for escape. "She keeps the pain alive so it can go back."

"Go back?" Jasmina queried.

Delaney understood. "You mean to the people who paid all that money to be rid of it. You're keeping the pain alive so when the boosters fade you can do it all over again?"

The Guru shook his head. "If I take the pain away, it will not come back."

"So what?" Jasmina asked. "For the Lord's Sake, what have you done, Ansolm?"

Delaney guessed. "You bring them into contact with the individual who has their pain. You bring them close and somehow jump the pain back. Is that what this is? The victims have to pay and pay and pay and what ... the homeless guy goes free?"

The Guru shrugged. "They get paid."

"And there's always more where they came from, right? This is extortion. This is health terrorism, Ansolm. You might have a gift, but this is beyond reason."

"You don't understand. She will kill me if she knows I have told you."

"What and kill the golden goose? I don't think so. She might kill you if you did the right thing and let the pain die. Tell me, what the hell has she got on you? You're old? What terrible crime have you committed that she can hold you like this?"

Jasmina intervened. "You told me that you were working with Father Vincent at Magdalen hospice. What happened?"

The Guru looked shifty. "It is true. That is how this started. I used to take people's pain and transfer it to the terminally ill." He saw Delaney's reaction. "Don't look at me like that. It was a genuine Christian thing to do. Doctors keep them alive when all they want to do is die and join their loved ones. They would ask for me, plead with me to let them go. The shock of another's pain would usually take them quickly. This was humane. Father Vincent always made sure they had a good funeral. It was not my idea to place other's pain in those who were not ill. She made me do that. She said it was a better business model."

"You understand, Ansolm, that I find this shocking. I

was struggling to see you as an arch villain but what you are doing is evil."

The Guru glanced at his sister. "I'm a villain. No doubt a lot of people would like to see me in jail. But I don't kill people. The people in the hospice found freedom from a life of torture and pain. But those people in St Joes aren't dying. They will live and be able to rebuild their lives. That is also humane."

"Tell me about Rafael?" Delaney asked.

The Guru shrugged. "He calls himself disciple number one, but all he does is applied meditation. He knows how to get people to let go of their pain, but he doesn't have the gift God gave me. He cannot remove pain and never will."

Jasmina glanced across at Delaney with a stern expression. "Go find Maria. Let me talk to him."

Delaney stood up. He realized he wanted to hit the guy.

"Ansolm, you asked me to help you, but unless you're willing to set all those people free, I don't think I can, or will."

Delaney left the courtyard and went to find Maria. She was sitting on a bed staring at the shirtless back of the boy Cedric. Delaney winced when he saw the bullet scars.

"Cedric was shot three times." Maria told him. "Show him your scars, Simi."

Sima slipped off the tunic covering one shoulder. Her skin was a patchwork of scarring and red weal's. She was a very pretty girl. He wondered if any of that skin would return to normal.

"Jasmina says I should have tattoos when I'm older. It will hide it."

Delaney nodded. Couldn't believe how calm these kids were or how easily Maria was speaking to them. Normally she'd clam up around strangers.

"How steep was the cliff you drove off," Cedric asked him, the wonder obvious in his eyes.

Delaney realized that they were all comparing scars today. "Over a hundred feet, I think. I was very lucky to survive."

"And it's true the dog escaped?" Simi asked.

Delaney nodded. "I don't know how, but if he hadn't been seen by a highway cop, I'm not sure what would have happened to him."

Maria smiled. "He's a very special dog."
Simi smiled, as if she already knew that there were special dogs out there to be found.

"M, we're going." Delaney told Maria. "You feel ok?"

Maria smiled brilliantly. "I'm better. I'm like brand new again."

Delaney sighed. He was very happy for her. But at what price? He had no idea what to do about the Guru or Mrs Jaywaller. Who would ever believe any of this? Who would want to stop it? They were all making so much money.

The Guru had already gone when he went back. Jasmina was soothing a crying woman. Delaney waved goodbye as he didn't want to interrupt, but Jasmina stopped him.

"He did something bad, Mr Delaney. He won't say what, but she has it on video. Something went wrong at the clinic. A famous woman died. That is all I can say. I know my brother has done terrible things, but he used to help people, desperate people and they were grateful for it. If in your heart you can help him get away from that woman. I beg you to try."

Delaney nodded but made no commitment. "On behalf of myself and Maria here, we thank you for all you have done for us today and happy birthday Jasmina."

She smiled. "You made it special for me. I know there were tears, but you kept your word." She stared at Maria a moment. "Maria, come back to me one day. I know you will have more questions. All you have to do is knock on my door. If help is possible – God will show me how."

Maria went over to her and gave her a hug.

"I will. I promise I will."

"And look after that dog." Jasmina added with a smile.

"It's my dog," Delaney protested.

Maria just went 'hah' and headed for the door. Delaney smiled at Jasmina and she laughed. "A dog can be shared. They are very generous."

In the car Maria kept staring at him as Rufus vied for her attention and kept licking her face.

"Did you know any of that stuff would happen?"

Delaney shook his head. "Maybe we won't mention to Asha how weird it was, right? Rufus, in the back. Now! Be good, leave M alone."

Maria looked at the road ahead and smiled. "I suddenly feel I can plan my life."

"Same for me." He raised one hand and shook it. "No pain. It's gone from my shoulders too."

"Will it last?" Maria asked.

Delaney nodded. "I think so. Keep the faith and it will last. No doubts, Maria. We're cured and we are going to stay that way. Right?"

"Fucking right. I'm going back on the team and I'm going to kick ass."

Delaney grinned. "Yeah. You're cured."

Maria reached out to his free hand and squeezed it. "If I forget to say thank you a million times a day, forgive me. I'm an ungrateful brat most of the time, I know, but you ..."

"A million thank yous are all I need, M. What was in that coconut juice, hey? I had to pour mine down the sink."

Maria laughed. "So gross. And the cake was like ginger or something. Can we stop for lunch? I am sooooo hungry."

Delaney laughed. He was hungry too. Like he hadn't eaten in a month. "Pizza?"

"You can read minds, oh mighty one." Maria settled back in her seat with a grin ear to ear.

Delaney made a left and took the route over the hill towards Crest Bay.

"We'll give Rufus a walk on the beach first. He was very brave looking after the car."

Maria was taking a look at the interior and feeling the shabby plastic seats and a glove box that was clearly broken.

"Is this your new car, it seems a bit..." Maria was trying not to be rude.

"It's a loaner, don't panic. I've ordered a hybrid."

"No diesel. Promise me?"

"I'm pretty sure the new diesels don't pollute as much as gas actually. But it's gas and electric. Ok?"

Maria shook her head. "Pure would be better, we've only got one planet."

Delaney shrugged. "If we really wanted to save the planet, we'd be back to riding horses. And you'd be walking to and from school every day."

Maria stuck her tongue out. "You could get me a bike."

"You'd use it? Knowing we live on a hill?"

Maria grinned. "Electric bike."

Delaney laughed. "Oh yeah and a few thousand later. Anyway, aren't you worried about all the child labor they use to dig all that cobalt and lithium out of the ground for the batteries?"

Maria sighed. "You know how to spoil everything."

"Just saying, there's no easy way out of this. We want to save the planet, but we still need to move around and go to work. And don't say trams to me. Remember last winter when they couldn't get up the hill or down it."

"It was too icy for them."

"Anyway, young lady, you'll have to go easy on your back now. I know you feel terrific and want to go back to running, but it won't mean you aren't putting a sudden strain on it."

Maria frowned. "You trying to tell me this won't last?"

Delaney shook his head. "I'm pretty hopeful it will. But last week I met a woman whose pain had gone thanks to the Guru, but she had the opposite problem, she can't feel anything anymore, not even when she broke her leg."

"Serious?"

"Very. By all means be active, start building up your strength, but be careful you don't stress your back too quickly. A couple of weeks of short runs and your Pilates exercises and you'll gain the confidence that you can trust your back again. Understand?"

Maria nodded. "What about you?"

Delaney stared at his hands on the steering wheel momentarily. "My hands probably aren't going back to normal, fingers and bone don't miraculously straighten, but as long as I can't feel pain, I'll be happy.

And who knows, maybe if the swelling goes down, I can go sailing again."

"You'll take me with you?"

Delaney glanced at her. "There's a lot of rules to learn about safe sailing."

"I'll learn. I want to go out there. I want to sail."

Delaney smiled. "I'll show you. Rufus has never been on the water; I wonder if he'll take to it."

Maria scoffed. "You can't take a dog sailing."

"He can swim pretty good. Put a life jacket on him, I

don't see why not."

Maria turned back to stroke the dog. "Poor Rufie, he'll get so seasick."

Delaney began to slow as he looked for a place to park. Maria stared at the waves pounding the shore. "Looks rough." Maria watched huge wave crash onto the shore. "My feet turned blue just walking along that beach last year. So cold."

"Come sailing, wear a wet suit, as I can assure you, you'll get pretty wet."

"There's always a negative with you, Delaney."

Delaney smiled. "Come on, walk first, then there's a great pizza place near here. They allow dogs."

CHAPTER TWENTY-NINE

Lottery Play

His phone alerted him to his follow up with his Doctor. He'd almost cancelled he felt so well, but then again, best to be sure.

Delaney dropped Maria off at home with Rufus as he went to the surgery. He was second in line so there was little waiting and the nurse called him over to deal with his bandages and lather him in sanitizer, which immediately irritated his abrasions. Delaney had to disrobe but keep his mask on. He sat patiently on a long plastic bench whilst a very pre-occupied Doctor Rockhill was looking at the x-ray of his neck area.

"How's your neck? You were very lucky not to have concussion I think."

The Doctor took the trouble to actually look up at Delaney when he didn't reply. He frowned.

"Well the neck bruising is going fast. That's unusual. Can I see your hands?"

The Doctor examined his hands carefully. "Can you move your fingers?"

Delaney showed him, wiggling his fingers up and down. "My mobility seems to have returned. The pain's gone too."

The Doctor gave a short laugh. "Well that's good to hear, but you don't get shot of rheumatoid arthritis so easy, Mr Delaney." He took a look at Delaney's headwound. "It's healing well, whoever did those stitches knew what they were doing. Don't wash your hair for a couple of days, give it time for the swelling to go down. No headaches?"

"Not since the first day. That was pretty bad. Maybe the jolt in my accident reconnected things. I really feel a lot better and..." he raised his arm about his head. "No pain. I can move."

Delaney saw the Doc try to suppress his skepticism. "That's pretty remarkable. I saw you what? Just a few days ago and you were moving like an old man. No pain in your fingers at all?"

Delaney shook his head. "All good."

The Doctor seemed at a loss. "I'm happy for you, but certainly this is not something I've done. I was going to prescribe a new anti-inflammatory called upadacitinib, but definitely not now. Let's hope this remission continues. In fact, I think I have read a paper on accidental impact related nerve reactivation. You might be right. I shall monitor you."

Delaney pulled his shirt back on. "You think it's possible that you could transfer pain from one person to another. Without giving them the disease or underlying cause?"

Doctor Rockhill laughed. "Impossible. You've been seeing a witch doctor? If you don't have the pain, you don't have the problem. Of course, there is psychosomatic transfer, where a person can assume the pain of another, but that's not in my field. I don't think I have ever witnessed it aside from a pregnancy pain transfer to a husband. I think I have seen that, but it isn't common."

"Well I'm just glad I'm on the road to recovery."

"Are you taking any supplements I don't know about? We talked about juicing."

"Never quite had the guts to swallow green slime, Doc."

"But you're taking something, arthritis can't vanish overnight."

Delaney smiled behind his mask as he dressed. "Put it down to a miracle."

Doctor Rockhill began typing up his notes into the computer. "No reactions to the Covid vaccine booster shot you had?"

Delaney shook his head. The Doctor's eyebrows raised a little in surprise.

"If I were you, Mr Delaney, I'd start buying lottery tickets."

Zuki was staring at her laptop screen and sighing as she deleted what she'd just written. Asha placed a glass of wine on the table near her.

"Wine is not going to improve my résumé, Asha."

"Might improve your mood."

"Nothing can fix that. I can't even lie about my last job, or jobs. Here is a perfectly good position in developmental analysis in Ai learning, it's got a great salary. I have the degree, all the skills they could possibly need and all they want to know is the reason why I left my last employment and what measurable achievements I accomplished. They also want to know what my high-school grade average was. How is that even relevant? I made the Dean's List, assholes. Get this, they also want to know my family background. Which I'm guessing is code for we're only hiring white people whose folks went to church and earned more than two hundred grand a year. There's no fucking box to tick for orphan, adopted and got fired for being in possession of an independent mind in my last five jobs."

Asha almost smiled, but suppressed it, knowing how sensitive Zuki could be. "I seem to recall you got fired from the last job because you called the manager at the pizza place a whore."

Zuki turned to her and stuck her tongue out. "She was turning tricks in the parking lot with our customers. She didn't even wear a mask."

"She was being entrepreneurial." Asha told her with a straight face.

Zuki laughed and reached for her wine. "Fuck, yeah. She was." She stared at the screen again. "I can do this job. I did this same job for Arcadia Health Care for six months on minimum fucking wage; remember? Yes, we will hire you the moment your internship ends. AS if. Those fuckers just churn graduates over and don't even care about the quality of the work. I seriously don't think I'm ever going to make a living, Ash. You are so lucky to have found Delaney."

"I am? We're about to get fired because we did our jobs."

"But he wants to bring you in as a partner."

"First we have to find clients. There's no guarantee. I might be competing with you for the next pizza job that comes up, Zukes."

"Life sucks, Ash. What can I say, except I'm way better at being a waitress than you."

Asha smacked her forehead. "Please god I never have to waitress again. I can't remember anything people order for more than 30 seconds."

Zuki nodded and sipped her wine, looking back at the screen.

"References? How the fuck am I supposed to get references? I've been fired from almost every job I've had."

"Arcadia Healthcare must be able to give you one."

"Except for that whistleblower incident when I told the state auditors they were double charging for the seniors they were treating."

Asha winced. "Yeah, that could be an issue." She glanced at her watch.

"I have to go to see Delaney. You going to be ok?"

Zuki stared at her. "No. I'm never going to be ok. But you go. One of us needs to be employed. One day I'm going to meet this guy and vet him."

Asha frowned. "Not yet. He's too fragile."

Zuki laughed. "Sucker. Go, Ash. Hope he's appreciative that you saved his ass out there."

"I just got him home, that's all. He's a good guy, Zuke. I promise."

Zuki shook her head. "There are no good guys. Just ones who haven't hit you over the head with a baseball bat yet."

Asha laughed, picked up her keys and left Zuki to it.

CHAPTER THIRTY

Rat & Rice

Asha appeared at the garden gate at suppertime. Maria and the dog went down the path to buzz her in. Rufus was barely able to summon a bark.

"I heard they closed the city pool," she began, as she followed Maria and Rufus into the house.

"We know. It sucks."

"Well don't worry, you can still swim at my place. For as long as I'm there. God knows how I'm going to pay the rent next month. Hey, I think Rufus is moving a bit better."

"He still whimpers if you touch him though."

Delaney looked up from the stove and hailed Asha as she came through the door. "Hey, well timed, Asha. I hope you're hungry. I've made way too much ratatouille."

Asha sniffed the air. "Look great, smells er ... very garlicky, I'm in."

"Help yourself to wine. Sorry we didn't make it back to the office. The birthday party was pretty traumatic, and then we needed to walk Rufus."

Asha poured herself some wine and grabbed some nuts. "I wasn't in the office after three anyway. Want to hear my news?"

Maria grabbed Rufus. "If you're talking business, I've got stuff to do."

Delaney wagged a wooden spoon at her. "Twenty minutes, M. I hope the table is laid."

"It's laid." She disappeared downstairs.

Asha had noticed the difference immediately. "She seems happy. You got her on drugs or something?"

Delaney shook his head. "She's not in pain anymore."

"You're kidding me."

"Me either."

"The Guru came?"

"He did, and I've got a lot to tell you. I'll spare the actual 'healing' episode but I'm pretty sure the sister has an even greater 'gift' than the guru. She's certainly more measured with it."

Asha took her wine to the sofa as Delaney continued to stir the pot. "I see your head bandage is off. I don't know why, but I'm kind of jealous. You really don't have pain in your hands anymore?"

Delaney waved his left hand. "All gone; my shoulders too. The fingers still look swollen and bent out of shape, but I can live with that. You've no idea what it feels like to be pain free."

Asha made a face. "Impressive. No thirty-grand bill in the post?"

"No bills, but it doesn't mean I approve of his methods or that I'm dropping the investigation. He's proved to me he's genuine, but there's some pretty dark shit in the Guru's past." He stirred the pan a moment. "So, what's up with you?"

"I was at the gym. Got talking to Alison Savage. Guess where she works?"

Delaney shrugged. "You wouldn't be here if it was the post office."

"Funny man. Believe me no one who works at the post office can afford my gym. Alison heads up the PR department at Jirdasham. She only fucking well lives in my building."

"Well I guess they can afford the rents."

"She really hates her job and Mrs Jaywaller in particular. The pay's shit actually. She thinks the whole thing is a scam. Over 75% of the clients need to have the boosters. They pay backhanders to some of the banks and financial advisors in the city for the names of high-worth individuals with health issues, then go cold calling them and invite them in for 'tasters'. It's a beautiful scam."

"She willing to go on record?"

Asha shook her head. "No chance. She says someone she worked with developed a conscience and the next thing you know she disappeared off the face of the planet."

"She knows about the homeless?"

"Not only knows, but she's the one who signs them up, gets them into the clinic, cleans them up so they look nice and shiny for the Guru. She has a list of places where vulnerable people hang out. She has a potential list of about 600 'volunteers' she can put into the program."

Delaney frowned as he checked on his rice cooker. "That could be a very expensive little army to feed, wash and keep locked up in St Joes and wherever."

Asha laughed. "You haven't heard the best part. It doesn't cost Jirdasham a cent. It's genius. Thanks to the Mayor's involvement, there's a government grant to get these people off the streets that pays for the 'treatment'. They're even up for an international humanity award from Norway. You couldn't make this shit up, Chief."

Asha wasn't finished. She took a sip of wine. "She told me that they're setting up a new company offering HORT. Get this. Hyper-Oxygen Regenerative Therapy."

Delaney stared at her none the wiser. "Which is what exactly?"

"They stick you in a high-pressure chamber for two hours a day for a whole month and claim it will make you younger – anti-ageing treatment."

"And I guess they'll have a line-up of billionaires around the block wanting to spend more time with their money."

"Yeah, it will cost a bomb and you get some kind of proof your telomeres have been extended and you have fewer senescent cells."

"Telomeres? Senescent cells? I feel I should know this stuff but..." He shrugged, he didn't want to admit that there had been times when the pain was so bad he'd wished his life could been shorter, not longer. "I'm serving up with basmati rice. You ok with that?"

"Smells good to me. I'm starving. You cook like this every night?"

"Teenage girls pretend they aren't hungry but this one eats all the time."

"Long may that last. I was so freaked out about getting fat; I nearly stopped eating for a whole year when I was fourteen. The soccer coach threatened to push me off the team unless I ate."

"That worked?"

"Yeah. Being on the team meant a lot to me back then."

"Happy to hear it. Tell me, that waiting list for the boosters at Jirdasham. They're waiting for the Guru, right?"

"Oh yeah. They hate the Guru. He can only manage one or if it is spaced out long enough two, three sessions a day. He's getting slower and older."

"But no one else can do it, right?"

"Correct. The so-called disciples are just masseurs and gym bunnies with good people skills. They give them training in mindfulness and relaxation techniques and the Guru shows them some of his techniques to make the clients believe they're getting the works."

"For which they charge thirty grand for."

"It's basic theft." Asha declared.

"Nevertheless, some clients do lose their pain." Delaney pointed out.

"Mind over matter probably. Treatment takes twelve hours. Massages, ice treatment, exercise, sauna, nutrition planning, oxygen boosters and some auto-suggestion stuff. Alison said that most clients are just grateful for the attention, their own doctors just ply them with pills."

"Call Maria. If you can prise her away from her iPad."

Asha rolled her eyes and went to find Maria.

Rufus appeared looking keen and sniffing the air. Delaney wagged a finger. "You already ate. Don't look at me like that, dog." Rufus sighed and flopped down on the rug.

Delaney heard footsteps pounding up the stairs. He smiled and took a slug of his wine. No pain, hot food and good company made him feel better about life than he'd felt in a long time. Even without oxygen therapy.

"Rat," Maria was shouting. "Rat and Rice."

"Put a place on the table for Ash, brat. You won't put Asha off. She loves Rat and Rice."

Asha grinned as she grabbed her glass of wine. She glanced at Delaney and said, "talk more after."

Delaney nodded. "For sure."

They sat out under the stars with mugs of hot herbal teas. Rufus stretched out across Asha's feet. Delaney was thinking about the money.

"I assume all those waiting for the booster already paid the thirty grand."

"Yeah, that what she said, but there's also a payment plan which is impossible to cancel without huge penalties. Even after death. They'll go after the families for the debt."

"It sounds to me that there's hardly any happy customers. And if they knew that their pain is being kept alive..."

"I don't think 'happy customers' are part of the business plan, Chief."

Delaney nodded. "That's pretty much what the Guru confirmed. The homeless aren't there for altruistic reasons. They're loaded with pain, so even after the booster works, they can give that pain right back to the client or victim, a better description. Each one is carrying that pain to hand right back so they can do it all over again."

Asha stared at him. "There's a third payment. Jeez."

"Third, fourth, ad infinitum until one or the other dies, I guess. Whatever the market will bear."

"That's crazy. It's sick."

"The great flaw in all of this is the Guru. As you say, he's old, he's tired and he's being blackmailed."

Asha did a double take. "What? It gets crazier."

"Seems he accidentally killed someone famous when a session went wrong. Mrs Jaywaller has it on tape."

Asha stared up at the stars and shivered, taking a sip of her hot tea. "That makes sense. If it's a famous death in Berg City I should be able to discover who."

Delaney sipped his tea and thought about things for a

moment.

"The Guru confuses me. Before all this shit he was running his own little side hustle taking pain away for paying customers and off-loading it at Father Vincent's Magdalen hospice. You know, the building that looks like a Greek temple by the lagoon."

Asha frowned. "Where people with terminal illnesses go to die right?"

"The way he puts it, these were mercy killings. The shock of all that new pain dumped on them would essentially kill them with shock. They'd ask for him specifically. Obviously, it was an open secret in this town."

"Cheaper than euthanasia in Switzerland, that's for sure."

"More humane, as the Guru puts it."

"Well I'm not shocked, Chief. My aunt had a stroke and the doctors fucking kept her alive and we all knew she was desperate to go. She lingered three years unable to move her arms and legs and hated every bloody second of it. If I had the Guru's number, I would have called him. Honest. I would have called."

Delaney inhaled. "I know, I know. Euthanasia should be a human right. I agree with you. Terminating your aunt would have been the humane thing to do. That I can handle. But taking the pain your aunt was in and installing it into someone healthy, well as healthy as any desperate homeless person can be. It can't be right. It just can't be excused, Ash. He showed me how he does it normally. Transfers the pain to a plant or flower and I fucking saw it wither right before my eyes. That's the humane thing to do. Not that the plant would see it that way of course."

"The flower wilted?"

"Died. Shriveled in seconds."

"Wow. Meanwhile Mrs Jaywaller gets to play saint and stores a never-ending supply of pain to bleed her rich clients dry."

"It's a perfect circle." Delaney remarked. "The thing is; what the fuck do we do about it? You think the media would run with this? No one would ever believe it. The cops are up to their eyes in dirty money and shunting people off cliffs, the Mayor and his Deputy are creaming off the top."

"It's madness," Asha commented. "You and me against the world." She swallowed more tea, watching a meteorite streak across the night sky and wanted to make a wish. "See that? Hell, I don't even know what to wish for anymore. What about you, Chief?"

"I want the Guru to undo all the shit he's caused."

Asha turned towards him. "What, force him to take the pain away from those people in St Joes?"

Delaney nodded. "Take their pain away, then go and see everyone on the waiting list at Jirdasham and take their pain away as well. I know he couldn't physically do it, but that's what I want to do. Kidnap him and set him loose in St Joes. Do as many as he can before he collapses."

"Or we get discovered."

"Yep. That too."

"Crazy stuff, Chief."

"You have a better plan?"

"No, but I'm thinking that all those people in St Joes are being fed regular meals for the first time in a long while and technically getting clean, despite the extra pain. You take that pain away from them and you'll make them grateful until the moment they get tossed out onto the street again without the money they've been promised."

"You think they ever actually intend to pay them, Ash?" Delaney stared into his empty mug. "Come up with a better plan. The Guru freed me of pain and I'm truly grateful for that, but there's a lot of sinning he has to make up for. He's killed people, performing mercy or not, he's traumatized hundreds with his 'gift'. I sincerely can't see a clear path from here."

Asha put a hand onto his arm and squeezed. "At least you're free of pain."

"I am. I promise. It just hasn't quite sunk in yet."

Asha laughed. "That's what my father used to say when I thrashed him at tennis."

"You never talk about him. Bad relationship?"

Asha shook her head. "Complicated. My mother left him for Mr Evil. I was fifteen. I knew she was having an affair. I didn't know my Dad was having one till I went to work at his travel agency. But he totally saved my ass by keeping me on part-time all the way through College. I'm like the only person I know my age who doesn't have fifty thousand of debt hanging over my head."

"Travel agency? He still in business?"

Asha shook her head. "Covid took him down along with the airlines. He decided to do the honorable thing and pay out refunds when they cancelled all the flights and cruises. Maybe he thought it would all come back the way it was. He lives out by Concord Lake now in his little shack. Got a cute dog and he goes fishing. I see him at Christmas and birthdays. See, you're disappointed now. No trauma. I still talk to him once a month and tell him he could start another business if he wanted to. But we both know he won't." She stood up and stretched her back.

"I'm going. We'll talk more tomorrow. Meet me at Harry's for coffee after you drop Maria at school, all right?"

Delaney nodded. "Yeah, good idea." He smiled at Asha. "Glad you came over. Do it more often. Maria likes you and I enjoy bouncing ideas off you. I'll see you out."

Asha smiled as she picked up her car keys. "Stay put."

Delaney shook his head. "I feel I need to move as much as possible now. I've been given a reprieve." He walked with her to the gate.

Asha suddenly turned and gave him a hug.

"I can't tell you how happy I am you're not in pain anymore." She held him tight and Delaney leaned in kissed her forehead – lingering perhaps just too long. Asha pulled back and looked into his eyes with curiosity, then grinned, only slowly disengaging, reluctant to break the moment.

He watched her walk to her car, unable to draw his eyes away from her cute ass. She glanced back and wrinkled her nose. He laughed. He probably needed some ice in his pants right at this moment. She lowered her window.

"Something will occur to you, Chief. Sleep is great for getting the mind to work."

"That it is. Night, Ash."

He watched her drive away and regretted he hadn't kissed her.

Asha glanced in her rear-view mirror and laughed at herself.

"Don't be crazy, girl." Nevertheless, she'd definitely felt something.

CHAPTER THIRTY-ONE

Harry's

Delaney took Maria's hand briefly as they reached the school. "Don't say anything about what happened to you. Be as normal as you can. Don't put any stress on your back. Ease into it, M. I'll be doing the same."

Maria shrugged. Keen to get out of the car. "I know."

"I know you know. But I still had to say it. Go make some poor bastard teacher's life miserable."

Maria laughed and climbed out of the car. "I will."

She watched him drive off and took a deep breath. She fixed on her indifferent glassy stare and headed towards the gates. For the first time in a long time she no longer felt vulnerable.

"Rufus is upset. He only got a walk around the block this morning."

Rufus slumped down under the restaurant table as Delaney slid into the booth seat opposite Asha. He looked around Harry's busy restaurant and seemed impressed.

"Harry's built himself quite a following I see."

"I miss the bench seats, and everyone crowded together. It sort of felt like University again. Now we're all so politely distanced and his prices have gone up."

"It's the only way restaurants can survive I guess."

Asha was scanning the menu board. "Good vegan choices here."

Delaney snatched a look at the board and raised his eyebrows. "Smashed avocado on cranberry sourdough with fresh strawberries. That would seem to have your number I reckon."

"Bastard. You think I'm a cliché don't you." Asha pouted.

Delaney smiled. "I'll have the same. Sounds good. What's the coffee like?"

"Rwandan. He roasts it here. Sometimes I just like to come in and inhale on the way home it's so good."

The waitress came over and they ordered. "There's a

fifteen-minute wait on the sourdough. It's only just out of the oven."

"Perfect," Delaney told her. "As long as we can have coffee. I take almond milk, ok?"

"We've got Oat, Soya, Almond and Cashew. Almond milk coming right up."

Asha looked at Delaney's hands. "They still good?"

Delaney nodded. "I think I slept the whole night through for the first time in years. Normally they ache so much I have to keep clenching and unclenching to get them to stop, but they didn't bug me once."

Asha smiled. "Must be so great to be free of pain."

Delaney nodded. "Yeah, frankly it's weird. You hear about people who've lost an arm or leg and they can always sense it's still there. When I got into the car this morning, I did all the usual things I do not to aggravate the pain, but it's no longer necessary. I'm going to have to unlearn at lot of bad habits."

The coffees came along and an assortment of brown sugars and honey. Asha drank hers black – dipping a brown sugar lump into the hot coffee and sucking on it.

"Still got the sweet tooth I see." Delaney remarked.

"I'm weaning myself off it, but it's hard."

"I used to eat a ton of chocolate when I was sailing. Now I never even think about it."

"I've got a plan. Want to hear it?"

Delaney reclined into his seat, casually looking around the café. No one seemed to be paying them any attention, but you could never be sure. He leaned forward again. "Ok, let's press play."

Asha lowered her voice. "You want to stop Mrs Jaywaller and her cronies from exploiting the people in pain and the homeless – right?"

"Of course."

"The one common denominator is the Guru."

"Who needs to be taken out of the equation." Delaney remarked.

"So, let's take him out of the equation."

"I don't think we're in the assassination business, Ash. At least not yesterday. Has something changed?"

"I'm not talking about killing anyone. Jeez, Chief."

"Then what?"

"We take him. Hide him. Without him they are nothing but charlatans selling an overpriced pain management scheme that doesn't work. There'd be no waiting list for the booster as there wouldn't be a booster."

"What about St Joes?"

"Not got that far yet. But if we have him, they don't. They'll have nothing."

"You know the Guru lives at Mrs Jaywaller's, right? There's a full-time minder attached to him. He's ex-Jackal."

Asha took out her phone and opened up a video. Delaney scrutinized images of a man getting into his Nissan SUV then driving away from a house. "Who am I looking at?"

"Is that the Guru's minder?" Asha asked.

Delaney nodded, looking more closely. "Yeah. When did you take this?"

"Last night after I left your place. He was leaving Jirdasham Institute. You can just make out the Guru beside him as he closes the driver's door. See?"

Delaney scrutinized the image more closely.

"Nine–forty-five pm. He drives the Guru all the way to Mrs Jaywaller's mansion and drops him at the gate. Doesn't drive in. Some woman, possibly the housekeeper, opens the gate for him and walks him up the drive and around the back. He walked slowly and she had to help him most of the way."

Delaney frowned. "He lives in the pool house at the back."

"Which means and don't hold me to this, but he's living there without a minder."

"Mrs Jaywaller will have security cameras, the whole works, Ash."

"That's fine. Because you are going to make a house call on Mrs Jaywaller. I'll be in the back and as you talk to her, I'll slip out, find the Guru and stash him in the back of the SUV."

Delaney smiled. "As easy as that."

"It's the start of a plan. I didn't say I'd worked out all the details."

"She'll have cameras everywhere. Most likely dogs"

"Park as near to the back as you can and make sure Rufus is on guard. He'd be a good distraction for any dogs."

Rufus stirred momentarily on hearing his name.

"It's ok dog. Sleep easy."

Asha leaned back in her seat and the food miraculously appeared.

"Two smashed avocados. The bread is hot. Be warned."

Delaney looked at his plate and discovered he was hungry. "Look great. Thanks."

The waitress smiled. "And you get an extra coffee for being the first customer to say thank you this morning."

Delaney glanced up at her and grinned. "Well, thank you all over again."

"Don't go over the top honey, once is enough."

Delaney laughed and picked up his fork. He looked over at Asha and she was studying him.

"People instinctively like you, don't they."

Delaney shrugged. "I've no idea. I guess."

"You're slightly weird; did you know that? Polite, clearly a pushover for rude needy girls, got that 'Justice' thing going on that the world should be fair and shit."

Delaney ate, wondering where this was going.

"You walked away from an amazing job in Paris and started this, let's face it, pissant little agency that probably will never make any money and could easily get us both killed and yet you're happy. You just roll with it, like everything is normal. Even the miracle of you not being in pain anymore, it's like it's no big deal."

Delaney swallowed some food. "Now there you are wrong. It's a very big deal. If I'm not shouting praise be and going down on my knees to praise God because of it, it's..." He ate some of the sourdough. "Hmmm, nice."

"It's?" Asha asked.

"In case. In case tomorrow the pain comes back. Mr Abrams, the guy who started us off on this journey. He said that when they took the pain away, he was ecstatic. When it came back – he felt crushed. Almost wanted to kill himself, like his daughter did. So – in the Delaney world, if something is too good to be true, I treat it like that winning lottery ticket that sits on my mantelpiece."

Asha blinked. "You have a winning lottery ticket?"

Delaney beamed. "I have no idea. I'm probably never going to check it. But as long as I don't, it's a winning lottery ticket that will change my life forever."

"I rest my case. You are weird."

"Pissant? Delaney queried. "Does that mean you don't want to be my partner?"

Asha frowned, oops, backtracking required. "No. I wasn't trying to be insulting. I want to be your partner, but I want to understand you better too. We could do good things."

Delaney rubbed his neck. "You're right, it is pissant. We could do better. You're ambitious. That's why I wanted you to be part of it. I'm not in pain now. I can be more focused. You will make us less piss and more ant."

Asha rolled her eyes. She wished she hadn't insulted him now. Stupid of her. He'd been nothing but generous and encouraging.

"This is tasty, Ash. Bread's delicious."

"It's the best place for breakfast in the city, Chief."

"Supposing I take you seriously and we can get the Guru out before we get shot or torn to shreds by the attack dogs. What then?"

"You ever been to Starlight Falls?"

"The fruit farms. It's up in the mountains and there's a great Inn at the pass I remember. Not been in years."

"My Grandmother Bunty might help us out. And don't make that face; that's her real name. She's got a very beautiful farmhouse there. Lived up there for thirty years, I think. Her second husband, Mr B for Benjamin, my step-grandfather, if there's such a thing, is an apple grower."

"The Guru's quite a challenge, Ash. Even for someone called Bunty."

"Yep, but if I know her, she'd love to take care of the Guru. Especially if he cures her bad knee."

"You're good at planning, Ash. Do we have a plan for if it all turns to shit?"

"No. You're the pessimist. I'll leave that to you."

"Thanks, I think."

"We're still the Office of City Oversight, Chief. Make an appointment with Mrs Jaywaller. What have we got to lose?"

Delaney stared at her, pursing his lips. "That's the bit I'm not sure of. Kidnap was never an item on my business plan."

"We're liberating him. That's not against the law,

right?"

Delaney smiled. "Judges are not that great on semantics, I fear."

"You're going to do what?" Zuki protested. "Whose stupid idea is this, Ash? Have you any idea what prison is like for a beautiful girl like you?"

Asha looked at her phone and sighed.

"I'm not going to jail, Zuke. We're liberating the Guru from the wicked witch."

"Listen to yourself girl. This is not a game. That witch has got every mean thug in the city on speed dial. She will hurt you, babe. If he's making you do this …"

"It's my idea, Zuke. He's the one who wasn't keen. I'm just telling you in case something goes wrong."

"If something goes wrong, what am I supposed to do, Ash? My superhero cape is at the dry cleaners. Seriously, girl. Don't do this. Listen to Zuki. Kidnapping is a crime."

"We're going to Bunty's."

"You're taking a bat shit crazy man to that wonderful old woman who is the only good thing in your short life so far."

"She'll mother him. You know what she's like."

Zuki went silent for a moment. "Bring back some Piccolo honey. And make sure you come back. If I have to rescue you, I'll be taking Bunty's side, not yours."

"You won't have to rescue me."

"Famous last words of a wannabe kidnapper. Don't do it girl. But don't forget the honey.

CHAPTER THIRTY-TWO

Money with a view

Delaney rubbed Rufus's head and fastened his seat belt. Maria was right; this loaner was a piece of crap. The stitching on the seats was coming away and yet it only had five thousand miles on the clock. It wasn't going to save his life if he fell off another cliff. He wondered when the new vehicle would be ready and if it would be tough enough.

He drove past his usual beach walk and Rufus looked wistfully at the waves as they disappeared behind them.

"Don't panic. We'll go back there after, Ok? We've got someone to see."

Rufus whined. He was a creature of habit. Bad enough that they were two hours later than normal.

"Stop the whining. You had an hour in the garden digging holes, dog."

Delaney slowed as the road narrowed and he took a left up the slope to the ridge. This was where the truly rich lived. They all had expansive views of the ocean with regular security patrols 24/7. Maybe in his younger days he had aspired to live here, but now he knew it would be too much of a burden. Your neighbors would all be rich people like you, looking to avoid paying taxes, resenting having to pay minimum wages for the host of gardeners, security guards, and hiring the inevitable interior designers so your home was always 'media' ready. Way too much stress.

"Look for a pink palace with palm trees." Asha called out from the back, well hidden under blankets.

"Pink? I guess you've really made it when you can paint a house pink."

Delaney tackled a tight 90-degree bend and there it was, in all its pinkness. He was staring at a three-storey mansion complete with tennis courts, hot and cold swimming pools and a glorious 180-degree view of the ocean. Ronnie had done pretty good for herself for a swimsuit model from the sticks.

He stopped by the wide gates and pressed the

intercom situated at the side.

"Jaywaller residence," a staff voice intoned.

"Delaney. Office of City Oversight to see Mrs Jaywaller."

There was a good minute's delay and he was about to push the button again when the double gates slid open. Rufus perked up when he saw two Alsatians watching from the terrace.

"Sorry pal. You're staying in the car. They're tougher than you and you have enough scars. Your job is to distract them. Understood?"

Rufus whined but didn't protest too much as Delaney drove to the parking spaces just below the mansion. He noted two Mercedes coupés and a brand-new Bentley Convertible. The loaner definitely felt intimidated in this company. He turned around and backed up to the edge of the mansion, some distance from the parked cars.

"Two cameras on the cars. If you go out the rear door you might just be outside their periphery."

Delaney left the passenger side window half open and went around the back to release the door. "Wait till I walk towards the house and don't let the door rise, keep a tight hold of the rope, Ash."

"I know. Go. Don't make them suspicious."

One of the Alsatians watched him carefully as he approached the steps leading towards the front door. He wondered where the other one was.

He was made to wait in the west reception room. It suffered from only having a 60-degree view of the ocean and he judged the hand-stitched rug on the yellowwood floor was likely worth more than his whole house. Mrs Jaywaller certainly knew how to spend money and he wondered if the Mira Schendel abstract on the wall was an original. He looked at his watch and hoped Asha had found the Guru and had enough time to persuade him to come with them.

The Guru was standing on one foot completely naked in the center of the pool house. He was pouring water over his head and chanting. He looked every one of his 88 years and then some. His skin was a pallid brown and he had old deep vicious scars on his legs.

Asha had no time to be coy or embarrassed, but she didn't want to shock him, considering his age and all. Only slowly did he become aware of her standing there, her arms crossed like she was contemplating a work of art. Which he was in a way.

"Child?" He asked, his voice almost falsetto.

"Guru Guranji, I've come to liberate you."

He nodded but made no attempt to cover himself as he gingerly lowered his leg to the ground.

"I know. I have been expecting you, child. Hand me my robe." He pointed towards the wall.

Asha saw it hanging there and below it a plastic shopping bag stuffed with his possessions. She quickly moved forward, grabbed his robe and handed it to him, noticing how long and slim his ancient hands were.

"You know I'm not from Jirdasham right. This is a prison breakout."

The Guru giggled. The notion tickled him as he pulled his robe over his head with astonishing speed. "I know. I spoke to you in your dream. Did you not hear me?"

Asha had no idea what he was talking about.

"Come to me and I will be ready. I told you I'd willing to go to your Grandmas."

Asha was spooked by this. How on earth could he know she intended to stash him there, unless he'd wired up Harry's and that didn't seem likely. She found his leather sandals in the bathroom that frankly was a hygienic nightmare, but she averted her eyes from the basin and toilet.

The Guru took them from her and bowed. "You have come, and I am ready."

"Any other stuff you need. You won't be back here unless it goes badly wrong."

"I have all I have. Time is short, child."

He slipped his surprisingly clean feet into his sandals, his overgrown toenails long neglected. Asha turned to grab his plastic bag when she saw one of the Alsatians blocking the doorway and growling at her.

The Guru waved a hand. "Flip be a gentleman. This is a friend. Be gentle."

Flip's attitude immediately changed, and he settled down, paws outstretched, eyes for the Guru only. "Good boy.

You will see us safely to the car."

Flip seemed dazed and stood up and stepped aside as Asha picked up the shopping bag and walked towards the door.

"My stick." The Guru grabbed his walking stick and patted the dog as he followed Asha out. "Such a good boy."

Someone was working in the laundry room next door but didn't pay any attention as Asha, the Guru and Flip silently walking by. They walked around the pool to the far end of the house.

"A pleasant day," the Guru remarked as Flip walked alongside him.

Asha anxiously looked up towards the mansion windows, but no one was looking out as far as she could see.

"Don't worry, we shall escape. They cannot see what they do not expect."

The Guru reassured her. "I have seen it. Just as sure as I have seen my death. Some things you cannot escape my child."

Mrs Jaywaller entered holding a pair of secateurs and three long stemmed red roses. She barely looked at him as she placed them in a delicate green glass vase on the table.

"Red Naomi roses. They're very fussy. My gardener is trying to grow them, but they don't last. Roses should last, don't you think, Mr Delaney."

"Well, it's been a while since I bought roses, but I guess the ones I pick up from the supermarket aren't so fussy. But then again, those are very red."

"Yes, they are." She turned towards him placing the secateurs on the table. She was definitely more beautiful than he remembered. This version of Ronnie had expensive work done on her teeth and probably the rest of her. She wore a white silk blouse and casual jogging pants that revealed a perfect figure. He wished he'd worn so well.

"I hear you're quite an expert in your field, Mr Delaney." She moved to the window so he could get a good look at her perfect profile. "But then again people aren't so enamored with experts these days, are they."

Delaney surveyed the ocean and saw two small yachts were moored in the bay, one with its sails up ready to move off. Crimson bougainvillea clung to a sidewall and he became aware of one of the Alsatians staring back in at him. It was slightly spooky.

"That Oyster 745 yours in the bay?" He asked.

"Just something to sail to the island. Get me away from the crowds on the weekends. Bobby Jenks yacht actually. You know him?"

Delaney nodded. "Met him a few times – he's quite a sailor."

"He's good company." Mrs Jaywaller stated. "When he's sober."

"We have met before," Delaney told her, "you most likely don't remember."

Mrs Jaywaller seemed surprised. "Not one of my husbands, I hope. I usually recall those, most of the time anyway."

Delaney grinned. She was so far away from the teenager he'd once known; she could be a different person entirely.

"Lindy Overbrook's wedding."

Mrs Jaywaller eyes widened just a touch. Probably surprised that he hadn't brought up the yacht club. "I was visiting Berg City with my wife and you told her to ditch me, that there were plenty of better and richer men to play with than me."

Mrs Jaywaller feigned horror. "I do hope she didn't take my advice. I was probably joking."

"Fortunately for me she did not."

Mrs Jaywaller clearly had no memory of this, but it did establish that they shared similar social status, of sorts. Stanley Overbrook was old money, oil and shipping. It meant something. Delaney had skippered his yacht in the Med for two years running when younger.

"And now we meet again, apparently. You seem to have been asking questions, casting doubts where doubts shouldn't be, Mr Delaney. Healthcare is very sensitive to reputational issues. The Mayor seems to have got a little hot under the collar."

"I was just drawing attention to the Deputy Mayor about the Mayor endorsing something that could backfire, if, heaven forbid, someone died, or had adverse effects."

"Adverse effects? You know that everything I am associated with has excellent credentials. I'm a very careful woman."

"I'm sure you are. I've seen some testimonials to that effect."

"And that's the way it will stay. I am informed by the Mayor that the City Oversight office is about to close, Mr Delaney and I am sure you are aware of the law of defamation."

"Indeed I am. Which is why the City Oversight office carries insurance to that effect. And I am sure you have a team of lawyers ready to pounce, Mrs Jaywaller. But you should know that I represent a client whom has expressed disappointment with a particular service at Jirdasham. Although I understand that this same organization is nominally clearly nothing to do with you, I was concerned as your name kept coming up. Certainly, the Deputy Mayor seems to think you were an investor along with Mr Huissan. For the moment at least the client has asked me to explore an allegation of fraud against Jirdasham."

Mrs Jaywaller offered a tight smile. "As you say, there is no connection between myself and this company you refer to, or to Mr Huissan, who I believe is in jail for fraud. I really hope you are not trying to link me to him. That would be defamatory, Mr Delaney. I can't think why you are here at all."

"Which brings me to something else Mr Huissan is involved with as an investor. You being the other partner. H & J Research. You recently were cited for an award for humanitarian work there, if I'm not mistaken."

Mrs Jaywaller hands clenched, but she continued to smile, though it had narrowed somewhat. "Indeed, it was an honor. Helping to get the homeless off the streets and into rehab is one of my most important goals, Mr Delaney. The Mayor himself asked me to take over this charity out of the goodness of my heart when Mr Huissan was jailed. Surely you would not criticize me for that."

"It's admirable, Mrs Jaywaller. Truly. And the Mayor is so supportive. I wish more people would do something about this terrible social problem. But, just to be clear, you wouldn't know anything about a car that drove me off the Coastal Highway for instance?"

Mrs Jaywaller's composure didn't alter one jot. "We don't run people off roads, Mr Delaney. Don't be absurd."

"I'm glad to hear it. Only I thought it was odd that I

went to Guru Gurajani's book signing and the next thing I know I'm at the bottom of a cliff. Gave me quite a stiff neck. Pity I can't seem to find him to take the pain away."

Mrs Jaywaller titled her head and laughed. "Well I'm sure even if you could find him, you couldn't afford him. He's a very busy man, I hear."

"Yes, I believe so. I went looking for him at his little house on the Hill. Someone there told me he's training people in pain management at Jirdasham."

"The more people who know how to manage pain in our ageing population the better, don't you think? Is that why you are here? You're are looking for the Guru?"

Delaney shook his head. "No, I know I can't afford Jirdasham prices. My client of course could, but sadly the pain came back quite quickly. He'd like to find a company where the pain treatment lasts longer than a couple of weeks."

"The Holy Grail, Mr Delaney. You seek the Holy Grail."

Delaney nodded his head. "So, it seems."

The dogs began barking outside. Delaney anxiously glanced towards the window. "I think perhaps your dogs have discovered mine."

"I do hope he's secure in your car, Mr Delaney. Dan and Flip are quite possessive over the grounds."

Mrs Jaywaller turned a little; clearly signally this meeting was over. "If you do find any serious issues of malfeasance in your remaining time with the City, do come to me first. My door is open, as you can see. I do not want to read in the papers or online that someone is unhappy when it is something someone could attend to professionally. You realize that I refer to my charity work, Mr Delaney. Nothing must get in the way of helping the homeless get off our streets."

Delaney understood his audience was over.

"Perhaps," she added as she moved towards the double doors, "if your client could be persuaded to give Jirdasham another chance, I sure there must be aftercare. A company like that has a reputation to look after."

"I have read the contract. I am pretty sure aftercare was not as visible as it might be, perhaps it was an 'afterthought.'"

A maid came to show Delaney to the front door.

Delaney noted a huge purple Iris standing in a tall Lalique vase. Nothing but the best here.

Rufus was trying to out stare the Alsatian sitting by his car but losing the battle. The other Alsatian was pacing up and down a nearby low wall in a state of confusion.

"Anyone in this vehicle?" Delaney asked as he climbed in, wondering if he had to stall for time.

"Start the engine and get us the fuck out of here," Asha growled.

Delaney started up. Rufus looked agitated. The seats were wet. Delaney notice a sprinkler has been placed close to the vehicle. Wet seat, upset dog, all part of the service sir – you're welcome.

"Dog's give any trouble?" Delaney asked as he made his way down to the gate. The gate opened painfully slow.

"Rufus got them a bit excited. Gave us time to get in the car unnoticed. Please get us on the road, Delaney. The Guru's got gas problems."

Delaney opened more windows and smiled.

"Namaste, Guru."

"Namaste." He returned guiltily from under the blankets.

CHAPTER THIRTY-THREE

Kidnapped

Delaney stopped briefly in Anchor Cove to let Rufus out for a while.

"You guys can come up for air."

"Jeez, at last," Asha exclaimed, flinging off the blankets and getting the hell out of the vehicle. "My God Guru, what did you eat last night?"

The Guru giggled as he sat up in the backseat and looked around him. "Lentils and beans."

"Lentils and beans?" Asha protested. "You are a hazard to the environment."

"Eat healthy and shit often. It is the way of Jirdasham."

Rufus dashed off towards the ocean barking at seagulls.

Delaney was watching Asha with an amused look on his face. "Well done Ash. You make 'kidnapper of the year'."

"Next time you do it. My heart was racing the entire time. First, he was stark naked and chanting with the door wide open, then he tells me he was expecting me. Already packed his bag and everything."

The Guru climbed out of the car and surveyed the glistening ocean. "Beautiful. Good day to you, Mr Delaney."

"Good day to you, Guru."

"Has your anger left you?" The Guru enquired.

Delaney looked away at the ocean waves. "It varies from hour to hour. I guess they'll be just about discovering you've gone about now." He turned towards Asha. "You scrubbed all the computers in our office?"

"Like we were never there," she reassured him. "Even remembered to take the biscuits."

Delaney smiled. "Mrs Jaywaller won't let this rest. The Guru is very valuable to her."

"For now, yes." The Guru remarked. "They believe

they have someone new. Someone quite young they can put to work." He squatted down to feel the sand through his fingers.

"One of your disciples?" Asha asked.

"No, they are nothing. This is a boy from Nepal. Mrs Jaywaller is flying him in and expects me to train him in the way of Jirdasham."

"He has the same gifts to remove pain?"

"His gift is different to mine. Untested. They do not even know if it is genuine. Village gossip in Nepal might have exaggerated his abilities. I have not been able to see him in my visions. His family, of course, worships him and believes they will grow rich, but I do not think it will end well. For him or for her."

"Well I'm not kidnapping the next one. Although technically he would at least be a kid." Asha declared.

Delaney rolled his eyes. "This was a one-time emergency. You said he knew you were coming?"

"That is what he said."

Delaney glanced at the Guru who was dancing in a circle on the sand, his wild white hair blowing in the breeze. "All I have is hindsight. Must be nice to know your mistakes before you commit them."

Asha shook her head. "If we did, we'd probably be paralyzed by inaction. I've spent half my life trying to decide which was the right course, which was the right boyfriend or right job. I don't think I made the right decision in any of them."

"Especially this job, eh?" Delaney told her, grabbing her hand and squeezing it. "Good job, Ash. Well done. Come on. We need to get that wild man back in the car."

Asha let go of his hand, then grabbed it again and pressed it against her heart. It was still beating fast. "I swear I thought I was going to have a heart attack when the dog was staring at us. It was drooling."

Delaney pulled her towards him and hugged her, kissing the top of her head.

"You didn't have to stand watching a woman who wanted to slit my throat there and then. I've never seen so much repressed anger in anyone ever."

Asha glanced up and darted in, gave him a little kiss on

the lips. "For luck."

Delaney grinned and reluctantly let her go. "We're going to need it, Ash. She will be so pissed when she discovers he's gone."

Rufus returned and laid a soggy stick at the Guru's feet. He bent down to pick it up, then suddenly paused to stroke his head. "This is the dog who lives for the girl. What was her name?"

"Maria." Delaney told him.

"Ah yes, Maria. She is so lucky; this dog guards her in her dreams every night. We should all have such a devoted friend."

Delaney took the stick and threw it into the ocean. Rufus ran off and dashed into the waves.

"Oh great, now we will have wet dog smells as well." Asha moaned.

Delaney laughed. "You have a very sensitive nose, Ash. You'll get used to it. Be thankful I don't feed him lentils and beans!"

Asha rolled her eyes. "God we are like the most useless kidnappers in the world, Chief."

Delaney tilted his head towards her. "You did good. No idea what the fuck we do next, but what the hell, hey. We're fighting evil."

Asha nodded and nudged him, laughing. "Yes, we fucking well are.

Her phone beeped. "Maria will be getting out of school about now." She remembered.

Delaney broke free and signaled to Rufus to come back. "I told her to go to the ice cream parlor on Main."

"Italian Ice Cream?" The Guru queried. "Pistachio is my favorite."

Delaney grinned as Rufus ran towards them. "Well I guess we all deserve an ice cream. Rufie, shake that water off. Ash, pass me the towel, I don't want him giving us a shower."

Maria and Rufus were squashed in with the Guru on the backseat; Maria was sleeping, slumped in the corner. Asha was in front as they headed towards the mountains. Delaney was checking the fuel gauge; he didn't want to run out of diesel in the forest.

"Turn off your phone, Ash. No need to let them know

where we're headed. From now on, we don't use our phones at all. Not even in an emergency."

"What about the cameras at Jaywaller's house," Asha reminded him.

"I'm hoping they won't automatically think I took him. It might give us breathing space. The camera will show me walking back to the car and driving off. If you guys were subtle, you would have crawled in the back without the camera picking you up. Of course, they could assume the Guru snuck in the back of my car."

"Well you'll be easy to track. They've got the cops on speed dial and they know your plate number and the make of SUV. How many of these shitcans are on our roads?"

"Probably more than we think. We should switch plates like they do in the movies. Let's assume that they think the Guru escaped of his own volition. They'll see from the camera I had nothing to do with it."

"You're quite the optimist, Delaney. And we definitely should switch plates, or switch cars. God, we didn't plan this at all did we." Asha turned her head to talk to the Guru who was staring intently at the passing scenery. "Why didn't you escape before, Guru?"

The Guru cocked his head to one side and stroked one of Rufus's ears. "A man cannot escape if he has nowhere to hide."

Delaney chewed on that. "You could have walked out if you had wanted to."

"I thought about it. But every time I foresaw them dragging me back."

"But this time it's different" Asha asked. "What about the video she has of you that worries you so much. You think she will use it?"

The Guru shrugged. "Her name was Mimi Leanne."

"Mimi Leanne, the opera singer?" Delaney asked, surprised. "I read she died in the gym. On an exercise bike. Opera singers have weak hearts I guess."

"She died on my treatment table. Mimi, I suspect never went to a gym in her whole life. Her pain was great. She came to me for relief. She could not sing anymore without pain and it was destroying her life. I had not understood that her greater wish was to die, not to be rid of her pain."

Asha frowned. "You couldn't tell the difference?"

The Guru sighed. He looked across at Maria sleeping. "This girl wanted to be rid of her pain so she could run again, to be the person she once was. Maria's signal was quite clear. Mimi told me that she wanted to be rid of the pain forever. What she meant, but could not say, was that she wanted to be rid of living forever." He took a deep breath, shuddering slightly with the memory

"Unfortunately, as I took her pain she relaxed, I didn't see her dive in so deep and close the door behind her until too late. I had granted her wish. I could not save her."

Asha stared at him, he seemed be genuinely upset. "Mrs Jaywaller taped this?"

"She tapes every session, everything I do."

Delaney briefly turned to him. "No one could possibly convict you, Guru." He turned back to the road. "You weren't doing surgery. There would be no visual evidence of anything except you laying on hands and singing to her, assuming that's what you were doing."

"I was doing surgery of her mind. It is spiritual intervention. I only sensed danger when I saw the doors were closing on me and she was trying to take me with her. It is hard to explain, but I too could have died. I could not work for a month after that. To enter someone's mind and discover they were so focused on killing themselves is not a pleasant experience.

"I'm confused. All those times when you were helping people to die in the hospices, that should have taught you something, right?" Delaney asked.

The Guru shook his head. "They all wanted to be rid of pain, Mr Delaney. Their lives had been robbed. They felt cheated. But I cannot cure cancer or a faulty heart. I can only take away the pain to ease their end. I gave them a shock, it's true, but I also opened the door to a quick passing.

"It was more of a celebration of a life. Their loved ones were there to hold their hands. A few minutes that's all it takes. It was a different situation; they had a quite another frame of mind. You are their ally in escaping the pain. Their families are supportive, grateful I am taking away their suffering. I felt no shame. We would then pray for forgiveness. Those people deserved to go by their own choice and not linger. You must ask the doctors why they let them continue when there's no hope.

"Mimi Leanne was angry. She felt cheated. She had lung disease. They said it was her heart, but I know it was her lungs. She told me that they were turning into glass and would shatter into a thousand pieces."

"I think no one would seriously prosecute you for her death, Guru," Delaney told him. "Mrs Jaywaller has no hold on you and if she did release the tape, her whole business would go down with it. You are her business and now you are not."

Maria stirred. "Hey, where are we?"

"Just starting our climb, M."

"How long are we going to the mountains for? I've never been."

"Two nights. A bit longer for the Guru here."

"Will there be snow?"

"Snow?" Asha protested. "It's spring. No more snow please. The blossom is on its way."

"You'll be able to take Rufus for walks in the forest. So many sticks, so little time." Delaney said.

Maria stretched and smiled. "I love forests."

Asha examined her hands a moment, deep in thought. "We need a plan."

"That we do. But first I'm hoping for a decent supper at the Inn. I'm hungry."

"Bet they don't do vegan," Maria complained.

"I bet they're making you a five-bean stew as we speak."

"Five-bean stew?" The Guru queried, his eyes lighting up.

"Please don't let the Guru have it, he'll explode," Asha said. "Think of my poor Grandma."

Delaney remembered something. "Shit I know I said turn off the phones, but we need to warn the Guru's sister. They'll go knocking on her door tonight."

"Jasmina knows." The Guru told them quietly. "I told her to leave last night. She will go to our cousins house in Marrow."

"How?" Delaney began. "When?"

"As I told the child. I knew you were coming. Everything that happens now is foretold."

Mrs Jaywaller stood arms folded staring at the computer screen. The Minder was rewinding and going forward again.

"He parked just inside camera range, but then again, there is only parking for three cars, so I guess he didn't want to block our vehicles." The Minder said. "He walks straight to his car. The dogs are watching him. There's nothing here indicating he's done anything unusual. He drove out. The Guru isn't with him. He couldn't know the Guru was even here, Ma'am. You said yourself he was fishing for information on him."

Mrs Jaywaller looked away, angry at the situation. "You swear you brought the Guru home last night, Maxim?"

"Absolutely. He was exhausted. Nancy took him back to the pool house. I saw her walking him. She says she fed him, and he went to bed by ten-thirty."

"And no one saw him leave. What about the girl doing the laundry this morning?"

"She saw one of the dogs go into his room this morning and he was chanting after his breakfast as usual. He was still here when Delaney arrived."

Mrs Jaywaller frowned. "The dogs were barking madly when Delaney was here."

"Nancy said they were barking at the dog in his car. The gardener placed the sprinkler by the car to deter them. I asked him if he'd seen the Guru, but he hadn't. He was working by the tennis courts today so he would have seen him if he'd gone by. The Guru could have escaped by the storm gully. I know he's old but if he was smart, he could have crawled out under the wire fence."

"You think? Well I don't believe a man of 88 could squeeze under that fence. Did you look?"

"The dogs can get under. It's possible."

"Didn't I say it should have razor wire there?"

"It's on order apparently."

Mrs Jaywaller kicked a chair out of the way. "So, we let our greatest asset just shimmy out of here and we have absolutely no idea where he might be. Or who will train the child when he comes."

The Minder picked up the chair and set it right.

"How many treatments was he scheduled for today, Maxim?" She asked.

The Minder checked the on-screen diary. "Four. Two

tonight."

"Cancel them. When is the boy due?"

"Next week, we hope. There's still a hold up on his visa. You can't put him to work if he's untrained."

"Nonsense, Rafael can do it. He knows all the Guru's tricks."

The Minder made no comment. He didn't have quite the same faith in Rafael.

Mrs Jaywaller let out a frustrated scream of anger and moved towards the windows. "Find him, Maxim. Find the Guru. He can't have gone far. If need be put pressure on his sister. He seems to place a great value on her. Find him and chain him up with the dogs. Let him know who is in charge here."

CHAPTER THIRTY-FOUR

Ciderbee

They were driving up narrow lanes boarded by huge ghostly pine trees, the headlights making everything seem spooky. Maria was puzzled and a little bit afraid of where they were going.

"It is a forest? These trees are so huge."

Asha seemed excited. "Some of them are almost two hundred years old. There are gum trees even older going back four centuries. I used to go exploring up here in summer on Jowett, my pony."

Delaney glanced at her for a second not wanting to take his eyes off the road or run into a roaming deer or antelope, a big risk on these forest roads. "I didn't figure you for a pony girl."

Asha wrinkled her nose. "It wasn't exactly 'my' pony. Grandma was still riding then, she liked to inspect the fruit trees by horseback. She let me ride her when I came up for the summers. Zuki came with me. God she was the world greatest tomboy, neither one of us wanted to grow up. We secretly planned a life here in the forest foraging for mushrooms and growing our own food."

Maria seemed excited by the idea. "That's so cool."

"It was cool until the shootings started. Four farmers and their families shot dead over two years. Some ex-farmhands who wanted to grab the land for themselves I suppose. They got two of them but after that my father wouldn't let me come up here in summer. Zuki went crazy. She wanted to go hunt them on her own. She's pretty good with a bow and arrow."

Maria sighed. "I hate guns."

"There's always someone who wants to destroy things," Delaney remarked. "We're coming up to a crossroads." He slowed.

"Go left. See the sign, CiderBee Farm."

The Guru was showing signs of life. He'd fallen asleep

immediately after eating and getting back in the car. "Cider? CiderBee?"

Asha grinned. "That's Grandma. She married an apple farmer, but she made the farm into a cider producer. The best. It's a thousand acres but they buy in apples from all over and even export cider now."

"You didn't want to get involved? Sounds like a good career move to me, Ash. I only drink CiderBee when I buy cider."

"Yeah. Bunty still wants me help her run things and take it over one day, but I don't know..."

"And live here with all these amazing trees," Maria exclaimed. "It would be like living in a fairytale."

"And a bit lonely without a partner," Asha pointed out. "And don't tell me how wonderful all the young farmers are around here. They don't exactly live in this century. Any man around here would want me barefoot and pregnant for the next ten years making him pies all day round. Hell, I hardly even drink cider. It makes me bloat."

The Guru tugged on Asha's arm and whispered. "Your future isn't here. Not yet. Perhaps one day."

Asha patted his hand. "I know. I've got this great career as a kidnapper going right now. Wondering where it will end."

"I like cider." Maria chipped in.

"Uh oh. Busted." Delaney said. "Not good at keeping secrets are we, M."

"Oops."

Asha laughed. "Don't worry. Secret's safe with me. Grandma Bunty will be pleased though."

Delaney crested a hill and immediately slowed as the headlights shone on an enormous old ranch house perched on an elevated rock before them. "Wow."

Asha drank it all in. "Jeez, it always gets me. This place good enough for you, Guru?"

The Guru leaned forward to get a better view, then giggled happily. "Your fairytale castle, Maria. Let's hope there's no wicked witch."

Maria giggled, but there was a definitely streak of worry in her laughter.

"It looks old," Delaney remarked as he approached the

driveway. "The ornate towers at either end look pretty impressive."

"18th Century. They meant to be here a long time. Original owner was French, and he planted it out scientifically. The original apple trees have long gone but Bunty and Mr B follow the same principles."

Delaney smiled. "You like this place."

Asha nodded. "I do. I love it."

"You told her we ate right? She's not going to make us sit down and eat at midnight or something."

"She knows. But wait until you see breakfast. Mr B goes out to check on the livestock at dawn and talk to the farmhands, so he's pretty hungry by eight when breakfast is served. You won't be able to move after."

Grandma Bunty made them all welcome. Her husband had gone to bed. She insisted they had tea and cake before retiring and the Guru cut himself an enormous slice of carrot cake, much to Bunty's pleasure. "You'll fit in here, Guru. Mr B likes a man with a healthy appetite."

The Guru beamed at the stout grey-haired woman with the bandaged knee.

"Just don't let him have too many beans," Asha warned her grandmother.

The Guru giggled and set Maria off laughing.

Delaney was staring at the huge kitchen that aside from a new American-Range stove was pretty much unchanged from the 18th Century. The twelve-seater bleached oak kitchen table was beautiful as well as practical. Everything had a purpose and you could see that she cherished all the old tools and plates.

"This place is like an old movie," Maria remarked, looking at huge dinner plates on the plate rack above her. She stared a long copper object strung up over the fireplace big enough to roast an ox; the dying log embers still glowed.

"They made a TV show here about five years ago about how people used to live two hundred years ago."

"God, I remember that." Asha said. "Zuki was so upset we weren't in it."

"I was in period costume an' everything. Mr B looked too modern without a beard, so they stuck one on him." Bunty told them laughing. "Other than his face, they said they didn't have to change a thing. We'll do a tour tomorrow. Just so you know, Mr Guru, everyone who stays here is expected to help out. I hope that doesn't offend your religion."

The Guru burped and smiled. "Madam, I have no religion except that one must eat well and spread happiness. Your cake was delicious. I will do anything you ask."

Bunty was curious about his name. "Are you anything to do with Guru Guranji? You do look so like the picture on my tea caddy."

The Guru beamed. "Once tea was my life." He pointed to the green teapot on the table. "This was my Rooibos and Darjeeling blend you served."

Bunty clapped. "Oh, how wonderful, Asha. You brought me the best tea blender in the world. You are so welcome, Mr Guru. My husband swears by them. Cures his bad moods and helps him sleep, we use them for everything."

Asha shook her head, remembering how she was once forced to drink a vile bitter green tea to cure her swearing one summer. She decided not to bring that up.

As Asha prepared to go to the bedroom she would share with Maria, she took the Guru to one side. "All I ask is that you never call or write to anyone in the city. No one must know you are here and please, please, please fix Bunty's knee so she can walk properly again."

The Guru took her hand. "You brought me to safety. Of course, I will help her. And Asha," he tapped her heart. "Don't neglect the one under your nose. He will not say it, but he will be the one you are looking for."

Asha blushed and withdrew her hand. She knew exactly what he meant. "I'm in no rush, Guru."

"He is healing, and he is ready." The Guru assured her. "Please inform your grandmother that I chant in the morning."

"Please not before sunrise. Mr B won't appreciate that at all."

The Guru put his hands together and bowed. "Namaste."

"Namaste," Asha replied with a sinking feeling.

CHAPTER THIRTY-FIVE

Break & Entry

The Minder's Nissan Murano pulled up outside the Guru's sister house at a few minutes to eleven pm. He hated this area. If he had his way, he'd bulldoze the whole street and get rid of everyone in it.

Sitting beside him was Neville, all six foot four of him, squashed into the passenger seat. He'd recruited the bald heavy who wore a black tracksuit and carried a crowbar. He seemed impatient to hurt someone.

They tried knocking on the door and no one came. The Minder knocked louder then turned to the heavy. "Fucking open it."

Word of the Minder's arrival had spread though the street. Eyes were on them from behind shutters. A kid zipped by on his bike and took a photo of them trying to force Jasmina's door.

The Minder swore. The last thing he needed was witnesses. "Hurry the fuck up, man. Step aside." He stepped back one pace then let loose a flying kick on the old oak door. It burst open and they swiftly moved inside.

It was obvious in minutes that the Guru's sister was gone, along with her entourage. The Minder flitted between rooms with increasing frustration. Everything looked normal but she was definitely gone. The kitchen was tidy and there was nothing to wash in the sink. They weren't coming back any time soon.

"Old witch has gone."

The Minder stood in the hallway wondering what to do next or where to go.

"Fuck it. I'm calling it a night. No way we're going to find him."

They stepped outside the house onto the porch and came face to face with around seventeen neighbors. All of them were carrying a weapon.

The smallest guy with a Mario moustache that he

probably thought was cool began talking.

"You going to fix that door, man?"

The Minder blinked. He hadn't expected this.

"The door was open. This is nothing to do with you my friend."

The small guy laughed. "I'm not your friend, man. Everything in this street is to do with me. You like that car of yours?"

He pointed to the Minder's car.

"You leave my car alone. I told you, we don't want trouble."

"Too late for that, man. You need to be more careful about whose doors you kick in. My friend Germaine has to go get his tools now and repair it. Germaine wanted to go to bed but you disturbed his sleep. He doesn't much care for that, do you, Germaine."

Germaine cocked his head to one side and tapped the club in his hands.

The Minder's Qashqai started up and drove off wheels spinning. Some kid gave the Minder the finger from the passenger seat as it passed by.

"Now you can pay Germaine here to fix the door." The small man said.

"Fuck off," Neville told him and produced a nasty looking nine-inch blade. "You take one step and ..."

He didn't finish. A knife sailed across heads and sank into his chest and he looked down in total astonishment, unable to believe it.

The small man gave a signal and the rest of them piled in, clubs swinging. As the first blow landed across the Minder's head, he cursed the fucking Guru and the bitch who'd sent him here.

CHAPTER THIRTY-SIX

Bunty's Knee

Bunty climbed the stairs with effort. The stairs were her nemesis. One day soon, she knew she'd have to sleep downstairs and put in an extra bathroom. She could hear the Guru chanting but didn't want him or any of the others to miss breakfast. She took a deep breath at the top of the stairs and shuffled along to the Guru's bedroom door. It was open so she didn't knock.

She was already red in the face from climbing stairs, but it deepened to crimson as she came face to face with an old naked man standing on one leg chanting to the heavens.

"Oh my." She muttered. "Oh my."

The Guru slowly became aware of her standing there, blinking, not quite able to say anything appropriate. He lowered his leg and stopped mid-chant. He pointed to his robe on the bed and with some relief Bunty went to fetch it and brought it to him, diplomatically averting her eyes from his person.

"That knee of yours," the Guru remarked, as he slipped the tunic over his head and pulled it down with remarkable agility. "I can feel the heat and anger inside it."

Bunty looked down, relieved that he was dressed. "I fell off my horse. Landed on a tree stump. You always think that an injury will heal when you're young but ..."

The Guru tied his robe and flicked his hair out of the way. "The body never tires of healing. Remember that. As long as you want to live, it will strive to renew and repair." He kneeled down in front of Bunty and she thought he was going to pray. To her surprise he placed his hands upon both knees. She had not yet pulled on the tight bandage she was supposed to wear every day to mitigate the pain.

She felt extremely awkward and embarrassed; but found herself transfixed. She realized that perhaps she needed to discuss some ground rules for his stay here and talk to him about his nakedness, but she couldn't quite formulate the necessary words.

    The Guru sang softly for a while and as he did so she could feel her damaged knee growing extraordinarily hot. She winced, a small desperate whimper escaped her throat and she wanted to tell him to stop, but for some reason she couldn't. It felt as if he was burning the pain out of her knee.

    Suddenly he stopped singing and sprang up, giggling like a fool, his eyes shining.

    "Breakfast. I am so looking forward to breakfast. I can smell bread baking. The scent of paradise, is it not?"

    Bunty gave him a tight little smile and turned. Then discovered that her bad leg turned as well – the one that always seemed as if it was made of lead. Suddenly it was as light as a feather and she could feel her blood circulating. Her heart was racing, the incessant throbbing on her knee was gone, had literally melted away.

    "Did you…?" She asked; but couldn't quite say it.

    The Guru smiled. "A man must pay for his breakfast, no?"

    Bunty nodded; she had already mentioned everyone must do their bit at the farm. She abruptly burst into tears. "A lifetime of breakfasts," she mumbled through tears. "Oh, my goodness, my knee. My knee. It moved, Mr Guru."

    The Guru put his hands together and bowed. "Of course. It is no longer made of glass. It was frozen. Be gentle. Let it begin to work and walk a little more each day to build up the muscle and tendons around it. They will not be used to working. Do that and you will be able to walk forever."

    Bunty didn't know what came over her, but she hugged the Guru, then hurriedly stepped back embarrassed all over again. She took a deep breath and became Bunty again. "I think after breakfast," she sniffed, "I will introduce you to the shower."

Maria was brushing her teeth after breakfast when the Guru appeared in the bathroom doorway draped in clean towels and wearing only his grey baggy underwear. Maria spat out the paste and wiped her mouth. "I won't be a minute."

    The Guru wanted to ask her something and was finding it difficult to find the words. "Can you cut nails?"

    Maria looked at his feet and his blackened overgrown

nails and winced. She wanted to bolt, not cut nails.

The Guru held up his hand and she saw a hanging nail. "I can't hold scissors anymore," he told her meekly.

Maria breathed a sigh of relief. A hangnail she could deal with. She immediately began to look for scissors and found them in the medicine cabinet.

"I hate hangnails. You need to get your toenails cut, Guru. They look scary."

He giggled and sighed. "You're a kind girl. I see good things for you."

"You said you knew Asha was coming for you. How? You couldn't know that? Can you tell the future?"

Maria took his hand and began to cut the nail. It was tough going.

The Guru shook his head. "I only know my own future. I knew someone was coming to free me, not who. I know how I die in the chapel and by who's hand, but not when or why. It is not something I can explain."

"If you know you'll die in this chapel, can't you just not ever go there?"

"Fate doesn't work like that. I knew I'd die there a long time ago, when visions were clearer to me. It's a place of peace and tranquility and I was praying for someone's soul when suddenly I saw my death so vividly. I have lived with that knowledge for perhaps twenty years now. I always remember it as the sun was shining through the stained-glass window of Christ on a donkey. It was like a message from God. You have this long and no more to do what you have to do."

"And if you didn't go there?"

"Fate would find me, my child. It always knows where you are."

"So, you don't know my future?"

The Guru smiled. "I know only you chose your future. The first choice was a bad one. Remember the cliff? Making decisions in a moment of despair is never a good thing. Choosing to leave your mother and return to Mr Delaney was the right choice. So, in the end, we make our own futures. Like cats."

"Cats?"

The Guru giggled as Maria finally cut the nail off and then trimmed a jagged bit on another finger. "Cats choose their owners. You are like the cat who wanders up the street and finds a better home. So, I can see your future because you have decided to have one and with whom. You will be surprised what you become and how successful. I will say no more. Except, thank you and perhaps you will show me how to turn on the shower."

Maria laughed as she washed her hands, wondering if this was the first time he'd ever used one. She turned on the shower, checked the temperature and placed the shampoo into his hands. "Use only a capful once your hair is wet. Understand?"

The Guru nodded, looking uncertainly at the steam rising from the shower cubicle. Maria headed for the door.

"Don't forget to take your underwear off." She called out, before running down the stairs.

Delaney was standing by the reservoir with Rufus watching tiny swallows flit in, scoop up the water on the wing and fly out, all in the blink of an eye. He turned at the sound of horses and there was Asha and Maria astride the ponies. Maria looked nervous and excited to be learning to ride.

"How does it feel up there, M? Please don't start asking for a pony. Rufus is all I can afford to feed alongside you."

Maria shook her head. "I'm never going back. I love it here."

"I believe it gets pretty chilly in winter. You seen the size of the fireplace in the kitchen? They have to burn whole trees to get warm."

"I love snow," Maria told him defiantly. "I bet Rufus does too."

"Rufus stays with me, M. You can sleep with the ponies to get warm."

Asha laughed. "I told you, young girls are expensive liability, Delaney."

She urged her pony on and pulled Maria behind her. "See you later, Chief."

Delaney sighed and threw a stick for Rufus. "Come on, dog. We're heading down to the farmhouse."

Asha's step-grandpa Mr B was sitting on the stoop drinking coffee when he arrived and asked Delaney to join him. They sat like good old boys on a battered sofa looking out across rows of apple trees in blossom.

"I've got no idea what's going on, or why you brought us the Guru to hide, but I've got to say thank you for giving Bunty a second chance. She's like a kitten this morning, singing praises for everything and she's so happy Asha is here. I guess you don't know this, but two years ago we were in despair about our Asha. She was so unhappy at College. She was determined to get on the honor roll and pushed herself too hard. I begged her to come here and find some peace, we worried she would do something stupid; she was losing weight again. But I look at her now and whatever you've done, she's happy. That means a lot to us. Would mean even more if she'd come and work here, learn the business, but I suppose there's plenty of time for that. After all she'll inherit it all one day."

Delaney drank his coffee and nodded. He had no idea about all this. He'd thought she was a computer geek when he'd met her and so full of confidence, he couldn't imagine her having any doubts about anything at all. "She's pretty special. She mention that we're full time kidnappers now?"

Mr B grinned. "The guy you kidnapped seems pretty happy about it."

"We haven't really planned what to do next actually."

"Usually there's a ransom involved," Mr B suggested.

"That's the problem. We're not handing him back. I've no idea what to do with him really. I just want him to stay hidden. You need to remind Bunty not to tell anyone about her miracle recovery. At least not about the Guru. There will be some very bad people looking for him. It's a secret he's here."

Mr B drank his coffee in silence a moment, contemplating that piece of information.

"You know there's a monastery about ten miles from here."

"You're kidding. They still exist?"

"They sell us their overstock, but they make the best Apple brandy you'll ever taste. About 40% proof. They distil it around five or six times, it's quite refined. A lot of it goes to Germany. I know they're always on the lookout for lost souls of the spiritual kind who want to become brothers. There are nuns there too. About thirty-five of them altogether I reckon."

Delaney put a foot out to rub Rufus who was sprawled

out on the stoop. "Not sure the Guru is well up on making alcohol, but they seem like his kind of people. You think we could persuade him to pretend to be someone else. Not the Guru? Or least get them to keep him their secret?"

Mr B finished his coffee. "Maybe we could take him up there tomorrow to see if they like him or vice versa. Not that I'm trying to get rid of him, Bunty's taken to him and she even got him in the shower this morning. I think he's quite a stranger to old fashioned soap and water."

Delaney laughed. "Yeah. I think so." He raised his coffee cup and finished it off. "Monastery sounds pretty good to me. As long as they feed him rice and beans, he'll be happy."

"You been out here before?" Mr B asked him suddenly.

"Once came hiking when I was a teenager. This place reminds me of an area I went to in Switzerland. A lot of apples grown there. Thurgau."

"Well this whole mountain area produces more than Switzerland, and our yield is a lot better, on par with Brazil, I think. People probably think growing apples is simply a matter of planting trees and waiting for the apples to appear. You've got pests, diseases, people demand organic but have no idea how hard it is to keep the trees healthy without chemicals. I patrol regularly looking for black spot or apple scab, fruit moth. My boys are on constant alert for problems. Then there's storage, chilling and don't even get me started on issues in making cider and changing consumer tastes. The trees are only at their best for around twenty years, so you have to start all over again and then there's frost. A late frost decimated the Swiss crop back in '19 for instance. When Covid lockdowns started we couldn't get our cider to market and with hotel and restaurant trades shut we almost ran out of storage. Other farmers around here let their crop rot on the trees, it wasn't worth the cost of picking 'em."

Mr B suddenly sighed. "Sorry, I went off on one didn't I. Conversation best left for a fellow orchard grower."

Delaney nodded. "I promise I will have a lot more respect the next apple I buy, Mr B."

An hour later Delaney was wondering if he could borrow the family computer when Mr B came running out of his warehouse looking very anxious.

"Mr Delaney my driver hasn't reported for work. I'm in a bit of a bind. I've got a special delivery for the Empiron Resort. There's a conference and ..."

"Is it loaded up?" Delaney asked.

"It is, but it's a lot of cases. They're heavy."

Delaney smiled. "I'll do it, Ben. A few days ago, it might have been impossible, but right now, thanks to the Guru I feel I can do anything."

Mr B looked relieved. "Excellent. Have you driven a delivery van before?"

"Drove a truck right across the States once to fetch a new rudder and sails. It was a lot cheaper than airfreight."

Mr B bid him follow. "Well it's only fifty miles to the coast, but the roads are treacherous. Lost a driver and van once. They always drive too fast. Try to avoid the potholes. Potholes are the enemy of cider."

Delaney followed, a little surprised at the size of the truck. A Ford Transit V6 Cargo van with a huge CiderBee sign on both sides faced him. It was fully loaded.

"There's a delivery entrance off Tulip Street at the side of the resort. Make sure you get the paperwork signed and dated and keep the pink copy. You've got sixty-five cases to deliver. Sorry."

"Is that a good order?"

"It's my premium vintage. So yeah. It's my best stuff. They have five bars and two restaurants. You can bet they make their teeth meet on the prices they charge."

"Then I'll take good care of it."

"I don't know how to thank you. I'd deliver it myself, but I'm not so good on the roads these days."

Delaney swung up into the seat and grinned. "No problem at all. Let Asha know where I've gone, Mr B."

Mr B watched him go, wincing as the truck wallowed in the potholes he'd been meaning to fill in once the dry summer weather came along.

Delaney figured that the brakes had seen better days, it made him cautious, but the van felt stable and as long as he didn't meet anyone coming the other way on the narrow roads across country, he was confident he'd get there and back in one piece.

It gave him time to think. He wasn't especially sure what the hell he was doing. Or what he should do next. He could also appreciate that he had intense feelings for Asha; she was certainly full of surprises. She seemed to be sending signals; but he wasn't sure he should do anything about it. He was strongly aware that now he was free of pain he was feeling surprisingly confident he could have a relationship without embarrassing himself with all those muscle cramps. Of course, she might reject him anyway, she'd seen him at his worst, be hard to forget all that. She would be always wondering whether the pain would return to haunt him again. Then he had to think about starting up a new agency. Asha would be an asset; but would there be enough business for the two of them? He sighed and wondered what Denise would make of all this. He missed her guidance most of all.

The Empiron Hotel was a magnificent edifice and new. Someone had spent a great deal of money on the resort. He had no memory of it, so it had to be recently built. The whole building was painted in a classic rustic burned red, dramatic against the wide blue sky. The gardens were laid out in a Venetian style, replete with canals and arched bridges. He noted the waterways were connected to the tidal lagoon that shimmered in the sunlight beyond the road. There was a ton of security, but it made it a great location for a conference center.

    He eventually found Tulip Street and after a lot of sweat managed to unload the heavy cases and even remembered to get it signed for. Once done, he took the risk of powering up his phone. He asked the guys at the delivery desk for the password and logged onto the hotel wi-fi. A great many messages poured in – several from the Mayor. Seems he had finally woken up to the fact that this was officially the last day for the Office of Oversight.

    He wasn't sure why he came to this decision at this time and once decided he felt a little guilty that he hadn't called before, but now was the time.

    The news editor of The Star answered on the third ring.

    "Newsdesk. Jonas Everard."

    "Delaney making a very anonymous call here."

    "David Delaney? Shit I heard you were dead."

    "You need more accurate news gatherers, Jonas. You sunk any yachts lately?"

"Ha. One time, Delaney. You sunk way more if I recall."

"History recalls the winners, Jonas, not the sinkers. You want something hot to put in your rag? It needs to be acted on ASAP."

"If it's about the Rugby forward and his gay lover, you're too late."

"All those guys with their heads up each other's asses all day long, I'm hardly shocked, Jonas. This is an anonymous tip from a concerned member of the public."

"How concerned?"

"Enough to give you a scoop that will sell a lot of papers. First get a photographer and TV cameraman to St Joes, like now. Get them to take some doctors and nurses experienced in battle trauma. This is a story about homeless people being experimented on for new torture techniques under the guise of getting them off the streets. And then receiving a phony humanitarian award from Norway to boot."

"What the fuck?"

"You heard. They've got hundreds of them stashed in the old dormitories. Follow the screams. It's all funded by the state on the Mayor's say so and run by H & J Research. That's H for Gus Huissan, who is already in jail for swindling the city out of thirty million and J is for Veronika Jaywaller who has her fingers in everything. Go tonight before they try to move them back onto the streets."

"St Joes? Your old school?"

"Yeah. There's some security, but I'm going to send you some photos I took as evidence. You can't hear the screams in a photograph. Want the second shoe?"

"Fuck yeah."

"Veronika Jaywaller owns Jirdasham Institute – the 'We feel your pain, so you don't have to' people. I can't find the documentation for it and I've been dumped from City Oversight, as you already know. But I heard there's at least 300 unsatisfied customers, each of whom paid thirty grand for the privilege of being scammed and are waiting for a top-up from Guru Guranji, who is at least a genuine healer. You getting all this?"

"Shit yeah. Go on."

"You won't find Jaywaller's prints on it, but it is hers. Her boyfriend, the Mayor, sings Jirdasham's praises all over the web. But get this; everything depends on the aforementioned Guru who is the master of removing pain. I have witnessed him actually doing this. Anyway, he's done a runner. Apparently, he was being kept prisoner by Mrs Jaywaller and escaped somehow. He asked me to help him, but I was too late, too sick frankly."

"You know I can't print anything about Mrs Jaywaller. She has lawyers up to her..."

"You can investigate though. I will send photos now. The Mayor is literally in bed with Mrs Jaywaller and she's funding his re-election campaign. Ask him where that money has come from. He has to declare it."

"That I will do."

"The Guru is involved somehow with the stuff going on at St Joes. It's a big mess, Jonas. Mrs Jaywaller is not paying taxes on the Jirdasham income. Do the math, five hundred suckers – maybe a thousand for all I know, taken for thirty grand each. Another fifteen thousand for the top up when it goes wrong. We're talking millions. Follow the money and expose the exploitation of the old and vulnerable in this city. Your exact readers, probably."

"That I can do. This is why they closed you down?"

"This is anonymous, Jonas. I have no idea how you got this information. I'm out of town looking for the Guru, but I fear he might be dead."

"Send me photos of what you have. This number on WhatsApp."

Delaney played with his photo album and selected some of the clearer images of St Joes.

"OK. Sent. Talk to a woman called Alison Savage, the PR girl at Jirdasham. They've all signed NDA's, but you might get lucky. Talk to Mr Abrams at BookBank. He's just one of the unhappy customers, although he might not want to admit it. We investigated over three hundred victims who all withdrew their complaints suddenly, which is what got my interest in the beginning."

"That's it?"

"That's a lot, Jonas. Once you get to St Joes you'll understand. Those photos come through?"

There was a pause whilst he checked his email. "Lot of sick looking bastards with horrific expressions. This from a horror movie you saw?"

"It's from a movie you're going to see tonight, Jonas. Go yourself; take witnesses. If I find the Guru, I will let you know."

"Do that."

Delaney hung up and headed to a coffee shop. He wondered if Jonas could still be trusted and would take all this seriously.

Thirty minutes later he was heading back towards his car when the Mayor called. He immediately wondered if he'd been sold out. Surely Jonas wasn't in his pay too. Not at The Star. He didn't believe in coincidences. He debated whether to answer him, but technically this was his last day.

"Delaney."

"Was wondering if you were still alive."

"Recuperating, Mr Mayor. You might have heard I was run off the Coastal Highway."

The Mayor was silent a moment. "I heard it was an accident."

"The accident was me surviving I suspect. Anything I can do for you, Mr Mayor? This is officially my last day."

"I got a call from Veronika Jaywaller. She told me you had visited her. She was very upset."

"I'm sure. I got a threat of defamation for my trouble, but if I were you Mr Mayor, I'd rapidly back away from Jirdasham and her charity charade at St Joes. It's a scam and your name is all over it."

"What do you mean, Delaney? That thing at St Joes is down for humanitarian awards. We're getting the homeless off the streets; don't you care about that? The pain treatment at Jirdasham works. I have spoken to people who've been treated."

"You've spoken to people who've have been treated by the Guru, but I can tell you that there's hundreds who have been scammed for thirty grand or more by his so-called disciples who have few skills, if any. Those people are still in as much pain as they ever were. You might be interested to know the Guru has done a runner."

"What do you mean?"

"He's disappeared. Mrs Jaywaller has lost him and everything at Jirdasham, and I do mean everything, depends upon him. Like I say, Mr Mayor. Your name is out there recommending this scam and I have a strong feeling it's going to blow up soon. I'm out the picture now. Audit Jirdasham."

"My deputy says you're prejudiced."

"You mean the guy who told the Jackals to run me off the fucking road? You bet I'm prejudiced. My job was to protect the city from thieves and robbers. I don't care how much your take was, Mr Mayor, but the party is over now. Do the right thing and hope you come out of this smelling sweet when it all goes down."

"I resent your accusations, Delaney."

"I saw you with Mrs Jaywaller. Your wife happy about your little trysts at the Palace hotel? This isn't about me, Mr Mayor. This is going to explode in your face."

The Mayor took a deep breath, trying to control his anger. "And you have no idea where this Guru is?"

"Don't know. Don't care. Ask your pal Veronika about Mimi Leanne."

"The fucking opera singer?"

"She died during a treatment session at Jirdasham, then covered it up. She was using that to blackmail the Guru. Not all your pals are as pure as driven snow, Mr Mayor. I've got to go. Physio session. Tell the Jackals not to drive me off the road again. I don't much care for it."

Delaney disconnected and turned his phone off. He wondered what the Mayor would do. Either way, he'd find out when the press began to doorstep him, if Jonas had the guts to go up against the Mayor.

He headed back to the van. Time to give some thought about putting the Guru in a monastery. He wondered if he'd cause too much trouble, but then again, it was a perfect place to hide.

CHAPTER THIRTY-SEVEN

Lump's & Bumps

Delaney was in bed reading one of Bunty's old crime thrillers when Asha sneaked in. Her huge Bugs Bunny t-shirt amused him as she plunked herself down on the bed and pulled the t-shirt over her knees. He noted a little rose tattoo on her ankle.

"Rufus snores. He's curled up next to Maria and she makes squeaking noises. The Guru giggles in his sleep next door and I am exhausted."

Delaney tossed the thriller to the floor. "Well if I was a gentleman I'd sleep on the floor and let you have the bed. But my back is sore from driving."

"What happened to the miracle cure?"

"He fixed my hands and my arms, but bruising needs time to heal."

Asha was confused. "You throwing me out?"

"No, but it's a single bed with lumps, all complaints to the management, not me." He grinned, moved over and flipped the covers to let her in.

Asha quickly moved over the bed to grab the warmth. "Long time since I slept in a single bed."

"You might not get as much sleep as you think," Delaney told her.

"I warn you, I have cold feet," Asha declared.

"Yikes, that you do." Delaney looked at her and nuzzled her head. "Did I ever mention how much I like your smell?"

"I smell?"

"Smell good."

"Better than the Guru?"

Delaney laughed. "A lot better than the Guru."

Asha could feel the heat coming off his body. "This is so weird."

Delaney rubbed her arm. "Good weird, I hope."

Asha felt the lumpy mattress under her. "I feel like a teenager sneaking into a boy's bed." She turned on her side to face him, kissing the tip of his nose. "I'm so jealous of your eyelashes. You ok with this?"

Delaney kissed her and pulled her closer to him. He was very ok with this.

"Can we turn the light off?" Asha whispered.

"Seriously?"

"I like it better in the dark."

"You like me better in the dark?"

"Now you're putting words into my mouth."

Delaney reached over and switched the light off.

"I didn't know you slept naked," Asha said.

"I run hot."

"Well that's good to know, in winter anyways."

Delaney slipped a hand between her legs and let his fingers explore. He kissed her harder. "If I told you that I've wanted to do this since the first time I met you?"

"That's what Zuki says."

"Am I ever going to meet this mysterious Zuki?"

"No chance, she's way hotter than me."

"Impossible."

"Ha, now you're pushing it, Delaney."

Delaney ran his hand over her petite ass and kissed her small well-rounded breasts, sensing her nipples hardening. He kissed her again and slowly worked his way down her slim body. He didn't want to talk anymore.

Asha placed her hands on his back, biting her lips and digging her nails into his flesh. She'd initiated this, the time to back out was quickly disappearing but she had no regrets, she wanted him, lumpy bed be damned, face any consequences tomorrow. She could feel his hot tongue working its way inside her and she began to feel that certain tingle. She pushed down hard on Delaney's head and wanted to cry out but didn't want to wake the house. She squeezed her eyes shut as a wave of pleasure shot through her. Then another.

"Come on up," she whispered gently after a while. "Come back up."

At some point in the early morning Asha made it back to her room. Maria and Rufus didn't even stir.

Delaney woke to the sound of chanting and groaned. Then he could smell her all over again and smiled, hoping that it really had happened and wasn't some erotic dream.

At breakfast Maria was excited that she was going to see where they made all the cider with Bunty. Delaney informed the Guru that they were going to visit a monastery, but first Asha had to update her grandma's computer.

"Monastery?" The Guru mused as he ate his second portion of poached eggs. "I've always been curious about the minds of men who lock themselves away from the world."

"There's women there too," Bunty remarked as she brought in more toast. "The Nuns are the brains up there. Speak to Felicity, she was an industrial chemist for twenty years before she found a calling."

Asha averted Delaney's gaze. He wanted to make sure she was ok and not embarrassed or worse, full of regret. Delaney wasn't going to make an issue of it or behave differently, but he did wonder.

Maria picked up on it. "You ok?" She asked Asha.

"Hmm, yeah, just thinking."

"Oscar, our foreman has promised us fresh crayfish for supper. He's taking a delivery to Hesper to that new boutique hotel there overlooking the harbor."

"Is that open? I remember reading about it." Delaney remarked. "Very exclusive I recall. Not for the likes of us."

"God, I remember being terrified of the giant crayfish there," Asha blurted out.

Bunty laughed, shaking her head. "You refused to let us boil them and insisted they had to go in the reservoir."

"I did?"

"You did. Mr B cooked them on the barbeque when you weren't looking. You can't put a salt-water creature in a fresh-water lake. It would kill them quickly."

"I don't remember that," Asha said, blushing.

"You always remember my birthday. For that I'm thankful."

Asha seemed to relax. "I'm going to look at your computer. Don't go to the monastery without me, Delaney."

"It's not very imposing outside," Bunty told them. "But inside they've worked wonders."

Rufus wandered in and tried his best to look hungry.

"Oh, he looks starved," Bunty declared.

Delaney laughed. "He has been practicing that look all his life."

Nevertheless, he got a good helping of Bunty's sausages.

Thirty minutes later Delaney and the Guru were waiting by the car for Mr B to join them when Asha came running out of the house.

"Delaney, you have to see something. You too, Guru."

She dragged them both back into the house to Bunty's cramped office filled with files and reference books. Asha had 'The Star' website up and Delaney stared at it pleased Jonas hadn't let him down.

Torture factory exposed in Berg City.
Shocking, cruel experiments on the homeless.

Veronika Jaywaller and staff at H&J Research arrested. Doctors and police called to St Joseph's (the former prestige school in Berg City).

The Guru stared at the screen with a very worried expression. "Do they know?" He asked quietly.

"About you?" Delaney asked. "They will. You've met every one of these unfortunate people, Ansolm. You swapped one pain for another. I'd say they'd remember you."

"But ... the pain." The Guru mumbled.

Asha looked back at the Guru as he stared at the photos of the overcrowded dormitories and the distorted faces of the men and women staring out of the computer screen.

"What about the pain?" Asha asked him. "How long will it last, Guru? How long will they go on suffering?"

The Guru collapsed onto the floor, his face pale with shock as if seeing these people for the first time. "They will throw them back on the streets," he wailed. "Their suffering will be for nothing."

Delaney frowned. "How long before someone gets straight, Ansolm? How long will they stay in pain?"

The Guru kept shaking his head. "If they've been there three months, they will be clean. But their pain," he shrugged. "I'm not sure, six months perhaps."

"How likely is it someone in so much pain will want to get hopped up on heroin or whatever to try and beat it?"

Delaney asked.

The Guru looked up at him, tears in his eyes. "Some will try, but it won't work. That was my plan. They would get clean and they wouldn't need or want the pills again."

Asha squatted down beside him and took his hand. She could see he was suffering. "You're saying they can't get high or the pain killers won't work? They're immune?"

"I don't think you thought this through," Delaney told him. "They'll probably overdose. That's what we witnessed at St Joes. They're giving them painkillers which can't help them."

The Guru nodded. "They were supposed to be released once the pain has dissipated. Mrs Jaywaller didn't realize that the pain couldn't be passed back. I never admitted that."

Asha kept hold of his hand. "There's nothing we can do for them?"

"I couldn't treat so many. I'm not strong enough anymore."

"They wouldn't let you near them anyway," Delaney remarked. "The City Hospital wouldn't be able to cope either. They'll probably have to leave them at St Joes."

"How did The Star find them?" Asha asked looking up at Delaney.

Delaney shrugged. "I found out by accident, so I guess anyone else could."

Asha got back up on the chair and hit refresh. An image of the Mayor looking very harassed came up with a video link. "This is a scandal and a tragedy. I will do everything in my power to help these unfortunate people. No one will go back on the streets and that is a promise."

Delaney drew some satisfaction from that and the look of panic on the Mayor's eyes.

Asha scrolled down. "They're investigating Jirdasham. Who's that being interviewed in hospital?"

Delaney stared at the screen more closely. "Mrs Palmer. She's lost weight. You overcooked this one, Ansolm. She can't feel any pain at all, keeps burning herself and she broke her leg and hips."

The Guru was shaking his head and weeping. Asha looked back down at him. "Did you not realize all this might go wrong one day?"

He nodded. "I knew. I knew. It's vanity. I'm stupid and vain. My sister is right. I have a gift and I exploited it. God will never forgive me. Never."

Asha glanced at Delaney. "What do we do?"

Delaney closed his eyes a moment to think. "You want to go the monastery, Ansolm? It's your best chance of disappearing."

"I must pay for my crimes," the Guru said softly.

"Ansolm, I want you to go and lie down a moment. Understand? You've had a terrible shock. Asha and I need to talk."

He looked into Delaney's eyes and nodded. "Please help me to my room."

Delaney did just that, pulling him up off the floor and walking him to the stairs. "Contemplate a while, Ansolm. You've done good and bad in this world. A gift like yours isn't an easy burden to carry."

The Guru said nothing as Delaney helped him up the stairs. Delaney figured that was a bad sign. He got him to his bed and took the old man's hand. "You were foolish; but the real bad people are Mrs Jaywaller and those who exploited all those people who needed help and care. Think about how we can make things right, Ansolm."

Delaney led Asha through a row of apple blossoms, she held his hand but was pensive and a little withdrawn. He didn't feel guilty but wasn't going to confess his role in this mess. "The Mayor called me whilst I was at the coast yesterday. I switched my phone on and there were like ten 'Where the fuck are you?' texts."

"Mr B said you'd gone an errand for him."

"I had to make an urgent delivery of cider. Driver failed to turn up. I didn't want to switch the phone on anywhere near here."

"Of course. What did he say?"

"I told him to expose Jirdasham and H&J before it blew up in his face. He seemed more concerned that I'd annoyed Mrs Jaywaller.

"Hmm, I wouldn't have given him the chance to get ahead. Those bastards tried to kill you. You think he can survive this?"

"The media won't give him an easy ride. He's the one who told everyone Jirdasham was such a good thing and the one who arranged for H & J to get Government finance. No way he's going to get ahead of anything. The Star won't let go. They love a scandal."

"But that leaves us with the Guru, Delaney. He's just as much a criminal as Mrs Jaywaller, but then again, he's done a lot of good. You won't feel right handing him over."

"You really want to do that? How many hours would you give him before he has a fatal accident down some stairs."

Asha shook her head and took his other hand and squeezed both tight. "If I said monastery, would you be mad at me? I sort of like him."

Delaney pulled her towards him and kissed her. "You regret last night?"

Asha wrinkled her nose. "No. It was my choice. I wanted to stay the whole night, but I nearly fell out of bed three times and my ass was freezing. Single duvet's suck. I sort of felt awkward in front of Maria this morning. Like she was my hyper-critical mother and I'd snuck some boy into my bedroom. How weird is that?"

"Well, the good news is that I have a bigger bed at home."

"You think I'm going to do that again?" Asha feigned shock.

Delaney kissed her again. "I hope so. And often."

Asha closed her eyes, feeling her heart beating faster as he pulled her closer. She held him tight and kissed his neck. He'd been tender with her in bed, and it had felt so good. She definitely wanted to do that again.

"Monastery," Delaney mumbled, as he gently kissed her ear. "But it needs to be his choice."

Asha broke free. "Yeah. God what a mess."

Rufus came running, happy he'd finally found them and immediately searched for a stick.

"You realize Rufus will be jealous." Asha remarked.

"Hey, he left my bed the moment Maria came back. Didn't look back once."

"And then there's Maria."

"She adores you and I suspect her mother isn't coming back for her anytime soon."

Asha took a deep breath. "Zuki will have to approve of anything long-term."

Delaney frowned. "That's my greatest fear."

"She's very critical."

"I am genuinely worried."

Asha smiled as she bent down and threw a stick for Rufus. "Let's get him to the Monastery."

CHAPTER THIRTY-EIGHT

The Guru Vanishes

They arrived back to a silent house. Bunty had taken Maria to the Cider processing plant and not yet returned. Asha went to fetch the Guru as Delaney headed to the bathroom to pee.

It was only as he was finishing up that he turned to look at the sink and discovered it was full of hair. His heart missed a beat. The only man in this house with a beard was the Guru.

"Asha?"

She was already calling him. Delaney began scooping hair out of the sink into the bin, noticing blood in places. "Ash, he's gone."

Asha appeared in the bathroom door and saw all the hair. "Eww, gross. He's gone, Chief. Left all his stuff behind."

"Can't believe he just shaved off all his beard and dumped it here." Delaney complained. "I think he shaved his head too."

Asha stared at the mess. "He told me he's been growing that his beard for sixty years. Shit, I have no idea what he would like without it either or ..." She fished out his robe from the laundry basket. "His robes."

Delaney turned to look with surprise. "What?"

Asha looked pensive. "This is a man who seriously wants to disappear."

Delaney struggled to clean the sink and get the remaining hair out of the drain. "You think he's gone out into the woods naked?"

Asha almost wanted to laugh. "Maybe it's a penance thing. But Mr B said it was going to frost tonight. With his robes he might survive the cold, but ... at least he's took his sandals."

Delaney rinsed the sink. "Well this is great. We've got to look for a man we no longer recognize."

"How far can a naked old man get on foot," Asha asked. "We're miles from anywhere."

Delaney called Rufus. "Rufus. You've got a job to do."

The dog responded quickly and ran up the stairs as Asha went through the Guru's deep pockets. She pulled out semi-precious stones and a fifty note. "He's out there without cash."

"Well he can't spend it out here, that's for sure." He grabbed the robe and acquainted Rufus with the smell. "We're going to find the Guru, Rufus. Get a good sniff of this."

Delaney glanced up at Asha. "You might be right, Ash. He's started some kind of ritual cleansing. He's in shock. He's a man who knows punishment is coming and he wants to atone for his sins. I'll take Rufus west."

"I'll saddle up and go the other way. There's a lot of hiding places in these hills."

"If he's hiding, we'll find him. If he's heading towards home, I hope we find him before anyone else does. God knows what they'd do to him."

Asha ran down the stairs. "Leave a note for Bunty, Delaney. If he returns great, but we need everyone looking for him."

"Got the picture, Rufus?" The dog wagged his tail and dashed back down the stairs. Delaney looked around the bathroom. It was still a mess, but he needed to get going.

Rufus wasn't entirely sure what to do. He ran in circles as Delaney encouraged him to 'Find the Guru'. After some hesitation he picked up a scent and headed off down a dusty track leading away from the house. Delaney found recent footprints but couldn't be sure they were the Guru's sandals.

They half ran, walked, did some more circles, but Delaney was pretty confident that Rufus knew what he was doing. After all this was the dog that found Maria when she vanished.

Asha saddled up Bertie, the oldest of her Grandma's horses and the most experienced. Asha knew all the hiding places from her younger days. But which was most likely to suit a man keen to atone his sins? If that was his intention. What if he'd simply gone mad?

She headed up to the caves, the places where aged twelve they'd go and lick water from the stalactites and pretend to live like a pre-historic women. She had memories of Zuki making up wild hunting stories as they warmed themselves by a stick fire.

Rufus lay down suddenly, panting. He kept looking at Delaney as if to say, 'here, this is where he is.' Delaney was glad of the rest but disappointed.

"Are you tired?"

He bent down and stroked him. "Sorry, Rufus. Maybe we should retrace our steps."

Some faint scent drifted by the dog's nose and he abruptly jumped up and sniffed the ground again and then shot off the way they'd come.

"Rufus?"

The dog ran with his tail up, ears back. Delaney struggled to keep up, jumping over tree roots and uneven surfaces. They were well away from the orchards now. Rufus made a sudden right and disappeared, doubling back a moment to make sure he was following. "I'm coming."

Rufus seemed very sure now and Delaney worried that he had no idea what he was going to say to the naked old man if he found him. Worse, he wasn't convinced the monastery was the right place for him now. Taking him to the city to face the cops, well how would they prove anything he did worked? How could you prosecute it? Maybe dig up some anti-witch-craft statues to lock him away, but three hundred homeless guys could all line up and say he filled them with pain, but who would ever believe that? Clearly it was impossible to a rational mind.

Up ahead Rufus skidded to a halt and began to drink from a stream.

Delaney caught up and wiped his forehead. "Good idea, dog."

He surveyed the terrain. The stream plunged off a rocky outcrop. He inched forward and looked down. It was a good eight-foot drop to a small rock pool below. The lack of recent rain meant the waterfall was a mere trickle, but he surmised it was quite a sight in full flood.

Rufus nudged his leg and he looked down. He had one sandal in his mouth and judging from the worn leather it was almost definitely the Guru's.

"Well done. I knew you could do it."

He bent down and gave him a hug. "You're quite the

tracker dog aren't you."

He took the sandal from him (with a bit of struggle) and examined it.

"The question is, Rufus, has our Guru fallen off the edge?"

Delaney lay on his stomach and crawled to the edge and looked down more carefully. He couldn't see any naked body lying down there, so took encouragement from that.

"Ok, you ready? We have to go down. You think you can find us an easier route?"

Rufus grabbed the sandal back from him and set off again. Delaney followed, breaking off a sturdy branch to steady himself as they slip-slided down the slope to the rock pool.

Asha dismounted outside the caves. They looked smaller and less imposing than she remembered. Zuki and herself had made so many plans here about their futures by their campfires. Right now, she couldn't remember a single one of them, but they had been so passionate about what they were going to be and do when they 'grew up'.

There was little trace of any campfires now. The cave had graffiti on the walls, which entirely spoiled her memories, but at least the life-size charcoal drawing she'd made of Zuki was still visible on the high cave roof. She smiled to herself as she recalled standing on two rickety apple crates to draw her with her spiky hair and brilliant smile. No wonder she had been in awe of her.

Outside the cave a hawk was circling, no doubt worried she was invading its space. Bertie chomped on some potent green grass that grew around the caves. His face was greying now; she reckoned she'd known Bertie for exactly half her life.

"Where next Bertie? Where would you hide if you ran away?"

Bertie stopped chewing for a moment as if to contemplate this but made no reply.

Delaney and Rufus were examining the remains of a campfire. The ground was still warm. It must have been extinguished less than an hour before. Further investigation revealed tire tracks and a discarded bag of trash. Logic would indicate that the Guru had stumbled on some camper, but what kind of camper would give a ride to a naked barefoot old man who was clearly out of his mind. It was a puzzle. He could see that they might leave because there was a naked man lurking out in the woods, but take him with them? It required quite a leap of faith.

Rufus drank from the clear mountain water. Delaney looked back the way they had come and decided his sore bones wouldn't like the climb back up the waterfall slope.

"Come on. Let's find the road."

They followed the narrow track away from the waterfall to the road. It was a good mile and he surmised only a local would know about this spot or at least someone who had been well informed.

Rufus lay down on the unpaved road staring at him, his tongue hanging out to cool.

"I know. This is a longer walk than normal. Be happy I can do this now, all thanks to our Guru friend." Delaney rubbed the sweat from his neck. "We'll follow this road and hope it takes us back to the farm. I'm guessing it's North. You got any other ideas, Rufus?"

Rufus reluctantly got up and walked beside him, the Guru's sandal still in his mouth as his reward.

Asha and Bertie returned to the farm an hour later. They'd seen nothing and no one. Mr B was stacking firewood by the barn and looked happy to see her.

"I saw the note. Any sign of him?"

Asha shook her head and dismounted, loosening off the saddle. "Nope. I tried the caves and the summer pasture hut. He didn't run that way. Delaney back?"

Mr B shook his head. "Bunty and Maria went up to the reservoir to see if he's there. Some of the farmhands live there and they'll soon tell her if they've seen a stranger. He cut all his hair off? I saw the bin. Never seen so much white hair before."

"Sorry. I'll clean it up, I promise."

"Already done. I didn't want Bunty to see it."

"God, thanks Mr B. I can't believe he did that. And running off totally naked. He's going to freeze his nuts off."

Mr B chuckled. "That he is, but he isn't naked, Asha.

He took my overalls. The ones with the Caterpillar logo. It's at least two sizes too big for him. He should be easy to spot."

Asha was surprised but happy to hear it. The Guru hadn't entirely lost his marbles. Obviously, he wanted to look different for a reason.

"Where do you think he's going?" Asha asked him, as she led Bertie into the barn.

Mr B scratched his head and shrugged. "My guess is he's heading home. He didn't disguise himself for nothing."

Asha removed the saddle and dumped it with the others. She scooped out some oats and corn from the barrel and poured them into the feeding trough. "You did good, Bertie. Got something nice for you. Eat up, boy, you deserve it."

She replenished the water bucket as well and gave him a quick brush down.

"Bertie's your grandma's favorite," Mr B told her as he went back to the house. "Never lets her down. We need to bring all the horses in tonight. The farrier's due tomorrow and I don't want to waste time rounding them up. I'm sure there's a frost due and they only just got rid of a cough. I know you think I'm soft, but the vet's bills were eye-watering."

"Don't worry. I'll do it later." Asha told him.

With Bertie settled, Asha headed towards the house where Mr B was setting up the barbeque. She gave him a hug. "I'm sorry we brought all our problems here."

Mr B hugged her back. "Nonsense, girl. You don't know how happy Bunty is that you came and for god's sake, that Guru fixed her knee. She's going to be forever grateful about that. Pity we have to keep him secret. The Guru could make some serious money up here curing everyone's aches and pains. Please come up here more often, Asha. No point in you being her favorite if she doesn't get to see you. Bring Zuki too."

Asha smiled, as she broke free. "You said you'd run off with her when she turns 21."

Mr B laughed. "I did? She wouldn't get much of a bargain out of me these days. Bet she's a stunner now. Don't tell Bunty I said that."

"I will. She is. But you might be disappointed. Zuki is not so much interested in men these days."

"No!"

"True. She might make an exception for an older man with an apple farm mind. She's not exclusive."

"You're mean, Asha."

"I'm kidding. Zuki is finding herself at the moment. Going to do a Masters, I think, if she can get sponsored."

"She was always bright. What was it she wanted to do?" He closed his eyes to recall. "I remember, build robots. She was very keen on that I recall."

"She's studying artificial intelligence now, so I think she's way ahead of the robots. Can't get or keep a job for long, but she is seriously bright."

"Tell me about your older man. Don't think we haven't noticed how much you like him."

Asha blushed, she felt like she was fifteen again.

"We like him, Asha. I know you don't rate our opinion on these matters, but Bunty thinks he's just right for you."

"And you?"

"I can see how much he likes you. He listens to you. In my experience, limited though it might be up here in the wilderness, a relationship lasts a lot longer when the man listens to the woman and takes her advice. Bunty practically raised you, so I know you'll understand what I mean."

Asha made no comment, but she took it on board. They liked him and their approval was important to her.

Rufus arrived first and made straight for his water bowl, draining it quickly. Delaney pitched up a little later sporting his rudimentary walking stick.

"Any news?" he called out as he approached.

Asha shook her head. "No sign of him."

"I think he got a ride with some camper by the waterfall. Just finding it difficult to accept they'd take a naked old man anywhere."

"He wasn't naked, Chief. Took Mr B's overalls."

Delaney digested that bit of information as he sat down on the stone steps and removed a pebble from a shoe. "Well that explains how he caught a ride, I guess. Rufus can't believe I made him walk so far."

Asha bent down to stroke the dog's head. "Poor Rufie. He looks exhausted. I'll get his supper."

Mr B appeared at the front door with two bottles of cold cider. "I think you guys need something to pick you up.

Our best vintage."

"Thank god. An ice pack for my legs wouldn't go amiss either."

Bunty and Maria arrived back a little while later as Mr B was getting the barbeque lit. "Going to frost for sure," Mr B told them tapping the barometer. "You find him?"

Bunty shook her head. "No sign. Nothing."

"Frost? What about your orchards?" Delaney asked.

"It will be a mild one. If I thought it was bad, I'd be firing up the pots. With luck it will kill off some of the bugs."

Maria flopped down beside Rufus and he licked her hello.

"The reservoir is huge," Maria complained. "No way the Guru could walk up there. Is there anything to eat?"

Bunty raised her arms in alarm as she suddenly remembered something.

"The crayfish arrived two hours ago. I nearly forgot. I'll get them ready for you, Mr B."

Asha looked over at Delaney and reached out a hand. "You ok?"

Delaney grinned squeezing her hand. "I'll tell you one thing. The Guru is pretty damn agile. He moved fast. He's determined, whatever he intends to do. I'm just happy that he's wearing something. It tells me that's he's got a plan."

"What do you think it could be?" Asha asked.

Delaney shook his head as he drank some of the chilled cider. "Hmm, nice."

He raised his bottle to Asha. "Cheers."

She raised her bottle and drank. "Wow, I don't remember cider tasting like this."

"Taste even better with crayfish," Mr B declared.

"Crayfish?" Maria asked from the floor, uncertain. "Not vegan."

Delaney gazed at her and smiled. "Make an exception tonight, M. Especially if Mr B lets you taste the cider."

Mr B's eyebrows shot up, but he knew a ploy when he heard one. "One glass of cider coming up young lady. There's a lot to learn about cider drinking, Miss Maria. You can't gulp it like orange juice. You have to learn to savor it, roll it around your tongue, let it ignite your taste buds."

Maria laughed. Enjoying being included.

Asha put her bottle down. "Come on, Maria. You can taste the cider later. We have to bring the horses in from the field."

"Can I feed them?"

"If you help me brush them down."

"Cool. I can do that."

"Put Jasper in the stall, Asha. He's foot sore. The farrier will sort him out and clip their nails."

"Horses have nails?" Maria asked, surprised.

"There's a lot about horses to learn, Maria. Nails, hooves, dietary issues. They aren't machines. There's a lot of maintenance." Mr B explained to her.

Delaney watched Asha and Maria go hand in hand to the field, happy they were getting along so well.

Mr B was nursing the flames. "You got yourself a ready-made family there, Mr Delaney. You're a lucky man. Can't tell you how much I used to like Asha and Zuki coming up here in the holidays. It was too late for Bunty and me to have kids when I married her, but it always felt as if we had two. We had tears, fights and disputes, lots of make-up and happy times. I used to fear Asha growing up or disappearing from our lives, but here she is, like she's never been gone and brought you and the kid with her."

"Maria isn't always as cute and adorable as she seems." Delaney said, swigging more cider. "But she is as honest as you can be and that's worth something."

"That Maria is just like Asha used to be. She will give you heartache and joy. Asha too. My advice. Never ever, ever allow politics at the dinner table or in bed. You'll live a happy and long life."

Delaney smiled. "Advice noted. Need more logs?"

"Just small sticks at this stage. I like a good fire then let it bed down for the grilling."

Delaney went to fetch the sticks.

"That Guru of yours," Mr B called out after him. "I reckon he aims to make amends for something he's done wrong. Maybe something in particular. I might be in error here, but that's what I think."

Delaney nodded. Trouble was, when a man has committed so many sins, which ones would you want to amend first and how?

CHAPTER THIRTY-NINE

Contemplating Futures

Maria was almost in tears when they departed in the morning. She clung to Rufus in the back of the car but even he couldn't cheer her up.

Asha understood. She could remember many tearful departures from Bunty and Mr B. Then the months of longing to be back in the crisp mountain air riding the horses. It always seemed such an uncomplicated life.

Delaney was concentrating on driving, deep in thought as Asha took once last look at the forest and mountain tops as they drove towards the pass.

"I need to stop at the farm shop at the Inn," Asha said remembering a promise.

Delaney acknowledged with a nod. "You ok? You're very quiet."

Asha placed a hand on his arm and squeezed. "Yeah, just sad we're leaving. I promised to get some honey for Zuki, she likes the Piccolo Brand."

"The one with the bear on sticks?"

Asha nodded. "The Piccolo farm has to be near here somewhere. They have some amazing heather and the bees go crazy for it."

"There are bears?" Maria asked.

"I don't think so," Asha replied. "If there ever were someone probably shot them. It's too depressing to think about it."

Maria sighed. "People always have to shoot everything."

"If you look hard between the trees you might spot some deer," Delaney told her. "We're in a national park here. No one is allowed to shoot anything. See the road sign?"

Maria looked up and briefly saw a picture of a deer leaping.

"You have to watch out for deer, they have no road sense and just leap across the roads." Delaney remarked.

Maria looked keenly but saw nothing leaping anywhere.

They stopped for coffee at the Inn on the pass. Asha made straight for the farm shop as Delaney went to order coffees. Maria took Rufus for a quick walk.

Delaney caught some news on the TV in the coffee shop. It was on mute, but the Guru was shown with his crazy white hair and flowing robes. There was even a number to call if anyone saw him. He looked like a crazy Moses. It had been a smart move to shave all his hair off. He wondered if he was safe. Veronika Jaywaller was also up there on screen, standing beside her expensive lawyers. She must have posted bail. The Mayor probably wanted her to disappear fast. He wondered if they had selected a nice little cliff on the Coastal Highway for her.

He was standing by the car with the coffee and switched his phone back on, not expecting a signal out here. A flood of texts streamed in. Jonas looking for more info, even the Mayor thanking him for the 'heads up.' He deleted them all.

Asha joined him armed with a whole bag of shopping. "Organic heaven in there. I couldn't resist. Fresh sourdough. It smells divine." She grabbed her coffee and looked around for Maria.

"Where's Maria?"

"Rufus pee duty. Got a text from the lawyer Nicolas, he wants that list of people who complained about Jirdasham treatment. I guess he's going for group action against Mrs Jaywaller."

"Make him pay for it. He can afford it."

"He offered a percentage of any settlement."

Asha shook her head. "The only advice my dad got right was 'never trust a lawyer'."

Delaney smiled. "You're probably right. Do we still have the list?"

Asha nodded. "I gave you everything on the memory stick. You put it in your safe."

Delaney looked back towards the woods with frown. "It's a long pee. I know she's feeling sad but ..."

Asha stashed the shopping in the back of the vehicle. "It feels very secure up at Bunty's place. She really bonded with it."

"Despite the murders?"

"That was because some crazy politician got the farmhands all stirred up. It's safe now. It's not like you can hear gunfire at night like in the city."

"You hear gunfire?"

Asha wrinkled her nose. "I might be exaggerating to make a point, but we do have the highest murder rate on the coast."

Rufus suddenly appeared looking happy to have found them. Maria was trailing behind, it looked as if she had been crying.

Delaney went to meet her. He didn't say anything, gave her a hug and then held her hand as they walked back to Asha.

Asha drank some of her coffee and set it down. "I got you a juice and a fresh pastry."

Maria mumbled a 'thanks' and headed for the back seat.

"You pee, M? It's a long drive home."

She nodded.

"I guess someone needs to know the surprise." Asha said, as she got back into the car.

Maria wasn't going to ask what it was. She was properly sad.

"Bunty wants you to come and stay in the holidays."

Maria looked at Delaney immediately. "With Rufie?"

Delaney realized he didn't have a chance on this. "With Rufus. But you have to promise to feed him and make sure he doesn't have any ticks. I had to spend an hour last night combing him to make sure."

Maria finally began to smile. "I will. I'm going to learn to ride properly and jump and I can help with making cider and ..."

Asha laughed. "You'll be running the place in no time."

"You'll visit?" She asked.

Asha nodded. "Of course, I'll not have you stealing my grandma. She's mine."

Maria leant forward and gave Asha a hug. "I'm happy now."

Delaney got in and started the engine. "OK, let's go."

"We still looking for the Guru?" Maria asked.

"Tomorrow. He'll turn up somewhere."

"I almost hope he doesn't," Asha said, handing the juice carton to Maria.

An hour had passed with at least another hour to go when they reached the base of the mountain and picked up slower traffic.

"You ever regret leaving your big job in Paris?" Asha asked suddenly. "You must miss the money at least."

Delaney shrugged. "Well I don't miss the taxes, that's for sure. My wife used to mock me. 'You have the dullest job in the dullest profession in the world,' she would say. But I sort of liked it in a way. I was part of a team of eighteen and we invested millions, billions sometimes to keep pension funds secure or invested in things that had a certain reliable income stream. Harder than you think with market volatility back then. I was comfortable, but unchallenged. When my wife died, I just couldn't carry on. She provided all the excitement I needed and then she was gone.

"When Coronavirus hit the world economy, they were desperate to cut back on staff and asked me to select candidates. I told them if they got rid of me, they would save the most money and I got a nice little goodbye present. Remember what I said about Ai, Maria?"

She suddenly realized she was supposed to reply. "I'm going to wipe old people's asses. Be the only jobs left when the robots take over."

Delaney grinned. "Don't you forget it, kid. Three months after I left Paris, they moved the office back to London and they replaced all the human staff with an algorithm, which could do what we did in a month in about five seconds and just as well, better yet, never needs a vacation."

Asha glanced at him. "That's what they told us at University. Everything we're learning will be redundant about a year after we graduate. Really motivating – right?"

Delaney looked in his mirror at Maria. "Well, we still need to eat, and we like cider, right? So, when you're up at the farm this summer, M. Take a good look about you and how they run the place. Cider making, or ass wiping, you choose."

Maria stuck her tongue out at him. "You're ridiculous."

Asha mock thumped him on his arm. "Ditto. Did Mr B give you the talk on how hard and stressful life is on the farm?"

Delaney nodded. "He did."

"You think he and Bunty look miserable?"

"No." He laughed.

"You think I'm going to end up there making cider one day?"

Delaney briefly glanced at her. "It's entirely possible. I could see how happy you were to be there. Don't knock it, Ash. It's a good life."

Asha looked back at Maria with Rufus's head on her lap. "When the robots come for us, that's where we run to, Maria. OK?"

Maria smiled and nodded her head. "Absolutely."

CHAPTER FORTY

Amend Corner

Without the hair and wearing the overalls he looked like any other bum without possessions or shoes and therefore invisible. The two cops stationed at the entrance were too busy eating sandwiches as he shuffled by, partially hidden by an arriving ambulance. He found the back stairs, guided by the shrieks emanating from the first floor and squatted down in a corner to wait. Inside the screams and moaning were incessant. He peeked through the window and saw the nursing staff doing little to help; one was wearing earmuffs and reading a book. A cleaning woman was disconsolately mopping the floor.

Someone wheeled out a laundry basket and left it on the landing, inches from where he was sitting, completely oblivious to him being there.

He rummaged through the basket and came up with some medic whites with a little blood on them. He exchanged his overalls for the white top and trousers, which were a size too big for him. He turned up the sleeves to hide the bloodstains. Moments later an orderly came out to throw a bloodstained towel in the basket and as she turned to go back inside, he slipped in behind her and entered the woman's ward.

The smell of disinfectant and piss was so strong he nearly gagged. It took him a moment to adjust. He recognized no one and they certainly didn't pay any attention to him, he was just another of their torturers who could do nothing to alleviate their suffering.

He went to the bed where a woman was perpetually screaming. She was in a fetal position and had fresh needle marks from whatever painkiller they were trying on her. He sat on the piss-stained bed and took hold of her shaking hand. He did not sing out loud but kept the song of healing in his head. After a few minutes the scream was silenced, and she fell asleep.

The only woman to notice the sudden quiet was in the next bed.

The Guru put his fingers to her lips to silence her as he went to the next patient, rocking back and forth in a silent scream. He repeated his ministrations and she too finally relaxed, lowered her legs and fell into a deep sleep. He felt a little pain in his head from the immense effort of concentration but knew he must continue.

"Do me," a woman called out.

"Do me," another chorused. "I want to sleep. I desperately need to sleep."

The Guru again put his fingers to his lips and noted a nurse was cleaning someone strapped to the bed. He flitted to a bed where a woman was grinding her teeth so hard, she was in danger of breaking her jaws.

Silently the Guru began his work.

The woman around him knew what he was doing. Some might even remember those delicate hands that gave them the pain in the first instance, but none did, and none tried to stop him. The silencing of the piercing scream of the first woman should have alerted staff, but there were still others making keening noises as the pain kept on and on and the Guru realized he would need to leave the loudest till last or risk discovery.

He was experiencing dizziness and lacked focus, getting weaker with each patient he saw. As he approached the twentieth woman, he could see that she had nearly gone blind with the pain and had gouged deep wounds into her bandaged arms to somehow compensate for the pain. This woman he remembered because of her beautiful ears and elegant neck. He wondered then how such a beauty had fallen so far, but now, in constant pain, her looks seemed to have crumbled.

He held her hand and took her pain away, but she held on a moment, unable to see him but aware something good had happened to her, sensing familiarity. "You!"

"Go to sleep. No more pain," he whispered, the room going around now.

"You," she said again, as she fell back in the bed.

An orderly was passing, just as the Guru slipped into unconsciousness. She called for help and caught him before he fell to the floor.

They carried him out and left him on the day bed in the staff room. A nurse gave him a shot of B12.

"How many hours has he been on?" she was asking. "Where are his shoes? Where the hell are they getting these temp staff from, he's so old."

The Guru came to briefly, remembering he hadn't eaten since he'd left the mountains. He desperately wanted to go back into the dormitory, he needed to do more, but he was too old, so very old. He knew he ought to leave but couldn't move a muscle.

He slept a while.

When he awoke Rafael was in the room. He appeared to be changing his clothes. There was someone in the doorway vaping. He wondered if Rafael would recognize him and waited to be discovered. If there were a reward for finding him, Rafael wouldn't hesitate.

"Who's the old guy?"

"Temp staff. He passed out on the ward. I keep telling them it's too hot in there."

"Couldn't they find anyone younger; he looks about a hundred?" Rafael said, putting on his ward shoes.

Another person arrived, somewhat breathless.

"We need you Rafael. Some of the women aren't waking up. The Doc says they're going into a coma."

"Shit, now what? I can't undo what the fucking Guru did, ok. If they're in a coma, at least they aren't feeling pain."

"The screamer is one of them."

"Thank Christ for that."

Rafael's clothes fitted him perfectly, although they were a little too colorful for a man trying not to be noticed. He couldn't wear the shoes given the length of his nails, but maybe no one would look at his feet.

He looked back at St Joes with regret. He wasn't strong enough to help any of the men and sadly he knew Rafael could provide no comfort at all. He said a prayer for them, it was the least he could do.

CHAPTER FORTY-ONE

Trashed

They dropped Asha off at home with promises to meet the next day to search for the Guru. Maria stared in awe at the apartment block as they drove away.

"I didn't realize it's so big.'

"Thirty floors, I think. I hate to think how much she's paying in rent. Girl, we have to think of some excuse as to why you missed school these past three days."

Maria buried her face into Rufus's fur. "My back?"

"Didn't you go around the school boasting that you'd be back in the team any day now?"

"Oops."

"Thought so."

"Maybe ..."

"Maybe nothing. You go in tomorrow and if they ask, say you overdid it and perhaps you'll have to wait to be back on the team until next term."

"But..."

"I told you, M. Take it slow. Get strong, work on those unused muscles and when you're ready, you'll be really ready. Understand?"

She nodded. "My hips hurt, if that helps. Riding really puts a stress on your thighs and legs. They are so sore right now."

"Perhaps not a good time to tell them you've been riding in the forest."

Maria giggled. "Yeah. Shit the girls would be so sick. I can't tell anyone, can I?"

"Not a soul." Delaney told her, as he turned left and headed up the hill towards home.

He was unpacking the car as Maria and Rufus dashed across the road to the grass overlooking the harbor.

"Hey, there's a fire in the docks."

Delaney joined her, glancing back to lock the car.

"Building or ship?"

"Building." Faint sounds of sirens reached their ears as a pall of smoke drifted across the harbor.

"Well that's a shame. Wonder where and why? They're pretty strict on fire codes down there."

"I can see another fire truck coming." A spectacular flash lit up the sky as the sound of an explosion reached their ears a moment later.

"Wow, you see that?" Maria exclaimed.

Delaney mumbled yes. It was no ordinary fire. Had to be quite a big building. He wondered what was stored there. If it was fuel, those fire fighters were going to have a bad time of it.

"Can we go down to look?"

Delaney shook his head. "If things are exploding, the last thing they want is spectators getting in the way. Let's get into the house. Have to hope the wind holds in that direction 'cause if it's oil burning the air is going to get pretty unbreathable around here. Keep your window closed."

Rufus ran across to the gate, but he didn't wait as usual but went straight in.

Delaney held Maria back. "Shit. M. Stay here. That gate was locked."

Maria ran back to the grassy area. She could immediately tell Delaney was tense.

"Rufus?" Delaney called out. The dog barked twice. Bad sign. It was their signal for danger. He looked back at Maria to make sure she was well away and ran for the gate.

He could see immediately that someone had drilled out the lock. "Rufus?"

Rufus appeared, then leapt back towards the side of the house. Delaney followed. The metal grill covering the patio doors was a twisted wreck. An abandoned sledgehammer lay on the grass and there was a huge hole in the patio door. Smashed glass was everywhere.

"Stay." He told Rufus. "Glass."

He moved forward carefully, releasing the lever and sliding the door open with difficulty. More glass fell to the floor. The sofa had been trashed, some chairs thrown about and the only two photos he had framed lay broken on the hearth. The new TV was still there, so that told him that this wasn't a smash and grab. Someone was looking for something.

He turned to Rufus. "Go get Maria." The dog bounded off.

Delaney quickly checked the ground level rooms. His mattress had been slashed; his clothes lay strewn all over the place. The kitchen was mostly untouched, except for the cupboard doors were all left open. Some dried pasta strewn over the counter.

Maria appeared at the patio door and let out a shriek. "Oh - Mi - God."

"Don't come in yet, M. I need to check the basement."

Delaney quickly went downstairs to find Maria's room was untouched, but the guest room had been trashed. In the bathroom the mirror had been smashed. He stepped over broken glass and gently opened the mirrored cabinet door. More glass fell into the sink. He moved some packets of soap and plasters and pushed a little button, which in turn released the whole shelving unit. He carefully pulled it open and revealed the safe. He breathed a sigh. The safe was still locked, a little blue light told him no one had used it since he'd locked it with his laptop and all the memory sticks containing their work in the office. If this was what they were looking for, they hadn't found it. Asha had been right to remind him to lock it all up.

A very anxious Maria met him at the top of the stairs. She had a dustpan and brush in her hands. "I've started on the glass. I don't want Rufus to get hurt. Is Bruno ok?"

Delaney smiled. "Bruno defended your bedroom like a pro. It's untouched."

Maria rolled her eyes, but he could tell she was pleased. "Don't mock Bruno. He's been my bear since I was three. Of course, he defended my room."

"Maybe I should swap the bear for Rufus?"

"You crazy, Delaney? Bruno only works for me; besides, Rufus is already mine. We both know it."

Delaney shook his head. There was no beating this girl.

"I'll get some strong garden bags. We've got a lot of stuff to clean up."

"Who did this?"

"Idiots. Maybe the same people who pushed me off a

cliff. Subtlety isn't their thing. I needed a new sofa anyway."

"And a bed. They slashed your mattress. What were they looking for?"

"Cash, maybe? Who knows? I hated that mattress too."

Maria got started on clearing up.

"I'm going to call a locksmith." Delaney told her. "Then I guess someone to fix the patio door and shit, then the insurance people. Insurers are going to be so happy with me after what I did with the car."

"What about the cops?" Maria asked.

"Yeah, them too. I'll need a crime number, a little ironic since it was probably them who did this. We'll get this place tidy and then I'll call for pizza."

"Pizza!!" Maria shouted, alarming Rufus.

Delaney grinned and began making calls.

CHAPTER FORTY-TWO

The Wisdom of Zuki

Zuki was painting her toes and thinking about Asha's situation.

"I can tell you like him more than you're saying, Ash. But why? He's a lot older than you. Sure it's not a father figure thing?"

Asha was making soup, added chopped zucchinis to the liquid. "Isn't that a cliché? I mean the last guy in my bed was the same age as me, fit and he stole my car and my phone. Delaney isn't going to steal anything from me. He's genuine, definitely old school, but he cares about me. He was so cute in bed." She laughed. "I kept thinking about you though. It was your bed when we used to stay there."

"Single bed with lumps in the mattress? Shit, I remember that bed. First place I ever had sex. What was that boy called? The one from the farm next over."

"Simon. I think he went into the army."

"I'm glad you went up there. Those were the best summers. Life seemed simpler then."

"Bunty sends her love. She wants you to go see them."

Zuki shrugged. "Only if they change that mattress. You really like this guy, Ash? Wasn't so long ago you were thinking he was going to die he was in so much pain."

Asha threw some turmeric into the soup. "I told you, he's cured, and I think he'll be good for me. We're equals now. Partners. It's different."

Zuki frowned. "I'm not convinced any guy is 'good for you'. But compared to every single guy you've been with, I guess he's a nice safe old guy who owns his own shack. It's a definite step up for you girl."

"You're evil, Zuki. You haven't seen his shack. It's on Meridian Ave; the whole city harbor is spread out below. The view alone is worth a fortune."

Zuki looked up. "Well at least you're pricing up his real estate. Half of that come the divorce will make a good payday."

Asha threw a sugar cube at her. "We haven't even started anything, and you've got me divorced already. I don't think I'm going to introduce you. Too many bad vibes."

Zuki smiled. "Well I'm not going to steal him, if that's what's worrying you, though I bet I could."

"I know you could." Asha scowled as she added chopped carrots and sweet potatoes to the mix. "But first you'd have to get past the kid and the dog. They're tough."

"The kid would be easy. Take her cookies, pretend to be interested in her shallow opinions for a week and she's mine."

"You wouldn't fool the dog."

"Raw steak in his bowl, it's easy. He'll worship me in three days."

"Like I said, you're evil."

CHAPTER FORTY-THREE

Mrs Rama Pays A Visit

It took the best part of three hours and at least one cut finger but what could be saved was saved, a sad pile of junk squatted outside in the yard to be taken away.

"The glazier can't come until tomorrow and the locksmith is due about now. To be honest I kind of wish there was some cash stuffed in my mattress. This is going to cost a fortune."

The bell rang at the gate and Rufus ran off barking his welcome.

Delaney was hoping it was the locksmith, but instead a small woman stood there in an odd hat. She looked older than he remembered.

"Jasmina. Didn't expect to see you here. Did you hear from your brother?"

Delaney got hold of Rufus and pulled open the unlocked gate for her.

"We're just getting tidy. Had a home invasion."

Jasmina could see that with her own eyes which took in the slashed sofa and mattress, not to mention all the other broken items and chairs.

She shook her head. "We live in terrible times. Someone came to my house as well, Mr Delaney. The boys in the street made them sorry and fixed my door but now I'm afraid of living there. But it's my home. I can't live anywhere else."

"Come on in. Maria will make you a cup of tea."

Jasmina smiled. "Is she...?"

"She's fine. She'll be happy to see you. She was fit enough to ride a horse yesterday; can you believe it?"

Jasmina beamed. "She'll never look back now."

Maria was a tad shy but came over and gave the old woman a hug anyway.

"Can I make you tea? We have about twenty different flavors."

Jasmina looked for somewhere to sit and settled for a

dining chair. "Some green tea would be nice, Maria."

Maria got to work on it. Rufus went back to guarding the patio door and Delaney grabbed the other chair. "Have you spoken to him?

She shook her head. "I had a message from him. He wants me to go to see him. He wanted you to come as well."

Maria placed a steaming mug of green tea on the table. "We have biscuits."

Jasmina shook her head. "No thank you, child."

"Did he message you?" Maria asked. "I was trying to explain WhatsApp to him, but he said he had no use for a phone."

Jasmina smiled. "Ansolm has never used a phone in his life. He sends me messages to here." She indicated her head. "It's always been like that with us. When we were younger, we finished each other's sentences. No matter where we are, we can 'hear' each other."

"Do you know where he is?" Delaney asked.

"That's why I've come. It's so muddled. So strange. I know he was with you in the mountains. I am sorry he ran away. I expect you would have helped him, but he went a little bit mad, I think. All his messages to me were so full of terrible images, I really thought he was going to kill himself."

Delaney took her hand. "That was our worry."

Maria stared at Jasmina. "Doesn't he know where he is right now?"

Jasmina closed her eyes. "It is so strange. He's trying to tell me, but..."

"Perhaps you need to lie down and concentrate without distractions," Delaney suggested.

Maria caught his eye and indicated she was going to her room. He nodded; glad she understood the situation.

Jasmina sipped her tea and smiled. "Refreshing."

"I'm not sure what to do for your brother. There are a lot of people looking for him. Did he mention he shaved off his beard and hair?"

Jasmina looked shocked. "His beard? He's been growing that for almost all my life. I have no recollection of what he might look like without it."

Delaney got up looked for something cold in the fridge. One lone CiderBee cider was all there was. He grabbed it snapped the cap off.

"She is happy now." Jasmina told him.

"Maria?"

"No, your wife," Jasmina told him. "You've found someone. The girl at the farm. My brother told me she was kind and got him out of that evil woman's house."

Delaney drank some cider, never quite sure how to react to these matters.

"Asha is pretty cool actually," he said. "Never really thought she liked me that way but..."

Jasmina warmed her hands on the tea mug. "She likes you. She has chosen and won't change her mind. She is like the little one. The stray cat that came and never left. The best friends are the people who choose you, not the other way around."

"I've ordered pizza. I hope you'll share some with us."

Jasmina giggled. "I haven't had pizza in years. But for the moment I need to lie down and listen for my brother. Do you ..."

"You can use my bedroom, but there's no mattress. I'll put some rugs down on the divan."

"No need. I will sit. If I lie down, I sleep, and I will hear nothing."

Delaney walked her into his room and turned his old armchair around for her. One of the few pieces of furniture they hadn't trashed. "This was my mother's chair. The sofa was too low for her, so she'd sit in this and watch the golf. She was quite a golf fanatic."

Jasmina sank into the chair and seemed quite happy. "This will do just fine."

There was a shout from the gate and Rufus began barking. Delaney rushed out of the house. The locksmith had finally arrived.

"I'll put the dog in the back yard," he told him seeing as the man was apprehensive. Rufus wasn't keen to be stashed away, but it had to be done.

"That's quite a fire down by the docks," the locksmith was telling him. "Traffic is jammed up everywhere."

"You know what it is? I saw the explosion."

"Old oil bunker, I think. They're building right next to it. Won't be much of the new building left I reckon."

Delaney's heart sank. The restaurant below his new

office location was the other side of the old oil bunker. He hadn't signed for anything yet, but if they went out of business because of it..." He put it out of his mind. He had other issues to deal with.

His phone rang. Asha. He took the phone outside

"You OK?" Delaney asked. "Bit of a disaster here, they trashed my house, smashed windows."

"Shit, sorry, Chief. Kids, or your friends the Jackals?"

"Wasn't kids, for sure. They took nothing, but damaged lots."

"Maria ok?"

"She's cool. Cleaning up the damage."

"I can see the fire in the docks from up here.

"Locksmith says it's the old oil bunker next to the Surf & Turf restaurant."

Asha paused a moment. "I guess that's not good news, right?"

"Let's not assume anything. I've got someone here right now. She's trying to find her relative before anyone else does."

"Ah." She understood. "He was on the TV news. Old footage of him talking about his books. The cops want to 'interview' him."

"I suspect our friends will want to eliminate him from the picture as soon as possible."

"That's what I was thinking. You want me there?"

"Honestly, Ash, it's a mess here and I haven't got a clue where to look for him. I'll explain later. Meet tomorrow. I've got to take Maria to school first, get back here to let the patio door people in and then see Mr Abrams. Meet at Harry's later?"

"Yeah, cool. Text me when you're ready. If you need me earlier, I will come."

"Thanks, I appreciate that."

The pizza arrived. Maria took over kitchen duties and even the locksmith had a slice.

"You're going to need a whole new patio door," he informed Delaney. "They've bent the frame."

Delaney sighed. "That's going to cost. Maybe I should just build a wall with a tiny window."

The locksmith shook his head. "You wouldn't want to

lose that view. Look, I'm forever replacing locks on these doors. I've got a deal with a company they can fit you new patio doors with a multi-locking system and anti-jacking so they can't get the door panels out of the frame. They use really thick double-glazed glass, which isn't fool proof, but will take a great deal of effort to smash and create a lot of noise. Your alarm didn't go off?"

"That's a good point. We've got lights all over the place but if the alarm sounded, the security company didn't report it."

"You weren't here, so this might have been done during the day." The locksmith remarked.

Delaney went outside looking for the alarm box. He looked up and swore. He could see where it had been, but where the hell was it now? He went back inside.

"They stole the fucking alarm."

Maria laughed. It was kinda funny. "Who steals an alarm?"

"Someone who comes equipped with a ladder," Delaney replied, taking another slice of pizza. "They really wanted some time to search the place I guess."

Jasmina emerged from his room looking frail and concerned.

"We saved you a slice, Jasmina. I've just got to pay the locksmith."

She smiled and came towards the table and grabbed a chair

"Eggplant and mushroom," Maria informed her. "Nice crust."

She sighed and helped herself.

The locksmith brought out his card reader for payment and Delaney presented his card. "Tell your friends I need a new patio door pretty damn quick."

He smiled as he put away the machine. "I've taken measurements and sent them on already. I'll make sure they come tomorrow. You're lucky it's a pretty standard size." He packed up his stuff and left.

Rufus was finally released from the back yard and Maria rewarded him with some biscuits. "Poor Rufie, exiled to the yard. Are all the locks safe now?"

"All except the patio doors."

"What were they looking for? You've got nothing."

"Thanks."

"But it's true. Nothing of value."

Jasmina shook her head. "Possessions do not make a home."

Maria dropped some pizza on the floor and tried to get to it before Rufus. She stood no chance. He gobbled it down.

"Rufie, I was going to give you some, promise." She banged her head on the underside of the table and swore.

"I heard that," Delaney said.

Maria came up with a small plastic device. "What's this?"

Delaney knew immediately what it was and took it from her. He put his fingers to his lips. Maria understood immediately, Jasmina just looked puzzled.

"Can we go on a treasure hunt, M? I've hidden some chocolate buttons around the house. See how many you can find."

"A treasure hunt?" Jasmina asked, puzzled. "What a funny thing to do."

Delaney took the bug outside and crushed it underfoot. They'd trashed the house just so they could bug it? He wondered how many more there were and what the hell he'd said since he'd got back that they'd overheard.

"I'll take you home shortly, Jasmina. I have to do something first."

"I'm quite content, in no rush to go home. I'm still waiting."

Delaney put a note under her nose. 'Someone is listening to us. Say nothing more.'

Jasmina's eyes opened wide. This had not occurred to her. She stared around the room startled.

"Found any buttons yet?" Delaney called out.

Maria found three bugs in total. Delaney wondered about their range. Was there someone out there listening in a car in the street? This didn't seem the Jackals' style. Perhaps Mrs Jaywaller had hired a private operative.

Jasmina was finally ready to go and stood by the door looking at the black smoke still rising from the docks. Delaney gave Rufus his supper and ushered everyone out of the house. He turned to Jasmina. "If I was going to hide from Mrs Jaywaller, and believe me, your brother needs to do that, where would he go? Where wouldn't Mrs Jaywaller look for him? It has to be somewhere she doesn't know about. But assume that she knows a lot about Ansolm."

"He's quite secretive, is my brother. One moment he shares everything, but another you wouldn't even catch a cold from him."

"Where was his tea business based?" Delaney asked.

"Oh, they knocked it down and built some apartments there. Such a lovely old building it was. I don't know where he might go. He wants to undo what he's done."

"Would he go to St Joes? They'll have police watching now."

"Perhaps all those people who were cheated. Maybe he wants to help them?" Jasmina suggested.

"He'd need the list and there's no way he'll get hold of that. No, it would have to be more dramatic."

"I know something," Maria said suddenly.

Delaney glanced back at her briefly. "What?"

"He told me about a chapel. He said he was always at peace there and he'd had a vision of his death there."

Delaney's eyebrows rose, he glanced at Jasmina. "Chapel? Ring any bells?"

Jasmina drew a blank. She realized she knew so little about her brother's life. "When he was a child, and that's so long ago now, he loved St Marks chapel."

"St Marks? That's near Rosedale. It's all boarded up isn't it."

Jasmina shrugged. "There used to be a hospice near there. But I don't think it was one he visited."

"Well – it's something. We can swing by there. It's not too far."

Jasmina frowned. "If he's hiding, it would be a good place I suppose."

They all climbed into the car. Maria looked back at the house, worried to leave Rufus alone.

"St Marks isn't far from Brunswick Mall. Strap in. Let's go."

It was pitch black out here and a brisk chill wind was bending the trees. The hospice was a ruin and the chapel hardly much better with all the windows boarded up. A good place to hide but Delaney wasn't convinced the Guru wanted to hide. That wasn't why he'd returned.

Delaney pushed open a broken door and shone his flashlight over the chapel interior. He could smell damp and piss. Someone was living here in this ruin, but he was sure it wasn't the Guru. Most of the old benches had been stacked to one side of the building; he ducked as a bat fluttered overhead, disturbed by the light.

His flashlight caught movement; something or someone in a sleeping bag trying not to be noticed. A dog appeared, looking groggy, its eyes shining back at him, a growl in its throat as it began to wake up.

Delaney backed off. He wasn't looking for trouble. He headed out and back to the car.

He swung back into his seat and both Jasmina and Maria were staring at him expectantly.

"No. Someone's living there, but not your brother. It's pretty stinky in there. I really don't think Ansolm wants to hide away, Jasmina. Certainly not here."

Jasmina nodded, she'd already guessed this wasn't the place.

Maria sat back in her seat and sighed.

"It was definitely a chapel," Maria stated. "He had a vision of his death and who would kill him. He said you can't escape fate. Is that true?"

"When did he say this?" Delaney asked, curious.

"When he asked me to cut a hangnail, he couldn't do it. He has scary, long fingernails. He said that he knew exactly where he would die, but not when. The chapel was a place of peace and tranquility. His vision was like twenty years ago."

"I remember him talking about Magdalen Hospice." Jasmina said, pressing her hands to her temple to try and connect with her brother again. "Father Vincent's place, he did favor the garden there. He planted a tree for future shade. Now I think on it, he loved the peace and quiet there. I don't know if it has a chapel."

Delaney frowned. "He mentioned the hospice before, but I didn't think he'd want to show up there, given his history with the place."

"I think that's it," Maria piped up, as she realized that she knew something important. "The sun shining through a stained-glass window of Christ on a donkey."

"At breakfast up on the farm he was saying that he was burdened by so many people wanting his help and how hard it was to say no." Delaney remarked.

Jasmina nodded. "Ansolm could never say no, even when he knew he couldn't help sometimes."

"Jasmina?" Delaney queried, snatching a glance at her troubled face. There was a delay as she listened to an inner voice. "Yes, I believe so. He's very anxious."

Delaney made a left onto the highway as he planned the best route. Traffic was light, but at least he knew exactly where to go.

"Would Mrs Jaywaller know this place?" He asked.

Jasmina had no idea. "I don't know. She seems to know everything."

"Yeah, she's got feelers out everywhere," Delaney said. "Wherever he turns up, someone will call her."

"If they recognize him," Maria remarked. "He must look so strange without his hair."

CHAPTER FORTY-FOUR

Lilac Ward

No one noticed the old guy wander in. No one saw him slope along the corridor to the carers changing room. No one entered where he took a cleansing shower and donned the crisp clean white uniforms of the hospice. He slid his wide feet into the grippy regulation slippers designed not to slip when a patient lost their balance. He placed the little white hat they wore on his head and snapped a mask onto his face. He was now for all intents and purposes invisible.

The Guru made a little prayer and headed to the kitchens. There would always be someone who hadn't eaten their lunch. It was the nature of a hospice that some food would be uneaten and often would be taken home to feed a family. No one was overpaid in Father Vincent's place and it relied on volunteers to care for the patients.

He ate cold mash and greens, followed by jelly and custard. As he chewed, he contemplated on what was the right thing to do. Nothing he did could ever make up for the suffering he had caused. All was vanity. Nothing could justify the pain he'd given those at St Joes. God would be watching and judging. God, he knew, would intervene. After all, had he not seen his end? Like thousands before him, everyone who entered Father Vincent's left in a box. He'd be no different. If not today, certainly tomorrow. He'd seen it, it was just a matter of time before justice caught up with him.

The door opened and an elderly woman in hospice uniform saw him and seemed very happy that he was there.
"You the relief?"

The Guru smiled, wiping crumbs from his mouth. The woman looked harassed, barely able to walk from tiredness.

"I am the relief," the Guru reassured her.

"Upstairs. The Lilac Ward. We've had trouble all day with the woman in bed five. They all seem very agitated. Clean sheets are in the top cupboards. Bed sixteen will need the catheter changing hourly. Bed twenty-two is incontinent.

She'll need putting on her side to give some relief from the bed sores. Beds three and seven are probably going to expire tonight. Just make them comfortable. We've already withdrawn everything except water.

The Guru nodded, made a good show of putting on his protective gloves and headed out of the kitchen.

Maxim was driving home when he got the call. He swore. He hated that she always assumed he was on duty 24/7. He contemplated not answering but knew she'd just keep calling.

"I'm heading home."

"Maxim. Got a curious call from Magdalen Hospice. It's out by the West Lagoon. You know it?"

"No, but I can look it up."

"The Nightguard is reporting the patients are wandering around the grounds."

"That's our business?"

"These are terminal patients. They go there to die, not wander around the grounds."

"You think the Guru was there?"

"It's a long shot, I know, but ... he hasn't actually seen the Guru. No one has. We're desperate to find him, Maxim. It could be nothing, but ..."

"You want me to go see."

"I'm sorry. I know you're tired."

"And if he's there? You want him back?"

"No, Maxim. I want him gone. My lawyers are screaming we need to eliminate problems. You understand."

Maxim frowned. This wasn't part of their original agreement.

"Do this – remember you're a partner. You stand to make a lot of money. We have a potential agreement with investors, Maxim. We're close to a deal. I want no loose ends."

He was only just recovering from the beating he'd got the last time she sent him on errand. Reluctantly Maxim replied. "I'll go look."

"You're a very good man, Maxim." She disconnected before he could change his mind.

Maxim sighed and slowed to turn around. "I'm a very good man." He repeated and swore as he spun his vehicle around. "Fuck."

The Lilac ward was buzzing with activity. Some of the women were singing. No one was dying, that was for sure. The Guru sat down on a bentwood chair and rubbed his face as terminal patients tried walking on emaciated legs. Other sat up for the first time in months and reveled in an ability to breathe without pain. Some were crying they were so relieved to be alive or disappointed to see just how wasted their bodies actually were. Others had already left to wander, discover the limits of their new powers.

They didn't see the Guru slip out of the ward. He knew, what most of the patients didn't, that this was merely a reprieve. They would still die at their appointed hour but without pain. That was what he wanted. This was his amends.

He paused by the stairs and summoned courage to go to the men's ward. He wasn't sure he any strength left at all. He descended with heavy legs and decided to go to the Chapel first. He needed rest. He needed to reassure God that he meant no harm. More than anything he needed sleep.

A male patient was there before him. Cancer seemed to have eaten half his face. Somehow, he'd found his way to the chapel and was on his knees before the stained-glass image of Christ on a donkey and praying.

"You should be in bed." The Guru told him.

The man didn't answer. The Guru could see he was lying in a puddle of his own making. He had kneeled; but couldn't rise again. The Guru suspected he'd been there a long time.

The Guru laid his hands on the man's shoulders and began to sing.

"We need to hurry." Jasmina declared suddenly. "Oh Lord we need to hurry. I know trouble's coming, Mr Delaney."

Delaney was going as fast as he could. Cops used radar in this area, he couldn't afford to get any more points, he wasn't carrying enough cash to make a fine go away either.

"Quarter of an hour, Jasmina. Not far now."

Maxim walked into the hospice and was assailed by the stench of disinfectant. The Nightman was distracted, talking with a tearful couple who had clearly just been bereaved. He looked up and saw an old woman dancing alone at the top of the stairs. She had shock of white hair and wore a hospital gown that exposed her emaciated body. Some other woman was sprawled in a heap on the floor laughing.

There was a sudden shout coming from the end of the corridor and Maxim followed the signs to the chapel.

He wasn't prepared for what he saw. An old man with half his face eaten away turning in circles – loudly praising God, pissing as he turned, unable to control his bladder. A medical orderly was watching him, not intervening. Just watching.

"You seen the Guru?" Maxim asked him. "Guy with a lot of white hair, barefoot. About this high?"

The Guru turned to see Maxim and smiled. "Ah, my death is come."

Maxim stared at the orderly in confusion. But then he saw the eyes. You didn't forget the Guru's eyes. He swore. He had been hoping that Mrs Jaywaller had been wrong.

"I knew it would be you," the Guru said calmly, briefly wondering why Maxim wore a head bandage. His nose looked swollen. He must have been in a fight. He smiled remembering his vision. "I have seen your death as clearly as my own, Maxim. You will meet your fate soon enough."

Maxim wasn't listening. He was casting around for something useful to make a point. Time to wipe the smirk off this little man forever. He noticed some carpenter's tools lying on top of stacked wood panels. He smiled.

The Cancer patient took uncertain steps towards the doors. Maxim watched him go, stood aside to avoid making any contact with the stumbling shell of a man.

The Guru made no attempt to go anywhere. He seemed to be praying to the stained-glass window depicting Christ on a donkey. Weird as ever. Maxim retraced his steps and closed the chapel doors. No need to disturb someone whilst they're praying.

CHAPTER FORTY-FIVE

A Nail in the Wall

It was close to ten pm when they turned off the road to Magdalen hospice. A long drive lined with ancient cedars. As Delaney pulled in, a black vehicle was leaving at speed, wheels spinning on the gravel. He couldn't see the driver.

"I've got a bad feeling about this," Delaney remarked, turning his head, trying to see the vehicle's plates, but it was too dark to see.

Three patients in hospital gowns were stumbling around the grounds barefoot and singing. They looked too frail to be doing anything other than dying.

"He's definitely here," Delaney instinctively remarked.

They entered the building. The Nightman was watching TV, didn't even turn when they swept by. A middle-aged couple were sitting on a bench weeping but paid them no heed.

"Chapel," Maria pointed to a sign. She quickly set off as Delaney took Jasmina's arm. She was flagging.

"We're too late. We're too late," she was muttering.

"Don't go straight in," Delaney called out to Maria, but she wasn't listening and pushed open the chapel doors.

Her scream would have woken the dead.

Delaney entered the room. He grabbed Maria and turned her away from the scene. The Guru, the small, bald, remnant of him was nailed by one hand to the paneled wall. "We feel your pain" written in blood on the panel beside him. A plastic wrapped claw hammer lay on the ground beside some oak panels waiting to be fitted.

Jasmina collapsed onto a chair without a sound.

Delaney took out his phone and quickly snapped a photo as evidence. "Make space on the floor, Maria. I've got to get him down."

Delaney felt the Guru's pulse. Remarkably he was still alive. He grabbed the claw hammer and attempted to ease the nail out of his bloody hand without tearing it. The man had lost a great deal of blood. He feet barely touched the ground. He must had struggled to stay conscious and upright to try and preserve his hand, hoping help would come, but his body weight, such as it was, had torn a huge hole in his hand.

Maria was at his side, crying, but trying to be helpful by handing up a cloth she'd found to mop up the blood. The four-inch nail was a bitch to remove and when it finally came loose Delaney grabbed the old man. They laid him out on the floor and Maria found a seat cushion to place under his head.

Jasmina came to his side and cradled him in her arms muttering a prayer for his soul.

Delaney pressed a bell for assistance, he didn't hold out much hope from the Nightman. He found a water bottle by the tools and gave it to Jasmina to give to her brother.

He drank thirstily and seemed to revive a moment, his tongue licking his cracked lips as he struggled to find a voice.

Maria could see all the blood on the floor and on his clothes. She couldn't believe so much could flow out of one person. His color was a dreadful shade of blue.

A patient came into the chapel in his hospital gown. He seemed happy, despite his spindly legs and emaciated face. Another arrived, a huge woman, stumbling in on enormous swollen legs and began to sing a hymn.

Jasmina wasn't fazed in the least. "What did you do, Ansolm?"

He tried to smile and breathe, filling his lungs in two short bursts. "I set them free." He whispered, choking. His eyes flickered. He was fading fast.

Maria took his bloody hand, wrapped it in tissue and held it tight. "Are you going to die?"

The Guru opened his eyes for a moment and focused upon her. "Yes. But you live for me," he whispered. "You live well for me. I did some good. I know I did. I will now be judged." He turned to his sister. "I will see you again, sister. I always loved you."

Maria saw the light go out in his eyes as all his breath escaped in one long sigh. She was still holding his hand and she felt a surge of heat pulse through her fingers and up her arm. She finally let go and fell to the ground weeping. Jasmina began to wail. Delaney backed off a little to give them room as more patients arrived. They seem to want something, but all of them were smiling.

"Is he gone?" One asked.

Delaney nodded. The Nightman finally arrived, bewildered all the patients were gathering in the chapel, patients that until an hour ago hadn't moved in weeks or months, waiting to die.

"What's going on?"

Delaney pinned him up against the paneled wall. "Who the fuck did you call? Who was driving that vehicle that just left?"

The Nightman could see blood on the wall and the body of the Guru as Maria stepped away.

"I don't know what you mean."

"Who did you call, man? Give me a name. You just let someone come in here and nail the Guru to a wall. You think someone wouldn't get upset about that?"

The Nightman was finding it hard to breathe with Delaney pressing on his windpipe. "I ... They ..."

"Name."

"Just a number. We were to call if anything weird went on."

"What number?"

The Nightman fumbled with his phone as he entered his passcode. Delaney grabbed it from him and dialed the last number. It was answered quickly.

"Yes?" He recognized the voice instantly.

"Don't think you won, Mrs Jaywaller. Don't go thinking that."

Delaney disconnected and gave the bewildered Nightman his phone back.

This was Maxim's work, the Guru's minder. A nice little touch of irony in the message. He looked down at Jasmina cradling her brother's body.

"Jasmina? You want to take him home?"

Jasmina looked up at Delaney, confused. "We can take him home?"

Delaney looked at the Nightman. "Is there a doctor on duty here at the hospice right now?"

"Upstairs." The Nightman gasped. "Room 221."

"You might want to consider shepherding these patients back to their rooms before they catch a cold." He turned to Maria.

"M stay here, I'll get the doctor. We'll need a death certificate if we're taking him away."

"What about the police?" The Nightman was asking. "He was k. k. killed."

"He was. But you arranged that by making the call. Makes you an accomplice to a murder. Live with that thought."

Delaney went to find the doctor. He didn't want police here; a homicide investigation by cops who'd couldn't be trusted. Maxim was protected, it would be a waste of time, they'd just fit up the nearest homeless patsy they could find and call it quits. Or worse, arrest him. After all he was covered in the Guru's blood. He was angry. No way was he going to take any shit from the doctor. Mrs Jaywaller was going to pay for this, one way or another.

Two exhausting hours later they were on their way. Maria sat in the front. Jasmina was in the back with her brother wrapped in a sheet. The young resident doctor had been faced with mayhem. Half-dead patients were singing and making merry; wandering all over the hospice. She had no idea how to regain control and no staff, because they hardly ever had any staff at night, and worse a man had been nailed to the wall in the chapel. Not the sort of thing that the charity that supported the hospice would like publicized at all. On the other hand, 'cardiac arrest compounded by excessive hemorrhaging' sounded so much better than 'nailed to the wall'. The death certificate would help smooth things along for Jasmina. She wasn't interested in justice. The Guru had run his course, and this was all the justice he was going to get.

"I've got a good lawyer for you to make a claim on the big white house. And perhaps we can get his bank account frozen first thing, if there's anything left."

Jasmina sighed. "He never lived in that house."

"True, but it doesn't mean you can't."

"Why would I ever leave my street? They would never forgive me. That is what Ansolm never understood. He wanted to be successful, but money was never important to him."

"That money could help your street, Jasmina. Don't dismiss it."

"I won't."

"I'll call Nicolas Goodman tomorrow on your behalf. At least you could put the money to do some good."

"Will you get the man who killed him?" Maria asked. She totally spent and struggled to stay awake.

Delaney shrugged. "To be honest, M, probably not. We could have called the cops, Maxim's DNA would be on the claw-hammer and the Guru's clothes, but then again so are ours now, and anyway, we can't trust them. I still want to get Mrs Jaywaller. And I will."

"He will be buried on Fort Lester Mound," Jasmina declared quietly. "We have a family plot there. I shall miss my brother more than I can say."

Maria could still feel the heat of the Guru's bloody hand in her's and see the light go out in his eyes. She didn't think she'd ever forget that. Ever.

"Do I have to go to school tomorrow?"

Delaney nodded. "It's safer than being at home right now. I'm sorry you're going to be exhausted and you can't tell anyone except Rufus what you saw. Understood?"

"I know."

"You don't have to come to the funeral child." Jasmina told her. "You've seen enough."

Maria shook her head. "We're going, aren't we, Delaney."

Jasmina smiled and stroked Maria's hair. "Then come. At least you knew the best side of him."

They walked Jasmina into her home and laid out the Guru on the old oak table in the yard. Jasmina immediately began to clean the blood off him. She looked exhausted but determined.

"You might want to get some ice." Delaney told her.

"I will let the neighbors know he is here," she said. "They will want to come and pay their respects."

Maria fell asleep in the car on the way home. Delaney carried her in and put her to bed. She should not have seen such things, but terrible things happened every day.

Rufus climbed onto the bed with her and even in her sleep her arm found a way to hold him close.

"Keep her safe, Rufus."

CHAPTER FORTY-SIX

Keys to the Penthouse

He was sitting at his desk as usual, examining a set of figures when Delaney approached. He could immediately see the old man was in pain, constantly pressing on his wrist to somehow relieve it.

"Good morning, Mr Abrams."

The old man looked up and frowned. "Good morning, Mr Delaney. And if I'm not mistaken it is a good morning for you. You're standing straighter, your eyes are clear."

Delaney smiled. "You miss nothing. I stand before you guilty of being pain free."

Mr Abrams' eyebrows shot up. "Good god man, you didn't pay them. Not now you've got them on the ropes."

"On the ropes, but not quite out for the count."

"Did you find the Guru? I hear there is something of a manhunt."

"Confidentially, he was found by one of Mrs Jaywaller's pet gorillas last night and murdered. I'm afraid he's unlikely to be punished for this as he's ex-Jackal and well protected."

Mr Abrams sighed. "I must confess I was looking for a little justice."

"Well don't give up. A lawyer friend of mine is putting together a class action suit against Mrs Jaywaller. I'll give you his number if you want to join."

"Lawyers ..." Mr Abrams' mouth turned down. He had little faith left.

"No win, no fee. It's worth being a part of it I think," Delaney handed over Nicolas Goodman's card.

Mr Abrams took it and slipped it into his jacket pocket. "You're keeping something back. I can still read your face Mr Delaney as well as when you were a teenager."

"The Guru was the genuine article. It was your bad luck you didn't get him to treat you. His sister, Jasmina, who I found thanks to you, has similar skills. She's in mourning for now, but she will see you soon after as a favor to me."

"She will remove my pain?"

"She concentrates on other aspects, but in the end, it amounts to the same thing."

"And how many thousands will it cost me this time?"

Delaney placed a hand on the old man's shoulder momentarily. "A contribution to the cost of the Guru's funeral might help."

Mr Abrams understood. "Of course."

"Good. Her phone number is on the back of the card I just gave you. She might surprise you, so be ready for anything."

"Nothing about this could surprise me, Mr Delaney."

"Now we're on the trail of the money. The Mayor will audit, but I doubt he'll reveal what he finds to the public. He's implicated in every aspect of this horror show."

"I saw the TV images of those people at St Joes. Torture? Really?"

"It's more sinister than that. The Mayor and Mrs Jaywaller even got the Government to finance it."

"If you're following the money, speak to Sorakin. He's got a little office in the old Steele Building on Fraser."

Delaney must have looked skeptical.

"It's run down, I know. But Sorakin is a cheap bastard and won't pay high rents. He's always in here wanting discounts on books we'd never sell to anyone else. But he's the go-to man when you want to hide money in this city. If he can't steer you right, no one can."

Delaney nodded and was about to leave when he remembered something. "You said when you had the treatment the pain left you for a month."

"It did. One short but glorious month."

"Are you able to repeat any of the exercises they did with you?"

"With great difficulty. I know they were trying to relax me, but I find it very hard to relax."

"It might help if you can repeat those exercises before you see Jasmina. I want you to go there with an open mind."

"You have me worried, Mr Delaney. You're beginning to sound like one of them."

Delaney grinned. "I will let you know what Mr Sorakin says."

"Please do, Mr Delaney."

"And you let me know how it goes with Jasmina."

"You'll be the first."

"Open mind," Delaney repeated as he left the old man to his figures.

Once back on the street he called Asha. "I'm on my way, Ash. We're going to pay a visit to an accountant after."

"Sounds thrilling."

"It might be. Might not."

"Did you get your patio door fixed?"

"They came, they ripped it out and installed a new one in about an hour and a half. The Jackals will need a wrecking ball to get through this one."

"I don't want to disappoint you, Chief, but I suspect they have several on standby. See you at Harry's."

She was there before him glowing in an all-white t-shirt and tight shorts and a pair of white Converse sneakers. Delaney's heart skipped a beat she looked so radiant. He nearly forgot why he was there. She looked up as he slid into the booth and hit him with her brilliant smile.

"You're looking good." He told her.

"I feel good. Did an hour in the gym and swam. You look really exhausted. You see Mr Abrams?"

"I am exhausted. It was a rough night."

Asha took his hand and squeezed it. "I'm sorry I wasn't there."

"I'm kind of glad you weren't. No one needs to see a man nailed to a wall.

Asha winced. "Nailed to the wall? Jeez. I feel so bad for him. And Maria? Is she ...?"

"She was a real trouper. Held his hand even though it was ripped to shreds and bleeding."

"She'll need trauma counselling."

Delaney shook his head. "She's tougher than you think. I got a text from her mother just now. She wants me to become Maria's legal guardian. She's going to Florida with the boyfriend. He's got a job there."

Asha blinked. "Can she do that? Just walk away from her own daughter?"

"Apparently. I could say no, but then Maria would

definitely need counselling."

Asha squeezed his hand again. "I think this is why I like you so much. You care. Maria doesn't realize how lucky she is. She's had it tough, Delaney. She told me about her life before you. One guy beat her mother senseless; another one felt her up when she was twelve. She wasn't stupid in coming back to you. Most kids in her situation wouldn't get that choice."

"She tells everything to Rufus. Rufus listens; it's the best therapy. She told me that she liked the Guru because he was like a naughty kid. I really wish she hadn't witnessed him die, but she didn't run away from it. She knows he cured her and if there are issues later, we'll just have to deal with it."

"See you do know how to handle kids."

"Probably a bit better than I know how to handle us. Does it make a difference to 'us'?" Delaney asked, as the waitress approached. He smiled at her.

"What'll it be guys."

"Americano – single shot. Almond milk. Some multigrain toast and some honey."

"Ooh, toast. I'll have some of that too," Asha chipped in. "And some hot water for my tea."

The waitress nodded and moved away.

Asha narrowed her eyes. "Honey isn't vegan, y'know."

Delaney shrugged. "I'm not a zealot. I like honey. Don't call the cops."

"Ah ha, sensitive too."

Delaney sighed. "Maria will be fine. I can't abandon her anymore than I could abandon Rufus."

"Either one would hunt you down if you did."

"True."

"I suppose Mr Abrams was disappointed the Guru's dead." Asha mused, running her fingers through her hair, raising Delaney's blood pressure a tad.

"Yeah, but I'm sending him to Jasmina. It might help, might not, but gives him some hope at least."

"She helped you."

"She did. I'm only sorry we didn't find her brother before they did."

"They would have got him one way or another. I guess they feel they can't be touched now he's out of the way."

"I intend to change that. You take a look at our future office? I imagine it's a wreck."

Asha nodded. "Windows actually melted, there's sticky tar everywhere. The restaurants closed already. They say its arson."

Delaney rubbed his face. He was tired. "I guess we'll have to rethink. How was Zuki by the by?"

"She got turned down flat for a job. She's the smartest girl you could ever want. No one will give her a chance. She blew the whistle on a company during her internment and she's sort of untouchable now."

"She should teach."

"That's what I told her, but she has even more ethical questions about universities and male hierarchies."

"You're worried about her."

"Yeah. Zuki's worried about Ai. I think she wants to start a revolution to stop the future happening. Y'know. Sentient robots against humanity. We're starting something we can't control. Terminator stuff."

The waitress arrived with their order and set it down.

Asha smiled. "Thanks, Nina." She waited until she'd left before asking. "So why are we meeting an accountant?"

Delaney held his coffee, warming his hands out of habit. "Mrs Jaywaller is still dangerous. I gave Nicolas Goodman our list. We have a handshake on any positive financial outcomes."

"Handshake? Who shakes hands anymore? How quickly people forget."

"It's legally binding if it's a lawyer shaking your hand. We sanitized our hands right after, if you're worried."

Asha shook her head, then grinned. "Just teasing, Chief. Don't you need witnesses?"

"I trust him."

"I'm going to need real money next month, not in ten years." Asha pointed out. "I know how long these things take. My father sued someone for criminal damage, and it took four years to get anything back. The lawyer took most of it, of course."

Delaney set his coffee down and spread some honey on his toast. "I agree ten years is a possible scenario, Ash, but we're going to try to speed it up."

"By seeing an accountant." Asha wrinkled her nose.

"I can see you have little faith, but we're going to see a particular accountant. A Mr Sorakin."

Asha looked non-plussed and spread honey on her toast.

"Sorakin is an advisor to the Kavreski twins. I made some calls on my way here."

"The supermarket billionaires?"

"He's the guy they go to when they want to hide stuff from the taxman."

"And he's agreed to see you?"

"Thirty minutes – max."

"And my role?"

"Read him. I don't always know when someone is trying snow me. A major character flaw. I have this belief that most people are honest."

Asha raised her eyebrows. "And you were in insurance?"

Delaney finished his toast. "Eat, we're due there in..." He checked his watch. "Forty-four minutes. He's the type who makes every minute count."

Asha poured hot water into her cup and took a bite out of her toast. "Zuki says I have to take it slow with you, but I'm the kind of girl who goes in headfirst."

"You want to consider moving in with us? You'd save a fortune in rent."

"Now that's a very romantic gesture. You could have left out the rent part."

"Sorry, was trying to be practical, especially as we don't have a client or an office yet."

"I'd have to check the closet space." Asha teased.

"I only use half."

"I know; I already looked." She smiled. "We'd better get going, Chief."

Delaney signaled the waitress.

"Anyway, think about it. Ash. I'd love to wake up with you every morning. I know I'm moving too fast but..."

Asha shook her head and pressed her leg against his. "I already gave notice. You do realize that we will have to re-decorate. When did you last paint anything?"

Delaney laughed as he paid the bill. "Never. That's how it came. I think perhaps I was going to, but I didn't know where to start."

"Zuki will be mad at me. What if she doesn't like you?"

"Does she vet all your boyfriends?"

"No one has ever met her standards yet."

Delaney rolled his eyes. "Well, it will be a challenge."

Delaney suspected that few millionaires ever visited the office of Mr Sorakin. It was on the top floor of a nondescript 1950's office building with the world's slowest elevator, the brass buttons well-polished and perfectly clean. The only modern additions were cameras on every floor and an electronic keycode on the heavily re-enforced door to his office suite. No one was going to get into this space easily, that was for sure.

Sorakin's secretary greeted them with a hard, tight smile. Silver hair tied up in a bun, thick waistline and dressed top to bottom in grey with sensible orthopedic shoes. Asha guessed she'd probably worked there her whole life.

"Mr Sorakin is on a call. He'll be with you in a minute."

Asha inspected the certificates on the walls. The oldest was dated 1975 and he'd been 'Berg City Accountant of the Year' way back in 1988. Almost fifty years of history or more right here in this building. She couldn't even imagine what that was like to work in one office for your whole working life.

Asha turned as the inner door opened and a tall over-tanned man with a shock of white hair greeted them. He had a slight stoop and his suit was at the very least a decade old, but the cut flattered him, and she guessed it was tailor made. He wore white Nike trainers on his feet, which rather spoiled the whole effect. This was a man who most likely didn't care what other people thought about him.

"Come on in. A pretty face is always welcome here. You too Miss."

Delaney smiled; the old jokes were always the best. The guy had to be late seventies at the very least.

Asha knew she was looking at a dinosaur, but she sensed he had an eye for the women; he'd x-rayed her up and down with a rapid assessment. She noted the Rolex Oyster on his wrist as well. Surprisingly the outer office was well equipped with the latest apple computers, and various printers. His office had a laptop on his desk, but it looked dated. There was an electronic date and time world map on the wall, little lights picking out Panama and the Cayman's as well as other places she was not familiar with such as Vanuatu. Not exactly discreet, but then again, she suspected few strangers would be getting in to see his office. Which begged the question, why had he let them in?

"So," Mr Sorakin glanced at the clock and noted the time, "what is it you want to ask so urgently, Mr Delaney."

Delaney went straight to the point. "Money trails. I realize you are no way compelled to answer anything, but we're investigating Jirdasham, a pain management clinic that's been in the news lately. The Mayor was particularly concerned that a Mrs Jaywaller, who controls the outfit, although her name is conspicuously absent from any documentation, has neglected to pay taxes to the city for a business that collects many millions in revenue."

"This would be the same Mayor that just fired you?"

Delaney smiled. "The Mayor transferred the Office of City Oversight to his nephew Billy Bengal, actually."

Mr Sorakin barked a snort of derision. "Billy 'fuck me I lost again' Bengal?"

"Yeah, the boxer. He has, if I recall, only won one fight," Delaney remarked.

"And I bet that was fixed." Mr Sorakin remarked, slipping some gum into his mouth.

"The Mayor, who is, I'm sure you know, on the take from Mrs Jaywaller, as is his deputy and half the Jackals, but he has remembered that taxes also need to be paid and we are unofficially trying to rescue him from his fuck up."

"I always knew he'd fuck up. I never gave the Office of City Oversight a chance. Window dressing is all. You were a sucker for working for him at all."

"Officially, we don't care if the Mayor burns, but we have a personal interest in bringing Mrs Jaywaller to justice."

"And you're looking for pointers as to where Mrs Jaywaller hid all her money." Mr Sorakin tapped his fingers on the desk, a habit rather than impatience.

"You came recommended by an esteemed bookseller."

Mr Sorakin smiled; then relaxed. "Mr Abrams, a man who hates giving a discount. I only ask because I know it upsets him. I doubt he's ever made a penny out of me."

"The coffee is excellent, however," Delaney remarked.

"I'll give you that. I make a point of buying coffee there." Mr Sorakin pushed away from his desk and walked over to one of his many filing cabinets. He could see Asha watching him carefully.

"You think I would keep any sensitive information on a computer, young lady? Paper is the only safe and secure way to be sure no one is looking. That little laptop you see on my desk is merely a word processor. It's not even connected to the internet. Mrs Anker out there does all the hard work. I just bring in the clients. Her office is lined with something connected to a Mr Faraday and has the latest biometric systems. Mrs Anker reads up on these things at night and no one, including me, can get access to her computer. If she ever croaks, I'm out of business."

Asha could believe it, but suspected he was more computer savvy than he was admitting.

"When I first started out everything was about trust, a man's word, or woman's, I suppose. Now they can fake your voice, fake invoices, fake everything. I am likely the last man working on paper in this city."

"I don't suppose Mrs Jaywaller or Mr Huissan are your clients?" Delaney asked.

Mr Sorakin found the document he was looking for, slammed the cabinet shut and turned the key.

"Neither one has any class. Huissan should never be let out of jail. People like them, who don't even pay their accountants, disgust me. You know how many people are chasing that women for unpaid bills? No fucking class."

Asha's eyebrows twitched. "We thought at first Mrs Jaywaller had shipped all the money offshore. Panama probably. I made enquiries. She's with Finchbank. My sources say the money's still in the country somewhere. Probably invested in art – something that will appreciate."

Mr Sorakin stared at her for a moment before sitting down. She couldn't tell if she'd offended him by opening her mouth or not.

"If it was offshore, you'd be wasting your time chasing it, young lady." He laid a piece of paper on the desk and spun it around so Delaney could read it. "It so happens you're right, she's invested."

Delaney showed the paper to Asha.

"A friend of mine, whom I believe detests that woman more than I, sent me this last year. It meant little to me then, but now I can see its value."

"Five Towers? The whole chain?" Delaney queried.

"Five Towers management were crooks; they asset stripped the chain. They went into administration when Covid hit them for six and she stepped in. She cut a deal with the Floral Group, who now successfully run the hotels. They at least pay their taxes. They're a solid company with good management and you can't say that about many these days."

"The Empiron too?" Delaney asked, astonished.

Mr Sorakin nodded. "I hear it's very nice, particularly if you picked it up for a song. The Hann Bank took a bath, 500 million I hear, they were the main creditors and the pension fund was deep-sixed. She got it all clear of debt. Capitalism at its finest hour."

"It's very nice and very exclusive," Delaney told him. "I was there on business just a few days ago."

Mr Sorakin grabbed a tissue and blew his nose. "If you want to hurt her, that's how to do it. Free of debt the chain has to be worth a billion, I'd say. Who's your lawyer?"

"Nicolas Goodman."

Mr Sorakin pressed his hands together. "Young, but sharp. I'll grant you that. I knew his father pretty well." He glanced directly at Asha. "You need a sugar-daddy? Don't be shocked Miss. We only have five minutes left and I'm a busy man."

"I ..." Asha couldn't believe he asked. She was astonished.

"You don't have to decide in front of your partner here. There's a nice penthouse overlooking the bay and three platinum cards to play with. Just say yes and it's yours."

Delaney was as astonished at Asha. This had come out of nowhere.

"Ms Knight is also a busy young woman and I understand taken. She is also no doubt deeply offended, Mr Sorakin. This is not acceptable behavior, sir."

Mr Sorakin just laughed revealing expensive dentistry. "I'm not one for pussy-footing around. How many beautiful women walk into this office on an average year? None. If you don't ask, you don't get."

"I'm flattered..." Asha began, although if she'd had a gun to hand, she might have at least aimed it at him.

"No, you're not. You're young; I'm old and rich. Sometimes money buys you anything you want, sometimes it doesn't."

Asha swallowed. If Zuki were here she'd pull that trigger or on reflection, sign on the dotted line. You never quite knew with Zuki.

Mr Sorakin grew more serious. "If you're wondering why I help you, I only ask, have you ever met Mrs Jaywaller?"

Delaney nodded. "Unfortunately, yes. The Mayor thought he could tame her, but I think he is sadly mistaken in that."

Mr Sorakin stood up. "Times up. Good day to you both. The offer Miss Knight expires at five pm. You know where to find me." He winked. She nearly gagged.

Asha didn't speak for almost five minutes when they left the office. Delaney daren't even mention it or make a joke.

"Isn't he aware of what an insult that was? And don't tell me a penthouse and three platinum credit cards are in the least bit interesting, Delaney."

"Not in the least. He was grossly offensive."

"And don't mock me. I am offended."

"I wouldn't dare. I was just thinking if he would have said that if I'd brought a young guy in with me."

"As if. Oh, and yes, thank you for almost sticking up for me."

"Hey I did. I was trying to be diplomatic, but I realize I should have punched him out, at the very least."

"Right answer." She punched Delaney's arm.

She saw him wince and realized that was probably not the right thing to do given his pain issues.

"That wasn't as painful as it could have been."

Delaney wanted to take her hand to reassure her, but figured it was bad timing. "To be honest, his type probably thinks everyone is for sale."

"Be like sleeping with a lizard. He has spent far too much time in the sun. And those shoes with the suit. No one wears white sneakers with a brown suit, and he talks about class! My God, I'd better not tell Zuki, she'll go in there and ..."

"What?"

"Probably negotiate a better deal. She's broke."

Delaney laughed and Asha finally leaned up against him.

"Now I know what it feels like to be a new chair or sofa. I'd look so nice in his little penthouse besides all his old furniture."

"If it helps, my father had a mistress. I only found out when they read his will. She ran the sales department in his store. She was the only one who missed him. For all of the time I lived in that house my mother slept in the backroom with the door locked."

"Family life is so wonderful. You sure you want me to move in? You'll have two females ganging up on you. It won't be sunshine every day, Delaney. I have moods."

"If you could consult and coordinate with Maria's diary for her mood swing days, I'd appreciate it."

Asha smiled. "Ha. You won't find it so funny when I move in."

"You want to come with me to see the lawyer?"

"And what will he offer, I wonder?"

"Nicolas is very into his wife and kids."

"Aren't they exactly the type to have a mistress?"

"Not if he wants to live."

CHAPTER FORTY-SEVEN

Law & Pizza

Asha was making pasta as Maria wrestled with math homework; Delaney was stripping plastic off the new mattress that had arrived. Rufus' barking alerted them to the new arrival. Asha went to the gate to let the smiling man in.

The sun was setting, the red glow reflected off his shiny receding hairline. She could tell he'd dressed down by removing his tie but there was no mistaking the Hugo Boss suit or the handmade leather shoes. He had the look of a guy who ate well but made an effort to keep weight off. He handed her a bottle of wine.

"Hi. I'm Nicolas. You must be Asha. We talked on the phone. Wife's taking the kids to see her mother. She'll be gone for the weekend. Freedom from the bickering. Sibling rivalry has hit the Goodman household big time."

"Come on in." Asha said, waving him towards the house. "But if you're looking for peace and quiet, you might have come to the wrong place."

Delaney appeared on the stoop and grinned. "Bickering is a permanent family feature, Nicolas. Get used to it. Welcome to my madhouse. You already met Rufus and Asha. So, I hope you're hungry."

Maria waved from the dining table as he entered. "Anyone know why I have to study math? Computers know all the answers to everything, I will never, ever need math."

Delaney pointed at Maria. "That's Maria, math genius."

Asha went back to her steaming cauldron. "You like pasta, Nicolas? There's enough fusilli for ten people I think." She said, glancing back at Maria. "This is why you need math, Maria, so you can work out servings."

"I can work out servings and how to dial pizza. I have civilization totally down."

Nicolas looked a bit bewildered but laughed. "Shit, it sounds just like my house. Open the bottle Delaney, got business to discuss."

Asha pushed the bottle towards Delaney who studied the label. "August Perrot – 2018. He only makes 1000 bottles a year, lucky us."

"I get one every Christmas. The thing about collectable wine is that you never end up drinking it until your liver is shot and you can't touch the stuff."

Delaney showed the bottle to Asha. "Ever had this? Should be nice."

"You kidding? We drink it every day in my penthouse."

Delaney laughed, but Nicolas looked confused.

"Don't mind Ash. She had a proposition from Mr Sorakin today. Turned him down."

Nicolas smiled. "That old goat? If you accepted, he'd turn you down. I think he's lived alone his entire life. My father used him as his accountant. Knows what he's doing but offends a lot of people on the way."

"I'm sort of disappointed," Asha said, opening up the oven, battling a cloud of heat and smoke. "If we don't eat the garlic bread now it will self-combust. We're eating, ready or not."

"Serve up," Delaney told her. "Chair or stool, Nicolas? We had a visit from the Jackals so I'm minus chairs and a few other things."

"I noticed wires hanging from the wall outside. Who can police the cops, right?"

Maria cleared the table and brought out the wine glasses. "Am I going to taste it?"

Nicolas shrugged. "You might as well kid, but slowly. Understand."

"Why does everyone always say that?"

"Because." Delaney told her.

"Oh, 'because' – that word."

"Because alcohol lifts you up, but always lets you down." Delaney told her.

Maria wrinkled her nose. "You read that on a poster somewhere?"

"It's true," Asha chimed in. "I have one hundred and one student hangovers as testimony to that fact."

Maria rolled her eyes, but she got a small glass anyway. She tasted it and nearly spat it out. "Gross. We have any apple juice?"

"A true connoisseur," Nicolas remarked. He took his glass from Delaney and tasted it. "Hmmm – not quite as robust as apple juice but pretty damn acceptable."

Delaney sampled his glass and smiled. "Well done, August."

Nicolas found himself a stool. "I heard from Mr Abrams today. He's going to join the class action suit. I also heard from the Guru's sister. Seems you're passing me quite a lot of business, Delaney. You regret not doing law?"

"I regret a lot of things, but not that. Can you help Jasmina?"

"I hope so. She wants me to check if the Guru really owned the big white house, and if so, she wants to sell and set up a foundation to help the people in her street."

"A noble cause."

"And those are few and far between, as they say."

"Jasmina deserves something. He never actually lived there."

"You know how many empty houses there are in this city? Everyone thinks they're in the bad neighborhoods, but it's a fact that half the Hill are investment properties and the only people who see them are security guards. No one knows where to put their money these days."

"People shouldn't be allowed to keep them empty," Asha declared, as she served up the plates of pasta. "So many people have nowhere to live or the rents are too high. It's immoral."

"It's complicated, but it might surprise you to know that I agree." Nicolas said.

"Mr Abrams isn't expecting anything back, but you need to know that Asha and I spoke with Mr Sorakin earlier and he pointed us in a new direction."

Nicolas looked interested. "Oh really?"

"What's it worth?" Asha asked.

"Worth?" Nicolas asked, confused.

"Asha is concerned about the value of our information. She's not a great believer in handshakes."

Asha passed the pasta around and Maria put the garlic bread on the table.

Nicolas smiled. "I'm not offended. For the record, it's

fifteen percent. That's very fair, although at the moment it is fifteen of nothing."

"It's a possibility that Mrs Jaywaller hasn't gone the Panama route."

Nicolas raised his eyebrows. "Go on. I'm listening." He tasted some of the pasta. He didn't pass comment.

"I hope it's ok." Asha told him anxiously.

"It's better than mine. So, where did our Mrs Jaywaller hide her cash?"

Delaney ate and smiled at Asha. "Tastes good, Ash. You like it, M?"

Maria tore of a chunk of garlic bread. "It's great. You going to teach me how to do it like this, Ash?"

"First I'll wait to see if you all survive." Asha remarked.

"Mrs Jaywaller is also interested in food, Nicolas," Delaney remarked. "She owns a small chain of hotels under the name of Ronnie Holdings."

Nicolas frowned. "Ronnie?"

"Her nickname before she married victim number one. You ever hear of the Floral Group?"

"The Floral Group of hotels. You fucking kidding me?" He glanced at Maria. "Sorry, didn't mean to swear."

"I'll live," Maria answered.

"She owns the leases," Delaney informed him. "The whole group. Five Towers is the name of the leasing company. Ronnie Holdings bought Five Towers out of administration for a song."

"The Empiron, too?" Nicolas exclaimed. "She's worth a fortune. Conferences book that out years ahead. The Metro Hotel downtown has an eighty-five percent occupancy rate. Or used to before ... y'know."

"I guess you regret that fifteen percent now." Asha said, looking for his reaction.

Nicolas laughed. "'Bout time someone looked out for Delaney here. Don't worry. We go back a long way. And Sorakin just gave this information up for free?"

Delaney shrugged. "I suspect Mrs Jaywaller once turned him down on his offer of a penthouse. When he told me Five Towers, I knew to look for familiar names or links and only a select few would remember she was once little cute, but seriously ambitious Ronnie at the yacht club."

Nicolas concentrated on his food for a moment, then glanced up at Asha. "You're right, fifteen percent is too generous, my partners will squeal, but a deal is a deal. She might be cash poor, but we can attach those leases. She will fucking scream the house down."

Asha put her fork down. "She can scream all she likes for what she did to the Guru and all those people on the streets. And you, Delaney, no way the Jackals tried to kill you without her being behind it. You're lucky to be alive."

Delaney squeezed her arm and nodded. "I am. I know."

Asha raised her glass. "To justice."

"To the Guru," Maria added, raising her apple juice. "I miss his crazy ass."

CHAPTER FORTY-EIGHT

A Funeral Plan

Perhaps the Guru might have appreciated it. Whether looking up, or down, whichever anyone's opinion on this matter settled on, he would have been amazed at just how many people turned out for his funeral. There was even a steel band.

Delaney held Maria's hand; she was suddenly quite anxious mixing with all these strangers. Rich, poor, a little crazy, they were all dressed in their best clothes totally ignoring any idea of social distancing at Fort Lester cemetery. Delaney was glad he'd made his party wear masks, even though they'd all been vaccinated.

It was one of the oldest burial grounds in the city. Once it has been open fields but was now threatened on all sides by luxury high-rise towers. There had been several unsuccessful petitions to have the dead removed so they could build on the four acres.

Delaney and Maria stood under an ancient Cedar, that had to be at least two hundred and fifty years old, watching the crowd jostling for a view of the burial ceremony. Asha was close by; a little bit confused as to what was going on. Like Maria, this was her first funeral. A fiery old priest was saying something to the gathering, about how the Guru represented the best of 'interfaith' worship and how he discriminated against no one. Testimony to that was all those of every race and creed crammed into the cemetery. Jew, Muslim, Christian, wealthy and poor had all been touched by Ansolm Guranji, whether they had pain or merely drank his health teas.

Asha was sorry the Guru had never really profited from his enterprises.

Delaney noted the unmistakable unmarked cars of the Jackals at the far end and the plain-clothes cops taking photos of the gathering. No doubt pissed the guy was dead before they could kill him. There was no sign of the Mayor or his Deputy of course. Even though they owed him a big debt.

The procession out of the cemetery was quite a vision. The Guru had specified jazz to guide him on his way and some were even dancing in the street as they made their way to their cars. Maria pointed towards Jasmina being supported by the folks from her street as they moved towards a yellow school bus borrowed for the occasion.

Delaney was about to take Maria and Asha out of there when a small kid came up to them. He thrust a note into Maria's hands and then ran off; too shy to speak whatever he had been told to say.

Maria handed the note to Delaney. He didn't open it immediately.

"It's going to take a while for the traffic to thin out. There's a little café nearby with the best cakes in the city, if it's still there. The Cat and the Fiddle."

Maria laughed. "Cat and the Fiddle. Like the nursery rhyme?"

Asha grinned. "Hell, I want to go, just for the name."

"My mother used to take me here when I was a kid." Delaney remembered. "The owner was Austrian, and you'll taste the best chocolate cake in the world."

"I'm in," Asha declared. "Though I'll have to do extra laps in the gym later."

The Cat and the Fiddle was no longer run by an old Austrian lady, but the new owners, who looked little older than Maria, hadn't changed anything. The cakes looked great, the strudel divine and the coffee was freshly roasted."

"I want to buy it all, don't let me," Asha declared, staring at the cakes. "I can't believe I never knew this existed."

They ordered coffee and a smoothie for Maria. As Delaney opened the note, he smiled, showing it to Asha.

"Our Guru really did own the White House on the Hill. The realtor thinks Jasmina could get ten million for it. Even after death duties, there will be enough left for her foundation. She wants me to be a trustee."

"That's either an honor or a curse."

"I'll accept it as an honor." He checked his watch. "We have to get to Jasmina's. She'll be upset if we don't go."

By the time they got to there the street party was in full swing. Delaney wasn't sure he wanted to go in and pay his respects after all, but Maria insisted, "I have to tell something for Jasmina, we have to go in."

They braved the crush and wormed their way through the crowds surrounding her home. The street band was still playing up a storm and people sang and danced along with it.

Asha couldn't believe how many people were there. "He's touched so many people's lives."

Maria was bewildered. "I thought funerals were supposed to be sad."

Delaney smiled at her. "The Guru wouldn't have wanted people to be sad. This is the proper way to celebrate someone's life M."

Perhaps fifty mourners were crammed into Jasmina's house with another fifty milling about outside drinking and laughing. It was a happy occasion.

Delaney didn't want risk being so close to people but felt obliged and retrieved his mask. He had to squeeze his way through with Maria close by. Asha decided it was safer outside. They finally found Jasmina holding court dressed in a sparkly black dress with a crimson feather in her hair. She greeted them like long lost souls.

"Mr Delaney. Maria. I saw you at the funeral, but who could have predicted such crowds? I am so sorry Ansolm isn't here to see it. He would have been shocked.

Delaney nodded. "The answer's yes. If you get the money, I'll be a trustee."

Jasmina beamed at them and took Maria to her bosom and hugged her. "He would have been so happy to see you here, little one."

Maria reached up and whispered in her ear.

Jasmina's eyes widened, she quickly checked Maria's face to see if she'd heard right. Maria nodded. "That's what he said."

A tear flowed down Jasmina's face and she didn't bother to dab it away.

"I shall tell no one," Jasmina told her.

Delaney reached for Maria's hand; it was time to go. The crowd was making him nervous.

"I'm happy the people came, Jasmina. I only hope they help tidy up after."

Jasmina shook her head, threw her hands up in the air and laughed. "So do I."

When they finally reached the street and found Asha, she quickly pulled them to one side. "On the right. Black Mercedes."

Delaney could see a crowd of men with sticks approaching the vehicle. Someone was here they didn't like. He couldn't see inside the car through the tinted windows.

"Who?"

"Mrs Jaywaller." Asha told him. "It's going to get ugly unless she leaves. She tried to get out of the car and approach the house, but someone told her to go back."

"Good advice."

A stone was thrown at the vehicle. Some men were shouting. The Mercedes abruptly lurched away, narrowly missing some street dancers.

The men jeered and waved their sticks at the disappearing car. Delaney couldn't hear what they were saying but he could guess.

"You think she came to pay her respects or gloat?" Asha asked.

"I don't know, but they certainly didn't appreciate her being here. Was she alone?"

"Yes."

"Brave. She must have known she wasn't welcome."

"We ever going to do anything about the guy who killed the Guru?" Maria asked.

"I'm thinking about it. He's protected, so it won't be easy."

"Pity we can't nail him to a wall." Asha declared.

"It's not over yet, Ash."

They were in the taxi heading home when Delaney asked Maria what she told Jasmina. Maria wasn't sure she should tell, so she decided to whisper it.

"He's waiting for her at Mulberry."

Asha frowned. "He said that? Or was it in a dream?"

"I wasn't dreaming. I was hugging Rufie and I suddenly heard him speak in my ear."

Delaney smiled at her. "He must have become part of you when he died. That's what my grandfather told me. If you hold someone and they die, part of them remains with you."

"Is that wrong?" Maria asked, confused.

"Not at all. You were holding his hand when he died. He was passing something to you. It's quite special, actually."

Maria nodded. That's what she thought too. But right at this moment all she could remember about that was the endless blood oozing through her fingers. "I think Mulberry is a place. If she wants to speak to him, she has to go there."

Delaney pulled her close. "Yes, I think that's exactly what he meant."

Asha put a hand to Maria's cheek and stroked it.

"You've been through so much. You're way stronger than me, M."

Maria smiled. "The steel band was crazy. When I die, I want a band just like that."

Delaney held her close and hoped that time was a long way off.

Asha looked at her phone suddenly.

"Uh-oh."

"What?" Delaney asked

"Zuki is coming for supper tonight. She says it's time."

"Oh my god, Delaney. Don't do it. What if she doesn't like you? Or me?" Maria protested. "We'll never see Asha again."

The taxi slowed and took the right fork to take them up the cliff road towards his home. "That's the test, M. It's time. She's right. I want Asha to stay with us, so yes, let's do the test."

Asha's heart was suddenly racing, not quite believing that this was going to happen, after all they'd been through. She didn't want Zuki there. In her head she'd already committed to Delaney and Maria, not to mention Rufus. It was like – no way Zuki couldn't say no now. This was the guy who calmed her. The man who looked at her with real affection, who didn't put her down and wasn't going to steal her car – ever.

"I think we're out of food." Maria remembered.

Delaney shook his head. "No panic. You know what to do. If Zuki can't eat a cheeseless pizza, we'll reject her. Right M?"

"Damn right. What if we don't like Zuki?" Maria asked.

Asha shrugged. "Not many people do. She's very marmite."

"Eww, marmite, gross."

"See. She's like an unexploded bomb. You never know what she's going to say. I think I'm the only friend she still talks to."

"We'll be ourselves," Delaney declared. "If Zuki doesn't like that, well maybe she's the odd one out. Don't panic, Ash. It will be fine."

The taxi pulled up outside the house and Delaney paid the driver off.

"It's going to rain, so I'll get a fire going." Delaney told them as he opened the gate. Rufus greeted them like they'd been gone months and nearly knocked Maria to the ground.

"Rufie, down. Down boy. God, calm down, dog."

"Yeah, a fire would be good," Asha agreed. "We can all stare at the flames when the conversation dries up."

"Suggest you open some wine," Delaney told her, grinning. "Looks like we're going to need it."

Maria kept watch from the stoop as she tried to do her homework. Rufus rested on her feet. Delaney was busy in the back-garden filling in the dog's holes, as Asha made a salad from the last ingredients in the fridge. She was sick with anxiety. Zuki's approval shouldn't be so important in her life, but somehow it was.

Maria was suddenly at her side, pressing the button to release the gate.

"She's here."

Rufus was first there. Maria watched from Asha's side as Zuki tried to get around an over-enthusiastic dog.

Maria stared wide-eyed at this tall, brown, exotic creature in a burnt orange t-shirt, high cut black shorts and red ankle boots.

"Oh my god, you're toast," she whispered. "She's hot."

Asha stared at Maria a moment with alarm. "Thanks for your support, M."

Maria laughed. "Only kidding."

Delaney appeared from the back garden carrying some mint and chives. "Welcome to my little shack, Zuki. Ash is inside making a tomato and mint salad; the actual chef is about to get on the phone to order pizza and the dog you just met is called Rufus."

Zuki barely smiled and went on ahead into the house

as Delaney sat down on the Stoop steps to remove his dirty boots. Zuki glanced at Maria on the phone ordering the pizza as she flopped down next to Asha on the sofa in front of the fire.

"The wine better be good."

Asha started to laugh. "Your short shorts? Really? There are children present."

"You have any allergies?" Maria asked Zuki. "I'm ordering eggplant, spinach and mushroom with red peppers. It's cheeseless on sourdough pizza."

Zuki stared at Maria a moment, as if assessing her.

"What have you got against cheese?"

Maria shrugged. "You can have Asha's lame salad instead."

Asha's eyes widened. Zuki had met her match. She realized that she didn't care what Zuki said after all; this was going to be her home now. She opened the wine.

Zuki frowned as she looked around the living space. "Who decorated this place?"

Delaney entered, handing over the herbs to Asha. "Former owner was a sea captain. He told me that it was painted in 1970 and was good for a few more years. I took him at his word."

Asha poured the wine. "I'm going to paint it white, floor to ceiling. It needs to be bright."

Zuki made a face. "How very non-committal of you."

"Asha looks good in white." Maria chimed in.

Zuki took her glass of wine and attempted a smile. "Yes, she does. How was the funeral?"

"Crazy." Asha replied. "There was a steel band and dancing."

"All the best funerals have steel bands." Delaney remarked, taking his glass.

"Welcome Zuki. About time we met you."

Zuki held up her glass. "Well here's to family life."

Asha glanced at Maria and smiled. Maria rolled her eyes. It was going fine so far.

"Any news on the job front?" Asha asked.

"Been offered two days a week at a government agency in health care. Two whole days analyzing data. I don't get it. Why not hire me for a month and get through whatever they've got. How useful can two day's work be? What about the rest of the week? Who's reading that data then?"

Asha felt bad for her. "What did you tell them and remember there's a child in the room."

Zuki stared at Maria a moment who was staring at her with fascination.

"I took the job. I have to eat."

Asha was relieved – Zuki was showing surprising pragmatism.

Delaney pulled up a stool and stared at Zuki a moment. He wondered how he could say this but decided to ask anyway. "Zuki, is your mother called Esme?"

Zuki stared at him like he had slapped her. Delaney realized immediately he'd made a mistake; but it was too late now.

"I ask because you're the spitting image of a girl I knew called Esme. Her family farmed at Riverbend, the other side of Oyster Point. They had a little hotel too, I think. We were at school together at St Joes."

Asha glanced at Zuki; her heart skipped a beat. The origins of Zuki's mother was a very taboo subject. Her heart sank.

"Was this the Esme who gave away her baby daughter to a family in Baresbrook?"

Oops. Delaney knew he'd walked into a minefield. He daren't even glance at Asha. "Er - Esme was still a teenager when I knew her. Big volleyball fan. I never saw her again after I left for University."

Asha gripped her wine glass waiting for Zuki to explode. Zuki frowned.

"Volleyball? Esme Harran?" Zuki queried. "I don't think so."

"Esme Lowe, not Harran. She was beautiful, like you. She was the only kid at school with a horse, which she rode out daily. You didn't mess with her. I'm sorry if I startled you, but you look so much like her I thought she had to be your mother."

Asha signaled to Maria to lay the table. "It's going to rain, so we'll eat inside."

"I never knew my mother, but she was definitely called Harran. Didn't even know I was adopted until I was sixteen. The Dodd's, my family, were legally obliged to tell me."

Asha came over to Zuki and sat beside her. "I was with her when they did. It was not a good day."

"I think I've been angry ever since, which is ridiculous, because the Dodd's treated me like gold. It never even crossed my mind that I wasn't the same as they were. Jenna Dodd, my adopted mother, used to tell me I was a throwback to a previous generation. Her grandmother was Jamaican, I think. I believed it, right up until that day."

Delaney stood up and helped himself to some nuts Maria had put out. "I'm no genetic expert. I have no business in arguing with you about who your mother was, but I would put good money on it being the Esme I knew. Everything Asha tells me about you fits that. Body shape, the way you walk, your nose. Esme had the most elegant nose and ..." He suddenly remembered something. "Maria? Can you fetch me my old photo albums from the guest room?"

Maria jumped up and ran down the stairs, quickly followed by Rufus.

He smiled at Asha. "The thing about living with a dinosaur, Ash, is we still have photographic evidence of our lives. Yours is all in the cloud and could be gone forever one day."

Zuki glanced at Asha. "He really is a dinosaur."

Asha nodded. "With photos to prove it."

Maria returned, struggling. "These are heavy."

"The past used to weigh more," Delaney told her.

Maria looked at him and then caught on he was making a joke. "It was probably funnier back then too, right?"

"Hilarious."

Zuki drank her wine. This evening hadn't gone to plan. But she was curious. She had never seen a photo of her mother. Never found out a single thing about her.

Delaney looked up at Asha. "Be prepared to be shocked. I looked a bit different back then."

Asha grinned. "Maria, take a photo of this moment - we're going to start an album right now. No more clouds. I want evidence I can touch that this evening actually happened."

Maria laughed and grabbed Delaney's phone to take photos.

Delaney spun the second photo album around. "Take it slow, but if you don't see her immediately, she's not your mother."

Zuki leant forward with a dismissive glance at the album, then gasped. "My god."

Asha squealed. "That's Esme? It's you. That has to be your mother. It just has to be." Asha declared.

Maria came around to look. "She's beautiful. You had long hair, Delaney. It was blond?"

"Sailing bleaches your hair. Turn the page. Don't be shocked."

Zuki turned the page and all three girls shrieked. Delaney was almost naked, standing with his arm around Esme and another girl on a beach. They were all smiling and there was another photo of the two girls wearing hats and nothing else.

"Esme wasn't my girlfriend. Esme was a bit ambiguous about boys or girls. We didn't care. She was fun to be with and whatever sport you played she'd beat you."

Zuki stared at this Esme and felt hope and anger and desperation.

"When was this?" She asked.

"'98, I think. I was a year away from Uni. Esme was going to go to Baileys. She wanted to teach."

"Bailey's?"

"The teaching college in Francistown. It's tough to get in. Their graduates get the best jobs."

"And you don't know what happened to her?"

"I went to Berg City University so I could keep sailing. I was on the sailing team. We all promised to stay in touch but… I don't think I heard from her again. I'm surprised actually, because we were close without being, y'know, in a relationship."

Zuki stared at him. "Why weren't you in a relationship with her. She was hot."

Delaney laughed. "At seventeen she was scarily hot and ran with a different crowd, big party-society, always heading off to dance and get wasted. Anyway, I was into another girl then and these two were best friends. A guy quickly learns that girl's share secrets. It can get awkward."

"You think this other girl would know what happened to her?"

"You can ask. Shannon was in Berg City the other day

and the lawyer Nicolas Goodman saw her. He'll know how to find her. She's on her third husband. Asha, you want to follow that up for Zuki?" He glanced at the fire a moment thinking about what he should say next. "Zuki, if you want to find your mother, be prepared for her not wanting to be found, or discovering something you don't want to know."

Zuki nodded with a huge sigh. "I understand. If it's her, I want to know. I guess I want her to know me." She sank back in the sofa, all aggression forgotten. "Can I take copies of these?" She took out her phone.

"Of course. Maybe not the ones with hats. There's more near the back. Her 18th birthday. That was the last time I saw her actually."

"When?"

"October 10th. Her grandparents had a place in Oyster Point, and it was huge event with a marquee and a band. If they're still alive, they would the people to go see."

The gate bell sounded.

"Pizza." Maria shouted. "I'll go."

Delaney gave her a note for the tip. "I want change," he told her. From the look Maria gave him he guessed that was not going to happen.

"Zuki, if Esme's your mother, I am sure there must have been a damn good reason for giving you up."

Zuki shrugged. "The Dodd's were the best parents you could ever want. I'm not one of those people who can't function because I don't know who my real mother was. I do know that finding out I was adopted made me bitter for a time. It was stupid. I don't know why it mattered so much. I must have hurt my parents a lot. I know it did. If I hadn't got Asha as my friend, who stayed with me through every stupid, self-destructive moment, I don't think I'd be here at all."

"Zuki got married to a guitarist at seventeen." Asha remarked. "Didn't tell any of us."

Zuki buried her head in her hands. "It was some stupid rebellion, a fuck you to my folks. It lasted a month. He was a complete asshole. Wasn't even a good guitarist. Turned out his main ambition was to own a KFC franchise. I have no idea what I was thinking."

"I had to get a friend to drive me five hundred miles to get her back." Asha said. "Mr Dodd was amazing. When we returned Zuki was literally throwing up she was so scared of her parents' reactions, but he held her and told her how much he loved her, that everyone is entitled to make mistakes."

Zuki shook her head. "Mistakes plural. But he was very cool about it and made sure I went to college with Asha. I was lucky."

Delaney left the photo albums on the coffee table. "Ok, let's eat. Zuki, you're the guest of honor so you get an actual chair."

Asha rose to get the salad and leaned up against Delaney and kissed him. "Thanks. I do adore you, even though you're super old. Photo albums? It's like antique roadshow in here."

Delaney laughed. "It is."

"Pizza's on the table people." Maria called out.

CHAPTER FORTY-NINE

The Pain Job

Three days later Delaney was doing his accounts when a WhatsApp message popped up. He opened it and smiled. Asha was busy making coffee in the kitchen, still in her pjs.

"Found him." Delaney called out. "Tierney came through."

Asha brought him his coffee. "She's taking a risk."

"She's not a fan of the Jackals and I helped her with the insurance scam she got hit with. I can't believe how many damn Maxim's there are in this city. Did the Russians invade Berg City whilst I was away?"

Asha shrugged. "There's a whole Russian community over in Ballade District. You sure our guy is Russian?"

"That or Ukrainian, I guess. Either way we have his address. Now we have to decide what to do with it."

"I got the paint."

"And you made sure you bought white as well?"

"Bought it out of town, wore a hat, paid cash."

"I don't want anything to lead back to us."

"You think this will work?"

"It won't give Jasmina justice, but she's ok with it. She's more worried about our safety."

"When do we get started?"

"Now, I guess. You and Zuki will stake out the house, then swoop in when you're sure he's gone for a while. Do it big. Make sure it can be read from the street."

"Makes me feel like I'm back protesting again. I was big on saving the whales when I was a student."

"Same rules apply. Don't get caught. You sure you can make it legible?"

"Sure. I used to do all the banners for the team. I know how to go big."

Delaney tasted his coffee. "As soon as you have given me the go ahead, I'll go to the paper."

"Isn't that a bit old school?"

"I use the contacts I trust, Ash. We go back a long way."

"Anyhow, Zuki will put it on social media. She's worried they'll trace it back to us from the photo you took."

"The only name the hospice Nightman knows is Jasmina's. She told me she's going to stay at her cousins for a week, or so, to administer to her clients there."

"Well here's to rebellion." Asha toasted, finishing her coffee.

Delaney affectionately pulled her close. "I know you think we should be doing something more drastic."

"Nailing him to his front door would be more appropriate."

Delaney nodded. "Apt, but I for one don't want to spend the rest of my life in Berg City Jail. You wouldn't see an avocado on toast for thirty years."

"Yeah, that's pretty drastic."

"It's making the link to Mrs Jaywaller that counts here."

"We could nail him to her door."

Delaney laughed. "Risky. Let's try it my way first, ok? If we don't get the reaction we want, then we try something else." He gave her the address. "Let's get this show going."

Asha turned away then remembered something. "By the way, Zuki traced a grandparent in Oyster Point. She's going to see him on the weekend. Let's hope he doesn't keel over when he sees her."

"Smart move. I hope the hell Esme Lowe was her mother, but I have a bad feeling about what happened to her."

Asha leaned over and kissed him. "She will either open or close a door."

"Yeah and that's important. You going with her?"

Asha nodded. "Unless I'm in Berg City Jail."

It took two days before they worked out a daily pattern for Maxim and his partner, who lived in his ranch house in Ballade. Zuki was exhausted from a lack of sleep and living in a van, but their patience finally paid off when both men left at ten am the following morning in matching jogging clothes. Maxim's head was still bandaged, purple bruising visible around his nose and eyes.

"Looks like our guy's been in an accident." Asha remarked.

"They're definitely together," Zuki remarked. "Maybe they had a falling out. Note the matching red Lycra outfits. We should call the fashion police."

"Later. We've got one hour. Let's get this over with."

Five minutes later they brought the white van up on to Maxim's driveway. Zuki had swapped the plates with a van from her neighborhood and hoped they wouldn't get stopped for any traffic violations that day. To any outsiders driving by they'd see two people in overalls in painting gear. Asha set up a screen so people couldn't see the front from the road and cut off the immediate neighbor's view.

They got to work. You couldn't just write the message six-foot high. You had to work out where to start it and finish it, so it had maximum impact from the road. "We start here. Cover the windows if you have to. This gloss red is going to be hard to get off."

Zuki studied the timber-clad exterior. "'We Feel' here – leave the window blank – 'your pain' there."

Asha thought about it. "Maybe a bloody dash streaked over the window. "

Zuki laughed. "Whatever. You want bunnies?"

"Of course. This is a message, not graffiti."

"What a nice middle-class protester you are, Ash."

"Hey, your family was rich."

"Let's not go there. I hope the Guru's watching this from wherever he ended up."

"He'd laugh. He laughed all the time. He gripped my hand back on the farm and said in a deep voice, 'Fear Life – not death', then just walked away laughing his head off."

"Well he's not wrong." Zuki stood back to look at the W she had just painted. "Upper case E or lower?"

"Upper. Delaney wanted big."

Zuki nodded. "Not subtle then."

"Just paint, Zukes."

Delaney was sitting beside Jonas Everard at The Star. The newsroom was busy; a plane crash up-country had them all excited. Jonas was distracted.

"You going to show me something now or do I ignore you, Delaney?"

"I'm waiting till I get the all clear. Hey, I promised you a good follow up to the Jaywaller story, didn't I?"

Jonas conceded that. "OK, you came through with some great stuff. She's wounded but not out. She also has vicious lawyers."

"We're about to attack from two sides. Class action suit led by Goodman Associates; Nicolas has signed up nearly a thousand victims who got fleeced by Mrs Jaywaller."

"OK, I'll call him to confirm that, but you promised me a front page."

Delaney's phone pinged. He opened up the link and smiled.

"Remember the guru?"

"Of course. Shame he died; I would have liked to have interviewed him."

"He was murdered."

Jonas glanced at Delaney sideways. "Any proof? I hear the funeral was pretty loud. We gave it a little space."

"Yeah, I thought you could have done more."

"Well we didn't have decent photos and he's not really a celebrity."

"You might want to run with this photo however." Delaney showed him the photo of the guru nailed to the wall. We Feel Your Pain scrawled in his blood beside him.

Jonas winced. "That little guy was the guru? I've seen photos, he has big white hair and beard and ...'

"Use your imagination, Jonas. What would you look like if they shaved your head and beard? You think your mother would recognize you?"

"Point taken. So, who, what, where, when, you know the drill."

"Murdered by Maxim Gregorski or Yukis, he seems to have two names. Right-hand man to Mrs Jaywaller. This is a photo of his house." He turned his phone around.

Jonas stared at the photo and laughed. "So that's why we were waiting. We feel your pain. Nice. He's not going to like that."

"This just happened. His address and this shot of his home is up online already, but you should get someone there fast and possibly to Mrs Jaywaller's place. He won't know it's up yet. I can't give you DNA proof, but this links him to Mrs

Jaywaller. We think she gave the order to have him killed. The Nightman at Magdalen hospice will confirm this happened and if he's not too scared, he will tell you he called Mrs Jaywaller's when the Guru arrived and started stirring up the patients. Maxim nailed the Guru to the wall.

"There's a Dr Fisher who was on duty at the hospice that night who's a witness to his wounds. She also issued the death certificate. She won't be happy, and she might well tell you about a guy who looks a bit like me who pressured her into signing the death certificate. However, she won't know his name or that the reason he made her do it was because Maxim Gregorski is ex-Jackal and there was no way any justice was going to happen for the Guru."

Jonas stared at him a moment. "You mix with a lot of very dubious people, Delaney."

"You going to use it?" Delaney asked. He sent him a copy of the Guru on the wall and another of how he used to look when he was up at the farm. "Before and after. Thought you might like that touch."

"Send me your house picture as well, in case it disappears. The hospice?"

"Magdalene Hospice on the old Military Road by the lagoon. He was nailed to the chapel wall and bled out. Just before that, he relieved quite a few terminal patients of their pain. A kind of penance."

"I take it your name isn't on this?" Jonas asked Delaney.

"All I want is for Mrs Jaywaller to feel vulnerable and for this Maxim guy to be neutralized."

"And he definitely works for her."

Delaney took his phone out again and scrolled through his photos. "Here he is standing with her at her home, and here he is with the Guru. You want these photos?"

Jonas nodded. "Send me them all. You should be working here, Delaney."

"Newspapers are a dying art, don't you know."

"Fuck you. And yeah, I reckon three more years and we'll be toast."

"Changing world. Good luck with all this."

"Thanks. The air crash is not as dramatic as we thought."

Delaney raised his eyebrows. "A case of not many

died then?"

"Worse, no one died." Jonas sighed. "Belly landing on a shallow lake. We think two geese drowned at most."

"Lucky thing that the Guru got himself murdered. I'd like to think the cops would investigate this but what with the Guru being dead and buried, it's hard to say."

"That's OK, digging him back up will make a good inside page. Stay out of trouble and find nicer friends, Delaney."

Delaney saluted him and departed the newsroom.

CHAPTER FIFTY

Zuki's Family Plot

Maria looked up from the newspaper he'd given her. The headline shouted, '**Murder of City Guru**' and there he was splashed on the front page nailed to the wall.

"You gave them this?"

Rufus was growing agitated as they neared the beach. Maria was studying the other photo of Maxim's house alongside it.

"I can't believe Asha and Zuki did this. It's like - wow – harsh."

"You think he doesn't deserve it?"

"Shit yeah."

Delaney smiled. "I'm hoping Maxim will turn on Mrs Jaywaller. Homicide said on the news he's a person of interest. But I imagine he's gone to ground."

"And no one knows about us?"

"We know nothing. We were never there. You remember being there?"

Maria's eyes widened as she understood what he was saying. "No." She let out a huge sigh. "This is going to be one weird half-term."

"Pancakes after we've walked Rufus?"

Maria grinned. "I love pancakes. What about Asha?"

"She's on a mission with Zuki."

"If my mother disappeared, no chance I'd go looking for her. You think Zuki will find her?"

"She might, but I have an odd feeling about it. Zuki's pretty strong, she'll cope."

"What if you'd met Zuki before Asha?"

Delaney glanced at Maria as he pulled into the parking lot. "That's not fair. But to be honest, Zuki is beautiful, but she kind of scares me. She's very full on. M, I need you to know that Asha means a lot to me and I'd like you to make sure she stays with us. Ok?"

Maria nodded. "She will. She'd better. I can't look

after you, I'm busy."

Delaney laughed. "Right, busy."

"You serious about being my guardian?"

"It's what your mother wants."

"What about you?"

"Me? Well I'm not sure now, you seem too busy."

Maria gave him a look. "You know what I mean. Will I have to go back to her? I mean ... eventually"

Delaney shook his head. "Guardianship is permanent. You'd be legally with me until you're eighteen. Then you can decide."

"Eighteen?" She looked confused and hurt. "That mean I have to move out again?"

"Legally you'd be an adult then, probably want to go to college."

Maria chewed on her bottom lip a moment. "College?"

"Well hopefully you won't be running off with a bad guitarist who wants to open a KFC franchise. What with you wanting to be vegan an all."

"Eww, gross. No running off. No fuck ups. I just want to know I've got my own room till I'm ready to go wild and crazy like everyone seems to."

Delaney stroked her head. "That room is yours for as long as you want it. That's a promise, M."

Rufus whined to be let out of the car, sniffing the sea air.

Delaney parked up and stared out at the ocean. "Whatever happens, my home is yours to live in. I made you a promise. Now let Rufus out and get going, girl."

Rufus and Maria were gone in a flash, running over the dunes onto the beach beyond. Seagulls swooped and shrieked. He briefly wondered what she'd be like at sixteen and if she'd listen to a word he would say. He guessed he'd find out in three years.

Zuki had a fit of nerves and couldn't bring herself to get out of the car.

"Zuke, we're here, get out. I need to pee. He's an old man. He's not going to bite. We'll just go up the ramp and ring the bell. Move your ass. This is what you wanted."

Zuki felt nauseous. Was this what she wanted? To

finally know?

Asha came around and opened her door. "Now, Zuki. We're already late. Remember we've come to give him a physio check-up. His Doctor's orders."

Reluctantly Zuki hauled herself out of the car and straightened her dress. She was wearing the most modest outfit she owned but the skirt was pretty short and kept riding up.

Asha was looking at the sprawling ranch house that had a great view of Oyster Point. "Nice place."

Zuki was looking back at the town they'd just driven through. "Didn't we come here once?"

"Pippa's graduation/engagement party. Pippa's owns a coffee shop come art gallery in Batten now. Her husband sells art."

Zuki vaguely remembered. "Battern is that old gold rush town, right?"

"We said we'd visit. Sounds nice. They've restored all the 18th Century buildings and cars are banned."

Zuki made no comment. She glanced up at the house and found the strength to walk up the ramp to the front door. She pressed the bell.

Nothing much happened.

"He's forgotten." Zuki turned away from the door, ready to go. "Let's go."

Asha held her arm. "He's old. They take time to answer doors."

A lock turned, a bolt loosened, the door opened a crack.

"Mr Lowe? Your physio appointment."

The door swung open. A good-looking man of about 75 stood there fumbling with his glasses that hung around his neck. He was tall with a bit of stoop and his full head of white hair seemed to compliment his brown skin.

"Physio?" He queried.

"We called. Your doctor said ..."

The man was staring at Zuki in some alarm. He seemed quite taken aback.

"Esme? Is that you, Esme?"

Zuki glanced at Asha, her heart thumping wildly.

"This is Zuki, Mr Lowe. Esme's daughter."

The old man looked confused and staggered a little. Asha caught him and steered him back to his living room. He tried to look back at Zuki.

"Esme? It's been so long. Where have you been?"

Asha settled him in his upright chair.

"Was Esme your granddaughter?" Asha asked him as Zuki followed them into the room and stood by the fireplace.

"Esme? I don't understand." Mr Lowe was saying as he continued to stare at Zuki.

Zuki was looking at the photos of Esme all around the room. Esme as a child; then as a teenager on her horse; receiving a prize for something; a beautiful happy looking girl who was the spitting image of herself. No photos beyond her teen years, however. Why had they stopped?

"Didn't you know Esme had a baby, Mr Lowe?" Zuki asked gently.

Mr Lowe continued to stare at her.

"I'll make some tea," Asha said. "You like tea?" Mr Lowe nodded.

Asha left for the kitchen via an urgent visit to the bathroom.

"I'm Zuki, Mr Lowe. Esme's baby. I'm all grown up now."

Mr Lowe slowly began to comprehend, his left hand shook a little, but his gaze was firm. "Esme is gone. Long ago." He searched for long buried memories. "We tried but the accident was..." he tailed off momentarily. "Her horse. She was walking her horse. No one knows how ..."

"The horse fell?"

Mr Lowe wasn't sure; something was crushed. He couldn't remember the details now. Twenty-two years was a long time. "My wife, Andrea rushed her to hospital, but it's two hours away. The baby was premature, and it passed. The baby passed and Esme ..."

Zuki thought he might be confused about this. And the father?"

Mr Lowe's expression changed to one of contempt. Him he did remember.

"Stephen Harran. He remarried quickly. We never saw him after the funeral. He couldn't live with the death of Esme and the child."

"Did you ever see the baby?" Zuki asked.

Mr Lowe frowned; he lay back in the chair, still staring

at Zuki. He closed his eyes momentarily. "My wife, Andrea knows everything. She was there. I was here."

He suddenly remembered something. "My foot. I broke my foot. It never healed properly. Had to give up golf."

Asha returned a few minutes later with some tea and put it on the table beside him. She looked at Zuki and saw she had glassy eyes. The rock had tears.

"Esme was so beautiful; you must have missed her." Zuki whispered.

Mr Lowe took a deep breath. "She should never have married him. Left College. Abandoned all her dreams. He stopped her seeing her friends. She was so unhappy but ..."

"And Esme's mother?" Asha asked, sitting close to the old man.

"Andrea, of course. You must see Andrea. She runs the hotel. The Marine. She'll be back at supper."

Asha was looking at a photo of what had to be Andrea with a baby Esme in her arms. She was white with a dark mass of brown hair. Zuki really was a throwback to the Grandfather after all, even had his elegant nose.

"You must go see your mother, Esme." Mr Lowe said with some force. "She was so heartbroken when you left. You didn't even invite her to the wedding."

Asha glanced at Zuki. A little déjà-vu going on there.

"Have your tea, Mr Lowe. We're going to go now," Zuki told him. "It was so nice seeing you."

Mr Lowe smiled. "I will tell Andrea you were here. Esme back home at last."

"Can I take a picture of you and Esme," Asha asked.

Zuki was shaking her head but Asha put them both together and the old man took Zuki's hand and pressed it to his cheek. "I am so happy you came back," he said. "Always loved you. We all did."

Zuki leaned in and kissed him on his cheek. "I know."

They walked to the quayside to watch the fishing boats come in from the ocean, a stream of gulls flocking around the small vessels.

"You want to go see your grandmother? We're here."

Zuki leaned on Asha and shook her head.

Asha hugged her. "What do you think happened?"

"Esme got pregnant. He married her; but was

probably having an affair. She died in that accident and he gave the baby away, so he didn't have to deal with it. Told the family the baby didn't survive. I get the feeling that Esme walked out on that family, they didn't approve of the marriage and Stephen was a control freak. Whatever, Ash, I was so lucky that The Dodd's were desperate for a baby and were top of the list."

"They were lucky." Asha told her. "They got one beautiful baby."

"I've got a family, the only one I need. I'd only ever be a ghost here."

Asha studied the photo on her phone. "He must have been seriously handsome when he was young. I'll send him a copy, so they don't think he's gone mad."

Zuki smiled. "He's still good-looking. That was the good part."

Back in the car Asha flipped through the map app on her phone. "The Marine Hotel is the other side of the harbor by the riverhead."

Zuki shook her head. "I can't. No, Asha. We've seen my grandfather."

"We're here, Zuke. I am not going back until you meet her. You don't have to stay in contact, but I know that deep down, you want to. God, how many nights did we sit up wondering how you could have been given up. I know it eats away at you. You're brave and strong and beautiful. They thought you were dead. You weren't given up by them. You had a bastard father who didn't want to be bothered with you; but your grandpa is really nice."

Zuki stayed silent, inwardly tortured.

Asha started the engine and headed towards road around the bay. They'd come all this way – they should know what a good person Zuki was.

The Marine Hotel was perched on the cliff overlooking the fishing boats. The terrace bar looked busy as people ate and drank, wary of seagulls' dive-bombing to steal their food.

Zuki was silent. Still close to exploding but in equal measure curious.

Asha parked up and turned to her. "A quick hello and goodbye. You don't have to stay any longer than that. Just make contact so she knows you're alive. She'll be shocked,

Zuke. Whatever you are feeling right now, she'll be feeling that too. I just hope she doesn't have a heart attack when she sees you."

Zuki glanced at Asha and placed a hand in hers. "I feel sick."

Asha smiled. "You feel sick? My stomach is churning so bad. Come on. Let's do it. She won't bite."

Asha held Zuki's hand as they walked up the steps towards the hotel entrance. Up close they could see it needed a lick of paint, but the flowering lilac and spring flowers in the surrounding gardens all looked so colorful and well cared for.

Zuki gripped her hand. "She might not be here. I forgot her name."

Asha read the name on the wall by the entrance. Andrea Lowe was the licensed Innkeeper. It looked very cozy in the lobby.

Asha read a sign aloud to distract, Zuki. "The Marine Inn was the former home of Captain Goodhand, 1890-1965. 'Famous campaigner to Save the Whales.'"

Zuki was clearly having difficulty in putting one foot in front of the other. She stood in the open doorway and stared in. A young girl on reception was talking animatedly on the phone. Someone was reading a newspaper at a large table in the bay window. It all looked so normal.

There was a sudden scream and a stream of clean linen fell from the mezzanine floor above them. Zuki glanced at Asha in puzzlement. They looked up and a white-haired women was standing up against the balcony, literally shaking, holding her hands up by her face as she stared down at Zuki.

Zuki stared back and the woman let out a shriek, pressing her hands against her mouth. Perhaps she thought she'd seen a ghost.

Asha nudged Zuki. "I think we found your grandmother."

She indicated to Zuki to climb the stairs. "Come on. She needs help."

The white-haired woman was leaning against the landing wall clutching her throat as Zuki approached. Asha hung back a little.

"Esme?" The woman whispered, hardly daring to look. "Esme?"

Zuki went forward and took her hand, she could see

she was trembling.

"Zuki. I believe Esme was my mother."

The woman's legs gave way and she fell to her knees, fat tears rolling down her cheeks. Zuki knelt with her. She didn't know whether to hug her or lay her out on the floor, she looked so ill.

"We've been to see your husband, Mrs Lowe."

"We?"

"My friend, Asha. She made me come today. We, I ... only found out about Esme a few days ago. I didn't know whether to come."

"Of course, you'd come. Of course, you'd come. How could you not look for your family? Oh, my lord, it's impossible, it's ... I don't understand. What a blessed day this is." Mrs Lowe pulled Zuki towards her and sobbed. She couldn't stop.

Asha decided to go downstairs and order coffee for everyone. Give them some space. She felt a lump in her heart. Zuki had two families now. She hoped they'd like her.

Three hours later Zuki held Asha's hand very tight for a moment, not wanting to let go home. "Tell me I'm doing the right thing."

Asha wiped a tear from her face and smiled. "You're doing the right thing. Stay, get to know them. She's a lovely person. To think she's been running this place on her own all this time. Tell her thank you for lunch. You want me to tell your dad you're up here."

"They won't understand."

Asha shook her head. "They will. Believe me, they will. I'll tell him. Mr Dodd calls me all the time saying how worried he is about you. Lucky you, Zuke. You have a hotel to stay in by the beach. You can go sailing and swimming."

"I've got to be back for that job on Monday."

"If you have to, you have to, but getting to know your grandma is pretty important too. Call me."

Zuki let her go and took a deep breath. "Love you, Ash."

"I know. Love you too."

Asha started the engine and contemplated the long journey back alone. She felt saddened as if she was losing Zuki forever somehow. This was the most grown up moment she had ever felt in her life. She made a ninety-degree turn and checked her mirror. Zuki was waving. She beeped and laughed as Zuki gave her the finger. Yeah, she'd be fine.

CHAPTER FIFTY-ONE

Dixon Comes Good

Asha heard her phone vibrate and groaned. Delaney stirred beside her. "You'd better answer it. Second time they've called."

Asha felt for the phone. "Sorry, god, I hope it's not Zuki having a meltdown."

She pressed accept and put the phone on speaker. "It's 2.30. I'm asleep. Can't it wait?"

"Don't hang up. It's me, Dix."

"Dix?" Asha was suddenly wide-awake. "Something bad happened?"

She had sudden memories of his suicide attempt at College, an overdose that he'd been lucky to survive.

"You got me interested in that woman. Jaywaller. Remember?"

"Yeah, but it's 2.30 am, Dixon. Can't it wait?"

"No." He insisted. "She's booked on a flight to the Cayman's leaving in two hours. She's on her way to a meeting with a Chinese delegation from Hong Kong. The Mantra Group. There's a deal going down, Ash. You ever find that Picasso?"

Delaney was listening, already up and dressing. Asha sat up in bed.

"She owns Five Towers, Dix. They own the leases on all the hotels in the Floral Group."

He whistled. "And the Mantra Group own a chain of hotels across the world. Bingo, Ash. She's selling out. I don't know what you can do about it, but unless you stop what's going down – that Picasso is gone girl."

"Must be a private flight, Berg City Airport doesn't fly scheduled to the Caymans." Delaney whispered.

"That your new guy?"

"Yeah, Dix. Where's she flying from?"

"I'm checking ... Pennydown – it's the flying school. Definitely suspicious."

Asha had no idea where that was, but she knew Delaney would know.

"Dix, we're on it. Thank you."

"I've got the passenger manifest up. There are two other passengers. One is Frank G Halstead - wait ... he's from International Development at Hann Bank. Don't know who the other is. Get moving Ash. Remember you owe me."

Delaney was already calling Nicolas Goodman. It took a while to get an answer.

"Nick, I know it's late but it's urgent. You file that action against Mrs Jaywaller yet?"

"Tomorrow, first thing. It takes time to get all parties to agree. Is that why you called and woke us up?"

"Mrs Jaywaller is less than two hours away from flying to the Cayman's to sign all those leases away. She's at Pennydown Airfield. If you have any ideas on how to stop her, now is the time, Nick."

"Jesus. There has to be a leak in my office. Fuck. If she offloads the leases in the Cayman's we're cooked, Delaney."

"We need to stop that flight. Our informant says she's meeting a Hong Kong delegation from The Mantra Group of hotels."

"Damn. That fits." Nicolas mumbled something to his wife, then came back to the phone. "I've got to think. See you at the airfield."

Delaney disconnected and glanced at Asha as she jumped out of bed and began pulling on her clothes. "I'll leave a note for Maria. Rufus will take care of her."

Asha nodded. "Can we stop her? I mean physically prevent her from getting on that plane?"

Delaney was thinking. "If we can delay her until Nicolas files that Class Action suit in the morning – it might be enough to deter the buyers."

Asha pulled on a sweatshirt. "Got to pee first."

"Meet you at the car. Make sure you close the gate."

Pennydown Airfield looked dead. One Cessna was parked out on the tarmac with some ancient single-engine crop dusters further along. No lights. This was not high security; clearly no one was expecting anything to happen. The security guy in the booth was fast asleep and resented being woken.

"We're meeting a flight." Delaney told him.

"Nothing scheduled." He made a fuss of looking at his schedule.

"It's a late booking. We'll wait by the hangar."

The security guy was checking his board. "I'm telling you there's nothing scheduled until seven am."

"Maybe they didn't update you. You'll be getting two more vehicles shortly."

Delaney flashed his City Oversight ID at him. "City Business, pal. Be obliged if you'd open up the barrier. Next guy due in is called Goodman from our legal team."

The security guy reluctantly raised the barrier.

Delaney drove over towards the hangar and switched off the engine and lights. No need to let anyone know they were there. Asha opened a window and rubbed her face in the chill night air.

"You really think we can stop her?"

"Short of driving in front of the aircraft, I'm not sure." Delaney replied. "Tell me about Dix?"

"Dixon was at Berg U with me and Zuki. He's a gay punk cyber freak who thinks he's rebelling but actually gets most of his money testing cyber security at banks and other companies. He's very bright and focused. Nearly killed himself over some boy when he was nineteen. He's a sort of romantic autistic loner."

"OK, interesting. And you trust him?"

"If he gets obsessed about someone, he's obsessed. If he says she's flying to the Caymans. She's definitely flying to the Caymans. Why didn't the Chinese didn't come here to sign?"

"They would be too visible. There's little oversight in the Cayman's. She's going to sell out cheap for a quick deal." Delaney remarked.

"Don't they have to go through due diligence? Some legal stuff?"

"It's the leases that produce a negotiated rental income from the hotels. It most likely runs for around fifteen years and can only be renegotiated at the end. The real question is, why haven't the Floral Group made a bid for the leases? If someone else gets them, particularly a Chinese hotel group, then maybe they'd want to run the hotels as well and make life difficult for them. Mrs Jaywaller doesn't care about that. She wants to cash out before we can attach the suit to the leases."

"And if the Mantra Group get the leases?"

"The lawsuit is against Mrs Jaywaller. Not the Mantra Group. We lose. She wins."

"Plane's due here in thirty minutes," Asha noted, glancing at her phone.

"I expect it will fly in and pick up in very short order. She'll be here soon."

A Lexus RX appeared at the security gate. The guy waved it through.

Nicolas climbed out hauling a briefcase with him. Mysteriously his passengers remained in the vehicle.

He nodded at Delaney. "I hope you're right about this. Had to make some very sensitive calls."

Delaney indicated Asha. "It's Asha's informant. He's a reliable source."

"Hong Kong is ahead of us timewise. I made a call to our associates there and they made contact with the Mantra Group. Pointed out a few things but ..."

"But?" Asha asked as she approached.

"The Mantra Group are not so inclined to play ball. She's giving them a very sweet deal. The way they look at it, it's between us and Mrs Jaywaller. They sign the deal before the court opens here – then it's our problem."

"We thought the Floral Group, who run the hotels might be interested to counter bid." Asha remarked.

Nicolas smiled. "The Chairwomen of the Floral Group is now fully up to speed on this, as are her lawyers. We think they may have first refusal on the leases. They have been talking."

"She can't sell to the Chinese unless they have turned her down?" Asha asked.

"She made them an unreasonable offer. Two billion. They said way too much. They were not aware of another parties' interest. Now they're in a panic looking at the contracts as we speak."

Delaney glanced at Nicolas' vehicle. "Who's with you?"

"Judge Raleigh and two enforcement officers. We don't want to reveal them just yet."

All eyes suddenly turned to the skies as a small plane

could be seen approaching the airfield.

"Can that little plane reach the Caymans?" Asha asked. It didn't seem possible to her.

Nicolas was studying the plane as it grew closer. "King Air 350i. It's slow, but it can fly 1500 nautical miles in one trip and refuel just about anywhere."

They watched the plane come into land on a very dark airstrip. The pilot bounced just once and made a smooth landing.

"More vehicles arriving." Delaney remarked. "Keep in the shadows so we don't spook them."

Two vehicles arrived at the security barrier. No doubt an argument ensued about what was scheduled and what wasn't.

The plane taxied towards them and then turned, ready to take off again.

The light was poor, and Asha strained to see Mrs Jaywaller climb out of a Mercedes. She was surprised to see the Mayor was accompanying her.

"That's interesting. You think the Mayor's going with her or seeing her off?" Asha asked.

"He's wondering if he'll ever see the money she's promised him, if he doesn't," Delaney remarked, rubbing his face. "I need a coffee."

Mrs Jaywaller waited for her driver to unload her bags. The Mayor was struggling to see who else was around in the darkness. Perhaps he'd hoped this was a secret farewell.

The Judge lowered his window and signaled to Nicolas.

"Can we stop the flight?" Delaney asked, stepping forward.

The Judge stared at Delaney with indifference. "Mr Goodman here has not filed suit yet. Technically she has a right to sell those leases."

"Even if the Floral Group has first refusal?"

"If they turned her offer down, she can legally offer them elsewhere."

Delaney shook his head. "Smart. Naturally they'd turn that down. Now she can sell to the Chinese for the real price."

The Judge smiled. "Yes, but she can't leave Berg City.

She is awaiting court business for the abuse of those homeless people. If she gets on that plane, she's in breach of her bail conditions."

"Then you can arrest her?" Asha asked.

"Not until she gets on the steps. That shows firm intent to flee justice."

Delaney took a deep breath. Mrs Jaywaller's driver took her bags towards the plane. He was worried now. She could board, close the door and take off. There wasn't a thing they could do about it. He didn't see the aged Judge sprinting anytime soon for the plane.

"We just watch?" Asha asked.

The Judge turned to the back of the vehicle and spoke with the officers. "The moment they go up the steps arrest them."

Nicolas received a brief call. He disconnected and turned to Delaney with a smile.

"Floral Group says they are still in negotiation with her lawyers as far as they are aware."

Delaney figured that meant something.

"But who are these other people?" Asha was asking, wondering about the last car to arrive.

The Mayor walked with Mrs Jaywaller towards the plane.

Another man, carrying an overnight bag was also hurrying towards the plane.

"That will be the guy from Hann Bank," Delaney told the Judge.

They watched as the Mayor and Mrs Jaywaller approached the plane. The late arrival from Hann Bank was hailing them and they turned to greet him at the bottom of the steps.

Asha was willing them to mount the steps, but Delaney was pointing her in another direction. Another vehicle was arriving at the barrier.

"Who are those guys?" Delaney queried. "Your friend Dix didn't mention anyone else, did he?"

Asha shook her head. "No."

Mrs Jaywaller began to climb the steps to the plane, the Mayor close behind. "Now. Go now." The Judge slapped the dash with his cane. The two law officers burst out of the car and began running towards the aircraft to arrest her, weapons at the ready.

Then it all suddenly began to kick off. From out of the darkness came two guys in suits carrying heavy weapons. They were moving swiftly towards the aircraft. One of them wore a head bandage.

"Down, get down." Delaney shouted out, grabbing Asha.

Nicolas turned towards them in surprise as Delaney hit the ground. The Judge was climbing out of the Lexus when the gunfire began.

Delaney looked up in time to see the banker, the Mayor and Mrs Jaywaller fall from the steps. The arresting officers tried to return fire, but one was shot dead almost immediately. The Judge fell to the ground beside him. Nicolas likewise.

"What the fuck?" Nicolas was yelling.

A hail of bullets slammed into his vehicle and it burst into flames.

Delaney grabbed Asha. "Roll back to the other side of my car." He told her. "These guys won't want to leave witnesses. Run. Hide."

Delaney turned to Nicolas. "Get the Judge out of here."

Another burst of gunfire sprayed over their heads. The Lexus burned brightly. Delaney saw one of the gunmen finish off the remaining officer and run up into the plane. He was going to take out the pilot and any crew.

Without weapons to defend themselves their only choice was to run and hide. Nicolas was hauling the Judge up off the ground and yelling at him to get out of the line of fire. Delaney ran after Asha into the hangar.

"Over here." Asha called out.

Delaney reached her side. "Who the fuck are those guys? Keep moving. We need to get out of here." He turned back as saw Nicolas pulling the Judge along with him, both clearly visible in the firelight. He realized it would be the same for them.

"Look for a back door. Concentrate on surviving, Ash."

"I am."

She ran, swiftly moving around an aircraft, keenly

aware that there were a lot of flammables all around her.

"Here," Asha called out. She ran towards a door but found it locked. "Shit."

Delaney appeared at her side with a crowbar. "Keep looking, stay low."

He tried to force open the door. It barely moved.

Nicolas and the Judge reached them. "The Judge has been hit."

"Bad?"

"My arm. I'll live," the Judge said tersely. "Can you open it?"

Nicolas saw a fire alarm on the wall and pulled down the lever.

A siren blasted out and emergency lights flicked on outside flooding the area. Delaney prayed the alarm was connected to a nearby fire station.

Delaney got the crowbar in deeper and put all his strength into it. The lever lock finally gave way. He wrenched the door open.

Overgrown vegetation and a stench of oil greeted them, but it was their only option.

Asha was at his side with a flashlight. "Let's go. Did anyone call the cops?"

"The alarm will bring someone." Nicolas told her. "Let's go, Judge."

Asha led the way. "Left, or right?"

"Right," Delaney told her. "We don't want to be in open field. Kill the flashlight."

Asha snapped the light off. "This way leads to a school, I think. I saw a sign earlier."

"I don't get who the shooters are." Nicolas was saying.

"You think we're the only ones she pissed off?" Delaney said. "She gets on that plane all the money disappears with it and their hopes of a payday."

Asha didn't think it was that. She wondered how many people knew Mrs Jaywaller was going to get on that plane. Couldn't be many.

"Might be revenge." Asha said. "I think one of the shooters was your friend, Maxim. He was wearing a head bandage last time I saw him."

"Revenge?" The Judge asked, gripping his arm to staunch the blood.

"Maybe Maxim didn't get the payoff he was expecting." Delaney remarked.

"Who is Maxim?" Nicolas asked, pushing some spiky plants to one side.

"Her right-hand man. The one who killed the Guru." Asha told him. She came to a stop. "Down." She whispered and they all crouched behind her. Asha could feel her heart beating fast. Someone was ahead of them.

The moon reappeared from behind a cloud. Asha began to breathe again. "Foxes."

Delaney could just make out a pair of frightened foxes staring. "Keep moving. They won't do anything."

Asha moved forward as the animals silently disappeared into the undergrowth.

Delaney heard it first. "Sirens approaching. We stay put till they arrive." Delaney told them. "Just in case."

"Those guys will vanish." Nicolas said. "Won't they?"

Delaney wasn't sure. "We're witnesses. They will want to eliminate anyone who can identify them."

The Judge suddenly keeled over. "Judge?"

Nicolas grabbed the guy, pulled him up off the tarmac. "Judge?"

Delaney crawled back towards them and felt the old man's pulse. "He's lost a lot of blood. We need to tie that wound off. Shit. We do not need a dead Judge on our hands."

He removed his sweatshirt and pulled off his t-shirt, ripping it to make a tourniquet. He began to tie it around below the Judge's wound. "The shooting's stopped. Ash, take Nicolas, scout out if we can go back safely. Text me if it's safe. I'll bring the Judge."

Asha didn't want to leave Delaney behind but obeyed. Nicolas followed her to the far end of the hangar.

Delaney propped up the Judge against the wall. This had not quite worked out the way he thought it would. What the hell did Maxim think he was achieving here? He was almost ready to give up hope when his phone vibrated. "Safe."

He hauled the Judge up and put him on his back. It was tougher than he thought to carry the man. He was tall and a dead weight. He stopped to take a breather at the end of the building and lowered the Judge to the ground again. The steps would be a killer and he wasn't as fit as he'd like to be yet.

The fire department had arrived but where was the noise? He'd expected Asha to return for him. He took out his phone again and was about to message her but thought better of it. If she wasn't safe, then sending a reply might put her in danger.

He looked down at the Judge. He was breathing at least. He left him propped up against the wall and moved swiftly back the way they had come to the hangar back door. He quickly glanced inside. He could make out Nicolas's car was still burning, but no firemen were putting it out. The hangar space was filled with smoke, hard to see anything clearly. Flashing lights shone from the fire engine but he couldn't see any people milling around. This made little sense. No shouting, no nothing going on.

He moved inside, found a cloth and covered his mouth and nose as he moved around, staying low beneath the upward curling smoke.

His eyes were streaming but he could see one gunman talking angrily on his phone, gesticulating wildly. In the distance the other gunman was standing over what looked like the entire fire crew squatting on the tarmac with their hands behind their heads. He couldn't see Asha or Nicolas. Why the hell had she texted 'Safe'?

Something abruptly exploded in the hangar roof space. The gunman on the phone was immediately engulfed in burning fuel spraying down from a melted feed line. He screamed, dropped his gun and tried to peel off his burning jacket. Any which way he trod he ignited more flames. Burning gasoline was spreading all over the hangar floor heading right for Delaney.

Delaney ran forward and scooped up the fallen weapon. He dashed out of the hangar towards the other gunman. The man was momentarily distracted, staring in horror at his partner staggering around the hangar in flames. Delaney didn't hesitate, fired three times, taking the guys legs from under him. He fell hard and a fireman lunged forward and grabbed the man's gun.

Delaney lay his own weapon down on the ground, glancing back at the burning hangar. "Guys, I think there's a fire to bring under control."

The firefighters adjusting to the changed situation stared up at him in surprise. Only now did Delaney remember he was still bare-chested.

    Nicolas appeared from behind a row of oil barrels. Asha anxiously stood beside him, bewildered by the turn of events.

    "Safe?" Delaney asked as Asha ran towards him.

    He could see Asha had been hit in the mouth. Her lips were bleeding. He grabbed her and hugged her hard.

    Around them firemen began to unfurl hoses and get into action. Finally, they were making all the right noises.

    "Made a stupid mistake," she said. "I thought they'd gone and suddenly they reappeared shouting and waving their guns. Did you see who it was?"

    "Who?"

    "The fucking guys with guns."

    Delaney shook his head. "We need to get the Judge. I left him by the steps by the end of the building."

    Nicolas quickly set off as Delaney and Asha followed.

    "Why the fuck didn't they leave?" Delaney was asking. "Makes no sense."

    "It will." Asha told him. "Good timing, Delaney. They were seriously discussing shooting us all."

    The Judge was still alive but barely conscious. They scooped him up and carried him back between them.

    "You shot anyone before, Delaney?" Nicolas asked.

    "No. Had to learn to shoot though. Wouldn't let us sail to South America without basic self-defense skills."

    "Well thank Christ for that."

    A couple of hours of confusion passed. The fire was brought under control; but the hangar was lost, along with one light aircraft. It seemed to Delaney that a whole division of cops had arrived on the scene. He had to make multiple statements, but for once the police weren't trying to kill him. The firefighters were reliable witnesses to the fact that he'd saved their lives. The presence of the Judge and a lawyer had also made it all seem more legit. Nicolas rode back with the ambulance and the Judge. He was already scheming how to put this debacle to their advantage. He just hoped Mrs Jaywaller had made a will.

    "You've seen the aircraft?" Asha asked, as she was finally given permission to drive him home.

    "No, but I'm going to have fun explaining why this

loaner doesn't have any windows anymore."

"You should probably buy a tank."

"I'm considering it."

As Asha turned the vehicle around Delaney finally saw the aircraft. He stared as the barely legible slogan 'We Feel Your Pain,' daubed over the doorway. He laughed. "You are kidding me."

Asha shrugged. "They forced the Pilot to paint it. I don't know what happened to him, the cops took him away."

"Maxim must have been seriously pissed."

"The one who burned alive was your pal Maxim. The one you shot, was his boyfriend. You were right, they thought Mrs Jaywaller was leaving without them and taking all her money with her."

"She was. I guess the cops didn't look very hard for him."

"You said yourself he was ex-Jackal. I suppose the paperwork went missing."

"Someone will pay for that. Wait, you said boyfriend?"

"As Zuki said, red Lycra doesn't look great on a paunch."

Delaney shook his head. "Five shot and one seriously wounded. What did they hope to gain by killing them?"

"All I know is that Mrs Jaywaller is dead, along with the Mayor and the banker and we're not. It's a kind of happy ending."

Delaney stared at the sunrise. He felt drained. "Let's grab Maria and Rufus and go to Harry's for breakfast."

Asha reached out and nudged his arm. "You looked very wild and angry when you came out of the smoke shooting."

Delaney sighed. "Yeah. I was. I thought you were dead. He's so lucky I didn't kill him." He turned towards her, admiring the wind blowing her hair all over the place. He wondered what he'd done right to deserve her. "You sure you're OK?"

Asha flashed a bright grin at him. "I'm very OK, Delaney. Remind me to get you a new t-shirt for Christmas."

FIN

Author's Note -

I began this project after falling ill after eating shellfish in France. I remember my legs stopped working first, then it moved to my shoulders, arms and hands and at one time I could barely move or dress without extreme pain. Somehow, I continued teaching through this before deciding to take a year off and go somewhere warm to 'cure' the pain. It took almost three years for most of the effects of the shellfish to finally wear off.

I wrote this novel in between the more difficult days and took many long walks on empty beaches because sitting and sleeping were often impossible. Much of the research for the 'cure' found its way into the novel. So many people think they have a solution for pain and so many billions are spent on an illusion that the more you spend the closer you are to being pain free. Sadly, this is not likely to happen. Now or in the near future.

The Sam Hawksmoor Novels - (All available on Amazon)

Girl with Cat (Blue) – Hammer & Tong
ISBN-13: 978-1-5451-56629
War, secret tunnels, pre-historic monsters and airships.
Shortlisted for the International Rubery Book Award
'This book was amazing! I was hooked from the first few pages and couldn't put the book down.'
Judge, 26th Annual Writer's Digest Book Awards

The Heaviness (No 3: Genie Magee story) – Hammer & Tong
ISBN 978-1-49750-8033
Who owns your DNA? Genie Magee is about to find out.
Review: 'The best Genie Magee story left till last. A controversial heart-stopper.' R. West

J&K 4Ever - Hammer & Tong -
ISBN-13: 978-1-5306-24225
Sixty years after the apocalypse, the city of Bluette survives, controlled by a malignant sect. Jeyna and Kruge are two young orphans determined to stay with each other despite all the odds. They must escape into the unknown, but behind them will come the cruel Enforcers ready to hunt them down and haul them back dead or alive.
Review: An amazingly sweet love story in the wastelands - C Thomas

Another Place to Die: Endtime Chronicles –
Hammer and Tong
ISBN-13: 978-1-5028-35437
Think you can survive the next lethal pandemic? Kira and her dog Red try to escape the virus as it becomes a reality. Whatever you do, don't take the cure ... (A Hawksmoor & North novel)
Review: 'I couldn't put it down. Excellent. Prescient.'

The Repercussions of Tomas D – Hammer & Tong
ISBN-13: 978-1- 4910-32015
Tomas (15) accidentally goes back in time to London in the Blitz. Captured and tortured for what he knows about the war... WW11 abruptly ends in 1941. The day after Tomas disappears, his girlfriend Gabriella wakes up to realize she's the only one who remembers that Germany was supposed to have lost the war...
Review: 'Terrifying alternative outcome to WW2 - the Blitz brought vividly to life.'

Marikka – Hammer & Tong
ISBN-13: 978-1- 5119-94224
The Girl who ran from the fire - The Boy who crashed the car & Anya, the girl who can read objects – An intense story about a father's search for his missing daughter and a ruthless kidnapping gang.
Review: As a secondary school English teacher and a mother of a 13-year-old, I'd recommend it to colleagues and family. Strong male characters too - not a book just for girls.

Note: The Repossession & The Hunting are now out of print in English but thrive in Turkey where they exist as:
Toz, Gölge and Rüya published by Marti Yayinlari

https://www.samhawksmoor.com

Printed in Great Britain
by Amazon